PRAISE FOR

THE HOLE IN THE MIDDLE

"I loved *The Hole in the Middle*. It is honest, it is deeply moving—and it is really, really funny. In this, her debut novel, Kate Hilton captures the delicate and often unforgiving balancing act that is everyday life for so many women, and she does so with a graceful and nuanced eye for the absurdities of modern life."

—Jennifer Robson, international bestselling author of *Somewhere in France* and *After the War Is Over*

"Kate Hilton delivers a clever and compelling novel about second guesses and second chances. With equal measures of hilarity and heartbreak, Hilton weaves an honest and engaging story of middle-life struggles. Hilton gives a touching, true-to-life account of today's busy woman and the choices she makes—and later questions. *The Hole in the Middle* is filled with witty, authentic characters we root for and fall in love with—flaws and all. With issues and struggles every woman can relate to, *The Hole in the Middle* is the perfect read for any woman who has ever questioned the choices she made or wondered what might have been. An impeccably written, highly entertaining novel that kept me turning pages into the wee hours of the morning. Kate Hilton's debut marks the entrance of an exciting, fresh, and funny new voice in women's fiction."

— Lori Nelson Spielman, #1 international bestselling author of *The Life List*

continued . . .

Written by today's freshest new talents and selected by New American Library, NAL Accent novels touch on subjects close to a woman's heart, from friendship to family to finding our place in the world. The Conversation Guides included in each book are intended to enrich the individual reading experience, as well as encourage us to explore these topics together—because books, and life, are meant for sharing.

Visit us online at penguin.com.

"Hilton's characters are authentic, unique, and unforgettable, and *The Hole in the Middle* is an engaging novel that is both unexpectedly funny and remarkably wise. I loved this novel because I saw myself, my friends, and every woman who struggles with the modern paradox of having it all versus keeping it together—but I also loved it because of Hilton's perfectly rendered revelations about life and love, and the beautiful honesty of her writing."   —Marissa Stapley, bestselling author of *Mating for Life*

"I thoroughly enjoyed it. Kate Hilton has created a warm, memorable, and insightful heroine."   —Joy Fielding, author of *Someone Is Watching*

"A wise and witty book that every woman who has ever tried to juggle kids, a job, and a husband will relate to. The pacing is fast; the suspense is strong from start to finish. This book is 'unputdownable.'"
     —Roberta Rich, author of *The Midwife of Venice* and *The Harem Midwife*

"Smart, spirited, and fiercely honest, *The Hole in the Middle* illustrates, with pinpoint accuracy, the pitfalls of juggling work and family. Sophie Whelan is a modern Everywoman, admirable, lovable, and exasperating, and I cared about her intensely. Hilton keeps the pages turning with crisp prose and convincing dialogue, delivering an authentic and entertaining story brimming with wit and compassion."
     —Sonja Yoerg, Author of *The Middle of Somewhere*

"As moving as it is entertaining . . . crammed with funny, truthful moments that will strike a chord with overextended women everywhere."
     —*Hello! Canada*

"Full of things that are not said enough. . . . [Hilton] writes about matrimony with rare honesty."   —*National Post*

"Hilton's novel beautifully captures the daily grind and obstacles women face in a story that continually entertains. . . . While incredibly funny, the novel is written with a level of sophistication that caters to the intellectual side of her readers . . . accurate, humorous, and gentle."
     —Leah Eichler, columnist for *The Globe and Mail* (Canada)

the
hole
in the
middle

KATE HILTON

NAL ACCENT
Published by New American Library,
an imprint of Penguin Random House LLC
375 Hudson Street, New York, New York 10014

This book is a publication of New American Library.
Previously published in a HarperCollins Canada edition.

First NAL Accent Printing, January 2016

For more information about Penguin Random House, visit penguin.com.

ISBN 978-0-451-47669-2

Printed in the United States of America
10 9 8 7 6 5 4 3 2 1

Interior text design by Kristin del Rosario.
Set in Perpetua Std.

Penguin
Random
House

For my sisters in outrage

the hole in the middle

December 2013

Dear Friends,

Another Christmas season is here, and for all of us in the Walker-Whelan clan, it has been a year rich in love, friendship, health, joy, and professional fulfillment. Here's our news in a nutshell, from smallest to tallest:

Scotty, our baby, turned three in July. He is showing a real talent for music, and the whole family loves to hear him play his pint-sized piano. Since moving into the toddler room at the Progressive Center for Child Development and Care, Scotty has become so comfortable expressing his authentic feelings! We are lucky to have found a daycare center that is aligned with our "whole foods" philosophy, and that is such a partner to us as parents. The dedicated staff members really feel like family.

Jamie is seven this year, and he's thriving in Grade 2 at Watkins Elementary School. Watkins is a very special place with a strong emphasis on volunteerism and parental engagement—that's the "Watkins Way"! We feel fortunate to belong to this warm and accepting community. In this nurturing environment, it's not surprising that Jamie is embracing his creative side. We are so inspired by his emerging passion for the cello!

Jesse is doing what we all dream of: making the world a better place. With his amazing business partner, Anya, by his side, Jesse's company is growing by leaps and bounds. He's saving the planet one project at a time, using cutting-edge technologies to reduce environmental impact in commercial and residential buildings. All this, and a perfect husband and father, too! I don't know how he does it.

As for me, I'm thrilled to report that I'm still running the Communications department at the Baxter Children's Hospital. Even after six years, I still love going to the office every morning. I get to work on challenging and important projects with great colleagues. What more could I ask for? As for hobbies, I stay grounded with yoga and literate with book club. And Jesse and I celebrated our eighth anniversary this spring with a romantic getaway to Las Vegas.

All in all, it was an action-packed twelve months, and we are looking forward to a peaceful holiday season. We wish the same to you!

With lots of love from the Whelan-Walker clan,
Sophie, Jesse, Jamie, and Scotty

CHAPTER ONE

monday, december 2, 2013

It's Day One of my BlackBerry diet, and I'm huddled in my minivan in a windswept parking garage across the street from my office. The heat's going full blast as I commit various environmental sins against the forlorn stand of leafless maple trees that passes for a view here. It may be short on ambience, my parking spot, but it has cell phone reception, which makes it an important plank in the BlackBerry diet strategy.

The BlackBerry diet is my latest effort to bring my stress level down to nontoxic levels. I'm allowing myself voice mail–only access to the office before I arrive in the morning. Phase Two will involve reduced e-mail access on weekends, but it's only Monday, so we'll have to see if we get to that stage. Success is unlikely, which is why the BlackBerry diet is a strategy and not a plan. A strategy requires less commitment, and therefore less guilt in the event of failure.

I dial into the voice mail system, punch in my code and wait.

The disembodied voice speaks: *You have eleven new messages.*

Eleven. That's not so bad.

First message. Click. Barry, definitely. He never leaves messages.

Next message. Click. Ditto. But two hang-ups before nine o'clock is unusual. I feel my shoulders start to creep up with anticipatory tension.

Next message. Message marked urgent. Uh-oh. "Hi, Sophie. It's Barry. I see that you're not in yet. I need to speak to you about the Gala as soon as you do get in. There's a problem and you need to get on top of it."

Next message. "Hi, Sophie. It's Anna from the toddler room at daycare. Scotty is pulling on his ear and seems a little fussy. He can stay for now, but if he gets any worse we'll have to ask you to pick him up. Sorry about that. We'll call you later with an update."

What? No. I dropped him off half hour ago and he was fine. A little phlegm-riddled, maybe, but nothing more. If I believed in God, I would pray. Maybe I should anyway, just to hedge my bets.

Next message. "Soph, it's Zoe. This is your warning call. Book club is on Thursday at Sara's house. Line up a babysitter, tell Jesse to be home, do what you have to do, but you are not bailing again this month. Seriously. I always fight with Megan when you're not there. I'm your best friend and you don't want to piss me off. Love you, bye."

Next message. "Hi, Sophie. This is Kelly Robinson. I'm the chair of the Parent Council for Watkins Elementary. I wanted to talk to you about your volunteer hours—" I skip the rest of the message and delete it. I've been avoiding calls from Jamie's class parent all year, but now it seems that she has handed my file to someone more senior in the Parent Council hierarchy.

Next message. "Hi, Sophie. It's Janelle Moss." Janelle is the lead volunteer on the Gala, an event controlled by a group of very wealthy women who have intense and competing agendas that I don't even begin to understand. Every conversation with these people is a minefield. Happily, managing Gala volunteers is one of the few things in the office that I'm not responsible for, and whatever the problem, I'm going to punt it right back to Justine. "I don't know if you've had a chance to talk to Justine yet, but we're looking at a little change in direction on the creative for the marketing materials. Happy to chat once Justine has filled you in. Bye now."

Next message. "Sophie, it's Justine. *Major* screw-up at the Gala meeting last night. We need to talk *urgently*. Call me." Justine is my colleague and sometime friend, when it suits her. She runs the Event Planning department, which means that the Gala is *her* problem.

Next message. "Sophie, my dear. It's Lillian. I was hoping to catch you in person. How I hate these dreadful machines! Do give me a call today if you can. The issue is rather time-sensitive, as you young people are fond of saying."

Lillian Parker has been one of my favorite people on earth since my last year of university, when I lived in her rambling house, paying criminally low rent in exchange for house-sitting services during her frequent sojourns abroad. Her annual holiday party is this weekend, and I can see the invitation in my mind's eye now, poking out of the pile on the corner of my desk that I lovingly call my Guilt Stack. It's not like Lil to get worked up about RSVPs, which is why the card is still buried in the Guilt Stack, but I'll move it up to the top of the pile and deal with it once I get into the office—or by Thursday at the latest.

Next message. "Hi, Sophie. It's your mother. Look, honey, I know you're busy, but we have to talk about Christmas. It's *urgent*."

Instinctively, I check the date on my BlackBerry. Have I lost a week somewhere? But no, it's only December 2.

"First of all—dinner. I'm going to do a turducken again this year, but did Jesse like it last year? I know he said he did, but he didn't have seconds, so I'm not convinced. Your brother and Dana liked it—come to think of it, did you like it? Anyway, if you and Jesse agree, we'll go with the turducken again, but I want you to be honest with me if you don't like that plan. Anyway, assuming that you do, we'll go with the usual sides—mashed potatoes, turnips, that rice dish that you like and probably some creamed spinach or something. I was going to do mini shrimp cocktails for the appetizer, but did you tell me that Jesse isn't eating seafood these days? If not, I could always just do a soup, maybe roasted red pepper—that would be nice with the turducken. I've been talking to your brother about dessert—he says that he doesn't care, but I know he prefers the pumpkin pie and you always say that you prefer the lemon meringue. So I guess I could make both, if it's really important to you to have lem—"

Next message. "It's your mother again. The machine cut me off. Anyway, call me about dinner. And then I need you to think about what the kids want for Christmas. Are you doing stockings at your house or mine?

If you are doing them at mine, I'll need to get the old stockings out and do a few repairs—they were pretty threadbare last year. And also I'll need to know if you are bringing everything for the stockings or if I need to buy some things as well. Are you going to stay overnight here on Christmas Eve? Because if you are, we'll need to make a plan for dinner on the twenty-fourth. Beef might be nice. Does Jamie still like those transforming robots? Because I saw a robot kit that he would just love! It said it was for thirteen years and up, but Jamie is *such* a smart little boy, and he could use a challenge with all that energy he has, don't you think? Maybe it's something that he and Jesse could do together; Jesse's been working so hard. And for Scotty I was thinking that it's probably time to get him playing hockey. Wouldn't Jesse love that? Maybe some little skates and a helmet and a stick? How cute would that be? I'm around this morning, then out for lunch with Jennie Birkin—you must remember Jennie; you went to school with Andy Birkin. Then I'll be back for a couple—"

End of messages.

I feel a little warm and light-headed now, and I pull down my visor mirror for an assessment. Every day of my thirty-nine years looks back. Gray coat, gray suit, and gray roots: I really need to get my highlights done. More alarmingly, I can feel an aching weariness in my chest. I've noticed it with some regularity lately, and it makes me nervous. Some days it's just a knot of anxiety, but today it feels like the hole in the middle of a donut: empty but for the wind whistling through it. I know I shouldn't feel this hollowed out and used up at thirty-nine, but I don't have time for that kind of reflection today.

I rummage through my purse and locate my triage kit to deal with the problems I can solve. I pull out the bottle of cough suppressant and take a long swig that burns going down, and then squeeze a couple of drops of Visine into each eye. Then I attack the area under my eyes with concealer and everything else with bronzer. And with that, I'm ready to brave the germ-screening desk.

The germ desk is a fairly new addition to the Baxter, since a terrible outbreak of the flu at another children's hospital made headlines last year. Now everyone entering the hospital is screened at every entry point and doused with hand sanitizer. I've invested considerable time and energy in my relationship with Max, the guy who has been guarding the germ desk for the past six months; I know the names of his grandchildren and their ages, and how Max developed a herniated disk last year, and that Max's wife wants him to get a storage locker for his model trains. And because our conversations have covered extensive areas of Max's life and times, there has been little opportunity to explore the subject of my health, which is exactly the way I want it.

But today, Max is missing. Nigel, according to his security tag, is sitting in Max's chair. And judging from the length of the line, Nigel takes his job very seriously. When I get to the front, I consider batting my eyelashes, but I suspect that insouciance of this kind has a shelf life, and mine is getting awfully close to the expiration date. I give him what I hope is a winning smile instead.

Nigel is clearly unmoved. He picks up his clipboard and clears his throat. He's going to make me do the survey. I can't believe it. Max never made me do the survey. I wonder if that's why Max isn't working here anymore.

"Have you experienced any coughing in the past twenty-four hours?"

"No." This is absolutely true.

"Sneezing?"

"No." Not more than everyone sneezes when they wake up in the morning, that is. Take Jesse, for example. He sneezes practically every morning, sometimes eight times in a row. It doesn't mean that he's sick. I myself am not a chronic sneezer like Jesse, but there is no reason to draw any dire conclusions just because I was sneezing this morning.

"Vomiting?"

"No."

"Fever?"

"No." I can't say for sure. I don't have a thermometer in my portable pharmacy. And again, there are lots of other possible explanations for the flush in my cheeks today.

"Flu-like symptoms of any kind?"

"No."

Nigel peers at me over the top of the clipboard. If Nigel wants to, he can insist on taking my temperature, and then I'll be in deep trouble. But as much as he wants to, he can't find justification today. I almost pump my fist in the air as he moves on to the next person in line. But with Max gone, I know this is only a temporary win. Nigel is cut from a different cloth entirely. Society requires people like Nigel; without them there would be no parking officials or mall cops or hall monitors, and we would live in a state of anarchy. And it's important to remember this, because I dislike Nigel so intensely at this moment that I'm beginning to imagine terrible events that might befall him and prevent him from coming to work ever again. Not death, of course. I'd never wish for that. A debilitating injury would be quite enough.

For the record, I approve of the hospital's infection-protection measures, at least in a theoretical sense. And I would definitely comply with them if I were providing frontline health care and believed that I posed any risk whatsoever to the hundreds of sick children upstairs. But I'm the director of communications for the hospital, so I spend my days reviewing press releases and dealing with media requests, ducking my boss and trying to persuade my assistant to do some work. I'm not saving lives. There are lots of people in this building who do, but I'm not one of them. And if I followed the letter of the law and kept my flu symptoms at home, I would have worked exactly thirteen out of the last forty-five days.

In the meantime, though, it's already 9:10 and I'm late for work.

My assistant, Joy, is at her desk: a mixed blessing. She raises her tweezed eyebrows at me and murmurs, "Slow start this morning?" before turning back to her computer, where she is communing with her Facebook friends, or possibly buying designer knockoffs on eBay. But I'm not ready to declare this day a complete write-off, at least not yet, so for now I'll act as though she works for me and we're both happy about it.

"Good morning, Joy," I say. "I need to speak to Justine right away. Can you find her and see if she can pop by?"

She eyes me with a combination of contempt and petulance, and my request hangs, unacknowledged, between us. "Your phones's been lighting up all morning," she says. "And Barry's been by twice looking for you. It's about the Gala."

The Gala is the hospital's major fund-raiser of the year. It is a lavish dinner-dance for two thousand of the city's established and upwardly mobile, and it raises over a million dollars for our medical research each year. It is organized by a committee of well-heeled volunteers who have lots of extra time and opinions about everything from the shade of the napkins to the font on the table cards. It is also—mercifully—not in my portfolio, except in a tangential sense, since I oversee the marketing for the event. I've attended a few committee meetings, mostly as moral support for my colleague Justine, but I begged off last night to nurse my cold.

"I'll go and see him once I've had an update from Justine. So if you could get her for me, that would be great. Thanks," I say, retreating into my office and closing the door behind me.

I see my computer sitting innocently enough on my desk, but I'm not fooled. Recently, I have fallen into the habit of ascribing human characteristics to my computer, and unfortunately, our relationship has taken a turn for the pathological. This week, I'm having trouble shaking the irrational conviction that my computer is poised for an attack; each morning, I quake inwardly as I push the power button and hear, in the hum of waking machinery, a marauding army of data collecting itself and preparing to barrel over the horizon at me.

I log in, and the screen fills with e-mail—definitely more than twenty. Could it be as many as fifty? I avert my eyes in horror. The computer seems to vibrate with a malevolent energy; I'm convinced that it senses my fear, like a rabid dog. I back away and peek out into the hallway. "And, Joy? Could you please call everyone and postpone the staff meeting? I've got to sort out this thing with Justine."

Joy has been at the hospital for twenty-seven years. Her seniority guarantees her a position with someone on the executive team, but she gets passed around like a hot potato because she has the worst attitude in the secretarial pool. She is also not particularly competent, and it's hard to tell if she's bad at her job because she hates it, or if she hates it because she's bad at it. You could spend a lot of time on this age-old philosophical debate about chickens and eggs, but the real takeaway is this: getting good secretarial help is not unlike winning at musical chairs; the people who think it has anything to do with luck are usually the ones left standing when the music stops. Your chances are always going to improve if you're willing to keep your elbows out, but I, against a mountain of evidence disproving it, have always clung to the belief that civility is rewarded in the end. And even if I were prepared to sink into the fray, my bargaining power is constrained by the fact that my department, communications, is a cost center, not a profit center, which is to say that we spend money instead of bringing it in. This is a designation that presages all kinds of large and small disappointments. It's the profit centers that hold the real power in any organization, and that are routinely showered with staff and budgets. Not for the first time, I consider the merits of my career choices.

Joy actually rolls her eyes. "They're not going to like it, you know. It's the second time this week. Erica is totally pestering me about getting some time with you."

"I get it," I tell her. "I'll meet with them today. I just can't do it right now. Can you please let them know?"

Joy sighs heavily and departs.

"Thank you, Joy," I call after her. "I really appreciate it!"

Deep down, I suspect that the real reason Joy works for me is that I am the only person in the office who is willing to put up with her. As I do each morning, I remind myself that Joy is paid to show up every day and make my life easier. The fact that she refuses to fulfill this basic requirement calls for a serious conversation with the HR department, but I would rather suffer than invest my emotional energy in a doomed attempt at performance management. I'm just going to wait until someone with less power than I have is hired, so that I can pass Joy off and continue the cycle of dysfunction.

I feel a little light-headed, and am taking deep, calming breaths as Justine appears in my doorway. As the director of special events, Justine is the only person with less power than me on the senior management team. I feel for her. Event planning is a career for masochists. Events can fail for almost infinite and wholly unpredictable reasons. Providing name tags? You'd better hope that the temp who is preparing them remembers to include the appropriate honorific after the name of the megalomaniac on the board. Using audio-visuals? Pray that the AV department sends the smart guy who actually knows how to use the equipment and not the stoner who is mailing in his last few years until he can trigger his pension and still hasn't really figured out how to work those newfangled computers. Serving food? Look out for the myriad of allergies—news to you—that are likely to endanger the life of a major donor. While you're at it, hope that the bartender has recovered from the fight with her boyfriend and decides to show up after all. And here's the kicker: even if you throw the best event in the world, the volunteers will take all the credit and you'll be left managing feedback like "Didn't you think the vinaigrette was a little too citrusy? Can you make sure that doesn't happen again next year?"

Justine is made from tough stuff, though. She's been managing events for close to fifteen years and has nerves of steel. But today, she looks panic-stricken.

"What happened last night?" I ask. "Barry is freaking out. He's practically stalking me. What's going on?"

Justine groans. "It was horrible, Sophie. You can't imagine."

"I don't understand. I thought we were just rubber-stamping approval for the art for the posters and website last night. It was supposed to be a short meeting."

"I know," says Justine. "Claudio did a great job on the photos. Very sexy—gorgeous models, loincloths, Cleopatra—everyone loved it."

"So what's the problem?"

Justine wrinkles her nose as though she has just tasted something bitter. "They don't like the theme anymore," she says.

I'm stunned. We have spent months trying to get the volunteers to agree on a theme for the evening. Every single detail flows from the theme—music, entertainment, décor, and most importantly from the perspective of the volunteers, wardrobe. It was a big day when they finally settled on "Walk Like an Egyptian," which the volunteers felt provided an esthetic bridge between the retro cool of eighties girl-band music and the sophisticated elegance of the wildly fashionable Halston-style goddess dresses. More importantly from my perspective, the decision allowed us to move forward with hiring an outside designer and getting the promotional materials done. In truth, the website should have been up a month ago. We are supposed to start selling tickets next week.

Justine shakes her head. "Apparently, the fundamental appeal of the Egyptian theme had to do with being able to get the Bangles to perform."

"The Bangles," I repeat. This is news to me. How did this never come up? "Didn't they break up, like, twenty years ago?"

"Well, it turns out that they're back together. They're doing a reunion tour, and Janelle saw them in L.A. last month. But they're committed to a long-term gig in Vegas through the spring and can't do the Gala."

"Can't we just get another girl band?"

"I tried that." Justine grits her teeth. "Just be glad you weren't there, Sophie. It was a freight train. It couldn't be stopped. Janelle converted every single person on the committee in the space of ten minutes. By the end, everyone agreed that the theme was too stiff without the Bangles tying it together."

"Stiff? What about the male models in loincloths, the belly dancers, the palm trees, and the dance party in the pharaoh's tomb?" I can't believe this is happening.

Justine's smile turns nasty. "Do you know what the real problem is?" she asks. "They suddenly realized that they'd all be wearing the same dress. Not that anyone was crass enough to come out and say it."

"Oh my God," I say. "There's no way they'll change their minds, then?"

"Nope."

"I need to think," I say. "Don't cancel anything." I suddenly remember Barry. "What are we going to tell Barry?"

"I think he knows," says Justine. "Janelle said that she was going to tell him."

As if on cue, Joy pops her head in the door. "Barry wants to see you now," she says.

"Are you coming with me?" I ask Justine.

"Not a chance, friend," she replies. "My ears are still ringing from the slap-down I got from him this morning. I'm planning on staying out of his way for as long as possible. Anyway, you can handle him. He likes you. More than he likes me, at least."

"Low bar," I say.

CHAPTER TWO

monday, december 2, 2013

I turn down the hall with all of the enthusiasm of a delinquent teenager heading to the principal's office. I wonder, idly, if Barry will make the effort to call me by my name today. Based on experience, the odds are around 60-40 against, but it's hard to predict. He usually just calls everyone "pal" or "buddy"—even people whose names he must know. He reminds me of my elementary school principal, who called all the girls "princess" and all the boys "cowboy." Barry's cut from the same cloth; he's just updated the nomenclature to reflect the ostensibly gender-neutral values of our age.

Barry Wise is the chair of the board of the hospital. He is my boss as well, although only temporarily. Under normal circumstances, the chair of the board would make only rare appearances on the administrative floors of the hospital, which is what everyone would prefer. However, my former boss is on an extended leave after some allegations were raised about the extent of his interest in children. Ever since the police paid a visit to his house and left with his computer, he's been a dead man in the corridors of the Baxter Hospital. I've already drafted the press release announcing my boss's early retirement and praising his visionary leadership during a period of growth and change. We'll hit *Send* as soon as the search committee announces its choice.

In the meantime, Barry has taken up residence in the office of the vice president of advancement, just down the hall from me. I find him with his back to the door, staring out the window. It's a studied pose, designed to give the impression that he is wrestling with a management issue of great complexity. But since he begins virtually every meeting this way, I've concluded that he is simply watching the pigeons and waiting for the opportunity to practice his pained, faraway expression, befitting one who must climb down from a lofty perch of contemplation to deal with the mundane matters below. It is an expression that has been imitated in the staff room on countless occasions, usually after Barry has made a particularly boneheaded pronouncement. In truth, Barry has absolutely no idea what any of us do, and why should he? He runs a hedge fund, and is only the chair of the board because he has what is known in our business as "capacity": he is rich, and so are all of his friends.

"Hi, pal," he says. "So I hear we have a problem."

I dip my toe in, very cautiously. "Justine briefed me," I say. "I understand that the volunteers want to change the theme. Of course that will be difficult, not to mention expensive, at this stage. Not impossible, but definitely far from ideal."

"Hmmm." Barry nods sagely. "I've spoken at length with Janelle about this issue." Of this I have no doubt. Barry is putty in Janelle's hands and she knows it. I can see that we are doomed. But I make one more attempt.

"I think that we need to be quite concerned about the impact that this could have on ticket sales, Barry," I say. "Our experience suggests that we need at least ten weeks of advertising to get the word out. The designers have been working on the marketing for at least a month. We are going to run out of time."

"I hear you, buddy," says Barry. "But Janelle assures me that she can make up any losses by selling tables to her friends."

"It's not that simple, Barry," I say. "If we change the theme now, we'll throw away thousands of dollars, not to mention all of the time that our staff has put in on this project. We can't recoup those losses with ticket sales. Our budget for the event already assumes that we'll sell all the tickets."

Barry's expression hardens. He hates being told what to do, especially by women. And even more especially by young women. I brace myself for the explosion, but it doesn't come. The restraint is uncharacteristic, and I wonder why he is making the effort.

"Look, pal," he says. "I know it's going to be a lot of work for you." *For me?* "But you'll just have to put your head together with—"

"Justine?" I suggest.

"Justine, precisely. Tell her that I want you two working together on this. You have my full confidence. I look forward to hearing what you come up with."

"Um, Barry? You know that I'm always available to help, but my responsibility for the Gala is pretty limited to the marketing side." I can see Barry's face starting to redden. "I'd be reluctant to horn in on Justine's territory. She's doing a terrific job and I wouldn't want to give her the impression . . ."

I trail off as I see Barry's expression darken and his cheeks begin to puff out in a malevolent expression known around our office as the Blowfish. "We're not selling aluminum siding around here!" he huffs. "We don't have territories. This is a game for team players, and we need to get in the same boat and row together. When someone tells me something isn't in her job description, I hear an excuse—and what's my motto?"

"There are no excuses in business," I say.

"You got it in one shot," says Barry.

Barry's contempt for the HR department and all of its policies and procedures is well-documented, so it seems pointless to tell him that very little of what I do every day is actually in my job description. And in any event, I know my strategic advantage. I'm a stroker, a smoother; I'm the career-girl version of the angel in the house. I'm nurturing and supportive; I can be relied upon to laugh at jokes, even when they are bad or inappropriate or at my expense; I'm still slightly better-than-average-looking, holding steady with the help of well-fitting bras and control-top hose and incredibly expensive moisturizer; and I work hard at being non-threatening in every way. And that is why I'm going to fall on my sword, fix the problem, and make Barry feel like he's in charge. Not for the first time, I contemplate the years I spent in graduate school on women's studies. I should have done something useful, like Latin

Barry is looking at me expectantly. It's my cue. "Of course, Barry," I say. "Justine and I will get right on it. Don't you worry. It will all turn out just fine."

"Excellent!" Barry beams. "I knew I could count on you, buddy. Now, there is just one other thing that I wanted to discuss with you."

I make my way back to my office in a state of disbelief and with my arms full of binders, living proof of the axiom that no good deed goes unpunished. Now in addition to assisting with the Gala, I have been selected to serve as the staff rep on the search committee for the new vice president of advancement. The only good news is that it should be done by next week. The bad news is there are at least three meetings this week, and accommodating them is going to require scheduling contortions that would be awe-inspiring even if I had a willing assistant, and probably impossible in my current circumstances.

Barry is a little disappointed in me; I think he expected me to exhibit more obvious pride at being plucked from the herd and elevated so far above my station. But it's widely known that the committee has been meeting for at least a month without a staff rep, a state of affairs that has been both observed and roundly denounced for weeks in the staff kitchen, a closet just spacious enough for a coffeemaker, a microwave, and two employees muttering to each other about a conspiracy at the highest levels to circumvent the collective agreement. Now it appears that someone has checked the hospital bylaws and realized that staff consultation is a disagreeable necessity. There's no way to disguise the fact that I'm joining up by way of a shotgun wedding, since they've picked a short list and start interviewing this week. But I can smile for the photo if that's what's required. I'm supposed to go through all of the applications today and let them know if there is anyone else that I think should be included on the short list; I think I can make time to flip the pages, show up for the meeting, and venture no opinion, which is exactly what the committee wants from me.

Geoff Durnford sticks his head into my office, and I feel my spirits lift. Everyone should have an employee like Geoff. He is the head writer on my team and does incredible work with almost no direction. He never gives me a hard time about anything, never whines, and never demands attention. I can take him to any meeting; I can even send him in my place. The rest of the staff admires him, and when I'm not available—which is all too often lately—he steps in and keeps the team on course. His fashion sense runs to the whimsical, especially in ties and socks, and today his ankles are adorned with a riotous paisley in pink and tangerine. He is tragically single, but I just know there is a perfect man out there for him, someone who loves theater and fine restaurants and will overlook the fact that his hair is thinning as quickly as his middle is thickening.

"Not your best day?" he asks. "Have you even checked your e-mail yet?"

"Is there anything urgent?" I ask.

"Probably not super-urgent," he says. "Although Erica's head is going to explode if you don't sign off on the Family Care Center press release today."

"Noted," I say. "Have you seen it?"

"It's fine," he says. "It's all boilerplate except paragraph six. That's the only part you have to read."

"Can you e-mail it to me?"

With a flourish like a conjurer, he whips a few pieces of paper out from behind his back. "I just happen to have it here," he says. "Since I had a feeling that you may be a bit behind on your e-mail." He grins, flips over the first page of the document, and places it in front of me, pointing to the relevant paragraph. "Just read this," he says. I do what I'm told.

"It'll do," I say. "Tell her to issue it, with my apologies for the delay."

"Done," says Geoff. "I'm heading down to grab a coffee. Can I bring something back for you?"

"You're an angel," I say. I don't have time to run downstairs, and in any event, I need to stay as far away from Nigel as possible. "Hot tea, please. With lemon."

Geoff looks concerned. "Are you sick again?" he asks. I shrug and Geoff shakes his head. "Has it occurred to you that your body might be trying to tell you something?" he asks.

"It can get in line," I say.

At ten past one, I'm walking as quickly as I can with the binders in my arms. I'm late, of course; I'm always late these days. I can remember a time before I had children when I was always early; I have a mental picture of myself standing outside the movie theater, waiting for friends, checking my watch every thirty seconds starting at the appointed hour. Back then I thought chronic lateness was a character flaw, evidence of a profound self-absorption. Now I regard it as a mark of efficiency. Imagine how much time you would lose if you were early for everything. I read once that economists say if you travel for business you should miss one out of every three flights; the repeated close shaves save you more time than the occasional missed flight loses you. I like this justification; the alternative theory is that I can't get my shit together to be on time for anything anymore, but I don't like that one as much.

Overall, though, I'm feeling a little more in control of my day now. I've spent the last two hours plowing through sixty-three e-mails: thirty-two of the for-your-information variety requiring no comment from me; twelve requiring a quick review and approval; one from the convener of my book club; four reply-all messages from other members of the book club; one from Jamie's class parent about volunteering for the winter fair; four from my mother; and nine that, to be honest, I haven't dealt with yet and have re-filed in my inbox. But I'm fifty-four e-mails lighter, and that can only be a good thing. I've even found twenty minutes to look at the binders and have managed to affix brightly colored sticky flags on a few random CVs to demonstrate my enthusiasm for the process.

I push open the door and get my bearings. I recognize a few familiar faces from the hospital's medical staff and administration: Carolyn Waldron, the head of oncology; Marvin Shapiro, the director of medical research; Anusha Dhaliwal, the head of the nursing staff; and Patti Sinclair, the patient liaison officer, responsible for running interference between unhappy patient families and the hospital. Carolyn gives me a friendly wave and Marvin nods courteously. I've worked with both of them recently on the publicity for major gifts to their units. Jenny Dixon, the director of HR, is here too; I avoid eye contact in the knowledge that I have been avoiding her weekly e-mail about staff reviews for the past five weeks. In truth, I'm a little scared of Jenny. She is a large, imposing woman who was born in a shantytown in the Dominican Republic, came to North America as a young teenager, and managed to put herself through two university degrees and raise three children without missing a beat in her career. Although she is unfailingly polite and supportive in the classic manner of HR professionals, I always feel like a pathetic whiner around her. The rest of the faces are completely unfamiliar, a man and two women, all of whom must be from the board. Then Barry comes in and we all take our seats.

"Good afternoon, everyone," booms Barry. "I don't expect that this will be a long meeting today. As you know, we are moving quickly to the interview stage here, so what we want to do today is finalize the short list so that we can check references. We have a meeting on Wednesday to decide on the interview questions and then interviews on Friday. Everyone on the long list has been asked to keep Friday clear, so there shouldn't be any problem with availability."

He pauses, and seems to grit his teeth before continuing. I catch a quick look that passes between Patti and Jenny, and I resolve once again to stay as far away from the field of battle as possible. It's clear that allegiances are already forming in this room, and I have zero interest in finding myself on Barry's bad side. In any event, I'm distracted by the fact that my skirt is stretching uncomfortably over my hips and riding up inappropriately. I surreptitiously yank the skirt down by a fraction and vow to stop drinking wine every night with my takeout.

Barry studies the notes on the table in front of him. Ordinarily,

Barry doesn't believe in speaking from notes; you can't command the room, he says, unless you can convey the impression that you are speaking from the heart. In practice, this means that Barry ignores all of the carefully prepared briefing notes that we write for him and is notorious for going off-message. But today, he is sticking to his script, a bad sign.

"I also want to address the issue that Mrs. Baxter raised at the last meeting about the board's policy on equity in hiring. Although I said at the time that I didn't think the policy applied for the purposes of this search, I have since been advised by HR"—he glares at Jenny—"that we should be scrupulous in our efforts to uphold board policy in all of our searches. So I want to take this opportunity to thank Mrs. Baxter for her very helpful intervention." Barry grimaces as though he has bitten down on something sour. One of the women from the board—presumably Mrs. Baxter—inclines her head in a queenly gesture.

I look at her for the first time and feel my eyes widen. A blond beehive hairdo towers over a vacant face decorated with inappropriately bright pink lipstick applied well over the lip line and a harsh stripe of rouge on each cheek. She wears a pilled blue Chanel suit that has clearly languished in the back of a closet for forty years, and I think I catch a faint whiff of mothballs across the table. The outfit is finished with an honest-to-God fox stole wrapped around her neck, the sharp little teeth clutching the end of the tail and the beady glass eyes gleaming sightlessly in the fluorescent light.

Astonishingly, no one else at the meeting seems distracted by Mrs. Baxter's extraordinary costume. I sneak another glance and find to my surprise that her expression has shifted. She is focused now, her eyes alert. When she sees that she has my attention, she cocks her head and gives me an almost imperceptible but unmistakable wink. And then she puts a long finger up to her lips. It is simultaneously a signal between conspirators that a prank of epic proportions is in the works and a warning not to spoil the fun.

It is a gesture that I would recognize anywhere, having seen it many times over the years. It's one of Lillian Parker's signature moves, but this is a novel context, and it dawns on me that Lil's message this morning had nothing whatsoever to do with her holiday party. I tune Barry out while I construct and reject several elaborate theories to explain why this search could possibly have piqued Lil's interest, why everyone in the room seems to think her name is Mrs. Baxter, and why Lil has deemed it necessary to come in disguise.

". . . committed to a short list of three. Since the policy that we are bound to follow requires that we meet with the most qualified female candidate and the most qualified visible minority candidate, we may need to alter our preliminary selections," Barry continues. "Obviously, we are all interested in seeing Stephen Paul."

I flip through my binder. This isn't a name that I remember seeing. I find the CV and can see immediately why I didn't flag it; the candidate has years of experience as the CEO of a major corporation, but there's nothing on the CV about fund-raising. I'm obviously missing something here. I raise my index finger in the air.

Barry registers my presence, and raises his hand. "Just a minute," he says. "I should have mentioned one other thing. When we reviewed the policy earlier this week, we discovered"—again he glares at Jenny—"that we were short a staff rep. So I've asked"—he consults his notes—"Sophie Whelan from the communications office to serve for the last leg of our deliberations." The group swivels to look at me, and I give a little wave. "Did you have a question, Sophie?" asks Barry, discouragingly.

"Just a quick one," I say. "I have Mr. Paul's CV here, but I don't have any information about his fund-raising experience. I assume you had this discussion before I joined the committee, but I was hoping you could fill me in if we are going to interview him."

Now Barry glowers, Jenny beams, and I want to stab myself with my pen for having wandered into enemy camp in my first five minutes. "Our view is that Stephen's experience managing a massive public corporation for fifteen years is extremely transferable," Barry asserts. "And obviously, as CEO, he has had oversight of the corporation's philanthropic foundation."

Barry is putting me on notice that further interventions will be unwelcome, and may even convert his general indifference to antipathy. I square my shoulders and raise my hand again. Barry frowns. "Yes?"

"Again, please accept my apologies if I go over things that you've already discussed. I just want to make sure that I'm on the same page." I point to the CV on the table in front of me. "Obviously, Mr. Paul has extensive experience working with his corporate foundation, but I'm not sure how transferable that experience would be to our operation." Several people straighten in their chairs and lean forward; I'm not sure whether they are interested in my analysis or just want to get a good view of the new kid's act of self-immolation. "Corporate foundations give money away," I continue. "In the most basic terms, their job is to manage an annual budget and decide how to allocate it among worthy charities and community projects. An organization like ours works in the opposite way. We raise money from the community in order to support our own projects." I pause. "The vice president of advancement is our lead fundraiser."

"Thank you, Sophie," says Barry, crisply. "I think we are all aware of that. And as we discussed prior to your appointment to this committee, Stephen's vast experience in deal-making will give him an edge in any donor negotiations."

I murmur my thanks for Barry's helpful clarification, and then sit back while I consider how to proceed. I could quit the committee, which a large part of me desperately wants to do, but in the end I know I won't. This is because most of my actions are governed by a complex calculation that I call the Requirement of Action Rating, or ROAR. The ROAR is a number that is produced by adding the Desire to Perform Activity (DPA) to the Guilt Factor (GF) associated with the failure to perform the activity and the Need to Behave Like a Grown-up (NBLG), and then subtracting Allowable Selfishness (AS). So: DPA + GF + NBLG − AS = ROAR. Although the temptation is often to allocate a negative number to the Desire to Perform Activity (DPA), the available range is zero to ten. Allowable Selfishness (AS) is generally in the range of one to five, except when it is your birthday (8), or you are in labor (9), in the hospital in critical condition (9.5), or in a coma (10).

My desire to remain on the committee in order to fill a quota, ignored on a good day and reviled on a bad one, is obviously zero (DPA = 0). My guilt factor, on the other hand, is not insignificant, since I suspect that Barry won't replace me if I leave. And then someone will be hired to supervise my unit with no staff input at all, a person who will in all likelihood be totally ignorant about the work we do and have a mild-to-serious personality disorder (GF = 8). My need to behave like a grown-up is heightened by the public nature of this committee and my personal vow to maintain a stiff upper lip around people like Jenny Dixon (NBLG = 9). And while I'm entitled to some selfishness due to Barry's rudeness (AS = 4), it doesn't change the fact that $0 + 8 + 9 - 4 = 13$, which is a very high score indeed. According to the ROAR, I'm staying. But my first order of business is to grab Lil at the end of this meeting and find out what she's up to.

". . . Margaret Anderson," I hear Carolyn say. "She is the strongest female candidate by far, and in my view, the strongest candidate on paper. She has had a distinguished nursing career, so she knows how things get done inside a hospital, and she has ten years of experience in fund-raising in the health care sector."

"Do others agree with Carolyn's assessment?" asks Barry. "Should Margaret Anderson be included on the short list?" There is general assent around the table, and the discussion moves on to the policy requirement for a visible minority candidate. But the conversation has barely started when the door to the conference room flies open and hits the wall. The committee jumps collectively in their seats; a couple of the women are so startled that they screech. And into this tableau steps Joy, with a gleam of malicious delight in her eyes.

"So sorry to interrupt," she says in a creamy voice. "Sophie, you need to call your daycare immediately. Your son has a fever. They want you to pick him up."

"That's fine, Sophie," says Barry. "Go ahead. There's nothing here that we need you for."

I rise from my seat, my face still burning with embarrassment, and step into the hall. Joy's back is already receding into the distance.

"Joy," I call, and then louder: "Joy!"

She turns but makes no move to close the distance, so I half-run to meet her, silently cursing myself for yet another failure to take charge of this toxic relationship.

"I would have preferred for you to show more discretion in there," I say. "Next time, please just say that you have an urgent message for me and ask me to step out of the meeting."

She shrugs. "Whatever," she says.

Back at my desk, I call Jesse's cell phone to see if there is any way that he can pick Scotty up and take him to the pediatrician. I don't know how I can leave the office now; I still haven't met with my staff or reviewed the six proposals sitting on my desk or figured out what to do about the Gala. Jesse doesn't answer. I call his office line. No answer. I call his assistant. No answer.

I suspect that Jesse screens my calls whenever he's too busy to be dragged into a domestic quagmire, and it makes me hot with anger. It must be nice to be able to be completely unavailable. Restful, to be able to ignore the call from the daycare, to be certain that someone else will deal with it, and to know that the someone has a "flexible" job, where it doesn't matter if she disappears for half the day to go to the goddamn pediatrician.

I call his cell phone again.

"Jesse Walker," he says.

"I've been calling and calling," I say in a controlled voice. "Where were you?"

"Sophie, I'm in the middle of something," he says. "Do we need to do this right now?"

I grit my teeth. I am going to be a mature adult. I am not going to say something passive-aggressive like, *So sorry to disturb you. It's only about our son.*

"So sorry to disturb you," I say. "It's only about our son." I hear Jesse sigh at the other end of the line. "Scotty needs to be picked up from daycare. His fever spiked and he needs to go to Dr. Goldstein's. I'm sure he's going to need a prescription." I soften my tone; you catch more flies with honey than vinegar, and vinegar is clearly not working. "Please, Jesse. I am really underwater here."

There is a pause. "Sophie," he says, "I'm sorry, but I can't. We have a meeting with the investors at the end of the day, and we are all scrambling to put the presentation together. I can't even really talk on the phone right now. Did you try your mother?"

"Not yet," I say.

"Well, you're going to have to sort it out without me. I've got to go. I'll call you later and check in." And I'm listening to dead air.

I think of the four e-mails and two phone messages about Christmas and I know that I am not going to try my mother. I'm going to close my door and burst into tears. I'm going to sweep all of the paper off my desk and into my bag so that I can do it after the kids are in bed. And then I'm going to get into my car and take my son to the doctor.

And that's exactly what I do.

CHAPTER THREE

monday, december 2, 2013

And so it is that I find myself in the car on Monday afternoon (how can it still be Monday? *how?*), inventing crazy routes to avoid traffic as I race to the doctor's office. There is no woman more desperate on earth than the one with a sick and deeply unhappy toddler in the back, trying to make it to the pediatrician before he leaves for the day. A lot of ink has been spilled drafting laws to make the roads safer from people who drink and drive or talk on their cell phones and drive, or wear sexy bathing suits and drive, which is apparently very distracting for drivers in Kentucky. But in my opinion, regulators have really missed the boat here, since the most dangerous, distracted drivers on the road are moms with screaming children in the backseat. You can see them everywhere, belting out their little one's favorite tunes from the Creative Caregivers Singing Circle and shimmying in the driver's seat, contorting backward through the gap between the seats to shove pacifiers and animal crackers into their darling babies' mouths, or just weeping hysterically at the horror of it all. And today, I'm one of them.

I've got my wireless headset wedged in my ear, and I'm trying to do a modified staff meeting over the phone, which is profoundly unsatisfy-ing for everyone concerned since at least half of the discussion is drowned out by Scotty's howls. It's the standard docket: three press releases for approval, two major proposals in development, and a variety of daily media inquiries, none of them particularly earth-shattering. Erica's peevishness comes across the line loud and clear; she feels ignored and she's not wrong. But she's a grown-up and writing press releases isn't rocket science, for God's sake, and for today, I'm delegating supervision of her work to Geoff. In my current state, he's going to do a better job of it anyway. And he has much more innate patience than I do for the delicate emotional states of my little group of writers, all of whom think that they should be producing the Great Novel and exist in a state of quiet despair that the exigencies of mortgages and groceries require them to write thank-you letters and donor profiles instead. Thank heavens for Geoff, the sanest creative type on planet Earth, and his unexpected talent for HR management.

I had been planning a brainstorming session on the Gala theme, but the shrieking is hitting an alarming crescendo, and after nearly rear-ending a city bus, I decide that I am going to have to concentrate on getting to the doctor in one piece. I ask them to continue the meeting without me and hang up. And I need to calm down before we get to the office so that I can pull off my Competent Professional Mother in Control of Her Life impression. For reasons that I don't fully understand, sitting in Dr. Goldstein's waiting room seems to trigger intense paranoia in me. I'm always convinced that he will take one look at my kids and diagnose them with scurvy or some other disease that has been eradicated in all but the most negligent households in the developed world. As a result, I talk too much and put words in the children's mouths, boast inappropriately about their achievements, and generally undermine my own efforts to portray myself as a successful and relaxed parent.

Dr. Goldstein comes into the examining room. "What do we have here?" he asks. "Another ear infection, young man?" He pulls out his scope and looks at me expectantly. "I'll need you to lay him down and hold his arms so I can get a good angle into his ears."

Scotty, who has been sobbing at a slightly lower volume since we arrived, ramps it up at the sight of Dr. Goldstein. He goes rigid as I try to lay him down, kicking furiously and making contact with my left breast, which hurts so much that it takes my breath away. I lose my grip on him entirely. Dr. Goldstein steps in. "Like this," he says, and in a nanosecond he has Scotty pinned on the table. "Now hold his hands here—no, not like that, like this—right." With practiced movements, he jabs the scope in one ear and then the other, and takes Scotty's temperature for good measure. "All done," he says. "You can let him up."

And now Dr. Goldstein turns his attention to me. "The right ear is red and his temperature is slightly elevated." He reaches over and grabs a prescription pad and scribbles something completely illegible. "He's had a few more ear infections this year than I would like. I'm giving you something a bit stronger this time. But if the infections don't taper off, we're going to have to consider tubes."

At this, I feel my calm façade start to crack; in truth, Dr. Goldstein's pronouncement makes me want to wrap my sick baby in my arms, sink down to the floor, and start bawling right along with him. Antibiotics are one thing, we have them every couple of weeks, but how am I going to manage a surgery? And where is Jesse going to be when all of this happens? He's not the one here now, listening to Dr. Goldstein announce that our son has defective ears, and my bet is that he'll manage to have a meeting that conflicts with everything that follows—the pre-op, the surgery, and the days of recovery spent unwrapping Popsicles and switching *Backyardigans* DVDs. Not that Jesse would be able to pry me away from Scotty's side, since nothing fills me with purpose like nursing my children when they're sick. I'm never more patient, more effortlessly loving, than when my children need me. And never more conscious of the fact that their father enjoys a different kind of freedom.

Dr. Goldstein appears surprised, and I can tell that whatever expression is on my face at this moment, it is inappropriate. "It's a minor procedure," he says soothingly. "And it may not be necessary at all. Let's just cross that bridge when we come to it, all right?" And I know in that moment that neither he nor I believe that I am a Competent Professional Mother in Control of Her Life, Her Children, or Anything Else. "And what about you?" he asks, adding insult to injury. "You look a little flushed. Are you sick as well?"

A responsible adult would admit weakness, would reach out and take help where it is offered. But I am determined to cling to the one little raft in the roiling sea of chaos that is my life. I will not give in. I may have a cold, but it is only a small, insignificant cold that will be gone tomorrow because I refuse to acknowledge its existence. No retreat, no surrender. "No," I say. "I'm absolutely fine. Thanks so much for fitting us in."

I pack Scotty back into the car. When we reach the drugstore, I lift him out of the car, whispering soothing words while he screams his head off, and carry him inside where I bounce him up and down on a hard plastic chair for fifteen minutes while the pharmacist fills his pre-scription on a rush basis. I stroke his sweat-damp hair and sing a song about sleepy bunnies, which has no effect on Scotty but makes all of the busy people waiting in line look at us with varying degrees of pity, annoyance, and outright dislike. When we finally make it home, it is four-thirty, far too late to find alternative care arrangements, even if I had any bright ideas about how to do that, which I don't. I give Scotty a dose of medicine, tuck him in on the sofa with a blanket and a DVD, and contemplate drinking heavily. But Jamie is due back from school any minute, so I decide to do a few minutes of work while I can.

As I empty the papers from my desk out of my bag, a pink message slip drifts to the floor. I scoop it up and feel a rush of adrenaline as I read the name. I haven't seen Will Shannon in at least three years, but the thought of him never fails to trigger a chemical reaction. I examine the message slip with the attention of a scholar deciphering the meaning of an ancient manuscript. Joy hasn't given me a lot to work with here. Assuming that she ticked the correct box, I can expect a call back. But the bottom of the check mark is touching the box below, which could indicate that Will is expecting me to call. There's no number on the slip, but Will knows that I have it, and Joy is really unreliable when it comes to getting full information from callers. And there's no actual message, so it's hard to justify jumping the gun and calling him first when there is no obvious issue that needs to be addressed. I could send an e-mail, something quick and light saying that I got his message and asking when might be a good time to connect since my schedule is so crazy. I don't want to give the impression that I've been sitting by the phone. I'm mulling over the possibilities when the phone rings.

"Hey, Soph," says Jesse. "How did it go at the doctor?"

"Scotty has another ear infection," I say. I'm still irked by the ease with which Jesse passes responsibility for our kids over to me, but he gets a few points for calling to check in. I communicate this by adopting a tone that is measured and mature, and only a bit chilly.

"No scurvy today?" he asks. I smile in spite of myself. "Did you pick up the prescription?"

My smile vanishes so quickly that the corners of my mouth hurt, and I put the phone down on the counter for a second so that I don't throw it across the room. As if I wouldn't pick up the prescription! As if there would ever be a slight chance that the job would fall to Jesse! I bristle with indignation; that the sum total of Jesse's contribution to today's misadventure should be to drop in at the end and ask stupid, self-serving questions, and that this should count as engaged fatherhood, seems wildly unfair.

"Are you there?" he asks.

"Sorry," I say. "The line cut out for a minute." The surge of rage is fading, and I wonder if any of this is really Jesse's fault. In choosing to juggle the competing demands of work and family, I was bargaining on a professional life that would be worthy of the effort. Juggle—the word annoys me intensely when applied to the multiple responsibilities of my life, suggesting as it does a trifling hobby with the sole purpose of entertaining a paying audience, none of which actually relates to the conditions of my existence. When I made my choices, I anticipated a steady rise in stature and an accumulation of accolades that would make the wisdom of my choice clear. Perhaps more importantly, I was terrified of finding myself on the stay-at-home end of one of those excruciating conversations in which a working mother attempts and generally fails to persuade a stay-at-home mother that she values and admires the choices that have led the latter to a life of unpaid, unappreciated, and unremembered domestic labor. Am I actually angry because the biggest challenge and crowning achievement of my day has been the mere acquisition of a prescription?

"I got the prescription," I say. "I've given him the first dose."

"Great," he says. "What's he doing now?"

"He's watching unlimited episodes of *Dora* and *Diego*, which is making him marginally less miserable. When will you be home?"

Jesse pauses, and now I can hear the telltale clicking of his keyboard and I think my head is going to explode. I can't believe that just moments ago, I was trying to persuade myself that anger is just shame turned outward. Jesse can't even concentrate for more than two minutes on a conversation about our poor sick child, who is running a fever, for God's sake, on the couch in the next room, without doing e-mail.

"I'm sorry, Soph, but I'm going to be late," he says. "The meeting this afternoon went well, and this group of investors seems serious, but Anya thinks that it's important to cement the relationship by taking them out to dinner."

"I'm sure she does," I say, not very nicely. Anya is all sharp edges: cutting wit, experimental jewelry, severe bangs over prominent cheekbones, bony hips. She doesn't have kids and, I'm quite sure, doesn't like kids; and most of the time I think she pretends that Jesse doesn't have them either. She has primary responsibility for business development at the firm, which gives her the power to disrupt our family schedule by routinely booking after-hours command performances for Jesse that I am certain could easily be accommodated during the workday. I can't stand her.

"Sophie," says Jesse, in a tone that is both a plea and a warning.

"Fine," I say. This is an old conversation and I know better than to go there. When Jesse started the business with Anya, I gave him my full and unconditional support by learning to appreciate Anya's strengths and accept her differences (what Jesse actually said) and not driving Jesse mad by unpacking every exchange with Anya and looking for imagined slights (what Jesse actually meant). It's been a bigger struggle since our disastrous trip to Las Vegas earlier this year. Jesse and Anya had a trade show that fell on our anniversary weekend, so I tagged along, thinking that we'd be able to carve out some time together. But in the end, Anya found a reason why Jesse had to be with her at all hours. I sat by the pool and got drunk in the desert sun and ordered room service by day; and by night I watched bad movies on pay-per-view and tried unsuccessfully to beat back my paranoid suspicion that Anya's ambitions for her relationship with Jesse extended well beyond the confines of the business. But I'm committed to getting past it, because I know that Jesse is incredibly stressed about the funding for their new project. It is a huge condominium development with street-level commercial space and state-of-the-art environmental technology, which is Jesse's area of expertise. If they can get the financing together, their little company will establish its reputation in a tough and crowded market. But they've had to extend themselves a long way to get all of the permissions, plans, and computer-generated renderings, and if the financing falls through, the company is likely to go the same way. I reach for my better self.

"Good luck," I say. "I love you."

There is a moment of silence and I hear that Jesse has stopped typing. "I love you, too," he says distractedly. "Oh, Soph, Anya is waving me back. I've got to go. See you later." And he's off.

I sit at the breakfast bar in the home that we have bought and renovated together and look at the pink message slip on the counter, thinking, *This is what no one tells you about marriage.* No one tells you that you will feel angry and disappointed and lonely; no one tells you that you will have to work so hard to be good to each other. No one tells you that you will wonder whether it is worth it.

Marriage is a trade-off, but not the one you think. When you get married, you think you are trading freedom for certainty, and a past of failed love affairs for a future in which your romantic hopes are realized. There is a heady sense of emancipation that comes with the knowledge that you will never again look at your spouse and ask: Does he like me back? Does he want to kiss me? Do we belong together? When Jesse proposed to me, it was the definitive answer to all of these questions, and I almost wept with relief.

And then, as time marches on, you realize that in the day-to-day-ness of your married life together, in your haste to escape from the insecurity of your pre-married existence, something essential has been lost. The very uncertainty that made you sick with anxiety also fueled your desire. Think about the most romantic moment of your life and you'll see what I mean. Eyes meeting across a room, an unexpected touch that crackled like electricity on your skin, a first kiss under a streetlight in the snow, your beloved getting down on one knee: the moment was about expectation, the anticipation of a future where the relationship moved forward and deepened. Marriage, even a great marriage, is decidedly lacking in anticipation. There aren't a lot of surprises, and let's face it, surprises in marriage are rarely good ones. Announcements such as "I've discovered that I really like men/my twenty-five-year-old secretary," or "I've decided that instead of working I want to build giant art installations out of car parts in our backyard," are not in the standard happily-ever-after package.

And then you realize something even more disappointing. Marriage doesn't change either one of you. It changes your outward behavior, because you are—at least ostensibly—committed to the social norms associated with the institution: fidelity, for most, but also a whole host of more mundane acts that fall into the category of making an effort, like contributing to the family income, and treating each other with respect, and being nice to your husband's loathsome business partner. But all of your essential insecurities and desires eventually surface over time, like landmines in the desert.

I believe in marriage. I believe that two good people can be happy together for a lifetime. It's the only thing even close to a religion that I have, and I cling to it with almost messianic zeal. But it is a belief system that makes unreasonable demands on its adherents, all of us sacrificing to the bone for a reward that may or may not come at the end of our days, and all of us steadfastly refusing to see the mounting evidence that long-term happy marriages, if they exist at all, are pretty hard to come by. We all want to think that miracles are possible. Otherwise, marriage is just a lot of hard work.

The front door opens and snaps me out of my reverie. It's Jamie, home from school with the thirteen-year-old neighbor who picks him up from aftercare every day. I pay her extra to give him a snack and stay with him until I get home. By now she's probably saved enough to pay for her college tuition.

"Mommy!" Jamie lights up to find me here, races over, and throws himself into my arms with a force that nearly bowls me over.

"Hi, sweetie," I say, and I kiss his curly head and know that this is the best moment I've had all day.

"I have a letter for you, Mommy," he says, opening his backpack and presenting me with an envelope. I open it, and find a stern missive from Kelly Robinson, the Parent Council chair, advising me in bold type that I'm shirking my duty to provide the recommended number of volunteer hours at the school. Watkins Elementary is a *community school*, where *parent engagement* is a *critical resource* to provide children with the *strongest possible education in the early years*, Kelly writes, and according to her records, I haven't volunteered for *a single event all year*. Ignoring her request to contact her *at my earliest convenience*, I crumple the note and throw it in the garbage.

"What do you want for dinner, baby?" I ask.

He thinks for a bit. "Can we order pizza?" he asks.

I can see that he doesn't really think I'll say yes, but I want him to believe in miracles for a little longer, so I say, "Sure."

"Awesome!" He punches his fist in the air, an expression of wonderment on his face.

"Where did you learn that?" I ask, miming his fist pump.

"Dad does it when we watch the hockey game," he says, and I remind myself that Jesse is a great father while I pick up the phone and call for dinner.

"How was school today?" I ask.

"OK," he says. "We did science. Oscar had a time-out."

"How come?"

"Mrs. Carron told him to take turns with Lily and he said no."

It strikes me, not for the first time, how few of the qualities that we consider necessary for survival—sharing, putting the interests of others ahead of your own, controlling your emotions—are innate. Our parents try, our teachers try, and we, as adults, try to reinforce these learned behaviors in ourselves, but fundamentally, we would rather throw our crayons on the floor than share them. No wonder marriage is so hard.

Jamie and I hang out at the breakfast bar, waiting for our pizza. He has some juice and I have some wine (because it's been a long day, and it's true that wine has a lot of calories, but you really have to do the analysis of whether it's more important to be skinny or to be sane, and anyway, it's sensible to hold something in reserve for your New Year's resolution), and he draws me a picture of Anakin Skywalker battling an army of droids.

It's not until Jamie says, "What's Scotty watching?" that I realize the theme song from the menu screen is playing over and over again, and if the video is over and Scotty isn't shouting for me to fix it, it can only mean one thing. I groan and peer into the den, where I see Scotty fast asleep on the couch, two hours before his bedtime. With two of my essential parenting principles in conflict, I am torn between Never Wake a Sleeping Child and Mess with Bedtime at Your Peril; but Scotty needs the rest, and I'm not keen on the prospect of spending two hours with a fussy three-year-old who would rather be sleeping. I carry Scotty upstairs, and he barely moves as I change him into pajamas and roll his sweaty little head onto the pillow. I sit on the edge of his bed for a minute or two, listening to his congested snorts and snuffles in the dark, and my chest aches with the fierceness of my love for him. When Jamie was born, I realized that children are to their parents as Kryptonite is to Superman—they are the only thing in the world with the power to destroy us utterly, and their presence leaves us in a state of constant and unrelenting vulnerability. But by the time we realize it, we're committed forever.

The doorbell rings and I rush downstairs to claim the pizza. "Do you want to watch *Clone Wars?*" I ask Jamie.

"Can we eat in the TV room?" he asks, as if hardly daring to imagine that an ordinary weeknight could offer such marvels.

"Absolutely," I say, and as we snuggle on the couch, eat our supper, and watch the Jedi restore peace to the universe, I think, *Just under the wire, it turned into a good day after all.*

CHAPTER FOUR

august 1994

"It's Paris," says Zoe. "I'm going."

It's a steamy Saturday night in August and we're walking to a party. We're down to a handful of weekends before classes start, our last September as the graduating class of 1995. It's muggy and airless, and I'm deeply regretting my choice of footwear. I've got my hair up in a scrunchie and am draped in a loose, sleeveless black peasant dress, but they are doing little to compensate for the fact that my feet are slippery with sweat inside my Doc Martens.

I've been planning this conversation for a few days now, but it's not going the way I thought it would. "I can't afford the apartment without you," I say.

"That's why I've been telling you since May to make other plans," says Zoe. "I'm sorry, Sophie. I know how much you hate the idea of moving, but I'm going to Paris."

I try one last time. "Are you sure you want to miss your last year on campus? It's the best one. You can take all these great seminar courses . . ." I trail off as Zoe starts laughing.

"That's you, Soph, not me," she says. "With my GPA, it's a miracle I got permission to do the exchange program at all. It's happening." She throws an arm around my shoulder. "It's not the end of the world," she says. "You can come and visit me next summer. And I'll help you find a place. I'm going to ask a few people tonight."

"I don't want to live with a bunch of strangers," I say.

"Strangers are just friends you haven't met yet," says Zoe, quoting one of my mother's notorious aphorisms. I open my mouth, stick my finger in, and make a gagging sound. "No need to be dramatic," says Zoe. "We'll find you something great. I promise. Now stop pouting and try to have some fun tonight. Will's parties are legendary."

"Is he on your hit list?" I ask. It's clear that someone is; Zoe is wearing a baby-sized black tee with the words DO YOU WANT ME TO SEDUCE YOU? emblazoned across the midriff. It's supposed to be ironic, but it works like a charm. It reminds me that Zoe isn't an entirely satisfactory roommate; she rarely comes home alone on the weekend, if she comes home at all. But I've adjusted to her, and it's a small price to share, however peripherally, in her sparkle. She gets me out of the house and out of my head.

"Oh, no," she says. "I fooled around with him in high school, lucky me; it was like getting vaccinated. He's trouble. I've got my eye on a couple of his engineering buddies."

"Tell me again who Will is." Zoe has a gigantic social circle: high school friends, camp friends, skiing friends, family friends. It's dizzying to try to keep track of them all. I've never moved in packs; I'm more curatorial in my approach to collecting friends. And if I'm honest, I've never felt comfortable in Zoe's pack. I recognize their ilk from my waitress days at the golf club near my parents' house up in cottage country— all streaked hair and diamond studs and high-quality fake IDs. Having collected Zoe, I try to hold up my end among the various PSR&Bs (Pretty, Skinny, Rich, and Blonds) in her orbit, but I still feel like I'm supposed to be bringing them cheeseburgers and Tom Collins cocktails.

The first time I met Zoe was in my college dorm, in the first week of school. I was in my room, but with the door open, which was a compromise with my shy self: I wouldn't venture forth into potentially awkward human contact, but would, by way of the open door, indicate basic sociability. No one had taken up my admittedly obscure invitation to come in and befriend me until Zoe showed up. I had noticed her, of course; she was absolutely gorgeous and seemed to have acquired an entourage in the short time since she had arrived.

"Are you squeamish?" she asked.

"No."

"Great. Then you can help me." She came in and held out her hand. "I'm Zoe Hennessy."

"Sophie Whelan."

Zoe held out a diamond stud. "My piercing closed up." She laughed at the expression on my face. "Don't worry—the one in my ear. Can you push this through?"

I was fairly sick with loneliness by this point and prepared to take friendship in whatever form it was offered. "Sure," I said. "Have a seat."

Zoe sat down and I got to work. She barely winced. "Hey," she said, pointing to the *Thelma & Louise* poster on my wall. "My English teacher liked that movie too. We had to write an essay on female empowerment. I always wondered: am I the only one who noticed that they drive off a fucking *cliff* at the end? What's empowering about that? Ouch."

"Sorry. But it's in. You're done."

"Awesome," she said, standing up. "I knew the girl in black would know how to do a piercing."

"The girl in black?"

"Yeah. You're the mysterious, artsy one on the floor. Aren't you?"

"I don't know," I said, too surprised to be anything other than honest. I'd always wanted to be mysterious and artsy, and I had chosen my back-to-school wardrobe accordingly with a heavy emphasis on long black skirts, black flowing blouses, and dangling earrings. If my new floor-mates found me mysterious, though, it was more likely because I was scared to come out of my room.

"You are," she said, definitively, and I felt a rush of gratitude that I'd been given an identity in this strange new world. "What are you doing right now?"

"Nothing. Just hanging out," I said, by which I meant that I planned to spend the evening alone, listening to the Indigo Girls and hoping that someone would come by to invite me to do something more interesting.

"I'm going to a party at the res next door. Do you want to come?"

It was a lifeline, and I grabbed on with both hands. Then at the end of first year, she astonished me, and everyone who knew either of us, by inviting me to share an apartment with her. Three years of university had sparked countless awakenings of the intellectual, political, and even sexual variety, none of which were due to Zoe, but she was responsible for virtually all of the fun.

"I did tell you this," says Zoe with a touch of exasperation. Zoe thinks I don't make enough of an effort to be social, which is why I am usually single. "Will Shannon. Just moved back to town after doing his undergrad in political science at Duke. Very smart. Rower. Starting law school in September. Throws good parties, which you always miss because you go home for Christmas and summer holidays."

We turn onto Abernathy Road, and Zoe stops outside an enormous redbrick mansion. "He lives here?" I ask. "Is it his parents' house?"

"No," says Zoe. "His parents are uptown. I'm sure this was the address, though." And she climbs the stairs and rings the bell.

When the door opens, it's obvious we're in the right place. The main floor is packed, the music is blaring, and it's incredibly hot. "Push through to the kitchen," yells Zoe, and we head for the back of the house. Above the din, I hear her calling Will's name, and by the time I hit a clearing in the crowd, I see her being lifted onto the kitchen counter. "Beer me, baby," she says, and the boy with his hands around her waist reaches below the counter and comes up with an icy bottle.

Rower, indeed, I think. He's tall, with ridiculously broad shoulders and long muscular arms that make the word *rower* shorthand for *physical perfection.* And then there's the dark hair set off by gray-blue eyes and a white T-shirt that fits in all the right places. I laugh out loud, and both of them turn toward me. They make a striking couple. "Sophie," Zoe calls, waving me over. "I want you to meet Will. Will, this is my roommate, Sophie."

"Hey, Sophie," he says. "Having fun?"

"We just got here," I say, and Zoe grimaces. "Amazing house," I say, trying again. "Is it a rental?"

"Not exactly," he says. "My great-aunt owns it. She lives on the third floor and I'm living on the second floor with a buddy of mine." He turns to Zoe. "Do you know A.J.?"

"Of course," says Zoe. "I saw him at Heidi's last week." Zoe turns to me, and says, meaningfully, "A.J.'s an engineer."

"I heard you're going to Paris," says Will. "When are you leaving?"

"In three weeks," says Zoe. "And I promised Sophie I'd find her a new place to live or a new roommate. Do you know anyone who's looking?"

"I might," he says. "Let me think about it. Sophie, do you want a drink?"

"Please," I say.

"Is A.J. here?" asks Zoe.

"I think all the engineers are in the backyard," says Will.

"I'm going to go and say hi," says Zoe, slipping off the counter. "Back in a bit."

"Careful back there," says Will. "You know engineers. They could be slaughtering a goat or climbing a greased pole. I take no responsibility."

"I've got it covered," says Zoe, and heads to the back, while Will hands me a beer. Another boy enters the kitchen from the living room, and Will shifts a few feet to let him past as he opens the fridge. Will gestures toward the backyard and shrugs. "She'll be back," he says. "Let that be a lesson to you. I'm totally unreliable."

I don't get the joke and shoot him a quizzical look.

"This is A.J.," he says, by way of explanation, and we share a smile.

"Hey," says A.J., turning. I can sort of see why Zoe likes him. He's shorter and more compact than Will, but he's attractive in a generic way. He has nice brown eyes with long dark lashes, which might be soulful on someone else, but he's shaved his head and is wearing a loose basketball tank that screams *jock*.

"This is Zoe's roommate," says Will.

I hold out my hand. "Sophie," I say.

"Oh, right." A.J. nods. "I've heard of you. You're the wingman."

"I'm sorry?"

"Zoe's wingman." I shake my head. "You're the one who goes with her to parties, hangs out with her while she decides who she wants to go after, chats up the guys she doesn't want."

I'm mortified. I always suspected that Zoe's high school friends thought of me as a curiosity; now I see that they think I'm a loser. "It's really not like that," I say. God, engineers are such assholes.

"I didn't mean to offend you," he says.

"It takes more than that," I say, hoping that I sound cutting.

Will steps in. "Zoe's going to Paris and Sophie needs a new place," he says.

"Yeah?"

"What do you think?" asks Will. I'm having trouble following this exchange, but that's nothing unusual. I can never figure out how boys become friends when this is what qualifies as meaningful conversation. The secret must have something to do with sports.

"It's your call, man," says A.J. He looks at me uncertainly. "Are you sure I didn't upset you?"

"Sure," I say.

He runs his hands over his head, exasperated. "OK," he says, finally. "See you around." And he picks his beer up off the counter and heads for the backyard.

"He's a good guy," says Will.

"I'm sure he is," I say, as neutrally as possible. Honestly, could I be more socially inept around Zoe's friends? It's not as though I don't have my own posse down at the student newspaper. My flight instinct is kicking in, and I resolve to give Zoe fifteen minutes to finish her business in the backyard before I start heading for the exit.

"You write for the student newspaper, right?" Will asks.

"You read it?" I'm surprised. Will doesn't seem like a guy who Cares About Issues, unlike my brethren at the paper.

"Not often," he says. "Just trying to figure out what you do for fun."

"Normally on a Saturday night I'd go downtown to search for social injustice and protest against it," I say. "But it was Zoe's turn to choose." Will smiles, and I continue: "Look, Will, it's really nice of you to entertain me, but you should feel free to circulate. I'm fine, honestly."

"So what does offend you?" he asks. "Just out of curiosity."

"One thing above all others," I tell him.

"More than tuition increases?"

I nod solemnly. "More than frats, even."

"More than frats? What could be more offensive than frats?" Will's grin widens.

"Engineers," I say, and both of us burst into laughter.

"There's someone I want you to meet," says Will. "Come on upstairs for a minute." He crosses over to the far side of the kitchen and opens what appears to be a closet door. "After you," he says. I peer in and see a steep, narrow staircase.

I climb up, my thudding footsteps echoing in the stuffy air. I pause on the little landing for the second floor. "Keep going," says Will. On the third floor he stops, reaches past me, and knocks on a door, and I absorb his scent of soap and sweat, cotton and shaving cream: pure, unadulterated male. Will turns the handle and pushes the door open.

"It's Will," he calls.

"Excellent," says a woman's voice. "We were just beginning to get on each other's nerves."

We step into a large sitting room bursting with antique furniture and exquisite oil paintings and books and silk carpets and lamps with fringes, and I have a sudden sensation of having passed through the back of the wardrobe into a new world. In the center of the room, there is a large, carved fireplace flanked by two stone dogs, and sitting across from it on either end of a tufted velvet sofa are two women. One is clearly elderly, stout, unsmiling, and glittering with diamonds. The other is younger and slimmer, in a linen sundress with her bare feet curled up under her. "Hello, darling," says the younger one to Will. "How is your party?"

"Going well, so far," says Will. "I hope it's not too loud. You're welcome to come down, you know."

The older lady shudders; the younger laughs. "I think not," she says. "Who is your friend?"

"This is Sophie," says Will. "She's a friend of Zoe Hennessy's. She needs a rental for September." He turns to me. "This is Lillian Parker, my great-aunt," he says of the younger woman, and then turns to the woman with the diamonds. "And this is my grandmother, Penelope Shannon."

"Do sit down," says Lillian. "Would you like some champagne?"

"Sure," I say. "Thank you, Mrs. Parker."

"So polite, William," she says approvingly. "You can go back to the party." Will turns to go and I stand up to follow him. "Not you, Sophie," she says. "Do you prefer regular champagne or pink?"

I've never heard champagne described as regular, so I say, "Whatever is open is fine."

"Pink, then," she says, and expertly fills a flute. "So," she says, handing me a glass, "you want to rent one of my rooms?"

"Oh," I say. "Well, my roommate is moving out, but I didn't realize . . . that is, Will didn't mention that you had a room available."

"Rascal," says Penelope. It's the first word she has uttered so far, and she delivers it with what appears to be a great effort.

"Penelope and I were roommates once," says Lil. "That was many years ago, of course. She is my oldest friend."

"Attrition," says Penelope.

"She was rather displeased when I married her brother."

"Gold digger," says Penelope, slowly but very clearly.

"All water under the bridge, as you see," says Lil. She lowers her voice. "Penelope has aphasia since her stroke five years ago."

"Six," says Penelope, who obviously has little difficulty with her hearing.

"She can only say a word or two at a time, but she chooses them well. I'm going to show her the room, Pen," says Lil, rising from the sofa and gesturing to me to follow her.

We walk through a large dining room into a vestibule. "The third floor is a self-contained apartment," says Lil. "I live here when I'm in town, which is about half the year." She opens the main door to the apartment and we walk down a grand staircase to the second floor. "There are four bedrooms on this floor," she says. "At the moment, I have Will and his friend A.J. in the two rooms at the end of the hall. I wasn't going to take another tenant but I could probably stand to have one more. I told Will that I would consider adding a girl for a civilizing influence." She walks to the front of the house and opens a door. "Have a peek," she says.

I step inside and catch my breath. It's twice the size of my current room, dominated by a huge bay window with a window seat perched over a leafy maple tree. There is a heavy wooden canopy bed and a dressing table and armoire, all old and perfectly preserved—not unlike Lil, I'm beginning to realize. "You'll need a desk, but otherwise you should have all the furniture you need," she says. "So, what do you think?"

"It's amazing," I say. "But I probably can't afford it. I didn't have a chance to tell Will that I'm on a budget."

"Could you afford two hundred dollars a month?" she asks. "I think that would be reasonable."

"Yes," I say. "I could afford that." She can't be serious. It's half of what I'm paying to live with Zoe. I'd live with strangers if I could save half of my rent; I'd even live with an engineer. At $200 a month, I might even be able to save enough to go and visit Zoe in Paris in the summer.

"Come back upstairs and finish your champagne," she says. "One always makes better decisions over champagne."

We rejoin Penelope in the sitting room, and I settle into an armchair by the fireplace with my glass of pink champagne. "It would be good for those boys to have a girl around," says Lil. "And you seem a very sensible sort." She looks at my boots. "More sensible than most, anyway. So, do we have a deal?"

I can't believe my luck. Excitement and relief explode out of me in a very unsophisticated giggle. I blush. "Yes," I say. "We have a deal."

"Marvelous," says Lil. "This will be great fun."

"Diverting," says Penelope.

"Most definitely. Diverting," agrees Lil. "When will you move in?"

CHAPTER FIVE

tuesday, december 3, 2013

When the alarm goes off, I can hardly believe it, and I lie for a few minutes with my eyes closed, willing it not to be true. I've had so little sleep that I feel hungover, shaky and nauseated, and hollowed-out. *Sleep* is the wrong word, really; I haven't slept, I've napped, a string of short and wildly unsatisfying naps, and now I have to get up and face the day. But I'm not going to do it without coffee, so I stagger downstairs.

Jesse is already dressed and sitting at the breakfast bar, alternating between the newspaper and his BlackBerry.

I pour a cup of coffee. "God, that was a terrible night," I say.

"Agreed." Jesse barely glances up from the paper.

"Scotty was up, what, twice, three times? I lost track." This is not, in fact, true. I know exactly how many times Scotty was awake, and for exactly how many minutes each time, which roughly equals the number of minutes that I lay in the dark awake, listening to Jesse snoring and wondering why I was the only one awake, plus the number of minutes that I snuggled upstairs with Scotty, composing bitter speeches in my head about Jesse's failure to wake up for even a token attempt at shared parenting. This is a test, and Jesse has already failed.

"Three o'clock and four-thirty, maybe, but he may have been up before I got home." If I'm honest, I'm surprised that Jesse can provide an accurate report on Scotty's nocturnal activity, but no less infuriated. I can feel color rising in my cheeks as I realize that Jesse was conscious enough to register the time but couldn't muster the effort to participate.

"I got up with him at midnight," I say.

"Tough break," he says.

"Are you mad at me?" I ask.

"No."

"Because you seem kind of grouchy."

"Sophie." Jesse looks exasperated. "I had the same night you did. I'm tired. I am trying to muster enough energy to get through the day. Must we turn this into a referendum on how well we communicate?"

This is totally uncalled-for. "Jesse," I say in a snarky tone. "That is a far bigger project than I have energy for this morning. I'm simply asking what you're so pissed off about."

His expression is cool. "If you must know, I'm wondering what possessed you to let Scotty fall asleep on the couch at six o'clock last night. By now, I would have thought that you knew to avoid mistakes like that."

Now that I've extracted proof of my suspicions, I'm on the offensive. "Well, you weren't here, were you?" I snap. "Scotty fell asleep and I was supposed to wake him up? He's sick. I didn't think the extra rest could hurt."

"Fine. What's done is done. Let's move on," he says. "I've got to get going anyway. I have an early meeting. My mother will be here at eight-thirty to watch Scotty for the day."

I could be furious with him for leaving me alone for the early shift, but I'm too tired to fight and almost pathetically grateful that he has taken control of the childcare arrangements for the day. So I say, "OK. Have a good meeting." And I lean in for a kiss.

Jesse puts a hand on my shoulder and stops me. "No way, Soph," he says. "You've been sick for two weeks. The last thing we need is for me to get it too." He pats my arm. "See you tonight."

Jesse is right. I am sick. And now I look it, because with Jesse's early departure I didn't have time to shower or put on makeup. Nigel has my number, and today, I fear, it's up—which is why I'm lurking by the garbage cans at the back of the hospital, waiting for the deliveries to start so that I can sneak into the building through the loading dock. The stench of rotting cafeteria waste is gut-wrenching, but the smokers brave it every day, and I can do it for five minutes until the first truck arrives. It occurs to me that if I were a more "integrated" person, which Zoe is always encouraging me to become, I would cling more resolutely to the small amount of dignity that I have left. But then I hear the happy sound of a diesel engine, and I brush away these unpleasant thoughts and concentrate on building a little staircase out of cardboard boxes. As the truck pulls in and the loading-dock door rolls up, I hop from box to box and launch myself off the rim of the nearest Dumpster and over onto the ledge. The receiving clerk gapes, astonished, as I vanish into the bowels of the hospital in a puff of exhaust fumes.

The first sign that something is wrong comes in the elevator. I get a couple of strange looks from the other passengers, one of whom covers her nose and mouth with her hand. I'm still incredibly congested, so I can't confirm it, but the evidence suggests that my morning exploits have had an unexpected consequence. I know I'll get an honest reaction from Joy, who is always enthusiastic about sharing bad news, and I'm not disappointed. She purses her mouth in a little moue of distaste, wrinkles her nose for effect, and says, "What is that revolting smell?"

But she has overplayed her hand, because she has kept me at her desk long enough for me to see that she is in the middle of an epic game of solitaire, and she knows that I know it. So I take full advantage of my upper hand and put a ten-dollar bill in her in-tray. "Could you please do me a favor, Joy?" I ask sweetly. "If you wouldn't mind running down to the pharmacy in the lobby for me and picking up a bottle of Febreze, it would be a big help. I had a mishap taking out the garbage this morning."

I can see the thought bubble forming above Joy's head with the words I HATE YOU in bold type in the air, but she knows that she has lost this round. She nods curtly, scoops up the money, and stalks off. As I watch her go, I think that a job, like any intense relationship, can go sour even from the most promising beginnings. When the Baxter and I first got together six years ago, it was pretty hot: the Baxter loved my hunger and creativity, and the awards I won for designing its website and magazine, and I loved having a senior title and a staff and a reasonable budget for the first time. Lately, though, I think the novelty may be wearing off for both of us.

Geoff arrives for a morning debrief, which I have scheduled first thing so that there is no way I can bump it. He sniffs cautiously.

"I'm working on it," I say. Joy reappears with the Febreze, and I mist myself generously from head to toe. "Better?" I ask.

"Much," he says. "Now you just smell like a suburban sofa."

"That will have to do," I say, as the rest of the staff rolls in.

Erica is up first, so that I can try to defuse some of her hostility. She wants approval for the media package she has prepared on a major donation to our new cancer center, and although we aren't doing the official announcement until next week, she has worked herself into quite a frenzy. She wants to start calling reporters to secure their attendance and insists on finalizing the media package today. I'm not in the mood to tell her that the reporters won't commit to coming this early, and even if they do, they'll blow it off the second a bigger story comes in, and that sending the media package too early is almost a guarantee of having it forgotten by next week, so I take ten minutes and lavish praise on what is, in fact, a fairly mediocre effort. And then I ask Albert and Jacob, our fund-raising writers, to present their draft of the Family Care Center proposal, and I gush to them about how inspiring and incredible it is, and who could fail to be moved to give thirty million to build it; I certainly would if I had cash on hand. And for good measure, I tell them how impressed I am with the Annual Fund thank-you letters, which in my opinion raise the bar for stewardship communications in our sector. This is the cornerstone of my management strategy: douse my resentment with heaping mounds of guilt and then alleviate the guilt by showering employees with unwarranted praise. By the end of the meeting, Erica, Albert, and Jacob are positively glowing, while Geoff looks amused. I ask him to stay behind.

"Too much?" I ask.

He laughs. "I doubt they noticed. Erica's a total narcissist, so I'm sure she took it at face value. And Albert and Jacob are in awe of you, so they were probably touched."

"Excellent," I say. "That should tide them over for a couple of days, then. Now, on to more important matters. Any word on the Gala?"

"You still on your BlackBerry diet?" I nod. "Then you have a lot of e-mail traffic to catch up on. But no decisions, not even close. The committee is spinning off in a million different directions. You and Justine are going to have to rein them in, but I think Justine's taken a powder on this one. I was trying to track her down yesterday, but she was keeping a low profile. I'd guess she doesn't have any bright ideas."

"Perfect," I say. "Did I mention that this is totally not my job?" Geoff smiles sympathetically. "All right, bright ideas are on us. Janelle and the girls like the songs of the eighties, so let's start there. Category is song titles that can carry off a broader theme."

"Springsteen, 'Dancing in the Dark,'" Geoff starts.

"Simple, basic, a good backup," I say. "Bryan Adams, 'Summer of '69'?"

"Too confusing. Is it an eighties theme or a sixties theme? What are the ladies going to wear? Certainly not shapeless flowing frocks with love beads."

"Good point," I say. "'Everybody Have Fun Tonight'?"

"Wang Chung? That song was really awful, even back then," says Geoff. "'Like a Virgin'?"

Now I'm laughing. "Not an appropriate theme for this group of ladies, Geoff. And while we're at it, let's avoid 'Bizarre Love Triangle.'"

"Tough crowd," says Geoff. "I'll come back to it. My brain hurts."

I give him a wicked smile. "Small price to pay when the work is so meaningful."

We snicker in unison, and then we both start giggling, and then guffawing. By the time Geoff gets up to go, I'm slumped in my chair, wiping tears from my eyes.

"You're the best," I say. "Honestly. I know I laid it on thick with the others today, but I want you to know that, in your case, it's one hundred percent sincere. I have no idea how I would manage without you."

Geoff blushes so deeply that I can see his scalp glowing. "Um, thanks," he says, and I remind myself that I should give him this kind of feedback more often. Geoff looks as though he wants to say something else, but instead excuses himself and practically runs out of my office. It's a bit odd, but then again, so is Geoff. There are probably good reasons why he's still single.

I'm tempted to call Will, but I want to check first to see if he's sent an e-mail. Unfortunately, there's no way to open my inbox without triggering an e-mail flood; the members of the Gala committee, it appears, are caught in a terrible reply-all vortex. And they've drifted a long way from songs of the eighties in the past twenty-four hours, proposing and rejecting Mardi Gras (deemed to be insensitive due to the devastation of New Orleans, and offering limited wardrobe possibilities), Beach Party (a thinly veiled excuse for the Pilates crowd to show off their abs, but providing limited wardrobe options for everyone else), Hawaiian Luau (same objections as the Beach Party with the additional downside of terrible music), Mad Men (rejected as too esthetically narrow, and too obviously grasping at coolness), and Beauty and the Beast (an odd suggestion, soundly rejected as creepy, arguably insulting to dates/husbands, and offering little in the way of music that you can dance to). After I've read about fifty messages, I pick up the phone and dial Justine's extension. "I'm deleting the rest of my e-mail," I say. "I can't stand it anymore. Did they make any decisions?"

"Negative," says Justine. "The only suggestion with any traction at the moment is the Fashion Week idea, but at this point it's logistically unworkable. The idea is to have a full-on fashion show with a runway, models, and designers showing new collections in the middle of the event, between dinner and dancing. But the timing is all wrong, and even if we weren't months too late to get the designers on board, all of the fashion weeks will be over by the time we have our event and no one will be interested."

"You lost me there," I say.

"Trust me when I say that you will not care about what I'm going to tell you, but I got an earful from Janelle on this so I'll share my pain. There are four big spring-summer fashion weeks—New York, London, Milan, and Paris—and they all run between February and March. So in a nutshell—and I'm doing some serious editing here—by the time our event happens in March, these ladies will have seen most of the collections, and it won't be that exciting."

"So in what way does it have traction?" I ask.

"At a basic level, by introducing shopping and models, which everyone agrees are fun," says Justine. "But there seems to be consensus now that it's not enough to build an event around."

"So we're no further ahead," I say.

"Correct."

I take a deep breath. "Justine," I say, "today is Tuesday. If we don't get a theme nailed down by the end of the week, there is no chance that we will have an effective marketing strategy in place for this event, which means we won't hit our ticket sales targets, we won't raise enough money, and the event will be a complete failure. I need you to understand how serious this is." But, to be honest, I'm having trouble finding the energy to care.

"These women are impossible," Justine says, not very nicely. "You deal with them, if you think you can do a better job. I've had it."

"Hey," I say, in what I hope is a soothing tone. "It's not your fault. We'll figure it out."

There is an ominous pause, and Justine says, "Sophie, I have to tell you—"

But I interrupt her, because I've just noticed the time, and we are both late. "Shit! Justine, we have a senior management meeting now."

"Oops," she says, and we slam down the phones in unison and sprint out of our offices. We're overdue for our weekly dose of public shaming, otherwise known as Barry's weekly senior staff meeting, and we both know that arriving late is an invitation for retaliation.

Barry is sitting at the head of the table, obviously annoyed, as Justine and I enter. The rest of the team is seated, leafing through a pile of handouts that show our progress toward our annual fund-raising goal. The atmosphere is vaguely funereal, suggesting that we have missed Barry's opening comments on our fund-raising performance. There are seven of us on the senior management team, representing community relations and stewardship, operations, major gift fund-raising, annual fund-raising, research, events, and communications. As a general rule, the head of operations, a pudgy, pasty fellow by the name of Arthur, gets to sit there smugly while the rest of us get raked over the coals for our failure—however indirect—to encourage people to give us money. The rest of us went out for a quiet and wholly inappropriate drink the day the computer system crashed and a bunch of data was lost, and operations took it in the chops.

"Thank you for joining us, ladies," says Barry, darkly—a bad sign. "As I was just telling the rest of the group, it's time to talk turkey. The latest campaign totals are in and they are extremely disappointing. We have just over three weeks until year-end and we are going to have to bear down hard to meet our targets." He gestures to Peter, our director of research. "Peter has produced the report in front of you, which indicates that we have forty million in verbal commitments and solicitations in progress. You can't be a little bit pregnant, people. These numbers mean nothing until we have them in black and white." He scowls at Marni, the director of major gifts; this too is a bad sign, since Marni is a relentless suck-up and, consequently, the closest thing Barry has to a favorite. "Tell your staff that we need to close some deals. I don't care if they have to work 24/7 for the next three weeks. They need to stick to their knitting."

"Understood." Marni winces, but she rallies quickly. "And let me just say, Barry, that I completely agree with your strategy here. The economy is a challenge, but great leadership like yours inspires us to meet and overcome it. Thank you for keeping us focused on what we need to do." She is rewarded with a gracious smile from Barry. The rest of us avert our eyes at her shameless display.

Of course, Barry's expectations are completely unrealistic. No one is papering deals these days, because the economy is—to use a technical term—in the crapper. Philanthropy is a business based on hope and optimism, both of which have been in very short supply for the past couple of years. So while there are lots of donors who are willing to entertain funding proposals, and even some willing to tell us that they will give us money, almost no one wants to sign on the dotted line. Everyone wants to wait until next year, in the optimistic belief that recovery is just around the corner.

"And that goes for your team, too." Barry spins on his casters and points to Jason, the director of community relations and stewardship, which is a fancy term for sucking up to people who have already given you money in the hopes that they might give you more someday. "We've got a bunch of donors on the verbal commitment list from your stewardship program." He waves his fingers at Peter, who hands another document around. "I want you working with Marni's team to make sure that anyone on this list with any possibility of closing a gift is feeling the love. I want you two to put your heads together and come up with a strategy for each and every one of these folks. I want a full-court press, people. Senior volunteers, hospital staff, whatever it takes. Just close the gifts."

Jason nods, resigned. We all know that no amount of team-building is going to change the global recession, but as Barry likes to say, he's a mind-over-matter guy. And now his color rises as he turns to Bill, the director of the Annual Fund, whose results have dropped by thirty percent this year. Annual funds flow directly into the operating budget of the hospital, and are made up of many small gifts that are typically renewed year over year. In a recession, though, donors reduce or cut their monthly or annual gifts to charities as part of an overall belt-tightening exercise. Bill's been tightening his belt too; he's lost about fifteen pounds in the last six months from pure stress.

Barry shoots the Blowfish directly at Bill, who shudders visibly while the rest of us cringe in solidarity. "Well, Bill, there's no way to put lipstick on this pig. The Annual Fund results are disastrous. You leave me no choice." The rest of us exchange anxious glances. Surely Barry wouldn't fire Bill in the middle of a senior management meeting, would he?

"We are going to have to run a holiday appeal ad."

There is a collective exhalation, and we all rejoice inwardly that Bill has escaped the guillotine for now. But then Barry's pronouncement sinks in. A holiday appeal ad? These usually take weeks to write and shoot, and they air on television in the run-up to Christmas, which is to say, now. Several months ago, Barry announced, over Bill's objections, that we would be cutting the holiday ad, as it was too expensive to run and we couldn't prove that it made a measurable difference to the Annual Fund results. At the time, all of us (except Bill) breathed a sigh of relief, since the production of the ad never fails to drain time and energy out of every department.

And almost before Barry spins toward me, the penny drops and I realize that it's payback time for my too-vigorous participation in the search committee meeting yesterday. "Sophie," says Barry. "We will need the full attention of the communications office on this project. The fund-raisers need to drill down on bringing dollars in the door, so it's all on you. Today is Tuesday. I want something ready to air on Monday." He smiles, and his perfect capped teeth seem to glitter in the fluorescent light.

"Barry," I say, carefully, "I will do my best, of course, but the deadline is, um, tight."

"I have confidence in you, buddy," he says, but I can tell from the cold light in his eyes that I'm no buddy of his. He turns to the rest of the group. "What's my motto?"

"There are no excuses in business!" we all parrot, with varying degrees of self-loathing.

"You said it," says Barry. "And now, I have one more announcement. I'm sorry to tell you that Justine will be leaving us at the end of the week to spend more time with her family. Let me assure you that I tried to persuade her to stay, but she had made up her mind. I realize that this will seem like very short notice, but Justine asked me not to make her resignation public until after this week's meeting with the Gala Committee."

And now Barry spins back to stick it to me one more time. "Since you are already involved in the Gala, Sophie, you will take over managing the Events group until we find a replacement for Justine." He winks. I feel cold all over and wonder if I am going to vomit. Instead I force myself to meet Barry's eye.

"It's all on you, pal," he says. "Time to bring your A-game."

CHAPTER SIX

tuesday, december 3, 2013

I sit, bent at the waist, with my forehead on the cool laminate desktop. I turn my head and gaze out at the expanse of artificial wood grain, contemplating the luminous effect of the red message light from the telephone flashing through a fluffy mound of used tissues. For a moment, even this seems like too much stimulation, and I entertain the possibility of crawling under my desk and staying there for a while, just until I feel a little calmer. It's tempting because anyone walking by would assume that I'm at a meeting, but dangerous, because Killjoy would probably find a way to blow my cover, and what would be more humiliating than being caught hiding under my desk? It would be a fate worse than, well, being in charge of the Gala, or having to produce a holiday appeal ad by Monday with absolutely no assistance from any of my senior colleagues, who are afraid that they'll be fired if they have a conversation with anyone who isn't a prospective donor in the next three weeks, although not as bad as being caught drinking at my desk, which is almost as tempting. This brief environmental scan of my professional life complete, I summon the inner fortitude to reach over and dial Geoff's extension, and then close my eyes while I wait for him to arrive.

"Uh-oh," I hear him say. "That doesn't look good." I sit up and feel a rush of affection for reliable Geoff, the picture of caring and concern.

"Not so much," I say. "Do you want the bad news, or the really bad news?"

Geoff groans. "Let's hear it."

"The bad news is, Justine quit, and Barry's decided to put me in charge of the Gala for the foreseeable future."

"Ouch. What's the really bad news?"

"Do you remember the huge fight that Barry and Bill had about running the holiday appeal this year?"

He nods. "Barry thought it was too expensive and told Bill to man up and hit his numbers without it?"

"Correct. And now—surprise, surprise—the Annual Fund numbers suck, which is, of course, Bill's fault. But Barry has a plan. We're going to run a holiday appeal after all."

"Last year's ad? Isn't it a bit late for that? We don't have any ad space booked."

"I don't think you have the full picture here. He wants a brand-new ad to air on Monday."

Geoff sticks his fingers in his ears, wiggles them around. "I'm sorry," he says. "My hearing must be going. I thought I heard you say that you wanted a new ad for Monday, which is obviously impossible." He looks stern. "If we were going to run an ad on Monday, which to be clear is six days away, we would have to find a director and crew prepared to shoot and edit all weekend, and we'd have to get on the phone today and try to buy time to run the ads, which is by no means a sure thing, and we would have to produce the script in-house, because we are out of time to hire a freelancer."

"Correct." We both remember how much work it was last time we got pulled onto this project, on a much more generous timeline. "On the upside, though," I say, "you won't have to pay someone to write something lousy that you rewrite for free."

Geoff snorts. "It's a kamikaze mission," he says. "We'll have to kill ourselves to make it happen, and spend a small fortune, and there's no guarantee that whatever we can churn out is going to be good enough to see the light of day."

"Let's work backward," I say. "Nothing happens unless we can get the airtime. So let's give Erica a chance to save the universe, since she's feeling so neglected." Geoff snorts again, but this time it sounds a little more like a laugh. "I'll ask her to pull out all the stops with her media contacts and try to get the stations that ran the appeal for a reduced rate last year to give us the same deal this year. If we can't buy the spots, there's nothing more we can do and Barry will have to live with it."

Geoff sighs. "Fine. We'll have to start on the script at least, on the remote chance that Erica is able to find something. I'll get the guys on it. Can we use the same basic storyline as last year?"

"Of course," I say. "But we'll have to use an older kid this year, someone who doesn't need as much coaching. We don't have time for multiple takes. I'll call Carolyn Waldron and see if she can suggest someone."

Geoff is scribbling notes, a good sign. "We'll need to shoot on-site, so can you ask Joy to find some soundproof space—meeting room, operating room—that we can book for the weekend?"

"Yes," I say. "I think it's doable—just—if we can get someone to do the shoot and edit on short notice."

Geoff looks up. "Don't even think it," he says.

"I know how you feel about Claudio," I say, "but I can't think of anyone else."

"Seriously, Sophie, no way. The city is full of aspiring filmmakers."

"We don't have time to vet them," I say. "We know he does good work. And he'll do it if we ask him."

"You mean if I ask him," says Geoff.

"Right, if you ask him."

Geoff grits his teeth. I've actually never seen him so irritated, and it would be funny if he weren't so genuinely unhappy. I understand it. Claudio is a good filmmaker, very good in fact, but he doesn't get a lot of commercial work because he is so high-maintenance. He has the demands of an Oscar-winning director on a blockbuster budget, and he usually insists on having Geoff as his personal assistant whenever he works for us, and he hits on him relentlessly. Last year I promised Geoff that he would never have to work with Claudio again.

"Fine," he says. "I would only do this for you."

"It's my winning personality," I say, lightly. "Just ask Nigel the germ Nazi; he's a big fan of mine."

I expect a forgiving grin at this, but Geoff's expression is strangely unreadable, and I am struck with the horrible thought that the day may come when he will have had enough of working for a stressed-out, neurotic, and emotionally unavailable boss who allows freelance filmmakers to sexually harass him, and will go off in search of greener pastures. And when he does I will be in deep, deep trouble. "I'll make you a deal," I say. "You get Claudio to commit and I'll oversee the shoot."

"Sophie, you don't have to do that," says Geoff. "It's below your pay grade. I can handle it."

"I don't really get paid that much," I say. "And I'll feel less guilty for making you miserable if I share the pain." I grin. "Just don't tell Claudio. We're not exactly interchangeable in his eyes."

"You're not making me miserable," he says. "I . . ." Geoff pauses.

"Yes?"

He shakes his head. "Nothing," he says. "Just that I should go and get started." He stands up and walks over to the doorway. "I'll give you an update tomorrow morning. Let me know what Carolyn says. We should meet with the patient as soon as possible." He steps into the hall and turns, and I hear him say, "Sorry, my fault" as he collides with someone just outside my view.

"My turn," says the last person I want to see right now, and my mother steps into my office. "Sweetheart, for heaven's sakes, you look terrible! I had my eye appointment with Dr. Rogers, and since you haven't returned my calls I thought I'd pop up and see if you were trapped under a rock. And now I see that you might as well have been. You have huge circles under your eyes!" Her eyes light on the pile of tissues on my desk. "Are you sick? What are you doing at work? No one is going to thank you for infecting the whole office, I can tell you that right now."

She draws a breath, and I say, "It's just a cold. I got your message. It's been a little busy this week."

"Well, of course you're busy, good grief, with this crazy job of yours and two little boys at home. No wonder you're sick. But your brother is busy, too, and he still manages to return my calls."

"You mean Dana returns your calls." Dana is my sister-in-law, who is as beautiful as she is lovely and generous and kind. For years, when Dana was an aspiring kindergarten teacher and my brother, Mike, a.k.a. "The Stuntman," was famous among his engineering brothers for his dominance in a drinking sport that involved doing a shot of tequila, snorting a line of salt, and then squirting a lime wedge in his eye, I was tempted to tell her that she could do better. But Dana saw something that the rest of us didn't, because somewhere along the way Mike persuaded a bank to let him invest other people's money, and now he has a fancy title and a Porsche, and Dana is a stay-at-home mom with a full-time nanny. Dana remembers birthdays, bakes, makes Halloween costumes by hand, and calls my mother back. She is much, much nicer than I am, and would certainly never be as rude to my mother as I am about to be.

"It's a lot easier to return calls when you have a full-time wife to do it for you. I should really get one of those. Maybe I'll ask for one for Christmas."

My mother puts her hands on her hips. "Nice talk," she says. "You don't think it's worth the effort to make Christmas special for everyone?"

"I didn't say that, Mom, but it's still three weeks away! I haven't turned my mind to it. I haven't bought any presents. I don't even have a list of the presents I haven't bought. I don't have any opinion about what we should have for Christmas dinner, and I'll happily eat whatever you put in front of me as long as I don't have to plan it or cook it myself. Barbecue hamburgers, whip up some Kraft Dinner, whatever—I honestly don't care."

I see my mother straighten and square her shoulders, a gesture I know well. She is willing herself to rise above my childishness, to be the mature adult in this conversation.

"I can see that I've caught you at a bad time," she says. "I should have called first."

"No, Mom," I say. "You don't have to call first, of course not—it's always nice to see you."

She softens a little. "You know, honey, I had another thought about a present for Jamie. Dana was telling me about this amazing kids' program at the art gallery where they experiment with art forms from around the world. He's such a creative little boy, and I know how hard it is for you to do extra programs for him, but Dana was thinking about enrolling Lola, so she could probably figure out a way to get him there every week. It's a shame for him to miss out on these opportunities. What do you think? Would he like to do that?"

"Let me talk to Jesse about it, Mom," I say, with a calmness that I don't feel. "That seems like a lot to ask of Dana. Why don't I see if they offer a program on the weekends so that I could take him?"

"Whatever you think is best, honey. I'm just trying to help."

"And I appreciate it. I'm just a little tired today."

"Tired, always tired!" says my mother. "That's all I ever hear from you. These are the best years of your life! You must have something more interesting than that to tell me."

"Honestly, Mom," I say, "tired is all I've got."

I'm the last one home, but the kids are still up. As I come in the door, I hear shrieking, and I pray that they are only playing and not hurt. There were very high-level spousal negotiations involved in having Jesse do the daycare pickup and dinner for the kids today, on account of my also having a job that occasionally requires attention; and it's possible, although I'm not inclined to admit it at the moment, that there were tears and recriminations on my part, which ultimately led to a grudging acceptance of responsibility on Jesse's part. But I can see, as the boys and Jesse race out to meet me, brandishing light sabers, that they are having an excellent time: Scotty is wearing a Batman costume, Jamie is Darth Vader, and

Jesse has a triceratops hat perched on his head at a rakish angle. They are all flushed and giddy and ready to carry me off to Jedi prison, and I can tell that Jesse has forgiven me for reading him the riot act.

"Wait, wait," I laugh. "Let me change my clothes and I'll be right there. Do they have dinner in prison?"

"Absolutely," says Jesse. "It's a very respectable jail. We'll even let you eat your pasta before we make you escape so that we can recapture you."

"Sounds like a plan," I say, and I kiss my little boys on the top of their sweet heads. "Did Jamie practice his cello?"

"I hate cello," says Jamie.

"We had a cello-related mutiny," says Jesse. "We're going to let it go for tonight."

"His teacher—" I begin.

"We're letting it go," Jesse repeats. "Go up and get changed."

When I come back down, I find that Jesse has managed to distract my would-be jailers with a video, and I sit on a kitchen stool while I wait for my pasta to heat in the microwave. It's left over from a giant batch that I made over the weekend and it still looks reasonably appealing.

Jesse joins me. "Feeling any better?"

"So-so. I'm holding my own. I'm hoping I can beat it if I get a decent sleep." I take a bite. "I nearly forgot to tell you, I saw Lil the other day."

Jesse's face lights up with a huge grin. He adores Lil. "What is Her Majesty up to these days?"

"It's hard to tell, but definitely something nefarious," I say. "She's plotting something on the search committee. I'll fill you in once I figure it out myself. How are things with the investors?"

"Hard to know. They're going over the plans with a cost consultant and we're meeting again later this week. Anya is cautiously optimistic, and she's been spending more time with them than I have. I feel like it's kind of out of our hands at the moment."

"Hey, Jess?" I ask. "Do you think we have the kids in enough programs?"

He cocks his head. "Why?"

"Mom came by the office today and was asking about art programs for Jamie. Reading between the lines, which wasn't hard to do, I'd say she thinks we are squandering his artistic potential."

"Based on how much he hates cello, I'm not sure we need to worry about his artistic potential," says Jesse.

I roll my eyes at him. "She's fixated on her Christmas shopping and I was too busy to return her messages so she dropped by in person to make sure I was still alive."

"What does that have to do with the art program?"

"She wants to give Jamie art lessons. She and Dana have been concocting some charitable initiative that involves carpooling our understimulated son to the art gallery every week to counteract the effects of our negligence and even out the esthetic playing field."

"Were you nice?"

"Not especially."

"Sophie," Jesse says, "haven't you learned by now that you should just give her what she wants? Why rise to the bait? You only make yourself crazy."

"I know, I know," I say. "Let's not talk about it. Do you want to hear the best story of the day? Barry was overheard in the elevator saying that it's really unfair that all those poor kids with Down syndrome have to compete for medals with ex-military dudes who've had their limbs blown off in combat. The chief of surgery had to explain the difference between the Special Olympics and the Paralympics. It totally went viral."

"Sweet," says Jesse. "I have no idea how you work for that moron."

We laugh, and I notice that there are a few more lines around his eyes than there used to be, and a few spots at his temples that are now more gray than brown. He still has a drop-dead smile, though, and I'm tempted for a moment to reach out and run a hand through his curly mop of hair, which both our children have inherited. But as I think of the children, I realize that they have been quiet for far, far too long.

"Can you check on the kids, Jess?" I ask.

He pops into the playroom and I hear him say, "Scotty, NO!" and then I hear Scotty start to cry, and when I get to the doorway, I see that the markers are out, and Scotty has scrawled all over the couch and the carpet and part of the wall.

"What the hell are the markers doing out?" I yell.

"We were doing drawings with Daddy," says Jamie.

"You can't leave them alone with the markers, Jesse, for God's sake!" I snap. "That's why I keep them on the top shelf! What were you thinking?"

"I was trying to encourage the children to develop their artistic potential," says Jesse sarcastically. "Wasn't that a big priority for you five minutes ago?"

Jesse takes the boys upstairs for bath and bed while I dig through the cupboard for my collection of largely ineffective, although environmentally friendly, cleaning products. After a futile attempt to remove the ink by spraying and blotting, I eventually resort to squeezing blobs of upholstery shampoo directly on the couch and pouring hot water on top of it and going after the whole mess with a scouring brush—actions which are all firmly discouraged by the product packaging. By the end of the night the playroom looks as though it has been hit by a monsoon, and if the rainbow streaks of marker are slightly less visible, I suspect it is because they are harder to see when the fabric is soaking wet.

I stagger upstairs, dry myself off, and slide into bed next to Jesse, who is already asleep, turned toward his side of the bed. The vigorous scrubbing has taken the edge off my anger, and I curl up against Jesse's back, breathing in the distinctive and oddly intoxicating smell of shaving cream, deodorant with a hint of sweat underneath, and the unfussy white bar of soap that he uses in the shower.

"Are you awake?" I murmur, kissing his shoulder and reaching across to touch his chest.

Jesse rolls toward me, a promising beginning, but as I lean in for a kiss he turns his head and my lips land somewhere around his ear. "Not tonight," he says. "I need some sleep and so do you."

I close my eyes to hide the rejection in them, and I feel his cool lips on my forehead. "Good night," he says and rolls away to the other side of the bed, and I watch his back expand and contract with each breath, as sleep pulls him further and further away from me.

CHAPTER SEVEN

october 1991

By the time the leaves on the maple tree outside my window start to turn red, I've begun to settle into a comfortable rhythm in the house on Abernathy Road. The smell of oiled wood paneling, lemon furniture polish, and wool carpets feels like home now. A.J. and Will both have much heavier class schedules than I do, but I have mountains of reading in addition to two weekly columns at the student newspaper, and we rarely see each other except in the evenings. The guys are friendly, and conscientious about including me in their dinner routine, which generally involves pizza or, for a special treat, Chinese food.

Everything changes the day I come home with groceries and bright blue hair. A.J. and Will are in the kitchen when I walk in and drop two plastic bags on the island, and they freeze.

"Don't say it," I tell them. "I know it's awful. I'm making lasagna. I'm too depressed to eat pizza again, possibly ever." I glare at them, daring them to comment.

"You can cook?" asks A.J. He's trying hard not to laugh.

"Of course I can cook," I say, happy that we aren't talking about my hair. "My mother's a caterer."

Will shoots A.J. a look as if to say, *Don't fuck this up*. "I love lasagna," he says, flashing me the version of his smile that I now recognize as his warmest and most charming. "Can we help?"

"Can you chop vegetables?" I ask.

"I think we can handle that," says A.J.

We work together in silence for a little while, until I say, "In case you were going to ask about my hair—"

"We weren't," says A.J.

"But if you want to tell us, go ahead," says Will.

"My friend Sara convinced me that I'd have more street cred at the newspaper if I looked more alternative," I say.

"Friend?" says A.J., at the same time as Will says, "Alternative to what?"

"I realize student politics isn't your scene," I say. "But I'm embarrassingly mainstream. I'm not even bi-curious."

"Fine with us," says Will.

"I look like a Muppet."

"I always liked Cookie Monster," says Will.

"Me too," says A.J. "Although I think the color is more Grover-esque. Not to mention alternative."

I burst out laughing, giving them permission to do the same. "Your mom's a caterer?" Will asks, once we catch our breath.

"A caterer and a wedding planner," I say. "The wedding business is mostly in the summer, though."

"Where do your parents live?" asks A.J. I'm surprised; he's never asked me anything personal before.

"Port Alice," I say. They both nod. City people always know Port Alice; it's a sleepy little town in the winter but a tourist hub in the summer, at the junction of three lakes whose shorelines are dotted with designer cottages. Port Alice residents are utterly bemused by the fact that fabulously wealthy people who could pay for weddings anywhere would choose to marry on a dock with a view of Port Alice. My mother says that it's just more evidence that romance is totally irrational; she herself is a hopeless romantic, but leans more toward beaches and swaying palm trees.

"Did you grow up there?" A.J. asks.

"Partly," I say. "I was born here. We had a family place near Port Alice and when my dad inherited it, he decided that he wanted to move there. I was ten."

My dad practiced law in a big law firm downtown for years and he loved the idea of being a small-town lawyer; my mother referred to it as his Our Town fantasy. She was less enamored with the idea of relocating, but with her city connections, she quickly established her business and made good friends with all the local suppliers. I didn't mind the move at the time, because I'd always loved the family cottage. It wasn't until I hit high school that I began to appreciate what had been taken away, and since my first days of university, I'd been a zealous convert to city living.

"How do you guys know each other?" I ask.

"We went to summer camp together," says Will. "And then we ran into each other at a bar the summer before university and started hanging out again."

"I know that you went to Duke and came back here for law school," I say. "What about you, A.J.? Have you been living here the whole time?"

"Since second year," he says. "Will introduced me to Lil when I said I was looking for an apartment. I lived here with Alex and Simon for two years." I'd met his engineering friends at a couple of parties, and in fact suspected that Zoe had a fling with Alex before leaving for Paris. "I had to take some time off in third year, so they graduated a year ahead of me," he says, and doesn't elaborate further.

When the lasagna is ready, I serve up generous portions, and A.J. and Will help carry the dishes to the dining room. Will has set one place at the head of the table and one on either side, and he pulls the head chair out for me. A.J. rolls his eyes heavenward and snorts.

I leap to Will's defense. "Women like men with beautiful manners," I tell him. At least I do, but I read a lot of Jane Austen.

"I've noticed," says A.J., and now it's Will's turn to snort.

The guys make short work of the lasagna and insist on doing the

dishes. I sit up at the counter and watch them, feeling like an anthropol-
ogist. They fascinate me, and I want to know more. I feel that if I could
somehow come to understand the underlying meaning of their habits,
their interaction with each other, their clothes, their language and cus-
toms, then I might also unlock more general principles of attraction
between men and women in the modern age. It doesn't seem to work
the way it did in Jane Austen's day. I've had boyfriends, even serious
ones, but I've always felt off-balance in relationships. It's unsettling to be
vulnerable to someone when you have no idea what they're thinking—
not just about you and the relationship, but about the movie you saw or
the meal you ate. I want to see inside a boy's soul. That's what true love
is about, isn't it? But I need more data, and I think that Will and A.J.
might have it.

"You know," I say, dragging my eyes away from the sight of Will's
strong forearms drying dishes, "I could cook more often, if you like."

Will and A.J. exchange a sideways glance. "We'd like it," says Will,
"but we can't ask you to cook for us all the time. That wouldn't be
right."

"How often were you thinking?" asks A.J.

"If you put some money in for groceries, I could cook three times a
week—say Mondays, Wednesdays, and Sundays?"

A.J. nods slowly. "I could do Tuesdays," he says.

Will looks stunned. "You cook?" he says.

A.J. shrugs. "A bit."

"Wonders never cease," says Will. "I totally can't cook. But if you
are going to give me home-cooked meals the rest of the week, I'll
spring for takeout on Thursdays."

"No pizza," I say quickly.

Will laughs. "Deal," he says. He stretches a hand out across the
table, palm down, grabs one of my hands, and places it on top of his;
A.J. dries his hands on a towel and lays one of them on mine. "Operation Family Dinner," says Will, drawing our hands down and then
pushing them up in the air in a move I vaguely recognize from televised
sports.

"Woo-hoo," I say, feeling immediately idiotic.

And so our family dinner routine begins. A.J. has a solid if limited repertoire of chili, macaroni and cheese, and chicken fajitas. Will, as advertised, is hopeless in the kitchen, but I agree to take responsibility for reheating and plating his offerings, and in return he produces meals that are several cuts above takeout; he makes some arrangement with his mother's caterer and seems to enjoy ordering screamingly domestic dishes like chicken pot pie, beef bourguignon, and salmon en croûte. I wonder sometimes if he is making fun of me, but I prefer to think that he is hearkening back to the meals he remembers eating at his family table. As the weeks stretch on and the arrangement remains in place, I conclude that Will and A.J. like a home-cooked meal and some quasi-domestic companionship at the end of the day as much as I do.

Lil returns late in October. Will says that she's been on the European festival circuit, which apparently includes a film festival in Venice and an antiques fair in Paris. We have a special Friday-night dinner in her honor. I roast a chicken and vegetables, and make a green salad and an apple crisp. Lil regales us with tales of shocking celebrity behavior in the grand hotels of Venice. At the end of the meal, she sits back and surveys us with satisfaction.

"I knew a girl would add a civilizing influence," she says. "I do so enjoy being right." We all shift awkwardly and say nothing. She laughs. "You don't have to acknowledge that I'm right. Just knowing is enough for me. Now, what are you all doing tomorrow night? I'd like to take you out for dinner."

"Whatever plans you have, you should cancel," says Will to A.J. and me. "You won't want to miss it."

"Quite so," says Lil. "I thought we'd go to Tableau. They have a tasting menu that I've been wanting to try, but tasting menus are always more fun with a group. Are you all in?" There is a chorus of assent. "Excellent," says Lil. "No jeans, boys. Ties and jackets required. And, Sophie, you are going to come with me in the afternoon for some girl time."

Girl time turns out to be a visit to Lil's salon. I know immediately that I can't afford it here and I wonder, anxiously, if they have student rates.

"Lillian," says a tall, graceful man, stooping to kiss her on both cheeks. He looks at my blue hair with distaste. "What have we here?"

"Hello, Hugo," she says. "This is my friend Sophie." Hugo shakes my hand.

"The blue was a mistake," I say.

"It certainly was," says Lil, and addresses herself to Hugo. "Sophie is having a makeover today." She waves off my objections. "It's my treat, Sophie," she says. "All I ask in return is that you put yourself in Hugo's talented hands."

Hugo regards me with a diagnostician's clinical gaze. "Whoever did this should be reported," he mutters. "And stripped of their license to do hair."

"It's nothing you can't fix, Hugo dear," says Lil. "Back to a golden blond, I think. And a much shorter cut. Her hair is too fine to be so long." I reach up to clutch the loose bun at the back of my neck. It's taken two years to grow it this long. "Hand over the—what do you call that thing you wear in your hair?"

"A scrunchie," I say.

"Hand over the scrunchie," she says, and I do. She hands it to the girl behind the cash desk. "Would you mind throwing that in the trash for me? Thank you, dear." A grin tugs at the corners of her mouth. "Don't look so horrified, Sophie. Trust me, it's for the best."

For the next hour or so, I let Hugo repair my hair with chemical mud, until he finally covers my head with plastic and sits me under a giant domed dryer while I read magazines. Then Hugo's comely assistant washes the dye out and returns me to his chair. "And now we cut," he says. "Courage!" He pronounces it *cour-ahj*. His scissors start flying and soon the floor is littered with chunks of my hard-won hair. I feel tears prickle in my throat, and I close my eyes. Hugo massages product into my hair and turns on the dryer, and his brush scoops the hair up and pulls it out and under. Finally, the noise stops. "There," he says with satisfaction. "What do you think?"

I open my eyes with trepidation and freeze. I can hardly believe what I see. I have a sleek cap of golden hair that curves gracefully around my face. It's short in the back but lengthens gradually toward the front, and by some magic, it seems to make my round face look heart-shaped.

"Do you like it?" asks Hugo anxiously.

"You gave me cheekbones!" I say. "I love it." Hugo beams. "Thank you," I tell him.

"Wait until Marisa is done with you. Then you'll have cheekbones," Hugo promises. "Marisa!"

Marisa appears with what looks like a toolbox. "What's in there?" I ask.

"Makeup," says Marisa.

"Oh, no thanks," I say. "I don't really wear makeup."

"Mrs. Parker wants you to have makeup," Marisa insists, pulling out various tubes, holding them up against my face, and rejecting them. "Do you know what color you're wearing tonight?"

"Black, I guess," I say, as Lil appears behind me in the mirror, her own hair darker than I remembered and expertly set.

"Lovely cut," she says. "Much better. What size do you wear?"

I blush. "Ten," I say.

"Ten!" she says. "Nonsense. You need to stop wearing clothes that don't fit you. You have a nice little figure." She turns to Marisa while I stare at the floor in mortification. "She'll be wearing midnight blue."

Back at Abernathy Road, Lil hustles me up to her apartment. "I have just the thing for you," she says. "Come into the bedroom."

Lil's bedroom is decorated in blues and creams, with stunning dark furniture that must be terribly old and expensive. But it is the painting above the bed that captures my attention. It's an abstract portrait of a nude woman with dark hair, reclining on a sofa in the foreground, her face hidden by an arm lifted back and behind her head. The woman, the sofa, and the walls of the room are all captured in angular blocks of blue oil paint in varying shades and intensities. The only contrast is from a riotous vase of pink and red peonies in the upper right corner of the painting.

"Do you like it?"

"It's wonderful," I say. "It reminds me of a painting by—"

"Matisse." She finishes my sentence. "Yes, he was very influenced by Matisse in his early years. His work evolved into his own distinctive style over time, but this is one of his earliest pieces of any significance."

"Who was the artist?"

She seems to hesitate. "Isaac Wallace," she says.

"I. B. Wallace?" It is a name I recognize, of course, but I wouldn't have guessed that this was his work. Zoe and I went to the retrospective show at the art gallery last year. I wonder why this piece wasn't included.

"Let's get you dressed," says Lil. She opens a door on the far wall and beckons to me to follow her. The door leads to a closet that is only slightly smaller than the bedroom. "It's organized by decade," she says, wandering along the racks until she finds what she wants. "Here," she says, unzipping a garment bag and lifting it off the hanger. "I want to see this one on you." It is a satin confection of pleats and drapes, with a deep V-neck; small, rounded cap sleeves; a fitted waist; and a bell skirt that hits below the knee. The name on the label is Dior. I suck my stomach in as Lil pulls the zipper up.

"No need for that," she says. "It's not too small; quite the opposite. These were supposed to be very fitted. But it works on you. And the color is fabulous with your eyes. What do you think?"

She spins me around so that I face the full-length mirror. I hardly recognize the reflection staring back. My eyes look huge and radiantly blue, framed with lush dark lashes, my lips full and rosy, and, as promised, my cheekbones look like cheekbones. "I feel like Cinderella," I say.

Lil beams. "Bippity boppity boo," she says. "Speaking of Cinderella, do you have any proper shoes?"

"I have some black heels," I say.

"I'm sure those will be fine," she assures me. She checks her watch. "Anil is picking us up in a half hour. I'd better get ready." She opens a drawer and rummages around, pulling out a faded blue box with a sparkling necklace inside. "Take this with you. It will go very nicely. It's not real, so don't have an anxiety attack." She waves me off toward the door. "I'll meet you downstairs."

As I come down the stairs, I see that the boys have followed Lil's instructions and cleaned themselves up. Will is stunning in a black suit with a charcoal tie. Even A.J. is highly presentable in gray flannel pants and a jacket. Lil is wearing a claret silk suit. All three turn at the same time to watch me descend. Lil nods her approval, but both boys seem shocked, and I stop on the stairs, thrown by their reaction. I feel suddenly too exposed. My hands flutter up to cover my chest, the tips of my fingers touching the crystals on Lil's necklace. Then Will gives a low whistle, and I smile with relief. A.J.'s expression shifts from astonishment to something more like annoyance.

The doorbell rings. "That will be Anil," says Lil. "Are we all ready?"

I drape my fake cashmere wrap around my neck. It's black and doesn't exactly go with the dress, but it's passable in the dark. I'm not used to wearing heels, though, and I miscalculate the front steps and nearly pitch forward onto the walkway. Will grabs my arm and steadies me. "All right?" he asks. I nod. He takes a step back and then holds out an elbow.

"You mean chivalry isn't dead after all?" I say, looping my arm through his.

"It's a special occasion," he says.

"You three sit in the back," says Lil. "I'll ride up with Anil." I take the middle seat. Lil glances back, her expression impish. "A rose between two thorns," she says.

The ride is short, but I've never been this close to either Will or A.J., and I'm uncomfortably conscious that the top of the dress is gaping. I pull the wrap closer around my shoulders. I look out the window to the right and collide with a glance from Will; the same thing happens with A.J.

when I switch to the other side. I shift my hips and lean back slightly to minimize the view of my bra, but as I do so my thigh rubs against Will's leg and he jolts away. A.J. opens his window.

When we arrive at the restaurant, they both leap out, and I'm left to climb inelegantly onto the sidewalk. No one offers to take my arm now, although A.J. holds the door as we enter. We sit, and I take in the lovely room, with its deep, upholstered chairs and crisp white linens and enormous floral arrangements, while Lil examines the wine list. The waiter appears at Lil's side. "Madame," he says. "May I offer you a cocktail to begin?"

"We'll start with a bottle of Veuve Clicquot Vintage Rosé. Do you recommend the 1975 or the 1978?"

The waiter looks startled. "Let me get the sommelier for you, Madame," he says and scurries off.

"Rosé?" Will is clearly dubious.

"Don't be such a snob," says Lil. "This is one of the great drinks of the world. We're not talking about the syrupy sludge that can only be consumed with fresh strawberries on Valentine's Day."

The sommelier appears with a bottle. "The 1975," he says. "The 1978 is much better paired with food. This one stands on its own beautifully. A marvelous choice."

He pours a small amount into Lil's glass and she sips it delicately. "Yes," she says. "That will do very nicely." He pours a glass for each of us. "Would you let our waiter know that we'll be having the tasting menu with the wine pairings?" He nods. She raises her glass. "To new friends," she says.

And then we eat. The hours vanish in a blur of sensation. Each fresh combination of flavors is a revelation: sea scallop and caramel, foie gras and lavender, lobster and lemongrass, chocolate and sour cherries, and with each course, another glass of exquisite wine. My head is spinning when Lil suggests that I accompany her to the ladies' room.

"What do you think?" she asks.

I'm too tipsy to feign sophistication. "It's incredible," I say. "Amazing. The best meal I've ever had in my whole life."

She beams. "I'm so glad," she says.

"Why are you being so nice to me?" I ask, and then wince as I hear the words. "I mean, not that I don't really, really appreciate it."

Lil laughs. "Because I'm old," she says. "And because you remind me of someone I used to be. Now, let's get back to our dates, shall we?"

By the time Anil drops us back home, it's past midnight.

"Gentlemen," Lil says, and the way she enunciates each syllable tells me that I'm not the only one feeling light-headed, "one of you is going to have to escort me upstairs." A.J. leaps up and moves to her side, holding out his arm. "Well-raised," says Lil approvingly, as they head up to her apartment. "Good night, my dears."

"Thank you so much," I say. "It was a magical evening."

"It was my pleasure," she says. "And, Sophie? I want you to keep that dress. It's beautiful on you."

"Thank you," I say again, as she ascends.

Will leans against the banister. "Do you need assistance as well?" he asks.

"I think I can manage," I say.

"I'll stay close just in case," he says.

I concentrate on keeping my balance. I wobble a few times but Will doesn't intervene and we make our way up to the second floor. Outside my door, I kick off the heels. "Made it," I say with pride. I smile up at him. "I had a really good time tonight."

"It shows," he says.

I throw my hands above my head like a ballerina in a music box and spin so that my skirt flares out at the bottom. But this is one feat too many for my addled brain, and I lose my balance, giggling. Will grabs me around the waist. "Champagne spins," I say, referring to my head and not my dance moves. "They're much better than the regular kind."

Will adjusts his grip and I feel the spread of his fingers on my hips. With my heels off, he looms over me, and I hold on to his forearms and tilt my chin up to look at him. He is very still, his face troubled and uncertain. For a moment, I think he is going to kiss me, but then he releases my waist and steps away.

"Good night, Sophie," he says.

"Good night, Will," I respond, opening the door to my room and closing it firmly behind me. I'm too drunk to hang up my dress, but I lay it carefully over the back of my armchair. I can see it from my bed, glimmering with captured light from the street, as I fall asleep, with the memory of Will's gaze lingering on my skin.

CHAPTER EIGHT

wednesday, december 4, 2013

J. SOPHIE WHELAN

To: wshannon@perrimanhale.com
Sent: Wednesday, December 4, 2013, 6:45 a.m.
Subject: Hi

Hi Will,

I heard that you called the other day. It's been too long!
How are you?

Would love to get together next time you are passing
through town.

Sophie

WILLIAM R. SHANNON

To: j.s.whelan@baxter.com
Sent: Wednesday, December 4, 2013, 7:03 a.m.
Subject: Re: Hi

Hey Sophie. Thanks for the Christmas card. Glad to hear

that the family is doing well. I'm coming into town later today and wanted to see you. Are you around?

WRS

J. SOPHIE WHELAN

To: wshannon@perrimanhale.com
Sent: Wednesday, December 4, 2013, 7:06 a.m.
Subject: Re: Re: Hi

Definitely around. Let me know what works. Looking forward to seeing you!

I'm checking my BlackBerry every five seconds as I stand in line at Nigel's station, but there's nothing from Will. There are, however, a series of increasingly hysterical messages from Erica, with little red exclamation marks and subject lines that read, "Call me!" and "Where are you????"

I do a quick ROAR calculation. My desire to coddle Erica with reassuring messages about my impending arrival in the office is zero (DPA = 0), and any reasonable guilt that I might otherwise have felt is tempered by my conviction that Erica and the rest of her helicopter-parented, praise-craving, sacrifice-allergic generation need some tough love (GF = 1). My need to behave like a grown-up is arguably satisfied by refusing to give in to Erica's neediness, so I allocate a neutral score (NBLG = 5). Finally, I allow myself a modicum of selfishness due to the fact that I cannot seem to get rid of my runny nose and cough and feel moderately horrible, and also because I am pretty distracted by the whole Will Shannon situation (AS = 3). So that's 0 + 1 + 5 − 3 = 3, and in my system, anything in the dull ROAR range of one to five can be safely ignored. Willfully, and a little bit maliciously, I delete Erica's messages.

The line is moving very slowly this morning; Nigel has his hands full interrogating some anemic-looking supplicant who has had the misfortune to cough within earshot of his desk. I check my BlackBerry again.

WILLIAM R. SHANNON

> To: j.s.whelan@baxter.com
> Sent: Wednesday, December 4, 2013, 9:08 a.m.
> Subject: Re: Re: Re: Hi
>
> Am just about to board a flight. Can you call me in the
> next 10 minutes?
>
> WRS

Nigel summons me to the desk.

I hold up my BlackBerry. "Sorry, but I'm in a rush. I'm due on a call," I say.

Nigel is unimpressed. "No exceptions. Hospital policy," he says, pulling out his survey.

I check my watch. It's nine-fifteen. I'm going to miss Will if I don't get out of this line now. "I'll take a mask," I say, pointing at the box of surgical masks beside the desk.

Nigel looks surprised and more than a little disappointed. Failing hospital employees on the survey and forcing them to wear a surgical mask all day is the only fun his job has to offer. "I think we'd better complete the questions first," he says. "For our records."

"Sorry," I say. "I don't have time."

Nigel puffs out his chest. "I understand that not everyone thinks this process is important, but I would appreciate a little respect."

"I have three, no, two minutes to get on this call. Give me the mask, please."

"Not until you answer the questions."

"Give me the fucking mask!" I screech, and Nigel hands it over as I punch in the numbers.

"Will Shannon."

"Will, I'm so glad I caught you! It's Sophie," I say.

"Hey, Soph," he says. "I've just got a second here. I can swing by your office around two. Is that good?"

"Very good," I say.

When I arrive on the fourteenth floor, Erica is waiting, wild-eyed and pale. "Sophie, thank God. It's crazy here. I've got media calls from sixty news outlets already and they keep coming. Apparently one of our researchers has found a definitive link between hours of television and ADHD. Someone leaked a preliminary report onto an international news feed, and it went viral."

My shoulders crunch upward with anticipatory stress. "Breathe, Erica," I say. "Have you actually seen the report?"

"No."

"Who's the researcher?"

"Someone named Christian Viggars. I've never heard of him." She pauses. "What's with the mask?"

I ignore her. "Let's call Marvin Shapiro and sort this out."

I sit down at my desk and shove the mask up to the middle of my forehead as I pick up the phone. Dr. Marvin Shapiro is the director of medical research at the Baxter, and he is so lovely and respectful and gentlemanly that I try to be on my very best behavior whenever we speak. "Good morning, Marvin," I say, when he answers.

"Ah, Sophie. I thought I might hear from you today."

"Do we have someone named Christian Viggars doing research in our hospital?" I ask.

"Indeed we do," says Marvin.

"Well, Marvin," I say, "every news outlet in North America wants to talk to him this morning about how television causes ADHD."

"I see."

"Do you know anything about this report?"

There is a pause. "Possibly. I think it would be best if I spoke to Dr. Viggars before you meet with him."

"That's fine. We'll need to speak to him this morning, though, so we can figure out our media strategy."

"Undoubtedly a good idea," says Marvin. "It might also be a good idea for me to attend. Dr. Viggars is brilliant, but somewhat—what's the word I'm looking for?—disconnected from the concerns that animate your work. Do you understand what I mean?"

I don't, really, since virtually every researcher in the hospital, with the exception of Marvin himself, would fit this description, so I say, "Thanks, Marvin," and leave it at that.

I hang up the phone and see Joy in the doorway with a sheaf of pink messages in her hand. "You're late for the search committee meeting," she says. "And Janelle Moss has phoned three times this morning," she says sourly. "Are you planning to call her back?"

"Eventually," I say. "I have a couple of other things to deal with today that are more pressing than the theme for the Gala. If she calls again, please tell her that there is a very urgent problem that needs my attention this morning and I will call her at my earliest convenience, which will not be before this afternoon."

I turn to Erica. "Here's what I need you to do. Get a meeting organized with Marvin and Dr. Viggars for this morning. Joy has my schedule. Return any calls from media outlets and tell them that we'll have a statement this afternoon. I have to run."

I sprint downstairs to the meeting room. From the far end of the corridor, I can see Jenny Dixon waiting patiently outside the door, and I murmur *I am a competent professional* over and over again like a mantra until I'm standing in front of her.

"What was that you said?" she asks.

"Nothing. I think we're late, Jenny," I say. "We should get inside."

"In a second," she says. "I just need to have a quick word with you, Sophie. I'm sorry to tell you this, but there's been an HR complaint about you."

My mind races. Surely I haven't been so neglectful of my staff that they've complained to the HR department? "Who was it?" I ask.

Jenny looks uncomfortable. "The identity of the complainant is confidential, but he claims that you abused him in the course of his duties this morning and used an obscenity."

I'm almost giddy with relief to know that I've been betrayed by

Nigel and not by one of my own, and it makes me less measured than the circumstances call for. "I thought I was pretty restrained in the circumstances," I say.

Jenny smothers a smile. "That's not quite the response I was aiming for," she says. "This particular complainant is known to the authorities, shall we say, and not all of his grievances are as well-founded as this one."

"I admit that I may have been less than polite. Perhaps we could agree that there was a misunderstanding?"

"Perhaps," she says. "I'll tell the complainant's supervisor that you regret your choice of words. It would be ideal if you would apologize to him. Do you think you could do that?"

"I'll think about it," I say, ungraciously.

"Do that," she says. "Shall we?" She reaches for the door. "Nice mask. I understand it may be more effective if you take it off your forehead and put it on your face, though."

The meeting is in full swing as we enter. The agenda, which Barry flings down the table at us, indicates that we are reviewing the reference checks and deciding on the set list of questions to be asked each candidate in the interviews. I feel strangely light-headed in my mask, a symptom that is probably psychosomatic, but I seem to have to concentrate harder than usual on breathing without hyperventilating. As a result, I am only partly listening to the discussion; in any event, it's more of a monologue, as Barry describes the comments of the references at length. With Barry's voice rising and falling in the background, I look around the table at the rest of the committee. There are the two board members hanging off Barry's every word, nodding along with the cadence of his voice. As for the others, Marvin seems intent on a document in the binder in front of him. Carolyn Waldron is sending e-mail surreptitiously under the table. Anusha Dhaliwal is doodling on the back of the agenda. Patti and Jenny are writing notes to each other, which they scratch out violently as soon as they are read. And then there's Lil, still wearing the fox stole, eyes closed and head lolling slightly to one side. Again, I wonder what she is up to, and if I had a spare minute I'd call her and find out.

Reading between the lines of Barry's monologue, it seems that

Stephen Paul has had a distinguished career running a large public company, that he is regarded as a strong business strategist, that he is at his best when engaged in high-profile deal-making, and that his exposure to philanthropy is through his corporate foundation, which operates under the direction of an advisory board, distributing money to worthy community projects and reporting to Mr. Paul on a quarterly basis.

"Superb references," Barry enthuses, although to my ears, the candidate's manifold talents sound only tangentially related to the position that we are trying to fill. Karim Assaf is next, and he too is deemed by Barry to be "a serious guy," having made frequent appearances in the society pages as the stylish, metrosexual executive director of the City Arts Center. His references speak glowingly of his charisma, energy, and vision in relation to large-scale events, but there are also some oblique references to negative revenues, which Barry is not inclined to elaborate upon. Margaret Anderson is last. She is a former nurse turned administrator who is now the executive director of a national organization that provides support services for cancer patients. She is described as collaborative, hardworking, strategic, and dedicated. "A good third choice," says Barry. "Not the most exciting candidate, obviously, but clearly worth seeing. Although, in confidence, I understand that she is a single mother, so she will have considerable difficulty fulfilling the responsibilities of this position."

From the way that the board members nod in unison, it is apparent that Margaret Anderson's family status has been a lively topic of discussion in some quarters. I raise my hand. "I'm sorry," I say. "I'm not totally clear on the problem with Margaret being a single mother. How is that going to affect her work?"

Irritation flashes across Barry's face, but he quickly masks it with an expression of indulgent and exaggerated patience. "I'm sorry, Sophie," he says. "It's difficult to understand you in that mask. Could you repeat your comment?"

I raise my mask back up to the center of my forehead and try again.

"Fund-raising is not a nine-to-five job, Sophie," says Barry. "Whoever takes this job will be expected to attend a lot of evening events, regardless of family commitments."

"Again, I'm sorry to have come into the debate late," I say, "but has she said that she can't attend events after hours?"

"No. That would have disqualified her from the outset."

"Are you going to ask her directly whether being a single mother is going to prevent her from fulfilling her responsibilities?"

"Don't be ridiculous," Barry snaps. "That would be completely inappropriate!"

Jenny rolls her eyes at the end of the table. Everyone else is looking down; I'm on my own here.

I remind myself that I am a person who once Cared About Issues exactly like this one, a person who wrote articles condemning injustice in all its insidious forms. I was informed about current events. I was passionate. I marched and sat in and made people sign petitions. Since I rarely even glance at the news these days, other than the occasional MSN celebrity headline, I am gratified to feel a tiny little flame of rage ignite in the recesses of my brain—likely in the part that stores nostalgic recollections of the person I once believed I could become, a person who is certainly not someone who swears at minimum-wage employees at the check-in desk and who feeds her children nothing but processed food. "I think it would be fair to give her an opportunity to respond to your concerns if they are serious enough to make you think that she can't do the job," I say.

"Absolutely not," says Barry, coldly. "All candidates will be asked the same questions. We are not going to give this lady a reason to say that our process was sexist or some other garbage. Margaret Anderson is the weakest candidate in the group and that's why she's not going to get this job. You need to eat a reality sandwich here, Sophie. Smarten up."

I lower my mask and sit back in my chair, agreeing with Barry for perhaps the first time in our entire unfortunate acquaintance. I definitely need to smarten up.

Barry runs through the list of questions, which are all standard chestnuts designed to elicit platitudes and generalities: What three strengths do you possess that would insure your success in this job? What would your goals be for your first hundred days on the job? How would your employees describe you? How has your experience prepared you to lead the advancement department? At least Barry hasn't insisted that we ask the candidates what animal they would be, although it's not clear that the questions we have selected would be much more illuminating. The meeting finally ends, and as I prepare to leave, I notice a flurry of activity at the end of the table.

Lil is awake and rising with difficulty from her chair; Patti and Jenny flutter at her side. I join them. "Oh, dear," she says in a quavering voice, "I'm sorry to be such a bother! I wonder if I could impose . . ." Her hand locks onto my arm. "Would you mind helping me down to my car, dearie?"

"I'd be happy to," I say, and Lil beams. She says nothing as we head out of the room and down the hall, leaning heavily on my arm. But as soon as the elevator doors close and we find ourselves alone, she straightens up and grins at me.

"You have some explaining to do," I tell her.

"So severe," she says, laughing. "All will be revealed, I promise. Sooner rather than later, if you join me for an early lunch. Shall we?"

CHAPTER NINE

wednesday, december 4, 2013

Lil's car is waiting outside the building. It's a new one, a stretch Mercedes in a lovely smoky blue. Her driver, Anil, meets us and holds out his hand.

"Ah, Ms. Sophie. How nice to see you again."

It has been years since I last saw Anil, and he is exactly as I remember him. He emigrated from India to North America in his twenties, with a wife and two young children in tow; I would say that he has been one of the lucky ones, but he has made his own luck. He started driving a taxi in the early days, but quickly figured out that the money and the hours were better in the private service business. With his impeccable manners and chiseled good looks, he soon had the most popular car service in the city, a position that he has maintained—although the day-to-day operations are now managed by his son, an MBA, and his daughter, a graphic designer. Lil pays Anil a generous annual salary to be available to drive her whenever she is in town, which is around six months a year.

Anil seems completely unfazed by Lil's bizarre appearance. "Where would you like to go, Lillian?" he asks. Anil has his own code when it comes to formal address. Lil has always been Lillian, and I have always been Ms. Sophie, although in my left-wing student days I practically begged him to call me Sophie and let me sit in the front seat. He would have none of it.

"The Four Seasons, please, Anil," says Lil.

"Your bag is in the back."

"What a treasure you are, Anil," says Lil.

Lil turns to me and says, "So. It has been far too long. You seem tired. Are you working too hard?"

"It's a busy time," I reply. "I'm operating at a fairly high level of stress."

"Stress," she repeats. "This is a new invention. My generation was never 'stressed.' Busy, yes. But not stressed."

"How old *are* you, Lil?" I ask. I've probably asked her this question twenty times over the twenty years of our acquaintance and I still have no idea of the answer. I know that I'm not going to get one today, either. Lil grins.

"A lady should never tell her age," she says, as she always does. The car pulls up in front of the hotel, and Lil hops out, takes a large bag from Anil, and gives me a wink.

"I'll join you in a jiffy. Get a good table and order the pink Veuve." She vanishes into the lobby.

I wave good-bye to Anil and head inside. It's busy in the bar, but when I mention Lil's name, the crowd parts and, amazingly, a table for two with a view of the street becomes available.

"Will Ms. Parker be having her usual this afternoon?" asks the server who materializes instantly at my elbow.

"She asked for pink Veuve," I say.

"Of course," he murmurs, and vanishes.

And then Lil is back, and looking much more like herself with a steel-gray pixie cut, a velvet ink-blue pantsuit, a chunky silver cuff, and just a hint of makeup. I cast my mind back and am dismayed to realize that it's been more than three years since we've seen each other. It's a testament to how wild my life has been since Scotty was born. I hadn't anticipated that having a second child would be like driving our old life off a cliff; we'd done that once already when we had Jamie, but everyone we talked to swore that having two kids was more like having one and a half. It's breathtaking how often people lie when it comes to kids. I drag my attention back to Lil, who hasn't really aged since she decided to let her hair go gray about ten years ago.

"Where's the fox?" I ask.

Lil laughs. "My beastie? Isn't he fantastic? I found him at a costume shop in London's West End a few years ago. I thought it would go perfectly with my mother's old Chanel suit, and I was right, don't you think?"

"I think the beehive wig was a nice touch," I say.

Lil looks thoroughly delighted. "I'm so pleased that I was able to get you onto this infernal search committee," she says. "I know Marvin, of course, but he doesn't get the joke. He thinks I've gone senile. It will be so much more fun with you there."

"This is your doing?" I ask, knowing that this should have been obvious to me the second I realized that Lil was in the room. Things rarely happen by accident when she is around. "I hope you weren't expecting me to thank you. I need another committee assignment like a hole in the head."

Lil shakes her head, amused at my ferocity. "Where is your sense of adventure?" she asks, and I bristle inwardly at the criticism, although I'm careful not to show it. I don't take criticism well, but as Jesse has observed on countless occasions, you'll never get me to admit it. "I did try to fill you in ahead of time. Didn't you get my message?"

"No," I lie.

"I'm just hopeless with those awful machines," she says. "Oh, well. Sorry for surprising you." She grins, not at all sorry. "How *do* you work for that Barry character, by the way? He really is an insufferable incompetent. And the fellow before him! It should have been evident to anyone with eyes in their head that there was something seriously off with him."

The waiter, introduced as Bradley, materializes with the Veuve, and Lil applauds. "Lovely." She beams. "My favorite." Bradley fills her flute and she takes a long sip. She nods with pleasure. "Thank you," she says. "And I believe we are ready to order. Would you mind bringing me a Cobb salad? Extra bacon, please." She gestures to me. "My friend will have the same, won't you, Sophie?"

"Sure," I say. My head feels woolly with congestion, and in any event, being with Lil always makes me feel a bit slow on the uptake. It's so much easier to just go along. "What's up with the 'Mrs. Baxter,' by the way?" I ask. "I didn't think you still used that name." This is a delicate way of saying that Lil has been married a few times since she was Mrs. Baxter.

Lil leans back in her chair and cradles her glass in her hands. "Have you ever heard the story of Madame Clicquot?" she asks. "It's a very old story, but a good one, I think. At least, I've always liked it." She takes another sip. "In France, around two hundred years ago, there was a young girl who was very lucky. Her family was rich and moved in all the right circles, and when the time came for her to marry at the age of twenty-one, her father made sure that she married well. Her husband's father was ambitious and had built up a very profitable business in wine, wool, and banking and various other things. For the next six years, the girl did everything that was expected of her. She had babies and hosted dinner parties and learned how to manage a household. Her husband was thoughtless and absent, but so were most other men that she knew, and she had plenty of responsibilities to keep her busy. And then one day, her husband went and killed himself. The girl thought about her options. She could retreat into seclusion, or go into mourning for a polite period and then remarry. She had lots of money, which even in 1805 meant freedom of a kind. But this girl had the inkling that she might try to forge a new kind of life for herself. So she rolled up her petticoat, and went down to the wine cellar and invented a whole new way to make champagne. And over time, she built her business into the most powerful champagne house in Europe, made herself a large fortune, and lived to the ripe old age of eighty-nine. She put her name on every bottle, so that people would remember her forever." Lil reaches over to the ice bucket and taps the label on the bottle.

"Veuve?" I ask.

"Tsk, tsk, Sophie, have you forgotten all of your French?" Lil scolds. "Widow Clicquot, 'veuve' en français."

"Does this have anything to do with whatever you're doing on this search committee?" I ask, hopefully.

Lil smiles at me. "Maybe just a little bit," she says. "You can tell me once I'm done."

My sinuses hurt, and I cover my eyes with my hands, massaging my fingers gently into the sockets. "It's your show," I say, relaxing into the cushions.

"You know that my first husband was a Baxter," says Lil. "Monty Baxter, to be precise."

"*Montgomery* Baxter?" I say, stupidly. "You were married to Montgomery Baxter?" I am stunned that this bit of information has somehow eluded me. The Montgomery Baxter Foundation is the single largest donor to the children's hospital that bears its name, and it continues to fund virtually every major research project that we do.

Lil laughs. "I understand your feelings. Honestly, it still mystifies me whenever I think of it, and it really was a very long time ago." She looks a little bit wistful. "He was such a type. The most handsome man I ever knew. Absolutely incapable of holding down a job or keeping his pants on. Not that he had to, really. He had an enormous trust fund and women literally threw themselves at him."

"He doesn't sound like your type." Lil's friends tend to be artists and writers, or patrons of the arts, at least the ones I've met over the years.

"He wasn't." A shadow of sadness passes over her face, and she's quiet for a moment, lost in the past. Then she shifts and meets my eyes again. "Monty's parents wanted him to settle down before he came into his inheritance at twenty-five, and my parents disapproved of my preferred type; I was spending all of my time with actors and writers and others that they regarded as unmarriageable. So it was strongly suggested that Monty and I spend more time together. Everyone else in our social circle was getting married, and in the moment it seemed like a good idea to accept his proposal."

It's hard to square this story with everything I know about Lil. Even as a very young woman, it's hard to imagine that her spirit could be bent to marry a man not of her choosing.

"Six months after the wedding, Monty got access to his trust, and after that, I rarely saw him," she continues. "He was out all night, every night, drinking and playing cards." She leans back in her chair and takes a long sip of champagne. "And here is where Madame Clicquot and I begin to have something in common. That summer, fourteen months after our wedding, Monty went up to his family cottage. He would stay up for weeks at a time, and it was one endless party. I couldn't bear to be there, so I stayed in the city, and I wasn't there when the accident happened. But I'm told that Monty dared his friends to a midnight race across the lake. So they got out the launches in the pitch black and gunned the engines. And Monty slammed right into an island and killed himself. Boom! Just like that." She smacks her hands together loudly, and the sound makes both me and Bradley—who has appeared at last with the Cobb salads—jump.

Bradley puts our plates on the table. "Enjoy your lunch," he says.

"Thank you," says Lil. She takes a bite and her face brightens. "Is there a better lunch in the world? I ask you." We eat for a moment, and then she continues. "So there I was—a widow at the age of twenty-three. It was a very strange time for me."

"I had no idea," I say. "I'm so sorry. That must have been awful."

"Not for the reasons you might think," says Lil. "I knew that I had made a terrible mistake in marrying Monty, but I had no way of getting out of the marriage. It really was a different time then, and unlike the widow Clicquot, I had no money of my own, and I couldn't get a job. But when Monty died, I inherited a small fortune. Which is why, at the end of the day, I have no regrets about Monty whatsoever. In fact, I remember him rather fondly."

I take a moment to digest all of this. "How is it that I never knew any of this?" I ask.

"I don't like to tell my tenants about my secret identity," she says. "People have odd reactions to wealth. Not to mention that the Baxters are mostly nuts. Too much inbreeding."

"The search committee?" I prompt her.

"Patience, Sophie," says Lil. "I'm getting there as quickly as I can. Monty's family was somewhat less than thrilled when I inherited all of his money after such a short marriage, and they were showing signs of making things difficult for me, legally I mean. His sister, Penelope, had always disapproved of the marriage; we had been friends and she knew that I didn't love Monty. She was right about that, although not about my reasons for marrying him. I never cared about his money."

"Why *did* you marry him?"

"That's a story for another day," she says. "We need to finish this one, so you can get back to the office. How is your lunch?"

"Delicious."

"Good," she says. "After Monty died, I decided to create a foundation in his name dedicated to the promotion of children's health, using half of everything I had inherited. His parents had been long-standing supporters of the local children's hospital, so the idea had some philosophical appeal, and then I asked Monty's father to manage the foundation's investments."

"Did it work?" I ask.

"Like a charm," answers Lil. "Even half the estate was an enormous sum of money, and I was free to live exactly as I wished, while Monty's family felt invested in the creation of his legacy. It helped them with their loss." Lil pauses and takes a bite of her salad. "In the end, I became rather attached to his parents. Penelope and her siblings were all every bit as spoiled as Monty, and their parents ended up being quite lonely in their later years. They volunteered a lot of time with the foundation, and when they died, they left their entire estate to it. It was rather a lot of money to begin with and now—well, it's a staggering amount of money. We give out at least ten million dollars every year, all to the Baxter Hospital, which is why they eventually named it after us."

"So you control the foundation that is the single largest donor to the Baxter Hospital, my employer."

"Correct."

"And that's why you are on the search committee?"

"Correct."

"OK," I say. "I'm with you so far. But I still can't figure out the costume."

Lil shifts in her seat as if slightly uncomfortable. "This is the part of the story that I am a bit embarrassed about, to be honest." She plays with her napkin, and then continues. "It's actually quite boring, being a major donor. I have to attend zillions of events and meetings, and people like your boss fawn all over me and agree with everything I say. It's impossible to have a real conversation with anyone. And so, a couple of years ago, I started to pretend that I was losing my marbles—just a little bit at first, just to see if anyone would notice. Your last boss, that fellow with the computer problem, kept on nodding and smiling and pouring me coffee and saying, 'Yes, Mrs. Baxter,' 'I've often thought that myself, Mrs. Baxter,' 'Your insight into the issues is very impressive, Mrs. Baxter,' and in the end I couldn't help myself. I would spend entire meetings staring into space with curlers in my hair and my mouth open, or pretending to fall asleep in the middle of sentences to see if I could shake him out of it. But it didn't make a whit of difference."

"Have you been enjoying yourself?" I ask.

Lil grins sheepishly, and suddenly looks years younger. "Well, yes," she says. "Quite a bit. When you are old like me, you'll understand that you take your pleasures as you find them."

She looks so pleased with herself that it seems churlish to be irritated with her. "And now?" I ask.

She pauses. "And now I find that I care about the outcome of this search. But it's awkward. Barry has handpicked this committee and told them all that I'm out of my mind. So I need a few allies. Marvin Shapiro is an old friend—he was married to my second cousin Eleanor before she ran off with her aerobics instructor in the early eighties. Such a sweet man. Although, come to think of it, he looked quite alarmed at my appearance this morning, so I'm going to have to give him a call. But to the rest of them, I'm a kooky old tycoon with a marginal grip on reality. So I read the board policies on hiring and realized that I could adjust the composition a bit. We were supposed to have a staff rep—I told them I wanted you."

"What makes you think that I'll agree with you on the merits?" I ask.

"Don't be ridiculous," says Lil. "Margaret Anderson is far and away the best person for the job, and you know it. I just need a few other obviously sane committee members to back me up when the time comes."

"Has it occurred to you that you might have to lose the costume?" I ask.

Lil looks annoyed. "Yes, Sophie. It has occurred to me. It's just a matter of finding the right time."

"How about the next meeting?" I suggest. "You are going to distract the candidates with that hairdo. And it's not fair to make me do all the work. Barry is my boss."

"I'll consider it," she says grumpily.

"Do that," I say. "And what other news? Do you still have students living with you?"

"Of course!" Lil laughs. "You know my philosophy: surround yourself with young people and you can feel youthful without the discomfort of being young. It's the best of all worlds. You and your roommates were always my favorites, though."

"Funny you should say that. Will is coming to see me this afternoon."

"Yes, he mentioned that." Her face gives nothing away. "Do you keep in touch?"

"Just occasionally," I say. "Christmas cards and that sort of thing." I keep my tone deliberately light. "You must see him more often than I do."

"He's the chair of the foundation board now," she says. "So we see each other at meetings a few times a year. And family weddings and funerals. But we talk on the telephone fairly frequently."

"He seems to be doing well."

"Yes," she says. "And how is that adorable husband of yours?"

"He's fine."

Lil raises an eyebrow. "Only fine?" Her head cocks to one side and she fixes her bright eyes on my face. She looks alarmingly like a bird about to go after a worm.

I stare down at my lap and am mortified to feel the prickling of tears. I clear my throat. "He's the same as always, Lil. But he's incredibly busy and distracted with his new business. You know how driven he is. He sees this as his big chance, and he may be right. But it is the most important thing in the world to him right now and it adds a lot of pressure." I feel the knot in my stomach tightening.

"The children are well?" Lil has never been terribly interested in children generally, but she is unfailingly polite about asking after them.

"They are. They're great. But they're still little. Jamie is seven and Scotty is three. They need a lot, and I don't always feel like I can give them everything they need."

Lil looks puzzled. "They're healthy, aren't they?"

I bite my lip so that I don't say something cutting. It's hardly shocking that Lil has no conception of the powerful currents of guilt and worry that define life with young children. Health is merely the preliminary hurdle that gets you into the main event; health buys you the luxury of being able to worry about the minutiae that define your success as a parent: Are they watching too much television? Are they eating enough vegetables? Do they get enough exercise? Are they old enough for music classes? Are they getting invited to birthday parties? When should they be toilet trained? What if one of them gets lost and doesn't know his telephone number?

"They're healthy," I say.

Lil shakes her head. "I don't understand you young women."

"I'm thirty-nine," I say glumly. "I don't think that qualifies as young."

She waves off my comment as if it is too ridiculous to merit a response. "Your generation has so much freedom, so many choices."

"Yes," I say, feeling heat flaring in my cheeks, "having it all is just super." I'm shocked at my own tone of voice. When did I get so bitter?

Lil looks a bit sad, and my shame deepens. "Sophie," she says, "you misunderstand me. I'm not minimizing how wearing it is to raise young children, hold down a busy job, and be a good wife and daughter and friend and all the other millions of things that you do. But you're a smart girl. No one is going to hand you a medal at the end of all of this because you ran faster and harder than everyone else. The point is to enjoy it. That's the end game. I look at you and all the other young women that I know and I see you weighing yourselves down with worry. You can buy fifty kinds of organic baby food in the store, but it's not good enough. You girls have to make your own. You let your kids sleep in your bed, so you never have adult conversations with your spouses, let alone sex."

I try not to appear mortified as Lil continues. "You breastfeed your kids until they're practically adults. I wasn't exactly on the front lines, but I thought the feminist movement was about trying to create new possibilities for women, to free them from the narrow confines of domestic life. And now I see a whole generation of women snapping the chains right back on."

I feel a large tear roll down my face and splash onto my napkin before I can stop it.

"Oh, Sophie, I'm sorry. I didn't mean to make you cry." She reaches over and pats my hand. "But that reminds me. My Christmas party is this Saturday and I haven't heard from you and Jesse. You need to have some fun. Get a babysitter and have a night out. You haven't come in at least a couple of years. It will do you good. Trust me."

"I have fun," I say, sounding petulant even to my own ears.

"That may be, dear," says Lil. "I can't say. But I'm not the one crying in my Veuve Clicquot."

CHAPTER TEN

wednesday, december 4, 2013

Anil pulls up in front of the hospital and comes around to open my door for me. For once, I don't try to stop him. I rummage around in my purse, pull the surgical mask out, and strap it on, and Anil smiles gently at me and says, "Be well, Ms. Sophie."

"I'll try," I say, and I turn and head off to deal with the rest of my day.

Erica is waiting outside my office again, but she looks slightly less frenzied now, which I take as a positive sign. "They're waiting for us," she says, and leads the way to the boardroom at the end of the hall.

Marvin is seated at the table, along with a man in a lab coat. "This is Dr. Christian Viggars," he says, gesturing to a tall, wiry man with short brown hair, a sulky expression, and an unfortunate goatee.

"Dr. Viggars," I say, taking a seat across from him. "I was surprised to learn about all of the media interest in your study, mostly because I'd never heard of it before this morning. Normally, when Baxter researchers have a discovery that they want to share with the world, they work with my office on a press release." I have an expression that I have perfected for just such situations as this: a slight widening of the eyes to invite confessions of misdeeds, a gentle tilt of the head to indicate calm attention to detail, and a modest but non-toothy smile to communicate warm capability and reassurance. I deploy it now.

"Are you a scientist?" he asks.

"A scientist? No. I'm the communications director for the hospital." My smile droops on one side, and I hoist it back up, exposing some teeth in the process.

"Exactly," he says, folding his arms across his chest.

Marvin clears his throat. "Dr. Viggars is of the view that researchers are in the best position to explain their work."

I feel a migraine taking shape at the bridge of my nose. "So you leaked your results to the media?"

"I *released* my results," he says. "The term 'leaked' suggests that they weren't mine to disseminate."

"I see," I say, looking at Marvin for inspiration. He tilts his palms upward, as if to say, *Search me*. "And what are your results?"

"That children under the age of five who watch five hours or more of television per day have a greater chance of developing ADHD than children who don't." Unbidden, an image of Scotty, rapt in front of the television, pops into my head, and I feel a wave of loathing for the entire group of pompous, childless lab-dwellers at the Baxter, secure in their belief that everything that matters can be quantified. I look at my watch: two minutes to two o'clock. Judging from Viggars's bullish posture, I'm even less likely to resolve this issue in the next two minutes than I am to find inner peace at Family Yoga.

"Erica," I say, "could you step out into the hall with me for a moment?" We rise and I close the door behind us. "I'm due at another meeting," I say. "I'd like you to finish up here for me."

Erica looks stunned. "Are you sure?" she asks. "What do you want me to do?"

"Get him to agree to a proper press conference," I say.

"I'm not sure I can," she says.

I check my watch again. I'm late for Will. "He's unrepentant and unlikely to change his tune. But he wants attention and we can make sure he gets it. Do what you have to do to get him to see that." I pat her shoulder. "You're ready," I say. "You can handle it." Actually, I have serious doubts about whether Erica can handle it, but I know I can't. My throat is tight and I'm afraid that if I stay, I'm going to burst into tears. "I'll be in my office," I say. "Come by when you're done and let me know how it went."

I rush back to my office, pausing at Joy's desk to catch my breath. She barely looks up. "There's someone waiting for you in there," she says, pointing to my office with her chin.

I poke my head around the corner and freeze. His back is to me, his long body folded awkwardly into the visitor's chair facing my desk, but I'd know him anywhere. "Will," I say, and watch him rise and turn with the unconscious grace of a natural athlete. For years, I've been waiting for Will to lose his hair or get squishy around the middle, but life isn't that kind. Will gets more attractive with age, at least partly because sex appeal is a relative measure, and the rest of his cohort is losing ground. Not to mention the fact that his six-foot frame looks even better in a charcoal Armani suit than it ever did in jeans and a T-shirt.

"Sophie," he says, coming over to greet me. I go up on tiptoes to plant a quick kiss on his cheek, feeling a hint of stubble rub against my face as he does the same to me; but when he moves to give me a second kiss, European-style, I turn in at exactly the wrong moment and bang his nose, and then promptly lose my balance. Will grabs my shoulder and steadies me with one hand, rubbing his nose with the other.

"First day on the new feet," I say, weakly, and he laughs.

"It's good to see you," he says.

You broke my heart, you broke my heart, you broke my heart, you broke my heart, I think, but I say, "Can I get you a coffee?"

"I'm fine," he says. "And I'm not going to keep you long. It's not purely a social call, although I'd like to find a time to do that while I'm in town."

I sit down at my desk. "How are you?" I say. "How's Paula?" Paula is the most recent of Will's live-in girlfriends. All of them have been impossibly gorgeous, chilly, high-strung, and artistic. I take way too much comfort in the fact that he has never married, or stayed with any of them for more than a few years.

From the way he deflects the question, it appears that the pattern has repeated itself. "She's spending most of her time in Santa Fe these days," he says.

"I'm sorry," I say, not trying especially hard to sound sincere.

Will grins. "Don't say things you don't mean," he says. "It doesn't suit you."

He holds my gaze and I feel a blush rising. It's always like this with him, as if no time has passed since our last conversation. "What brings you to town, Will?" I ask.

"I've got a proposal for you," he says.

"I'm all ears," I say, knowing that any proposal Will is prepared to make is one I'm likely to accept.

"I hear you've been spending some time with my aunt Lillian."

"Some," I say, thinking of the fox. "She's been misbehaving."

"She told me. She also told me that she gave you the history of the Baxter Foundation."

I nod. "I still don't understand how I never made the connection between your family and the hospital," I say. "You might have mentioned it when I came to work here, you know. I feel like a complete idiot."

Will shrugs. "I can't speak for Lillian, but I assumed you knew. I've never had any direct involvement in the hospital, so there wasn't anything to talk about when you took the job. As for the foundation, it's been a family affair over the years, but Lillian and I agree that it's time for a more modern structure. Lillian made me the chair of the board a few years ago, and we've done some excellent recruiting. But it's time to professionalize the day-to-day operations."

"How is it staffed now?"

He laughs. "Lillian wanders through the office a few days a week, but basically it's a self-governing island of misfit toys. And we have bags of money, so we should be thinking more strategically about what we do with it. Our mission is pretty broad—we fund initiatives that advance the health and well-being of children—but ninety-nine percent of our grants go to the Baxter Hospital and we aren't spending anything close to the income we have available every year. It's an amazing opportunity for someone to come in and build up the organization."

"You're looking for an executive director?"

"For now," he says. "But really, I'm looking for a new president. Lillian isn't going to be around forever, and we need to think about succession."

My mental list of possible candidates shrinks as I begin to appreciate the full scope of the job description. "That's going to be a tall order," I say. "Most people would balk at the idea of having Lil looking over their shoulder."

"Agreed," says Will. "That's why I think you would be ideal."

"Me?" He nods. "I'm flattered," I say, "but I don't think I'm the right person."

"Why not?" says Will. "You're smart, organized, experienced, and you know how to manage Lillian."

"No one knows how to manage Lil."

"You're more qualified than anyone else would be."

"It doesn't feel right," I say. "I love Lil. I don't like the idea of trying to set up something in order to manage around her."

"Sophie," says Will. "Do you think the board is doing this behind her back? It's her foundation. You are her choice. I'm here because she sent me." My face must show a little of the unexpected disappointment I feel at his words, because he says, hastily, "Of course, I wanted to see you, which is why I volunteered to come and offer you the job on behalf of the board." He raises a hand to stop me from speaking. "Spend a couple of days mulling it over. Also, Lillian said to tell you that she'll pay you more than they pay you here."

"I'll talk to Jesse about it," I say. "It's a really nice offer, just . . . unexpected." It's unsettling to see Will's hands, bare of visible signs of commitment, resting on my desktop, and I feel another blush coming on. Will was always good with his hands. I cover my discomfort by swiveling around to my computer and opening my calendar. "How long are you in town?"

"I'm leaving Sunday morning. I promised Lillian that I'd come to her party this year."

"Do you have plans on Friday night?"

"If I do, I can move them," he says, and a familiar glow spreads through me. There has never been any elixir as powerful for me as being the object of Will's undivided attention. It is his gift: he turns his spotlight on you, and you are transformed into the star of your own fascinating story, and not merely background to other, more gripping narratives. It's incredibly addictive, and dangerous. "Dinner?"

"Yes," I say, without hesitation. "I'll make a reservation and e-mail you the details." There's a knock at the door, and Erica pokes her head in. "Sorry to bother you," she says, and Will stands up.

"Perfect timing, actually," he says. "I've got another appointment." He turns to me and flashes the smile that has melted many hearts tougher than mine. "See you Friday, Sophie."

"Bye," I say.

Erica watches him go with an appraising eye. "Who was *that?*"

"An old friend," I say.

"Yummy," she says, completely inappropriately. I sit straight in my chair and regard her with a gaze that I hope is in the range of cool-to-withering. She drops into the visitor's chair that Will has just vacated, oblivious.

"So," I say. "Where did we end up with the disagreeable Dr. Viggars? Do we have a press conference?"

"We're good," she says. "The press conference is scheduled for tomorrow afternoon."

"Did he give you trouble?"

"Nothing I couldn't handle," she says breezily. "And anyway, it's not a bad news story for us. I mean, who lets their kids watch five hours of TV a day?"

I swallow hard. "Who indeed?" I say.

I dismiss Erica as quickly as possible and start mining through the stacks of paper on my desk. An hour passes, and then two, but the paper still towers.

Joy appears in the doorway, looking anxious. "Aren't you leaving early today?" she asks.

"Leaving early?"

"It's Wednesday," she says. "You always leave early on Wednesdays." I have long suspected that Joy bolts out of the office as soon as I do, and her agitation at the fact that I am still at my desk at four-thirty on a Wednesday clinches it. But I have no time to enjoy this small victory, because I'm late for Family Yoga. And I would definitely skip it today, with a legitimate excuse in the form of my runny nose, except that I was not very nice to my mother yesterday, and if I don't go to yoga it's going to take a lot longer to get off her naughty list.

Family Yoga is the brainchild of my mother and Dana, who decided in the summer that we should all spend more quality time together. Of course, they could have picked a different kind of activity, like drinking at a pub, but Family Yoga is supposed to be a form of intervention, taking me out of the office early and forcing me to relax. The underlying theory, I believe, was that a weekly yoga class would force me to clear my mind of all stressors and emerge at the end of the hour with re-adjusted priorities. What actually happens every Wednesday is that I spend the entire afternoon in a state of panic trying to figure out how to get out of the office in time for a five o'clock yoga class, knowing that I should leave at four-thirty but rarely departing before four-forty-five. Then I scream down to the yoga studio, burst into the class late, and disrupt whatever state of mindfulness the other people in the class have managed to achieve thus far. For the next hour, while others in the class empty the stress of the day from their minds, I fret. I fret about the work I left on my desk. I fret about how late I'll be to pick up Scotty from the daycare. I fret about the broken faucet in the powder room, and the fact that I've forgotten, for the tenth day in a row, to call the plumber. I fret about the kids and their eating habits and whether I'll be home in enough time to make something decent for dinner so that we don't have to order pizza again for the third time this week. All in all, I'd have to say that the only clarity I've attained in six months of yoga has been the realization that I could be bound and blindfolded in a cave in Afghanistan and I would still be thinking, *I really hope Jesse is remembering to make the kids eat some vegetables,* and *If I die, how will he know when to do the kindergarten registration?*

I do a quick ROAR calculation to see if there is any way I can justify skipping Family Yoga today. My Desire to Perform Activity is obviously zero, but my Guilt Factor is an eight (on account of yesterday's temper tantrum), while my Need to Behave Like a Grown-up is five (which is the minimum for any activity where my sister-in-law is present), and my Allowable Selfishness is one (see temper tantrum analysis above; a runny nose is usually worth three). So calculation for today is 0 + 8 + 5 − 1, producing a blood-curdling ROAR of twelve. I grab my gym bag from under the desk and run to the elevator.

Here are the things I hate most about Family Yoga:

1. That I forget about it approximately thirty percent of the time, thereby confirming for my mother that my life is completely out of control and giving her a perfect opportunity to regale Dana with tales of my pathological workaholism.
2. The way my mother flirts with Leo, the admittedly hot instructor, who speaks in self-help aphorisms.
3. The dreamy expression that everyone else in the class affects, presumably to advertise to the group that they have arrived at a state of mindfulness, whatever that means.
4. The way my rear end looks in my yoga pants.

I tear into the yoga studio with moments to spare, throw my clothes into a locker and pour myself into my yoga outfit. Is it my imagination, or is it getting smaller? I manage to convince myself, as I do each week, that spandex shrinks, because the alternative is too depressing to contemplate. I duck into the bathroom stall with a couple of towels, set my BlackBerry to vibrate, and swaddle it into a roll. Then I tuck it under my arm, flush the toilet, and run to the studio.

"Hi," I say, panting, as I unroll my yoga mat next to Dana and my mother.

"Hi, Sophie!" Dana leans over and gives me a peck on the cheek. "You look tired."

"I'm getting a cold," I say.

"Again! You have got to start taking better care of yourself," says my mother.

"Fatigue is the body expressing itself to you," says Leo, rising from his mat at the front of the room and making his way over to our little family group. "You must learn to listen when your body speaks," he says, laying an unwelcome hand on my shoulder.

"That's exactly what I keep telling her!" my mother trills. "Maybe she'll listen to you!"

"Ah," murmurs Leo, nodding meaningfully and gazing deeply into my mother's eyes. "Wisdom may be given, but it is not always received."

"I'm still here," I say, a bit too loudly.

"Are we ready, everyone? Let us leave our place of quiet meditation. Now that we are all here, we may begin our yoga practice."

"Sorry," I mutter.

"We begin with Sun Salutations," says Leo. "Mountain pose, please."

I put my hands together in front of me, and Dana whispers, "Busy day at the office?"

"And arch back and fold forward. Very nice," says Leo.

"Crazy," I say.

"And lunge—right foot, not left, Sophie—yes, and plank, good."

"What's going on?" whispers Dana, who can speak while doing a plank, which is evidence that her fitness level is well above mine.

"The usual," I gasp, pushing myself from an upward to a downward dog.

"And lunge again—other leg, Sophie, yes—and fold and back to mountain. Very good. Again." And now Leo is beside me. "You must focus, Sophie. Let your mind—and your lips—be quiet." This seems rather unfair, since it is Dana who insists on conversing during yoga to ratchet up the quality level in our time together. But Dana is such an incredibly nice human being that it's hard to blame her for anything.

For the first half hour of the class, Leo glides between the yoga mats, adjusting everyone's positions and spouting yogic aphorisms. "As we move through our practice, we must listen to our Inner Voices," Leo pronounces. "The Inner Voice is the guide to our deepest selves. If we can clear the path, it will speak to us. But we must first let go of all of the noise in our lives—the demands, the stresses, the desires, the ambitions, the self-criticism, the anger. The noise blocks us from receiving the wisdom within our own bodies." Leo is very keen on the Inner Voice.

At the thirty-five-minute mark, there is a muffled moaning sound nearby, like the call of a sick moose. It is coming from my towel roll.

"Now we move to balancing poses," says Leo. "Reaching forward, right leg lifts, and into warrior three." I wobble, and Leo comes over to adjust my posture. "Focus your mind," he says. "The mind-body connection is the source of your greatest power. When you achieve this connection, you allow your Inner Voice to speak to you. Hear it. Trust it. The Inner Voice leads us to self-knowledge as we begin to understand our unique place in the universe. Breathe."

I lower my leg and watch everyone else balance as I summon the energy to try again. My BlackBerry moans again.

"Do you need to check it?" whispers Dana, who knows my dirty little secret.

"Not yet," I whisper back. "If it's an emergency, you'll know."

"Crane pose," says Leo. "Knees wide and squat. Very good. Fingers wide on the mat. Lean forward and find your balance. Now lift your toes and hold. Breathe."

I topple over and land on my hip on the hard floor, missing my mat entirely. "Ow," I say before I can stop myself. Leo comes over. "Let's try again," he says. The BlackBerry vibrates insistently. Leo looks confused. "What was that?" he says.

"That was me," says Dana.

"Crane pose, Sophie," says Leo. "Squat and reach . . ."

A long low moan emanates from the towel, the product of messages being sent over and over again in rapid succession. The towel starts moving across the floor. "I'll be back," I say, grabbing the towel and racing for the door.

Outside, I unwrap the BlackBerry and see ten missed calls from Jesse, and a text message in all caps: URGENT: TRAPPED IN MTG W INVSTRS. CAN U PICK SCOTTY UP.

I look at the clock. It's five-forty-five. I grab my running shoes and shove my feet into them as the door to the studio opens. It's Leo. "Sophie," he says. "We all have our own journey to make, but we come together in a state of mutual understanding and respect in this room. I cannot allow you to bring an electronic device into our studio."

"Understood," I say, lacing up my shoes.

"If I may," says Leo, "it is not an accident that balancing poses are so difficult for you. To balance the body, you must first balance the mind. You must become more attuned to your Inner Voice. Until you do, I fear that you will not realize the benefits of this class."

"Go fuck yourself, Leo," I say. "There, you see? I'm completely attuned to my Inner Voice right now. Great class."

CHAPTER ELEVEN

wednesday, december 4, 2013

I throw my coat over my yoga clothes, stuff everything else in my gym bag, and run for the car. I arrive at the daycare at six-fifteen, fifteen minutes late, and find myself face-to-face with the director of the Progressive Center for Child Development and Care.

In my almost dizzying loathing for the director, it is easy to forget that it was I who insisted that we enroll our children in a daycare instead of hiring a nanny, a course of action which Jesse sensibly argued would relieve considerable pressure on our household in the form of basic cleaning, grocery shopping, and flexibility in parental arrival and departure times. But I held firm in my conviction that daycare was more consonant with our values than hiring a poor woman from a developing economy who would have to leave her own children behind in order to care for our privileged white offspring. Now I am faced daily with the bitter reality that the director is the most obvious obstacle to my ever attaining the mythical feminist state of joyous working motherhood.

"Sophie," she says, "I'd like to speak to you for a minute. Can you step into my office?"

"I'm sorry I'm late," I say. "I'll pay the fine."

She closes the office door behind me, an ominous beginning. "You've been racking up a lot of fines lately," she says.

"Maybe I should run a tab," I joke, but I can see that the director is not amused.

"We had another incident today," she says.

"Scotty bit someone?"

"Unfortunately, yes."

"It's not his fault," I say. "It's been pretty stressful at our house lately. He really is a good little boy."

"I'm not saying that he's not. But it's probably time to consider whether this is the right childcare arrangement for him and for you."

My heart sinks. "You can't kick us out," I say.

"I'm sure it won't come to that," she says. "Usually families come to the realization on their own that another arrangement would work better. I'm just encouraging you to start that conversation with yourself and your husband. I've been doing this a long time, and I get the strong sense that this isn't working for your family. Scotty's the last child here every day. It's stressful for him and it's not fair to the staff."

"I understand," I say. "I'll do better. Can I go and get Scotty now?"

"Go ahead," she says. "Let's talk again soon."

I find Scotty in the toddler room, watching a *Dora* video. He leaps to his feet when he sees me, throws his arms around my neck, and won't let go. "Can we watch the end?" he asks.

I sit down on the carpet with him and pull him onto my lap. The director can throw us out when she wants to leave. For now, I'm going to stage a sit-in, just like old times.

I bury my face in Scotty's curls and, finding myself in as dark a psychological space as I've been in for a while, allow myself to dive down a bit deeper still. I have always taken pride in my adherence to a long-term professional plan, terminating in my installation as the executive director of a socially relevant, politically influential nonprofit, preferably for the advancement of the dispossessed. After grad school, I logged six years at organizations with unassailable feminist credentials, one a UK magazine with a focus on women's health, whose dwindling readership

numbers were artificially inflated with free mailings to community centers across the country, and the other a think tank dedicated to lobby
efforts in support of girl-centric curriculum in public high schools. Having started a long-distance relationship with Jesse while employed at the
first of these fine organizations, and having moved in with him during
my tenure at the second, both of which paid next to nothing and offered
no benefits or job security, it occurred to me one day that if I wanted to
(a) not be entirely financially supported by my male life partner and (b)
ever be in a position to have children who would not be entirely supported by my male life partner, I would have to get a job with an organization that had sources of funding other than intermittent government
grants from minor agencies tasked with securing the women's vote for
the next election. And that's how I ended up working at the Baxter,
although when I took the job there it never crossed my mind that I'd be
planning social events for the ruling class. Life is indeed full of disappointments.

And on the subject of disappointments, as I plunge deeper down my
little rabbit hole of angst, I am reminded of my friend Sara, who had my
book club in stitches one night telling us about the worst things that her
children, now in their teens, had ever said to her. She had a fine collection
of ignominies, but the gold medal for maternal insults went to her son for
telling her at the tender age of five that she was not the mother he had
hoped for. I only had Jamie then, and he was too small yet to recognize
my shortcomings. I was more confident in the upward trajectory of my
parenting achievements. I thought there could be no failure more devas-
tating than having your child say such a thing. But as I sit on the floor in
Scotty's daycare, I know that there is much more profound despair to be
found in the knowledge that you are not the mother you had hoped to be.

"Hey, Scotty," I say. "Do you want to do something fun tonight?"

"What?"

"It's a surprise," I say, and as the credits roll on the *Dora* episode, I
pick him up and march past the director's office with my head held high.
Let her think that I'm a bad mother. What does she know? There is still
time to turn the tide, and my short interlude of meditation on the toddler

mat has given me some inspiration and perspective, a result of connecting with my innermost thoughts and feelings, no doubt: Leo would be proud. I am going to turn this day around, and, being a planner, I have a fool-proof plan. Tonight, I will nourish my children with healthy, homemade food, while simultaneously teaching them about the satisfaction that comes from enjoying the fruits of your own labor. And that's not all. I will teach them about the nature of giving and the true spirit of Christmas by helping Jamie create beautiful, personal Christmas cards for all of his friends. There is still time to be the mother I always wanted to be. And who needs television when you can make your own fun?

Fortunately, there is a supersized twenty-four-hour grocery store near Scotty's daycare, which has everything I need to implement an evening of exemplary parenting. I'm not really dressed for the occasion, but the one benefit of having a daycare neither near work nor near home is that you are unlikely to run into anyone you know. I feel unreasonably happy every time I come to this grocery store, and the main reason for this is the seasonal aisle, which has bailed me out on countless occasions. The seasonal aisle is a little oasis for the working mother, one of the few places in the world designed for her comfort and convenience. Forgot to buy Halloween candy? You can get it in the seasonal aisle at two in the morning on October thirty-first—and not substandard candy either, but the very same candy that the stay-at-home moms bought two weeks ago. No Easter presents? Fear not. On Easter morning, you will find an outstanding selection of chocolate bunnies and eggs for the Easter hunt and even festive Easter hats. The seasonal aisle has never let me down and today is no different. I pick up a package of red construction paper, glue, red and green sequins, and Santa stickers, and throw them in the cart along with all of the pizza ingredients.

Scotty whimpers, and I see that his nose is running. I rummage in my purse for a tissue and check my pockets. I must have one somewhere. I unzip my coat and check the inside pocket. Still no tissues, but I find a lollipop of unspecified vintage, so I resort to wiping Scotty's nose with his shirt and placating him with the candy. "Just a few more minutes, baby," I promise.

"Sophie?" I turn around and see Jenny Dixon standing behind me. I suppress a groan and smile brightly, attempting to look as professional as possible in sweaty yoga clothes. "Is this your son?" she asks. "He's gorgeous."

"This is Scotty," I say. "We're making homemade pizza tonight, aren't we, honey?" Scotty sucks hard on his lollipop and eyes Jenny with deep suspicion.

"How fun!" says Jenny. "I meant to call you this afternoon, actually. Have you done the performance reviews for your staff yet?"

"Not exactly," I say.

"I know it's been busy in your department, so I've cut you some slack. But they were due three weeks ago. When do you think you can get them done?"

"By the end of the week, for sure," I say.

"I'm counting on it," says Jenny. "See you tomorrow. Oh, and good luck with your pizza. I admire you. I've never had the patience for that—the dough just takes so long to rise."

By the time I find and pay for all of my purchases, load a resistant Scotty back into his car seat, and pull into the driveway, it's already seven o'clock. The babysitter, radiating irritation at my tardiness, pushes past me and out the door as I haul my shopping bags into the kitchen.

"I've got to run, Sophie," she says. "Jamie had a snack earlier but he's been asking for dinner. See you tomorrow."

"Can we order pizza, Mommy?" asks Jamie.

"I've got a better idea, sweetie," I say. "Let's make our own pizzas!" Jamie looks unimpressed. "You can have exactly what you want on it, and it won't take any longer than ordering. I promise. I'm just going to heat the oven." I scan the instructions on the package of dough to check the temperature, remembering Jenny's parting comment with a sense of foreboding. And now I see for the first time that I am supposed to put the dough in a bowl, cover it, and let it rise for an hour. Then the pizzas need to cook for fifteen minutes. I plunk the cold dough in a bowl and do some quick calculations. One hour plus fifteen minutes will take us to eight-fifteen, by which time the children will be completely ungovernable; I can't blame them, given that they go to bed at eight-thirty. The unwelcome thought crosses my mind that I have picked the wrong evening for homemade pizza, but I brush it aside. Surely a half hour is enough time for the dough? But I still need a stopgap.

"How about a handful of Goldfish crackers to tide you over?" I suggest. I fill two bowls with Goldfish and push them across the breakfast bar.

"I want to watch my show!" says Scotty.

"You know what? I've got a better idea," I say, brightly. "We're going to do some crafts! Look at what I've got." I pull out my bag of tricks from the seasonal aisle and spread the craft supplies on the table. I give Scotty a couple of markers and some construction paper and tell him to draw snowflakes, which, miraculously, he does. "And I have a great project for you, Jamie," I say. "We're going to make Christmas cards for all the kids in your class! Won't that be fun?"

Jamie pops the last goldfish cracker into his mouth. "I'm still hungry," he says.

I hand him a banana. "Look," I say, pulling out a sheet of red construction paper. "We'll fold the paper like this, cut out a white paper snowflake, glue it on, and add some sequins. Then you can print your friends' names and 'Merry Christmas' inside. Don't you think your friends will like them? They'll be so much nicer than store-bought cards."

"I hate printing."

"OK, how about you do all of the cutting and gluing for the front of the card and I'll do the printing?"

"How much longer until the pizza is ready?"

I look at the clock. The dough has been rising for fifteen minutes. It will have to do. "Coming right up," I say, and I rip off a handful of dough and roll it out. "See?" I say. "It's going to be just the perfect size for you. Do you want to put on the toppings?" Jamie shakes his head. I bash out two more misshapen personal-sized pizzas, fling some tomato sauce at them, and dump a mound of shredded cheese on top. "Will you at least put the pepperoni on?" I ask.

"Can I have some more Goldfish?"

"Me too!" Scotty drops his marker and throws his snowflake drawing on the floor.

"I'll give you more Goldfish if you put the pepperoni on the pizza," I say.

Jamie takes a few slices and places them on the pizza with a decided lack of enthusiasm.

"I think you'll be surprised at how delicious this dinner is going to be," I say, refilling their bowls with crackers. I open the oven door and slide the pizzas in. "Just fifteen more minutes, guys. And while we're waiting, we can get started on our cards."

"I want to get down," says Scotty. "Can I watch my show now?"

"We're not watching TV tonight," I say. Scotty's brow furrows; his lower lip juts out and starts to quiver. He is ten seconds away from a complete meltdown, but I have an emergency backup plan. "Come with me, honey," I say, holding out my hand. "Let's get your piano out."

Scotty's "piano" is a cheap synthesizer that my mother gave him for Christmas last year. It has six different tracks programmed in, each more annoying than the last, and no discernible volume control. I put it away in my closet sometime last February, after I realized that I was humming the tunes in the shower every morning. For a couple of months, Scotty would ask where it was and I would change the subject, but now I appreciate that I will have to make some sacrifices if I'm serious about reducing television consumption. So I race upstairs and produce the long-lost piano. Hopefully, this buys me at least a half hour to focus on Jamie.

"I'm going to teach you how to make paper snowflakes," I tell him, as I fold a sheet of white paper over on itself. I take a pair of scissors and make crisp little hatches around the edges, then unfold the paper to reveal a rectangle with a jagged hole in the middle and a ragged edge that looks like it has been chewed by a dog.

"Where's the snowflake?" asks Jamie.

"You know what? Never mind the snowflake. Let's just glue some sequins and stickers onto the red construction paper." I fold a couple of pages in half and hand them to him. "Here are the first two. Can you choose the stickers you want?" I notice that his second bowl of Goldfish is empty, but at least he seems marginally interested in the stickers. He selects some Santas, elves, and reindeer, and begins layering them onto the cards.

"Not so many, sweetheart," I say. "Pace yourself. We've got to save some for the other cards. How about some sequins?" I unscrew the cap on the glue and empty a pile of sequins onto the counter. Jamie takes the glue, turns it upside down, and squeezes a white, sticky puddle onto a full quarter of the page.

"Whoa!" I say, grabbing the glue and turning it upright. "You don't need quite that much, honey!"

Jamie grabs a handful of sequins and drops them onto the glue spill. I remind myself that the goal is not to create impeccable works of art, but to work on fine motor control, offer attractive alternatives to television, and, of course, celebrate the spirit of Christmas. "Gorgeous!" I say. "Your friends are going to be so happy that you made them these beautiful Christmas cards!"

Jamie looks doubtful, but he dutifully moves on to the second card, which is soon covered in the same gooey mess as the first one. The timer on the oven goes off, and I race over to peek at my pizza masterpieces. But there is something wrong. The pizzas are completely flat, too flat even to pass as thin-crust. Maybe they just need a little more time. I close the oven, just as Scotty comes in.

"I want a cookie," he says.

"It's dinnertime, honey," I say. "No cookies." His face crumbles and I rush over to pick him up. "Would you like a banana instead? The pizza will be ready really, really soon." I grab a banana, peel it, and hand it to Scotty. "Are you done with your piano?" I ask, sitting him up on the counter. "Do you want to read a story?"

"I want my show!" he says, and starts to cry.

"Me too," says Jamie. "I don't want to make cards anymore."

"Come on, guys," I say. "We can find something else fun to do."

Suddenly I smell something burning. I race over the oven, but it's too late. The little pizza pucks are completely scorched around the edges and, by even the most optimistic interpretation, inedible. "Who wants a peanut butter sandwich?" I ask.

"I'm full," says Jamie.

Scotty's eyes are streaming with tears, and as I pick him up off the breakfast bar, I realize that I have sat him squarely on top of Jamie's cards, and he is now covered in glue and sequins. I strip him down to his underwear and kiss his head. "How about you, honey?" I ask. "Are you still hungry?"

"No, Mommy," he says. "I want my show."

I pull a wine tumbler out of the cupboard, walk over to the fridge, and balance the door open with my hip while I pour leftover wine from the wine bottle and fill the glass to the top. I take a long drink and look at my lovely sons, whom I have made miserable for no good reason. They deserve better, but today I have no idea what better might be, or how to get there.

"Come on, guys," I say. "Bedtime in a half hour. Let's see what's on until then." And then I beckon my sons to follow me, walk into the playroom, and turn on the television.

CHAPTER TWELVE

december 1994

"Right back against the wall," instructs Lil. She's been doling out instructions all day in preparation for her annual Christmas party, and is presently occupied with moving various pieces of heavy Victorian furniture to improve "flow" on the main floor. Or rather, she's directing: Will and A.J. are on the implementation end of things, sweating over an overstuffed settee that must weigh several hundred pounds. "Sophie, roll up the carpet," says Lil. "I'm so pleased I remembered this year! Every year, some pretty young nymph catches her heel and flies headlong into just the wrong person and I think, I must remember to roll up the carpet. Gentlemen, you can take the carpet down to the basement when Sophie's done." Obediently, the boys release the arms of the settee, shoulder the mammoth carpet, and convey it downstairs.

Lil beckons. "Be a dear, Sophie, and read me the list. The light is dreadful in here."

"Do you want me to run up and get your glasses?"

Lil looks scandalized. "I never wear those hideous things in the presence of gentlemen," she says. "No matter how unformed they may yet be." I suppress the fleeting thought that Will looks rather well-formed lifting furniture and focus on the list.

"We're about done with the moving," I say. "The caterer is coming at four-thirty. The glasses and plates have been delivered, but we still need to set up the bar."

"Another job for the boys," says Lil. "What else?"

"I think that's it," I say. "We're completely organized."

"Perfect. Thank you, Sophie. Now, what are you wearing?"

"I haven't decided yet," I say. I've learned that this is the correct answer. Lil takes excessive pleasure in dressing me for parties. And there is an unexpected benefit to being Lil's project: I feel pretty and sexy. Until now, I've always believed the right guy would be drawn to my fire and strength and intellect, and not my appearance. Assuming he ever showed up, how would I know that he loved me for the right reasons if I compromised the purity of my assessment with form-fitting clothes and makeup? But I've started to care less about that since my theory has net-ted only a handful of prospects over the past three years, all relatively charmless and screamingly earnest, and not candidates for long-term love by any stretch of the imagination. I haven't been able to sort out why sen-sitivity and enlightenment can be such a huge turn-off in bed (*May I touch you here? Is it all right if I touch you there?*) but in the meantime, I'm enjoying the way men look at me when I'm playing Cinderella to Lil's fairy god-mother. I know I shouldn't, but I do. Which is why I've been wearing makeup lately, and not just to parties.

"Excellent," says Lil. "I've got just the thing. You'll like it. It's black."

At one o'clock in the morning, I'm standing barefoot in the kitchen, tak-ing stock of the damage. I've just retrieved the last half-empty glasses from the last side table and piled them onto the kitchen island. The full overhead lights are piercingly harsh in the opening act of my champagne hangover, so I pour another glass, bring down the dimmer, and rest my elbows on the island countertop. Lil has long since retired, and the guests are gone but for a handful of stragglers watching old movies in the den. Will wanders in, yawning, catches sight of me and waves, then freezes;

Lil's dress wasn't cut for slouching, and he's just taken in a lot more of me than he was expecting. I straighten quickly.

"Hey," I say. "Any ideas on how we get rid of the guys in there?" I point to the den.

"We don't," says Will, averting his gaze. "They'll pass out, if they haven't already."

"Lil won't mind?"

"On the contrary," he says. "She'll regard it as the sign of a successful party. Hopefully there's still some couch space."

"Why?"

"A couple of A.J.'s engineering pals took a nap in my room. We've been trying to wake them up for the last half hour, but it looks like they're staying put."

"You should sleep in A.J.'s room, then. He can sleep on the couch," I say, offended on Will's behalf that A.J. would be so careless with his guests.

"Easy, there," he says. "He offered. I refused." He looks sheepish. "I was planning on using Lillian's spare room. Then I looked at the time and changed my mind about knocking on her door. So here I am." He takes in my feet. "Shoes?"

"Search me," I say. "I vaguely remember kicking them off when we were jumping around to 'Smells Like Teen Spirit,' but that was hours ago and I was way more wasted then." I like the way the word *wasted* rolls off my tongue; like the dress, it fits, but belongs to a modified version of myself that I'm taking out for the occasional test-drive.

"You peaked early tonight," he says, laughing.

I take another sip of champagne. "I'm trying to catch a second wind while I clean up a bit. It's going to be a lot nastier if I try to do it hungover tomorrow."

He looks around the kitchen as if seeing it for the first time. "I see your point. I can help you fill a few garbage bags before we call it a night if you want."

"Aren't they coming to pick up the rental glasses in the morning?"

"Right." He yawns again. "OK, Little Miss Responsible, give me my marching orders."

I balk at the totally justified but deeply unwelcome moniker, so at odds with the sexier, more easygoing persona I've been cultivating, clearly less successfully than I thought. But I really want some help, so I instruct him to bring the empty storage boxes for the glasses from underneath the bar. "I'll hand them to you and you can box them," I say, and he bows theatrically.

"As you wish," he says.

"I love that movie," I say, carefully. I can recite every line of *The Princess Bride*. Does Will know that "as you wish" means "I love you" in the lexicon of Buttercup and Westley's great romance? Is he trying to tell me something? Can I find out without making a complete ass of myself?

He laughs. "You and every girl on planet Earth," he says, and holds out his hands for a pair of wineglasses.

For the next twenty minutes, we don't speak much as our small but efficient assembly line does its work and the counter begins to emerge from the wreckage. It's been weeks since I had an excuse to be this close to Will, and I try not to stare as I memorize new details that only add to his physical perfection: a tiny scar above his left eyebrow, a small dimple in the corner of his mouth where his smile always begins, a tan line encircling his powerful left wrist. It's hard to believe that he can be completely oblivious to my reaction whenever his fingers brush up against mine, since from my perspective it feels like an acute episode; the hairs rise on my arms, my breath catches, and my hands start to shake. But there are no visible signs as he powers through the last box and grabs a handful of garbage bags. "One circuit, then bed," he says, and I nod. We do a loop through the living and dining rooms, sweeping paper plates and napkins and beer cans into the bags. We end up in the den, where we fill one last bag with trash and discover three full-sized engineers dead to the world. Will sighs, rubbing a hand through his hair so that it sticks up. "No room at the inn," he says ruefully. "I guess I'm waking Lillian up after all."

"Don't do that," I say. "You can stay with me." His eyes widen in surprise. "On the floor," I say hastily. "I have a sleeping bag."

"Thanks, Sophie," he says. "That's the best offer I'm likely to get tonight. I'll take it."

My mind is working furiously as we turn out the lights and head upstairs. The air between us is heavy, and I wonder if any of the tension I feel is being generated by him I hope so. I've never been as attracted to anyone as I am to Will Shannon at this moment, and it would be mortifying to be in it alone. I open the door to my room, make a beeline for my dresser and pull out the first pair of pajamas I see. I'm so nervous, I'm afraid I'm about to start giggling hysterically; it's the opposite of the breezy, nonchalant, and utterly nonthreatening image I'm shooting for. "The sleeping bag is in the closet," I say. "I'm just going to go and change in the bathroom. I'll be right back."

In the bathroom, I wriggle out of my dress, brush my teeth, and remove my makeup. I stare long and hard at my reflection, regretting my pajama selection. I could not look less like an object of lust, in an oversized pink tee and loose pants covered in rosebuds and butterflies. I groan. I'm off to a bad beginning if I want to make Will see me in a different light. "You can do this," I tell my reflection sternly.

When I return, Will is already lying on the floor in the sleeping bag, eyes half-closed, one arm bent behind his head. His eyes flicker open as I come in. "I hope you don't mind," he says. "I borrowed one of your pillows."

I stand over him, trying to figure out my next move. I had anticipated at least one additional opportunity to brush up against him accidentally-on-purpose. But now I am at a loss. "Of course not," I say lightly, turning off the overhead light and climbing into bed. I hear Will's breathing become more rhythmic as he starts to fall asleep, and know that the window of seduction is rapidly closing. *Don't be a coward,* I think. I clear my throat. "There's room in the bed," I say. I hear him shift in the sleeping bag and then sit up. There is a long silence.

"Are you sure?" he says.

"Absolutely," I say.

There is a metallic purr as he slides the zipper down, and the old floor creaks as he crosses over to the bed. I remain on my side, curled away from him, and I feel a puff of air as he throws the pillow down next to me. The mattress dips and rocks as he adjusts his weight, and it's only when I sense that he's settled that I risk rolling onto my back. I keep my eyes closed, feigning half-sleep, but when I get up the nerve to peek, I find him lying on his side with his head resting on his hand, eyes wide open, staring down at me.

"Hi," he says.

"Hi," I manage, grateful that it's too dark for him to see the sudden rush of blood to my cheeks. With his free hand, he reaches over and brushes a loose strand of hair from my face, and then very slowly and deliberately traces the line of my jawbone from ear to chin with his index finger. I bite my lower lip.

"What are we doing here, Sophie?" His tone is conversational, but his finger continues its steady journey down my neck to the hollow at the base of my throat where it hovers, waiting for an answer. I don't say anything, but I roll my hips toward him so that we are only a few inches apart. His hand moves lower, and his thumb skims over my nipple. I shudder. "This could turn into a situation," he says, and from the way he says *situation,* I can tell he doesn't mean that we could fall in love, have babies, and live happily ever after like Buttercup and Westley.

Guys don't have a lot of cardinal rules, but I know which one he's worried about. As usual, Zoe filled me in when I expressed mild concern about living in the Abernathy house, understanding—largely from television and not from experience—that unwelcome sexual tension could arise between men and women living in close proximity. "You don't need to worry about that," she'd said. "You aren't their type anyway, but even if you were, there's a code. Guys like Will and A.J. don't mess with girls they live with. They're too freaked out about it turning all weird on them. They're like dogs. They never shit where they sleep."

"It doesn't have to mean anything," I say, reaching over and running my thumb over his lower lip. He expels a long breath, snakes his arm behind my back, and slides me toward him, closing the gap.

"You know this is a bad idea," he says, bending his head to mine.

I slip my hand under the hem of his T-shirt and slide my palm all the way up his spine. "I do," I say as his mouth meets mine. My lips part under his, and his arms lock around me, and I'm swept away in a rush of sensation so intense that I wonder, fleetingly, how I'll find my way back. And then we don't speak again for a long time.

The morning is almost gone when I wake up. I'm alone, and it's not until I bury my face in the pillow next to me and breathe in Will's scent that I'm wholly convinced I haven't been dreaming. The head rush when I sit up is crushing, and I lie back down panting and nauseated, happy that no one is here to see my hangover in full bloom. After several further attempts, I manage to get myself to the bathroom, where I swallow a couple of Advil and step into the shower. I let the hot water course over me and consider my options. Little has been said between us so far, although much has been done, and Will's early exit tells me everything I need to know about his interest in a morning-after analysis. I know that the next few days are critical, and the safest course is to let him set the tone. *You will not be weird about this,* I tell myself. *You will not rehash. You will not scare him off. You will not fuck this up.*

I repeat this mantra to myself as I follow the smell of coffee down to the kitchen and prepare to greet Will with a friendly but completely non-stalker-like smile. But I find only A.J., pale and moving slowly, nursing a huge mug of coffee. "Hey, Sophie," he says, as I pour myself some coffee and join him at the breakfast table. "I'm sorry I left you with the cleanup last night. Things got a little out of hand."

He looks so ill that it's hard to be angry at him. "Did you get rid of your guests?"

"The guys in the den are gone. There's still a couple upstairs."

"Did you have fun?"

"Way too much," he says. "You?"

I feel a blush rising and take a long sip of coffee. "Same," I say. "Is Will up?"

"Up and gone," says A.J.

"Gone where?" I ask, trying to sound casual.

"He said he was spending a couple of days at his parents' house. He's getting stressed about his first exams, I guess. He said he wanted to eliminate distractions."

"He said that?"

"'Eliminate distractions,'" he repeats. "His exact words." He takes a long drink. "I've never known him to be so serious about exams before, but maybe the pressure of law school is finally getting to him." He stands, stretches. "Bacon and eggs?" he asks. "It's the least I can do."

"Sure," I say. "Thanks."

Will doesn't come back in a couple of days. The week passes, with no word other than the occasional bulletin from A.J.: *His exams are going well. He says it's easier to focus up there. He's going to stay a few more days.* I go about my business as if nothing is out of the ordinary, but every nerve is on high alert. Every time the phone rings or the front door opens, I prepare a face for him. But he never comes. I convince myself that I need to check a resource at the law library and look for Will there, but there's no sign of him. I lie awake at night trying to concoct a convincing reason to call him at his parents' house and testing theories for his absence. My favorite theory is that Will is rocked to his core by the depth of his feelings for me, previously suppressed but now unlocked, and needs time to come to terms with them. There are other, less desirable theories, of course, which is why I don't give in to my desperate desire to call him. I hand in my last few papers, register for next term's courses, clean the house from top to bottom, do all of my Christmas shopping, and eventually acknowledge that there's nothing left to do but to pack up for Port Alice.

A.J. drops me at the bus station on his way to the airport. He's meeting his family in Barbados—his brother is flying from Los Angeles, where he's at medical school, and his mother and stepfather from New York, where they moved after they got married. "Two weeks in the sun," I say enviously. "Do you have room for me in your suitcase?"

"I don't know," he says. "I'm not complaining, but if I could choose?

Two weeks in the house where I grew up, with a Christmas tree, and snow, and turkey leftovers—that's a real Christmas to me."

I've never thought of A.J. as a sentimentalist, but I still don't know him that well and, in truth, he surprises me more often than he conforms to a stereotype. As if to prove this point, he gets out of the car at the bus depot to help me with my bags. "You don't have to do that," I say.

"My mother would never forgive me if I didn't," he says, carrying the heaviest bag into the terminal. He waits while I buy my ticket, and then carries it to the gate.

"You don't have to wait with me, really," I say. "Your mother will never forgive *me* if you miss your flight."

He laughs. "That's probably true," he says. He reaches inside his jacket and pulls out a brown paper bag. "This is for you. For Christmas. I'm sorry I didn't have a chance to wrap it."

"A.J., that's so nice of you," I say. "I feel terrible. I don't have anything for you."

He shakes his head. "It's nothing much," he says. "I just wanted to say . . . it's been great having you in the house. And not just because of the food. Merry Christmas." He takes a step closer, enfolds me in a bear hug, and then turns and strides off before I can say anything.

It's three hours to Port Alice, and I settle into a window seat with my Walkman. I'm too embarrassed to play Enya in the house where the boys can hear it, but now I indulge, and the lush, romantic layers of sound are an ideal soundtrack to the short film, looping over and over again in my mind, of *My Night with Will*. I barely notice the mostly undistinguished landscape of flat, snow-covered fields, broken by the occasional rest stop and the looming statue of the World's Biggest Woodchuck, one town's failed attempt to create a tourist attraction. Instead I see the planes of Will's chest, the wide slopes of his shoulders, the arch of his back, and the exquisite geometry of his face moving above me.

I wish, more than I have ever wished for anything, that he were here with me now. I want to hold his hand. I want to tell him my secrets. I want to know everything about him —the first girl he ever kissed, and what scares him, and his happiest childhood memory, and what kind of man he wants to be. I have enough self-awareness to know that I wouldn't be an obvious candidate for a fling with Will even without the intervening issue of cohabitation. Whatever happens between us will be fraught with complications. Naturally, Will wants to be sure of me before we embark on this path together. But he would not have run away so abruptly if he were indifferent to me, if he really believed that what happened between us meant nothing, and this suggests that it means something to him, perhaps even as much as it means to me.

Quiet tears roll down my cheeks and I rummage in my bag for a tissue, unearthing instead the brown paper bag from A.J. I rub at the tears with my sleeve and slide a notebook from the bag. It has lovely, thick, creamy paper, a ribbon to mark the pages, and a hard cover with a delicate pattern of watermarks in alternating shades of blue and purple. I've been meaning to keep a journal for a while now, but until this moment, my life seemed empty of any drama worthy of recording. I uncap a pen, ready to bleed my longing for Will onto the crisp pages, but then I think of A.J. He is a mystery to me, but it feels disrespectful to turn his gift into a monument to my relationship, such as it is, with Will. So I turn back to the window until the bus pulls into the parking lot of the roadside hotel in Port Alice.

And there, standing next to a battered pickup truck that he loves more than he ever loved the luxury cars he owned in the city, stands the man against whom all competitors for my affection will forever be measured. "There's my girl," says my dad, and he puts an arm around my shoulder. "How was your trip?"

"The roads were clear," I say, surrendering to the easy routine of our traditional greeting.

"Glad to hear it," he says, loading my bags into the back of the truck. "Your mother is beside herself. She was expecting you a few days ago." He pulls out of the parking lot and turns onto the main road.

"I had to finish a couple of papers," I say. "They took longer than I'd planned."

"Don't worry," he says, patting my knee. "She'll settle down when she has you back in the nest for a day or so."

"Isn't Mike home?"

Dad laughs. "He's driving her crazy, as usual. She wants to bond; he wants to sleep late, watch football, and go out drinking with his buddies. She's pinned all her hopes on you."

"Yay," I say.

Dad looks serious. "I'm counting on you, sweetheart. Your mom looks forward to having you home for Christmas all year. It's been lonely for her since you went away to school."

His tone alarms me. "Is Mom OK?"

"Of course," he says. "I didn't mean to worry you. She's been a little blue lately, that's all. The wedding business is quieter this time of year, and with you guys gone, the country life is a bit isolating for her. I've been wondering if we should get an apartment in the city so she could spend more time down there."

This is an unsettling window into a marriage that has always seemed rock-solid in comparison to those of my friends' parents. I look out at the familiar streets and houses, and wish that I could show them to Will; or rather, I wish that Will wanted to know every mundane detail of my history the way I do about his. I wonder what my dad would make of Will. However generous my interpretation of Will's actions, I suspect that my dad isn't the sort of man who runs from consequences; what passes for vulnerability in my eyes would undoubtedly be weakness in his.

"Mom says that she knew the moment she met you that she'd follow you to the ends of the earth," I say, trying to make both of us feel better.

Dad smiles. "I think Port Alice feels like the end of the earth to her some days," he says. "It's a good thing she's an incurable romantic."

"Didn't you know that she was the right person as soon as you met her?" My mother has told me this story so many times that it feels like my own. But suddenly I'm interested in his version of events. Maybe men are slower to perceive that they are in the presence of The One. Maybe the awareness of true love dawns more gradually for them.

"I think that events in the past benefit from hindsight in the retelling," he says, too judiciously for my liking.

"Which means?"

"Which means, when you know the ending already, it's easier to interpret a series of events in a way that makes the ending seem inevitable, whether or not it actually is."

Dad may be the lawyer in the family, but he's not the only one who can cross-examine.

"Are you saying that love at first sight doesn't exist?"

Dad pulls into the long driveway, and Mom rushes out of the house, waving frantically, as the truck pulls up. "It may," he says. "Whether it does or not is largely a function of personality, and your mother has the right personality for falling in love at first sight, or at least believing that she fell in love at first sight."

"And you?"

"I believe that there is only one major factor that determines whether or not a relationship will succeed, and it's not very romantic." He puts the car into park and cuts the engine.

"Which is?"

"Timing," he says. "It's all about timing."

CHAPTER THIRTEEN

thursday, december 5, 2013

If I'm honest, the headache that I have on Thursday morning has nothing to do with my cold and everything to do with the fact that I drank three-quarters of a bottle of Chianti by myself last night while the kids and I watched back-to-back episodes of *Go, Diego, Go!* I'm not proud of myself, and in a penitent act of self-flagellation, I call Janelle Moss to talk about the Gala.

When she answers, the background noise is deafening. It sounds as though she is standing in an airplane hangar or a wind tunnel. "Sophie!" she bellows. "I'm in the middle of a blowout. I'll call you back in five!"

I sit at my desk and contemplate my options. I eye my computer and telephone warily; both seem to vibrate with malevolent energy today. I opt for the telephone.

First message. "Sophie, it's your mother. What happened at yoga last night? Leo said that you quit! Call me."

Next message. "Hi, Sophie, it's Dana. Is everything OK? Your mom was worried after you left yoga last night. Give me a call."

Next message. "Hi, Sophie, it's Jenny. Funny to run into you last night. We need to chat about an incident with one of your staff members. And could you send me a note letting me know when you've done all the performance review meetings so I can put it in the file?"

Next message. "Honey, it's your mother again. I just opened the mail and saw your adorable Christmas letter! It's so nice to see you keeping up our family tradition! I was going to chat with you last night about the Christmas presents for the boys, but you left early so I didn't get the chance. I'm running out of time, so if I don't hear from you by the end of the week, I'm just going to go ahead and buy them whatever I want and you won't have anything to say about it. Deal? And I still want to talk to you about yoga."

There are additional messages, but I hang up instead and consider my Christmas dilemma. It's tempting to take the passive approach here, and just let my mother loose on the toy store with no restrictions. But inevitably she will hit upon the very thing that Jesse has identified as this year's Santa gift and send him into orbit. Jesse doesn't have a lot of rules about the holidays, and only one of them is iron-clad: no one can outshine Santa. With my dad gone, though, I find it almost unbearable to ruin any small pleasure that my mother gets from doting on my children, especially around the holidays. I groan aloud and feel my hangover gathering in one painful knot in the center of my forehead. I throw back a couple of Advil.

The phone rings. "OK," says Janelle. "Sorry about that. What's the status? Any progress?"

"Some. My staff and I have been brainstorming some great new ideas. I should be able to share them with you on Monday, and then we can present them to the committee."

"If you want to get the committee to agree on anything, you'll need to be prepared. Here's the skinny. There are four people you need to worry about: Addie Sims, Katerina Blackwell, Jane Phipps, and me." She pauses. "Are you writing this down? Addie's husband left her for his twenty-five-year-old dental hygienist last winter, at which point she practically moved into her spinning studio. She is interested in any theme that allows her to expose as much of her body as she can. Katerina has a high-school education and met her husband when she was a flight attendant servicing the first-class cabin. And I do mean servicing. She's extremely sensitive about her background. We're hearing a lot from her about how the event has to be 'elegant' and 'classy.' She and Addie nearly came to blows over the male models in the loincloths. Jane is an accountant, which is a very big deal for her. I swear she mentions it at least once every meeting. She has elected herself our unofficial budget chief. Between us, she's more than a little cheap. She was very down on the pharaoh's tomb and the belly dancers. So there's your challenge, Sophie. If you can think of a theme that will make the three of them happy, you'll win the day."

"What about you?" I ask.

She laughs in a short, sharp burst. "If I put my name on something, I want it to be the best. I want to throw a party that people are still talking about in five years. I want to raise more money than we've ever raised before. What can I say? I'm competitive." There is a longish pause, while I try to figure out the appropriate response. Janelle beats me to it. "Still alive there, Sophie? Look on the bright side. At least I'm not making you *guess* how to make me happy."

"And I appreciate that," I say.

"So tell me about yourself," says Janelle, "since we're going to be working so closely together. Do you have kids?"

"Two boys," I say.

"And you work full-time?"

"That's right."

"My goodness, how I admire you working mothers," says Janelle. "I just don't know how you do it! Do your kids miss you?"

"It's what they know," I say lightly. "They don't complain too much, and they get lots of time with us in the evenings and on weekends."

"But surely something has to give with the schedule you must keep," says Janelle sympathetically.

"Well," I say, deciding that it would violate female conversational norms not to offer up one of my deepest failings to this near stranger, "if I had to choose one thing that I would have to admit has fallen through the cracks, it would be family dinners. With our schedules, we don't get to sit down together for a family dinner too often. But hopefully we'll get around to that when the kids are older and can eat a bit later."

"You know," says Janelle. "When my oldest daughter was interviewed for admission to Harvard, she was asked what event in her life had influenced her the most. Quite a question, isn't it? Some kids talked about how their mothers survived breast cancer, or how they had helped to build a school in rural India, but do you know what Chelsea said? She said that the most important influence on her life had been family dinners."

"Extraordinary," I say flatly.

"Isn't it? But of course, I made such an effort to make family dinner special every night. I'd always put a candle on the table or some fresh flowers, so that the kids would think of it as a meaningful part of our family life. When I look back, the investment seems so small relative to the rewards. In high school, our kids' teachers were amazed at how well-informed the kids were about current events, but that was because the emphasis was always on the conversation, the exchange of ideas, rather than the food. Of course, this is what all of the studies say—that family dinners are a key ingredient in putting your kids on the road to success."

"Wow," I say, largely because I can't think of anything else to say. "What a story. I won't forget it." I clear my throat to get rid of the twinge that could be either tears or laughter. "Well, Janelle, I look forward to working with you. I'm sure the Gala will be a great success."

"It better be," she says with a hint of menace. "No one wants to preside over the *Ishtar* of the Gala season. We're in this together. When will you have a new set of concepts for me?"

"Monday latest," I say.

"Until then," she says and rings off.

"Your husband wants you to call him!" Joy yells from her cubicle. I reach him on his cell phone; he's spending a lot of time these days with various groups of people that start with *in-* or *con-*——investors, inspectors, insurance adjusters, contractors, consultants—so he's rarely in his office. "Hi, Soph," he says, "I've just got a second."

"You called me," I point out, I think reasonably.

He sighs audibly. "It's about the dinner party tomorrow."

"Dinner party," I echo, racking my brain to figure out what he is talking about. Are we going to a dinner party? Was I supposed to book a babysitter?

"You didn't forget, did you?"

"Of course not," I say. And suddenly it comes back to me. We've had this party in the works for ages. We have so many outstanding dinner invitations to return that we decided to get all of them out of the way in one fell swoop, although to our guests we are selling it as an effort to introduce our like-minded friends to each other: "I've been dying to introduce you! You have so much in common!" But the truth is that some seriously interventionist hosting is going to be required to keep the conversational ball rolling. A home-cooked meal for six guests who don't know each other on a Friday night: I've clearly been blocking it out.

"I want to invite Anya. It's been a rough week at the office and her husband is out of town. Is that OK?" I have to give him credit for asking permission instead of resolving to proceed and ask for forgiveness later. And anyway, speaking of permission, his gambit opens the door for me to resolve a problem of my own, namely what to do with Will on Friday night.

"That's fine," I say. "I'll invite Will Shannon, then. He's in town and wants to see us."

"Great," says Jesse, although there is stiffness in his voice that suggests another reaction to the prospect of dinner with Will.

"That's eight, ten including us, Jess. We've got to find some time to sit down and plan the menu. Are you home tonight?"

"I'll try," he says. "Call you later."

I do a little math. If I'm going to cook dinner for ten people tomorrow, I'm going to have to leave work early, which is going to be very hard to justify since we are shooting the holiday appeal ad on the weekend. I have until Monday to save the Gala, the ADHD press conference is this afternoon, and I have approximately one hundred and fifty unanswered e-mails in my inbox. There is no way around it: I'm going to have to cancel my lunch date with Zoe. I shoot off an apologetic e-mail and start working my way through the backlog, only to be interrupted by the phone.

"No," Zoe says.

"No, what?"

"No, I do not accept your cancellation," says Zoe. "Everyone has to eat, including you. I'll meet you at Carlo's at one."

"Zoe, I'm sorry. I just don't have time to go to Carlo's today. I'd love to, but I can't. Can we do it next week?"

"Forget Carlo's then. I'll meet you in the food court in your building." Zoe's voice sounds thick and scratchy. "I need to talk to you. It's important."

"Are you all right?" I haven't seen Zoe cry since her father's funeral fifteen years ago, but I'm pretty sure I recognize the signs. I suppress viciously the resentful thought that I am tapped out this week; I couldn't possibly be a lousy enough friend to find Zoe's emotional crisis inconvenient—could I?

"I'll be there," I say. I still have to check in with Erica and make sure that the press conference is on the rails and to return all of the e-mails with big, red exclamation marks next to them. Except for the e-mail from Kelly Robinson, the relentless Parent Council chair who is rocketing up on my nemesis list, and who wants me to organize the teacher gift for Jamie's class. Her e-mail has a red exclamation mark too, but I delete it without responding.

"I have a lunch meeting with a vendor," I tell Joy as I race out the door. "I'll go straight to the press conference after lunch." She doesn't believe me, of course, but she won't be able to say that she doesn't know where I am if Barry comes looking for me.

I find Zoe hunched over a plastic table next to the Chinese noodle stand, shredding a napkin into a tiny mountain of white fluff. I order two shiny plates of noodles, slide one in front of Zoe, and sit down across from her. "What's going on?" I ask.

"It's Richard," she says. "I think he wants to leave me."

This is much worse than I imagined. It's terrible to say, but I was kind of hoping that Zoe's music-producer brother had taken another overdose, since I know exactly what to say in that situation without getting myself into trouble. Zoe's husband, Richard, is a more complicated subject, one that we have tacitly agreed to avoid over the years. The best that I can say about Richard is that he is urbane and sophisticated, and a good dinner companion if you are prepared to let him do all the talking. The man never runs out of commentary on the poor quality of the latest season at Bayreuth, or the ubiquity of heavy blackberry notes in the new Australian reds, or the rise of boutique hotels in Iceland, but no one (in our house at least) would call him fun. I dip my toe in, cautiously.

"Is there someone else?"

Zoe shakes her head. "I don't think so. He just keeps saying that we're in a rut, that he needs to spend some time alone. He says that I distract him from pursuing his deeper purpose."

"Which is?" I try to keep the sarcasm out of my voice. Richard has never struck me as someone with a deeper purpose.

Zoe's eyes are red. "I have no idea," she says. "This all started in the summer, when he said that he wanted to go camping! Richard, camping! And when I asked where this was all coming from, he said that our life was alienating him from his natural world, if you can believe it. Natural world! Richard doesn't even like having flowers in the house. He says they're messy!"

I pat Zoe's arm sympathetically. "Maybe he's having a midlife crisis. After all, he did turn forty this year."

"I suggested that in therapy last week. But our therapist says that my need to categorize everything is part of the problem, not part of the solution."

"You're in therapy?"

"There's nothing wrong with therapy! You and Jesse should consider it. It's a healthy way to work out the normal differences and strains in a relationship in a safe environment. A little self-reflection can be good for you, you know. You should examine your own need to compartmentalize everything. You're the least integrated person I know."

I am not going to rise to this bait. If I were a therapist, I would say that Zoe has a tendency to project her insecurities outward. And so I say, mildly, "And this makes me what? Un-integrated? Disintegrated?" But as I say it, I have an alarming vision of myself disintegrating into dust and blowing away. I take a deep breath and remind myself that it's easy for Zoe to extol the virtues of self-improvement; she has no kids and, therefore, even with all of the demands of running HENNESSY, the hottest ad agency in town, she still has a reasonably unfettered ability to engage in pursuits from French cooking to jewelry-making to Italian lessons to kickboxing. Added to this is an enviable amount of time for what she refers to as "maintenance"—both inner and outer— which is why she has visible triceps and flat abs and spends a lot of her disposable income on various forms of therapy.

It occurs to me that Zoe and I have swapped philosophies since the early days of our friendship, the era before I moved into the house on Abernathy. I can picture myself back then, sucking back Thermoses of strong, terrible coffee, filled with restless energy and racked with perennial worry about the future. I fretted about my grades and my major and my career prospects and the various boys that I considered sleeping with—whether they liked me and how much they liked me and whether we had enough in common to justify sleeping together, as if there was any ethical or moral requirement to find such a justification. And after a while, I would stop worrying about whether the boy in question liked me enough and start worrying instead about whether I liked him enough, and then I would agonize over how to break up and when to break up and whether we would still be friends, and all of this rumination meant that I never felt that I was having a moment of pure experience since I was simultaneously ten steps ahead, dismantling and analyzing the moment as it was happening. That was before I met Will Shannon, of course, and figured out that being immersed in pure experience was both more and less than I'd bargained for. Zoe, though, was a master of the art of living in the moment, and of making every moment as pleasurable as possible. I would come home to the apartment after a long, contentious meeting at the newspaper, or a nighttime shift with the Safety Walk program, and Zoe would be sitting up waiting, with a cold martini already mixed.

And now Zoe has embraced the power of the examined life, whereas I now believe that too much contact with my innermost thoughts and feelings can only lead to trouble. And how would I find the time to live an examined life, anyway? These days, my life exists at the other extreme of the doing-versus-thinking spectrum. My days are measured out in tasks that must be checked off; I know the day is over when I've run out of energy to check even one more box, and then I pass out and start again the next morning. No doubt there are many complicated feelings to mine from the depths if I had the time or the inclination, but what good could possibly come of that? If my psyche were a map, it would have huge swaths of unexplored territory like medieval illustrations of the world, with warnings at the edge: Here Be Dragons.

I take a deep breath. "Zoe. This isn't about me. How long have you been in therapy?"

Zoe sighs. "Sorry. Since September. I should have told you, but I was embarrassed. Richard started seeing someone, and he thought that the work he was doing would be more productive if the therapist could interact with me as well."

"Why, so that he can blame everything on you?"

"It's starting to feel that way," she sniffs. I feel hot with anger at pompous, mean-spirited Richard. Who does he think he is? I can't believe how much effort I've invested in trying to identify and appreciate his good qualities, time which now appears to have been utterly wasted.

I look at my watch. I've pushed it as late as I can, but my time's up. I give Zoe a hug. "I'm so sorry I can't stay longer," I say. "We'll book some time on the weekend to do this properly, OK? But in the meantime, try to remember that you were something special long before you met Richard. Trust me. I was there." She gives me a watery smile, and I silently curse the responsibilities that are pulling me away from something so much more important. I blow Zoe a kiss and race for the door.

CHAPTER FOURTEEN

thursday, december 5, 2013

I've spent way too long at lunch, and at two-fifteen I'm racing back into the hospital so that I can drop in on Christian Viggars's press conference at two-thirty. Too late I remember Nigel, who spots me before I can think of a plan to avoid him. I cast about the lobby wildly, and see Jenny Dixon from HR waiting for the elevator, just beyond Nigel's station.

"Jenny!" I call, and I see her puzzled expression as she notices me waving frantically. "Be right back," I say to Nigel over my shoulder, and I dash off in Jenny's direction. "I need to ask that woman something really important."

"Hey!" Nigel yells after me. "You can't . . ." but I already have, and I'm feeling very pleased with my quick thinking.

"Are you all right?" Jenny asks. She looks mildly concerned.

"Of course! I just wanted to say that I got your message and I'll send you the reports as soon as I write them up." I shoot a look over my shoulder and can see Nigel pushing his chair back. I am about to make a break for the stairwell, but Jenny anticipates my move and puts a hand on my arm.

"I'm glad you caught me, actually." She pauses. "One of the medical researchers says that one of your staff members threatened him with termination. Any idea what happened there?"

I groan. *Erica.* "Tensions were running a little high yesterday," I say. "I'm sure it was just a misunderstanding."

Jenny furrows her brow. "It sounds to me like your staffer got in over her head," she says. "And that raises questions for me about how the staff in your office are being managed. I'd feel better if I could see your performance reviews." She pauses and gives me a frank look. "You seem to be under a lot of pressure these days. I think it might be a good idea for us to get together and chat sometime soon. I'm going to have my assistant set up an appointment."

Nigel is halfway across the lobby. "Sounds great, perfect, looking forward to it, OK," I babble, giving Jenny an ill-conceived thumbs-up as I back away. There's no time to wait for the elevator. I sprint over to the stairwell, duck inside and dash up two flights of stairs. Just as I'm rounding the last corner, I catch my toe on a step and crash down onto my wrist.

"Ow!" I scream at the top of my lungs, and I hear my voice echoing all the way to the top of the building: *owowowowow.* "Fuck," I whisper. My wrist is throbbing and I think I might be sick. I sit down heavily on the staircase and cradle my wrist in my good arm. It's already starting to swell. But I have to keep moving. Christian Viggars's press conference is about to start, and after my encounter with Jenny, I need to show that I'm in control.

I stagger out of the stairwell and make my way over to the auditorium. Christian Viggars, Marvin, and Erica are in a huddle beside the podium and the seats are filling up. I sidle up to the refreshments table, grab a napkin, and then, as subtly as possible, stick my hand into a plastic pitcher of water and extract a handful of ice to make an improvised icepack. The caterer comes up beside me with a scowl of disgust and removes the contaminated pitcher.

Erica spots me and waves me over. "All set?" I ask.

"Everything's great," she says. "Marvin is going to do most of the talking. Christian will explain the technical data, but we're going to limit him to that. Short and sweet." Her gaze lands on the wet napkin around my wrist and the pooling water at my feet.

"Erica," I say. "Did you, by any chance, tell Dr. Viggars that you could have him fired?"

"Of course not!" she says. "I don't have the authority to do that. I told him that *you* could have him fired. It seemed to really get his attention."

"Right," I say. I should absolutely stay in this room and prevent, physically if necessary, anything else from going wrong. But I'm becoming more light-headed by the second. The best I can do is to attempt to neutralize Erica. So I give her a stern look, and say in my most imperious voice: "Let Marvin handle things here. Stay in the background. Understand?" Erica nods. I check the room to make sure Jenny isn't here. "I'm going to watch the webcast from my office. If anything goes wrong, call me immediately and I'll come down."

I am overwhelmed with the need to get as far away from other people as possible, and I try not to break into a run as I leave the auditorium. I have a distinctly linear set of priorities at this moment:

1. maintain a veneer of professionalism all the way up in the elevator;
2. greet Joy with civility;
3. turn on my computer and link to the webcast;
4. take as many Advil as the directions on the packaging permit; and then
5. lie on the floor of my office.

I barely manage priority one and decide to skip priorities two through four temporarily. I hear a knock, my door opens, and I open my eyes to see Geoff standing over me, seriously alarmed.

"What are you doing on the floor? Are you hurt?"

"No need for concern," I say, pulling myself up into my chair and popping several Advil.

"Aren't you going to the press conference?" he asks.

"I'm going to watch the webcast," I say. "Do you mind pulling it up for me while I make a call?"

Geoff fiddles with the computer while I call my doctor, who has an office in the medical building down the street. At last, a piece of good luck. Dr. Chen is in the office today, and she can fit me in at three-thirty.

"I fell on my wrist," I tell Geoff, who still has a wrinkle of concern above the bridge of his nose. "I was feeling dizzy. But I'm fine now."

Geoff comes around the desk and reaches for my arm. "Oh, Sophie, look how swollen it is! Let me take you to emergency."

I wave him off. "It's probably a sprain," I say. "I just made an appointment with my doctor. Really, I'm fine. Do you want to watch the press conference with me?"

On my screen, I can see Marvin Shapiro striding up to the podium. He introduces himself and talks for a few minutes about the research program at Baxter. He is perfectly scripted. Then he turns the microphone over to Christian, who begins describing his research methods in great detail, with reference to several slides of charts, which are projected on a screen behind him.

Geoff nods his approval. "Erica did a nice job on this," he says.

"Her diplomatic skills need some honing," I say. "But that's another story. You've been trying to grab me all day. What's up?"

"We need to go over the plan for the holiday appeal. But now probably isn't a good time."

"I'm a captive audience," I say. "I'd go for it, if I were you."

"If you're sure," he says, and walks me through the script that he's worked out with Claudio. It's shaping up beautifully. Claudio has already filmed some sweeping introductory shots of the atrium, the playroom, and the oncology ward. Geoff has secured permission from a local pop star to play her hit song "The Power of Dreams" in the background; it is a truly god-awful piece of music, which has exactly the right blend of manipulative sentiment and fake inspiration that never fails to make people want to open their wallets. And best of all, we have confirmed our "cast"; Carolyn Waldron has agreed to participate and has recruited one of her teenage cancer patients.

"Carolyn says the patient's name is Taylor and she's fifteen," I say. "Can you swing by the ward this afternoon and do a preliminary interview with her? I want to get her responses to some general questions:

'What was it like when you first came to Baxter? What will you remember about your time here? What are your plans now that you are going home?' This will help build a narrative around her own words, as much as possible. We're really close. I think we'll be able to finalize the script tomorrow morning. Can you let Claudio know that we'll go ahead with the shoot on Saturday?" Despite the pain in my wrist, I feel pretty jazzed. I can't believe we're going to pull this off.

"You are a superhero," I tell Geoff. "I have no idea what I would do without you."

Geoff looks down at the desk, and I see a faint blush rising in his face. "Take credit where credit is due," I tell him. "You totally saved the day on this one. I'm not throwing away a compliment, believe me."

In the background, Marvin has started to take questions from the media. I note with approval that Marvin is answering most of the questions personally, and that Christian's answers are very short and to the point. Relieved, I turn away from my computer screen, only to be struck by how tired and anxious Geoff looks, completely at odds with his usual collected demeanor. The pressure of Barry's totally unreasonable deadline must be getting to him. "The holiday ad will be fantastic," I tell him. "Don't worry."

Geoff opens his mouth as if he is going to say something, but thinks better of it. "What is it?" I ask. "Tell me." Chagrined, I realize that I've been putting far too much pressure on him. He never complains, and I always assume that he welcomes the additional responsibility. But now I see that he is burning out, and I know that it's my fault. "Geoff," I say, "I'm sorry it's been so crazy lately. I'm sorry *I've* been so crazy. I need to try not to lean on you so heavily. It's not fair to you."

Geoff's head jerks up. "No, Sophie," he says. "Never say that!" He pauses and shifts uncomfortably in his seat. "This is awkward," he says. "I'm not sure how to tell you this."

Oh my God, I think. *He's quitting. I am so screwed.* I manage to keep an expression of polite interest on my face, but I feel my stomach churning.

"The thing is, Sophie," he says, "I think you're an amazing person." He pauses and looks at me expectantly.

"Thanks," I say. I'm still waiting for him to tell me that he is quitting, but I'm not going to make it easier for him. He's going to have to come out and say it.

He seems to steel himself to continue. "You know how much I enjoy the time we spend working together," he says.

"As do I," I agree cautiously. I'm losing the thread of this conversation, and it's making me strangely nervous.

He takes a deep breath. "Sophie," he says finally. "I have feelings for you, unprofessional feelings." He pauses, and then presses on, speaking quickly and not making eye contact. "I'm sorry to do this. I know that you aren't free. But I can see that you're not happy. And I would give just about anything to be able to make you happy. I swear this is the stupidest thing I've ever done in my entire life, but I needed to say it." He stops.

I feel an almost clinical sense of detachment, as several thoughts erupt in my mind at once. *My gaydar really sucks,* for one. *Could this day get any worse?* for another. And, in addition: *How am I going to get out of here?* And lastly: *This isn't my fault, is it?* I recognize these thoughts as being significantly less than admirable, and remind myself that until a brief, highly unfortunate moment ago, Geoff was a trusted colleague and work friend, if not a friend-friend. He deserves to be treated with respect and care, and I should appreciate the great compliment that he has paid me. But I don't. The feelings I have are every bit as inappropriate as the thoughts; the most pronounced are uncomfortably like revulsion.

I will myself not to meet his eyes. "I had no idea that you felt this way," I say, gingerly. "I think the world of you, but I— "

Geoff interrupts. "Don't say anything yet. I know this is a shock for you. You've persuaded yourself that I'm unavailable. But I want you to give this some time to sink in before you rationalize your way out of feeling anything for me."

"*I'm* the one who's not available," I say. "I have a *family.* I have a *husband.*"

"I know how important your family is to you," he says. His nervousness has vanished, and now he's sitting forward in his chair with unsettling intensity. "But is it enough? I see a smart, funny, beautiful woman who can't see herself for who she is. And I think that if you were with the right person, you would have a better idea of just how special you are. I'm not going to put any pressure on you. I've been living with this for a long time, and I can be patient. I'll be here when you're ready." Speechless, I watch him stand and walk to the door. He turns and delivers one last line, perfectly rehearsed: "Attraction doesn't happen in a vacuum, Sophie."

And I think, *I used to believe that too.*

The nurse calls me into Dr. Chen's examining room and tells me to have a seat. Within a few minutes I hear the telltale clattering of high heels and Beverley Chen appears, balancing her tiny, perfect frame on a pair of three-inch Louboutin pumps.

"I have no idea how you stand up all day in those," I say.

"They make me feel young and energetic," she says. "Mind over matter." She laughs. "But don't quote me—it's not a medical opinion."

She comes over and stands beside me. "So what have you done here?"

I hold out my wrist. "Something stupid," I say. "I fell on the stairs. I'm hoping that I didn't break it."

She takes my wrist and gently manipulates it. "I don't think so," she says. "I suspect it's just a bad sprain, but I'm going to send you for an X-ray just to be sure. What were you doing on the stairs?"

I tell her about Nigel and my cold and my narrow escape.

"How long have you had this cold?"

"A couple of weeks," I admit.

Beverley comes over and takes my temperature. Then she presses her fingers into the sides of my neck. "Any pain in your face?" she asks. "Here, or here?" She runs her fingers under my eyes and across my temple.

"Yes," I say.

Beverley looks exasperated and sits down at her desk. "You have a sinus infection," she says. She picks up her pen and begins filling out an X-ray requisition form. "I'll give you a prescription as well."

"Am I contagious?"

"Not at all."

"Could you write me a note that says that so I can get past germ security at work?"

Beverley smiles. "It would be my pleasure. Usually people want me to write the opposite." She scribbles a note on her medical pad and signs it with a flourish. "Is that it? Anything else falling apart aside from the wrist and the sinuses?"

I hear the words *falling apart* and I am horrified to feel my eyes filling with tears. "Oh, how embarrassing," I say. "I'm just fine. I have no idea why I'm crying."

Beverley doesn't say anything. She just waits and watches me with an expression of deep kindness and concern. She hands me a box of tissues.

"I've been a little stressed," I say as I mop my face, but I hear a little sob in my voice.

"I see," says Beverley, as if she does, indeed, see very well. "How are you sleeping?"

"Not very well. I have trouble falling asleep, and then if Scotty wakes up I can't fall back to sleep. I can't get my brain to turn off."

"What are you thinking about?"

"Work. The kids. Jesse. My mom. Christmas. Everything. How I'm not doing any of it as well as I want to or as well as I should. God, I sound like such a cliché." I don't add that my life feels like one long, flailing arc through the air, with no soft landing in sight.

"OK. How about eating? How's your appetite?"

I'm not sure I like where this is going. "It's fine."

"Are you eating a balanced diet?"

"I'm trying to," I say.

"How about alcohol? How many drinks are you having per week?"

I do a quick calculation and am shocked by the total. Do small glasses of wine count as a whole drink? I immediately revise the figure down. "Maybe seven?" I say.

Beverley makes a note in my chart, but to my relief moves to a new subject. "How often would you say that you feel anxious?"

"Is that a trick question?" Beverley shakes her head. "Pretty much all the time, I guess."

"If you had to pick one word to describe how you feel most often, what would it be?"

"Totally overwhelmed. Sorry. That was two."

"Do you cry easily?"

"Lately, yes," I admit. "Usually a few times a day. It's mortifying. The strangest things set me off. Like opening my e-mail and realizing that I have fifty new messages. Or thinking about what to get my mother for Christmas. Tuesday, I nearly burst into tears in a staff meeting because I found out that I have to come in on Saturday to work on a project. I could barely concentrate on the meeting because I was so stressed about lining up a babysitter."

"Have you had trouble concentrating on other things? Or making decisions?"

Now I really don't like where this is going. "Sophie?" Beverley prompts me.

"Not with concentration, particularly," I say. "But in the last few weeks I'm finding decisions a little challenging." I think about my e-mail inbox and feel the tears well up again.

"Do you do anything for yourself, Sophie? Do you have any regular social things that you do, fitness classes, anything like that?"

I cast about. There must be something. "I go to yoga with my mother," I say.

Beverley's mouth quirks up at the corner. "Do you enjoy that?" she asks, raising an eyebrow.

"Not particularly," I say.

"Let's try again, then."

"Book club?" I offer.

"How often do you go?"

"It's once a month, but I haven't been in a while," I admit.

She looks up. "When is your next book club meeting?"

"Tonight, actually," I say.

"I want you to go to book club tonight," says Beverley sternly. "Doctor's orders. And this is a prescription for sertraline. It is a selective serotonin reuptake inhibitor, or SSRI. It is a kind of antidepressant that often works quite well for people with your symptoms. I'm putting you on a fairly low dose for now, and I want you to come back and see me in a couple of weeks so I can assess your symptoms again."

"I'm not depressed," I say. "I'm just really busy." Now I'm crying openly. I'm crushed by my own sense of failure.

"Sophie," says Beverley, "this is your health. And you are headed for a crisis if you don't start taking care of yourself right now. I want you to take this seriously."

"OK," I snuffle.

Beverley comes over and takes my hand. "A prescription is not a failing grade in life management," she says, gently. "I see five or six people exactly like you every week. I think you'd be surprised how many people you know are in the same boat. Now go get your X-ray, and go see your friends. It will make you feel better."

CHAPTER FIFTEEN

thursday, december 5, 2013

I show up at Sara's house around eight, and book club is in full swing. I've come straight from the office, and my prescription is still in my purse. I'd say that I haven't had time to fill it, but even I know that for once, lack of time isn't the issue.

I ring the bell. Zoe answers and steps out onto the porch with me for a moment. "I was hoping it was you," she says. "I'm not ready to tell anyone else about what's going on with Richard, OK?" She gestures toward the house, where the rest of the book club is waiting.

"Of course," I say. And in any event, I feel a little fuzzy on the details of Zoe's marital crisis. Lunch feels as though it happened a week and not six hours ago.

"How are you feeling?" I ask.

She shrugs. "It helped to see you at lunch," she says. "But I think this is one of those situations where it's going to keep feeling worse until something big changes. I'm just not ready to think about what the something big is." I give her a hug, and we go in. "Look, everyone," she calls. "It's a special guest appearance by Sophie!" She drags me into the living room, where the rest of the book club bursts into enthusiastic applause.

"I haven't read the book," I say.

"Don't be silly," says Laura. "No one ever reads the book."

"I do," says Sara pointedly. "And it would be great if we could make a tiny effort to talk about it once in a while, even for five minutes. Hi, Soph." She pauses, taking in the tensor bandage that I've wrapped around my wrist. "What did you do to your arm?"

"A sprain," I say. "It's nothing."

"What was the book again?" asks Laura.

Sara raises an eyebrow. "Are you really interested, or are you just trying to humor me?"

Laura laughs. "Was it good?"

"Not especially," says Sara. "We can stop talking about it now. What's Megan going on about?"

Like Sara, Megan is one of my old friends from the student newspaper, and I've caught her in mid-rant. Nora is leaning back slightly to avoid Megan's violent gesticulations, which are, as usual, aimed at hapless, absent Bob: "And then he looks into the stroller and says, 'I'm starting to get to the point where I remember that he's around. Do you know what I mean?' And I think, 'What kind of fucking question is that? It's kind of hard for *me* to forget that our baby is *around* when he's hanging off my *tit* 24/7, but I guess you don't have that problem, do you, Bob?' Honestly! I just looked at him and said, 'I have absolutely no idea what you are talking about.'"

Megan takes a breath, looks around, and realizes that she is the main attraction. "Hi, Sophie," she says. "Good to see you."

I wave. "Still married?"

Megan snorts. "Barely," she says, but she smiles a little before turning back to Nora to continue itemizing Bob's shortcomings as a husband and father.

"What can I get you to drink?" asks Zoe. "Prosecco?" I nod, and she disappears into the kitchen. I sit down next to Sara.

"How have you been?" she asks.

"Bad day to ask," I say. "I'd say I've been stressed to the point of hysteria, while at the same time struggling to find enough meaning in my work to justify my level of anxiety. I mean, shouldn't you have to care about a job to get this worked up about it?"

"Of course not!" Zoe reappears with my glass and plops down on the sofa with us. "Do you remember the *I Love Lucy* episode where Lucy and Ethel are working on an assembly line at a chocolate factory? No? You know the scene in *Pretty Woman* where Richard Gere takes Julia Roberts up to the penthouse for the first time, and they have a fight, and then they make up, and then they stay up late watching TV?"

"Oh, yeah," says Sara. "Right before she gives him the blow job."

"Exactly. That moment where you think, am I *really* supposed to be rooting for these two to get together in the end?"

"Totally." Megan and Nora have finished with Bob and rejoin the group. "But they aren't watching the chocolate factory episode," Megan says. "They're watching the wine-making one, where Lucy runs around in a giant barrel and throws grapes at everyone."

Zoe rolls her eyes. "The point I'm making," she says, with the deliberate enunciation of a woman who has had too much Prosecco, "is that the chocolate factory is a perfect example of a job that is both stressful and meaningless. The chocolate starts coming faster and faster and they can't wrap it quickly enough, and by the end they are stuffing the chocolates down their shirts and in their mouths and looking completely panic-stricken, but to no real end."

"And this relates to Sophie's job how?" asks Laura.

Zoe waves her hand vaguely. "E-mail, voice mail, staff meetings—the whole tedious routine is a modern-day, white-collar version of the conveyor belt."

"Well, that's a pretty bleak assessment," I say.

"Only if you plan to be stuck beside the conveyor belt for the rest of your life," says Zoe. "But since you don't actually work in a chocolate factory, you have a few options. And if you would admit that you are having a midlife crisis, you could start looking at ways to change it up."

"I'm not having a midlife crisis," I say.

Laura laughs. "Everyone's having a midlife crisis, Sophie," she says. "You might as well join the club."

"I'll humor you," I say. "Let's say, for the sake of argument, that I'm having a midlife crisis. What would you suggest I do, then?"

"Any number of things," says Zoe. "You could change jobs, obviously to something either less stressful or more meaningful. Or you could find ways to make the rest of your life more fulfilling, by getting a hobby or taking a class with me once in a while. You could train for a marathon, or take up kickboxing, or write mommy porn. You could have an affair with your assistant, but that's more of a guy thing."

"You obviously haven't met my assistant," I say.

"Or you could figure out a way to be less stressed, which is going to be hard for you given your personality. That route would probably require medication."

I laugh uncomfortably and say, "That was my doctor's view."

"Nothing to be ashamed of," says Laura.

Megan snorts. "There's nothing wrong with any of you," she says. "Why you are all medicated is beyond me. It's like the Valley of the Dolls around here."

"You're on antidepressants?" I say to Laura.

"All of us except Megan," says Zoe. "But then, she's also the only one threatening to do a home vasectomy on her husband, so you do the math."

"Shut up, Zoe," says Megan.

"Now, now, girls," says Sara. "What's going on at work, Soph? I thought you liked your job." Sara is an HR manager at a huge telecom company, and she has an anthropological zeal for organizational dynamics that I find mystifying.

"I used to," I say. "But now, unfortunately, it's draining my will to live."

"Because?"

"Let me count the ways," I say. "My boss is a jackass. Every time I step into my office I get something added to my portfolio. I'm spending fifty percent of my time on event planning, which I hate, and another twenty percent on volunteer and staff management, which I hate even more. The other thirty percent I spend in excruciating meetings where nothing gets decided. I just found out that my favorite employee is in love with me, and my assistant wishes I would drop dead."

"Book club just got a lot more interesting," says Sara. "Gather 'round, ladies." She settles back on the couch. "Why does your assistant hate you?"

"It's not personal," I say. "At least I don't think it is. She's been there a long time and has been shuffled around from department to department. She's the hot potato of the secretarial pool—bad attitude, mediocre skills—your classic admin support horror story."

"Unionized?" asks Laura.

"You bet," I say.

"Damn," says Laura. "They saw you coming a mile away."

"I know you're going to tell me I'm naïve," I say, looking at Zoe, "but part of me thinks, we're both professional women here, shouldn't Joy want to help me out? Shouldn't there be some kind of sisterhood instinct that kicks in?"

Zoe leans over and pats my hand. "You women's studies girls are such babes in the woods," she says pityingly. "Sisterhood doesn't exist. It's a comforting illusion, a rallying cry to keep the foot-soldiers working in solidarity. It's what you used to call a 'political construct.'"

"Like gender?" I ask, smiling. Zoe and I have been having this debate for the last twenty years.

"No, baby," she says. "Not like gender. Gender actually exists."

"Hang on," says Megan. "I disagree. Sisterhood exists. Look around you."

"I'm not talking about female friendship," says Zoe. "I'm talking about the mystical bond that supposedly links women together and makes them act in each other's interest. It's the idea that women's natural instinct is to act collectively. It's nonsense. Anyone who's spent time in private school can tell you that." Zoe logged ten years at a private girls' school, and for her this is the end of the argument. I think fleetingly of Janelle Moss.

"Are we done with the assistant?" asks Nora. "Because I'm way more interested in the guy who's in love with Sophie."

"Patience," says Sara. "What's the problem with your boss?"

"He's a baby boomer," I say.

"Oh, one of *those,*" says Laura, with a knowing nod. "They are *so* never going to retire. Our generation will be prying the corner office out of their cold, dead hands."

"Statistically true," agrees Nora. "I read this demographic study that said our generation is basically screwed because by the time the baby boomers agree to step down, we'll be too old to run anything, and the reins of power will get handed over to the generation behind us."

"I don't care about the reins of power," I say. "I just hate working for a condescending know-it-all who treats me like I'm just out of college."

"Corporate employment is a form of institutionalized humiliation," says Laura. "Did you hear about the big event last month on the topic of 'retention of women'? A bunch of law firms and banks had this brilliant idea to join forces and offer a full-day symposium to inspire women to stay in corporate jobs and halt the so-called brain drain. They spent a fortune bringing in high-powered speakers on work-life balance and they basically forced all of their female employees with children to attend—and they held it on a *Saturday*."

"This is all very cheery," says Megan. "Before I go and kill myself, can I hear about the guy who's in love with Sophie?"

They all look at me expectantly.

"I thought he was gay!" I wail. "I never saw it coming! If I'd thought it was even a remote possibility, I would have been so much more careful!" Even as I say the words, my brain fills with images, hundreds of them, of me touching Geoff's arm, sharing a private joke, complimenting his new outfits and haircuts, and once, under the mistaken impression that he was on his way out for a date with a man, telling him that he looked sexy. I groan aloud.

Nora puts an arm around my shoulder. "Don't beat yourself up," she says. "He knew you were married. He's the one who forced the issue. If you're not interested, it's not your fault. That was the risk he took." She pauses. "You're not interested, right?"

"I am *so* not interested," I say. "I just liked that Geoff was always *on* for me. That he put his best foot forward, wanted to impress me. I liked that he *tried*." I realize I'm praising Geoff in the past tense, and that I'm undoubtedly right to do so. "I thought it was because I was a good boss, not because he wanted to sleep with me. It's very disappointing."

"Why do men feel like they can stop trying once they win you?"

asks Megan. "Don't they realize that if they don't try with you, they're going to end up having to try with someone else?"

"Are they?" asks Laura. "How bad would things have to be for you to leave your marriage? Most people will stick it out with a relationship that's just OK unless a credible alternative presents itself."

"So you're saying that there is always a third party involved when someone leaves a marriage?" asks Zoe, sounding edgy.

"I'm saying that inertia is a big feature of most marriages. Bodies tend to stay at rest without an external force to knock them into motion. It's basic physics. The external force doesn't have to be sex, but it usually is. Men get pretty comfortable in marriage. Sex is one of the few things powerful enough to get them off the couch."

Zoe drains her glass.

"My marriage is fine," I say.

"No one is saying otherwise," says Sara.

"Let's change the subject," I say firmly. "How often do you guys have a family dinner with your kids?"

"Aside from Christmas and Easter?" asks Megan.

"Does ordering pizza count?" asks Laura.

"Intermittently," says Sara, "but not before my youngest turned seven."

"So if someone told me that she had a family dinner every night of her children's lives with candles on the table, you would say she was—"

"Lying."

"Deluded."

"Desperately insecure."

"Someone with too much time on her hands."

"Trying to fuck with you."

"OK," I say, almost weak with love for these fine, fine women.

"Back to the conversation about your job, did I miss something while you were on book club hiatus?" asks Laura. "Why are you spending all your time on events? I thought you were running the communications office."

"I am," I say, "but my aforementioned boss has a fairly broad definition of communications. Actually, if you ladies want to help me out, you can come up with a theme for the Gala for me." I give them the thumbnail sketch of my quest for the Gala theme. "My current working theory is that the answer is buried back in the eighties somewhere. Any bright ideas? Emblematic song titles?"

"'I Want Your Sex,'" says Zoe. "That was my absolute favorite eighties song."

"Of course it was," says Megan. "I was more into the alternative scene. How about 'Tainted Love'?"

"I'm sure that you were big in the alternative scene at the age of seven," says Zoe.

"Piss off, Zoe," says Megan.

"Tears for Fears," offers Laura. "'Shout.'"

"Eurythmics, 'Sweet Dreams,'" says Nora.

"Not bad," I say. "Food for thought."

"Oh, I have the best idea!" Zoe leaps up. "Eighties dance party, anyone?"

There is a chorus of cheers and applause, and Sara sighs. "I guess we're not discussing the book, then?" she asks.

"Maybe next time," says Zoe, to the opening notes of "I Want Your Sex." "Hope springs eternal." And as I watch my friends shimmying and twirling around each other in circles, I say a silent thank-you to Beverley Chen, because in spite of everything, I do feel better.

CHAPTER SIXTEEN

february 1995

"I don't understand," says my mother. "I thought you were going to be home for the whole week."

"I was," I say. "But I haven't made as much progress on my honors paper as I should have. I need to be near the library. It's Reading Week. That's what I'm supposed to do."

My father picks up the extension. "Her work has to be her first priority, Mary," he says. "Don't give her a hard time."

My mother's disappointment is palpable. "If you work hard on it now, maybe you can make it home for the long weekend at the end."

"Maybe," I say. "I don't want to promise. I'll see how it goes."

"OK, honey," says my mother in a choked voice, and hangs up abruptly.

"Sorry, Dad," I say, my throat suddenly tight.

"Don't be sorry," he says. "We're very proud of you. We'll see you soon."

I hang up the phone feeling wretched. The truth is that my honors paper is coming along on schedule, and I could take a few days off. And if I were going to be alone in the house for Reading Week, I'd take a stack of photocopied research to my parents' place, make a few token efforts at underlining and highlighting the articles, and spend the rest of the week hanging out with my mom. But I won't be alone. Will's grandmother, Penelope, was admitted to the cardiac ward at the hospital last night, and Will's family ski trip has been canceled. With A.J. in New York, Reading Week on Abernathy is suddenly alive with romantic possibilities.

Will and I haven't spoken about the night of the Christmas party. I know that he's avoided being alone with me since we came back after the holidays, and I've been playing it cool. If he wants to broach the subject, I have some light, breezy banter ready to go. My instincts tell me that we're not yet at the denouement of our romantic comedy, and that any conversation about what's happening between us isn't going to end with Will pulling me into his arms as the credits roll, at least not yet. We're still in the middle of the story, the part where his true feelings slowly rise to the surface of his consciousness until he can no longer deny them. I've seen this movie, and I know that it's important to be present when the eureka moment arrives. So I'm not leaving town.

I find Will in the kitchen, leafing morosely through the sports section. "Hey," he says. "When are you heading home?"

I pour a mug of coffee and sigh. "Not sure," I say, keeping my tone light. "Maybe later in the week. I'm going to stick around and do some work at the library. Professor Marsh wants to see a draft in a couple of weeks."

"Really?" he says.

"Really. You've got to hate professors who think Reading Week is for reading." I roll my eyes and open the arts section. "Pass the milk?" He pushes the carton to me, giving me a chance to gauge his reaction to my performance. No signs of suspicion or, worse, impending flight: so far, so good.

We sit in what seems like companionable silence for a while, and then I say, "How's your grandmother doing?"

"Hard to know," he says. "If you believe my dad, she's fine and about to be released; if you believe my mother, she's at death's door. It's wishful thinking on both sides. I'm going to the hospital this morning to check it out for myself."

"Oh," I say. I've never met Will's parents, and he rarely talks about them. I've always assumed that it's because he's a guy and therefore less inclined to reveal personal details about himself, but there's a harshness in the way he says *wishful thinking* that makes me think Will is driven by more than simple biological imperatives. "I'm sure she'll be happy to see you."

He laughs. "You met my grandmother, didn't you? She's not exactly known for her warm fuzzies. But Lillian will be there today, so it has the potential to be bearable at least."

"Do you want company?" I ask, and then, kicking myself, add, "I was going to go downtown this morning to check out the Matisse exhibit at the art gallery before it closes."

But Will is too distracted to notice that my offer is overeager, or else he's willfully blind to my motivations, because he says, with obvious relief, "That would be amazing."

The cardiac unit reeks of disinfectant and despair, and Will and I stride quickly through the mint-green halls, averting our eyes from the shuffling patients in inadvertently revealing gowns as we look for Penelope's room. I feel unsettlingly young and healthy. Penelope is at the end of a long corridor, away from the nursing station. "That's good," I murmur to Will as we enter. "If they were worried about her, they wouldn't put her down here."

"Exactly what I said," says Lil, rising from her chair and coming over to greet us. "And believe me, there's nothing wrong with her tongue."

With no makeup to conceal her pallor, and semi-reclined in the bed, Penelope is clearly very ill. But she still manages to direct a glare of unadulterated hostility in Lil's direction. "You see?" says Lil. "She'll be just fine." She turns to Penelope. "Pen, you remember Sophie, don't you?"

Pen nods regally and shifts her gaze to Will, who is frozen beside me. I bend down, as if to tie my shoelace, and poke him in the shin. He looks down at me and I tilt my head toward his grandmother. He pulls his shoulders back, walks over to the bed, and kisses her cheek. "You gave us a scare, Gran," he says.

Her face softens. "Too mean," she manages.

"To die," finishes Lil. "Don't worry about Pen, my dears, she'll out-live us all. You should see the trouble she's giving the doctors."

As if on cue, there's a knock on the door and a man enters wearing jeans and a striped button-down shirt. "Ah, Dr. Barber," says Lil. "Where's the white coat?"

"We save those for the TV doctors," he says, unhooking Penelope's chart from the end of her bed. "So, Mrs. Shannon, how are we feeling today?"

"She can't speak for *you*," says Lil pointedly, "but *she's* doing much better today." Penelope gives Lil a smile that is almost grateful.

Dr. Barber steps over and raises the bed so that Penelope is sitting. "Let's have a look," he says, and Will backs away in alarm.

"We'll wait outside," I say, grabbing Will by the arm.

He leans up against the wall, crossing his arms over his chest. "Are you OK?" I ask.

"I'm not good at this kind of thing," he says.

"What kind of thing?"

"I don't know . . . hospitals, doctors, seeing my grandmother naked."

"She was wearing a hospital gown," I say, laughing. "Is there some deep childhood trauma that I should be aware of?"

He manages a weak smile. "Not that I remember. But maybe I've repressed it."

The door opens and Dr. Barber steps into the hallway, gives us a wave, and strides off. Lil comes out of the room. "The examination is over. You can come back in, Florence Nightingale," she says to Will, and steps aside to let him pass. She turns to me. "Don't mind him. He's always been squeamish. You, on the other hand, are a brick. He's lucky to have you."

She gives me an appraising look, and then her gaze travels over my shoulder and darkens. "You haven't met Will's parents yet, have you?" I shake my head. "You're in for a treat," she says. I move back to make room for Lil as she air-kisses the new arrivals, a tall man in a three-piece suit, with strands of silver running through thick dark hair; and a brittle blonde with a perfect manicure and no laugh lines. "Staunton, Susannah," says Lil. "How nice to see you both. Have you met Sophie Whelan, Will's roommate?"

"No, we haven't had the pleasure," says Will's mother, extending a smooth hand bristling with diamonds. I shake it briefly, then do the same with Will's father, who smiles at me warmly.

"Will speaks so fondly of you," he says.

"It's mutual," I say.

"I'm sure," his mother says meaningfully, and then turns to Lil, dismissing me. "How is she?" I feel myself flush, and realize that for all the catered dinners, the nice car, and the connection to Lil, I've only just processed that Will comes from money—lots of it.

"Stable," says Lil.

"Are her affairs in order?"

Lil's smile freezes at the edges. "This isn't the time, Susannah."

"I disagree. Penelope is lying in a cardiac ward. She refuses to tell us anything about her finances, her advisers, or her estate plans. If things go badly, who do you think will be left sorting through the mess?"

"I will, as it happens. I'm her executor."

"And does that seem like a competent choice, Lillian? You aren't exactly in the first bloom of youth yourself."

"Susannah!" says Will's father. "Mother is entitled to make her own choices."

Lil's voice is creamy. "Penelope will be here for a few more days, Susannah. This might be a good time to go over to her house and count the silver if you're concerned."

"I don't have a key, as you well know, Lillian," says Will's mother. "Shall we get this over with?"

I am way out of my depth trying to navigate Will's family dynamics, and acutely conscious that my status as his roommate is insufficient to warrant my presence here. I follow the group into Penelope's room, but linger by the door, waiting for an opportunity to signal to Will that I'm leaving.

"Penelope, darling," I hear his mother say. "You look marvelous. How are you feeling?"

"Pugnacious," says Penelope.

Staunton laughs. "That's a good sign. I'm sorry we missed Dr. Barber, Mother. What did he say about your condition?"

"Fatal," says Penelope.

"Penelope!" says Lil. "Dr. Barber says she's recovering very well and should be able to avoid surgery. He's going to keep her here this week and get her medication sorted out."

"Disappointed," says Penelope.

"Why would you be disappointed?" asks Staunton. "It's great news."

"You," says Penelope, looking at Susannah, and even I can tell what she's implying. Susannah colors, rises up on her Chanel heels, and stalks out of the room. Will watches her go, white faced, and finally makes eye contact with me. I shoot what I hope is a sympathetic look his way, point to the exit, and beat a hasty retreat.

Halfway down the corridor, I hear him calling me. I stop, and he jogs up. "Let's get out of here," he says. "Are you still going to the art gallery?"

"I could," I say. "Or we could do something else if you want."

"What time is it?"

I check my watch. "Just past noon."

"Perfect," he says. "Over the yardarm. Let's go."

"I thought you said you played pool," says Will, watching me miss yet another disastrous shot.

"I said I *had* played pool, as in 'a few times before.' I think I might have been drunk, though. I don't remember being this bad."

"Maybe that's the solution," he says. "You just need more alcohol."

"No," I protest. "I'm fine." It's been a long day, and the last thing I need is more beer. We've been chasing diversions for hours now—a boozy lunch at an all-you-can-eat Indian buffet, a sprint through the Matisse exhibit, an action movie, and now pool. I've already had three beers in an attempt to keep pace with Will, but he's way ahead of me.

"All right," he says. "A lesson, then." He takes a long drink and puts his beer bottle down on the edge of the pool table. "Pool 101," he says.

"Hold up your stick and find the balance point." He points to a spot on the stick. "There," he says. "Hold it with your right hand. Now move your hand back six inches." I do. "OK. Now step forward with your right foot."

"Are we going to do the hokey-pokey?" I ask.

He steps in so that he's standing at my left hip. "I'm ignoring you, because it's painful to watch an attractive woman make a fool of herself playing pool. It's not just a favor to you—it's a public service." My rational mind knows that I've been insulted, but I'm pretty sure Will just called me attractive. Now he has my full attention.

"You need to make a bridge with your left hand," he says. "Make a fist?" I do. "I think an open bridge will be easier for you." He takes my left hand in both of his and I clear my throat. "Stick your thumb out. Right, just like that. Now lean forward and put your bridge here." He places my hand on the table. "Now put the stick on the bridge and aim." He laughs. "I meant aim for the pocket, Sophie. Here." He puts a hand on either side of my hips and pushes me slightly to the right. I catch my breath. "Now try," he says. And I do. I concentrate every bit of my mind on sliding the stick across my bridge hand and tapping the ball dead center. Miraculously, the ball scoots to the corner pocket, teeters on the edge for a split second, and drops in. I whoop, pump my fist in the air, and leap up and down.

Will grins. "Feel good?"

"I've never sunk a ball before," I say. "At least not that I remember. That was awesome. Thanks for the lesson."

"Thanks for coming to the hospital with me."

"No problem," I say. "I can go with you any time. I'm around all week."

Will is quiet and I wonder if I've gone too far. But he says, "I appreciate it. Maybe in a few days, if I can figure out how to avoid my mother."

"OK," I say. Despite my brief moment of glory, I'm dying to get out of the pool hall. My previous pool experiences have always been late at night, surrounded by packs of university students. The clientele early on a Monday evening is markedly bleaker. "Why don't we go home? I've got some leftover lasagna in the fridge, and we can watch TV. Sound good?"

"It does," he says. "Let's get a cab. My treat." I smile. Will knows that I think taxis are the height of extravagance, caving only after very late nights of drinking in the middle of winter and even then persuading drivers to take four or even five passengers. He flags one down and opens my door for me, and we sit in silence broken only by the dispatcher as we make our way back to the house. We've been relaxed with each other all day, racing from one activity to another, but now Will seems edgy and brooding.

At the house, I go into the kitchen and pull out the lasagna, serve up two portions, and stick them in the microwave. Will opens the fridge and uncaps another beer. "So now you've seen the Shannon family in all its dysfunctional glory," he says.

The microwave beeps, and I'm grateful not to have to look at him while I answer. "All families are dysfunctional," I say, putting a plate in front of him.

"Yours isn't," he says.

"You haven't met them!"

"I don't need to. You're the most normal person I know."

I know I shouldn't be insulted, but Will's insight cuts deep. This fundamental truth is the chink in my alternative-girl armor. I'd love to be able to claim some genuine darkness, and my happy childhood is something I don't like to talk about. On the other hand, this is the most intimate conversation Will and I have ever had and I want to keep it going. We eat in silence for a few minutes, until I say, "Your dad seems like a really nice guy."

"He is a nice guy. He just handed in his balls the day he married my mother."

"She couldn't be that bad," I say.

"She put her foot down and refused to name me Staunton the Third. So I owe her for that," he says. "But she's otherwise a fairly unlikable person."

I can't imagine saying something like this about my mother, and I have an inkling, which I brush aside, that Will may have some issues that I don't have the tools to fix. But I say, "I guess your grandmother isn't a big fan of hers."

"Would you be? My mother's been waiting for her to die for years."

"You really care about your grandmother," I say.

"I do. I spent a lot of time at her house while my mother was playing bridge and running charity events and getting her hair done." He smiles, remembering. "She had a big influence on me. She used to make me debate current events with her. She wanted me to be a lawyer." He pushes his plate away and stretches his absurdly toned arms in front of him. "Thanks for dinner, Sophie. You're a good friend."

A friend. Disappointment settles over me like fog and I rub my own arms, willing myself to be whatever he needs until he's ready for more. "So are you," I say, forcing cheer into my voice. "So what do you feel like doing tonight? Do you want to see what's on TV?"

"No," he says. He gives me a stare that makes my belly clench, and I remind myself that Will wants a friend, only a friend, today.

But then Will throws me off balance again by walking over, putting a hand on either side of my waist, and boosting me up onto the counter. *Beer me, baby,* I think, remembering my first time in this house, and the first time I laid eyes on Will Shannon.

"I don't want to watch TV," he says, standing between my legs so that we are eye to eye. "I want to go upstairs with you and not talk about my family."

"I can do that," I say. *I'd go anywhere with you,* I think.

Will kisses me hard, and I kiss him back, and in the end we don't make it upstairs at all.

CHAPTER SEVENTEEN

$\mathcal{D}\mathcal{Q}$

friday, december 6, 2013

On Friday morning at nine sharp, I'm sitting in the conference room with Barry at the head of the table, while the search committee reviews the CVs of the candidates that we are about to see. It's interview day, and everyone is here—everyone except Lil. I wonder if Lil has decided to disappear now that stakes are higher and the game is less diverting.

I'm drinking strong coffee, as hot as I can stand it. I was up late last night, cleaning the house for the dinner party tonight, and I slept badly. I'm determined to maintain a laser-like focus on this meeting today and not think about the dream that left me raw with longing and sick with disloyalty at four in the morning. I dig my nails into the palm of my hand to pull my attention back to the meeting. I will not think about Will. Except that I have to confirm our plans for dinner.

J. SOPHIE WHELAN

> To: wshannon@perrimanhale.com
> Sent: Friday, December 6, 2013, 9:16 a.m.
> Subject: Dinner

Slight change of plans for dinner. Can you come to our
house? We have a few friends coming over—including
Zoe, so you can catch up. Hope that's OK with you.

S

Barry hands around a sheet of paper. "Jenny Dixon advises me, on
behalf of the HR department, that we should be asking every candidate
the same questions," says Barry, his tone betraying exactly what he thinks
of HR bureaucracy. "Apparently, this is the new best practice in making
hiring processes equitable." Barry sighs audibly, then remembers himself,
squares his shoulders, and reads from the paper in front of him. "Thank
you very much to Jenny for all of her efforts to protect the integrity of
our process." Barry raises his hands in the air and draws air quotes around
the phrase "integrity of our process," which causes Jenny to snort aloud.

Barry tries again. "I have here a list of questions, which have been
approved by HR. I have also been advised that we should alternate
questioners. Is there a volunteer who wants to ask the first question?"

"Why don't I take the first one?" says Jenny. "'Tell us, how has your
work experience prepared you for this position, and why are you interested in this move at this point in your career?'"

"Fine," says Barry. "Next?"

"I'll take the second question," says Marvin. "'What would you
hope to accomplish in your first one hundred days on the job?'"

"And I'll ask the third one," says one of the board members. "'Discuss your management style and how you motivate a team.'"

"Thank you, Carl," says Barry. "Carolyn? Do you want to take the
fourth question? 'Describe your specific experience in planning and
executing a campaign.'" He looks at Jenny. "I still think that question is
completely unnecessary, Jenny," he says.

"And based on the job description, which involves running a fund-
raising operation, I still have to disagree with you, as do all of my colleagues in HR," says Jenny briskly.

"I'll ask that one," says Carolyn.

Anusha raises her hand. "I'll take number five—'What would you say to persuade a donor that he should support the Baxter?'"

"Excellent," says Barry. "And I'll take the final question, which invites the candidates to make a closing statement." He pauses, and looks directly at me. "There will be no opportunities for unplanned questions. I hope everyone understands that. Now, please take a few minutes to review the materials and then we'll get started."

The door opens. Without looking up, Barry says, "We'll be right with you. Please wait outside and we'll come and get you in a moment."

"I think I'm supposed to be in here, actually," says a familiar voice, and Lil steps into the room. The beehive hairdo and the fox stole are gone; Lil is striking in a crisply tailored pinstripe suit and a ruffled silk tuxedo blouse.

"This is a private meeting," says Barry.

"I was afraid this would be awkward," says Lil with a laugh. I can see Marvin's eyes light with recognition, but everyone else around the table looks uncomfortable or confused.

"I'm embarrassed to say that I've been having a little joke at your expense, Barry," says Lil. "And I apologize for that. It was inappropriate for me, as the representative of the Baxter's principal funder, to take my responsibilities anything less than seriously. I just get so few opportunities to wear my fox." And she sits down in her usual seat.

Barry is flummoxed. "Mrs. Baxter?"

"Quite so," says Lil, crisply. "Please don't let me interrupt you any further. We should bring in the first candidate; he's waiting outside."

Barry's mouth is open slightly and he seems a bit dazed.

"Why don't I go and get the candidate," says Jenny, diplomatically, and she walks over to the door and beckons into the hallway.

The man who enters is tall—at least six foot two—and in his early sixties. He's tanned and energetic, with a slight paunch that would be more pronounced on a shorter frame. Barry gestures to the empty seat at the end of the table, and once the man is settled, he announces, "We are very pleased to have Stephen Paul with us today. For those of you who read the business pages on a regular basis, Stephen requires little introduction. He has recently retired as CEO of the Ascot Group, and it is a great compliment to the Baxter that he is considering spending the next few years investing his considerable experience in our organization. Welcome, Stephen."

Stephen opens his mouth, presumably to affirm his membership in the Barry-Stephen Mutual Admiration Society, but Jenny steps neatly into the void. "Mr. Paul," she says, formally, "we are seeing several candidates for this critical position at the Baxter Hospital, and we have a set list of questions . . ."

I take advantage of the introductory patter to check my BlackBerry under the table. There's nothing from Will yet, but there is one from Geoff, marked with a little red exclamation mark that inspires dread. I've managed to dodge him since his declaration yesterday, and my current plan is to avoid being alone with him until after the holiday ad shoot. It's callous, self-serving behavior that does me little credit, I know. But if I reject him now, the risk that the holiday ad will be compromised is high.

GEOFFREY DURNFORD

> To: j.s.whelan@baxter.com
> Sent: Friday, December 6, 2013, 9:35 a.m.
> Subject: Are you OK?
>
> I didn't see you yesterday after our conversation. Is your wrist OK? I'm worried about you. Can you meet me for lunch today?

J. SOPHIE WHELAN

> To: g.durnford@baxter.com
> Sent: Friday, December 6, 2013, 9:47 a.m.
> Subject: Re: Are you OK?

HI there,

Sorry you were worried. It's been a busy 24 hours. I'm tied up in search committee meetings today, so I can't have lunch. Too bad!

Speak soon, Sophie

". . . in conjunction with our board of directors, that it was time for the Ascot Group to do some blue-sky thinking about its mission and vision," Stephen says. "So it made sense to do a leadership transition. On a personal level, playing this key role at Baxter will allow me to leverage my expertise for the public good, which is something that I feel strongly about, while still having more time to pursue independent interests than I have had for the last number of years. In short, I can say with confidence that I offer the set of skills that this hospital requires at this juncture."

WILLIAM R. SHANNON

To: j.s.whelan@baxter.com
Sent: Friday, December 6, 2013, 9:58 a.m.
Subject: Re: Dinner

Sure. What's the address? What can I bring?

WRS

Marvin asks a question. "Well, to be frank," answers Stephen, "I would be reluctant to get too granular about my plan for the first one hundred days at this stage. There is no question that we would engage immediately in a strategic planning process to identify goals for the Baxter organization. And you can't design a critical path to arrive at the specified goals without engaging in a process of SWOT analysis . . ."

J. SOPHIE WHELAN

> To: zoe@hennessy.com
> Sent: Friday, December 6, 2013, 10:18 a.m.
> Subject: I might have neglected to mention
>
> Will Shannon is in town. He's coming to dinner tonight.

ZOE HENNESSY

> To: j.s.whelan@baxter.com
> Sent: Friday, December 9, 2013, 10:22 a.m.
> Subject: Re: I might have neglected to mention
>
> !!!!!!!

With effort, I wrench my focus back to Stephen Paul's interview. "When we understand the core competencies of the organization, we can begin to operationalize our strategic plan. Of course, arriving at a strategic plan that makes sense at Baxter will likely involve an extensive stakeholdering process. Completion of that process may not be actionable in the first one hundred days, but we'll bear down and aim high."

Carl the board member beams. "Terrific, Stephen. Thank you for that insight. And may I say how much I have admired your career at Ascot. It's an honor to have an executive of your stature in our process." The spectacle of these men rubbing up against each other is excruciating, and I can see clearly how foolish I have been to hope that a new VP could make any difference at all to my job satisfaction. I have a chilling vision of myself five years hence, writing press releases littered with corporate jargon for Stephen Paul as I grow increasingly bitter and less relevant, perhaps turning into someone to be tolerated and worked around: someone like Joy.

With a shudder, I go back to my BlackBerry.

ZOE HENNESSY

> To: j.s.whelan@baxter.com
> Sent: Friday, December 6, 2013, 10:29 a.m.
> Subject: Re: I might have neglected to mention
>
> Neglect bordering on the criminal—more on that later.
>
> But for now—why did you invite him to dinner??? Does
> Jesse know? Doesn't he hate Will?

". . . human capital is arguably *the* key resource that a manager has to leverage. Recruitment, retention, and responsibility are the three Rs of management on my team. You need to find the right people, get them on the same page, and delegate. But there's no victory to be had in herding cats, so commitment to the team is paramount. If you want to succeed in change management, you need to empower people to participate actively in the process." Stephen Paul chuckles. "I've always said there's no need to miss golf season when you have a team you can trust."

J. SOPHIE WHELAN

> To: zoe@hennessy.com
> Sent: Friday, December 6, 2013, 10:50 a.m.
> Subject: Re: Re: I might have neglected to mention
>
> He doesn't hate Will! It's complicated. But dinner will
> be fine.

Carolyn Waldron has her chin balanced on her fist, and her brows are knitted together in concentration. "I confess to being one of those who may be a little out of touch with the language of business," she says. "But I'm hoping that you'll be able to help me by being very specific in your answer to the next question. Could you please describe your experience with fund-raising and campaign planning?"

"The Ascot Group has a very robust philanthropic arm, and I have always taken a direct interest in ensuring that our business has a significant charitable footprint. Now, it's true that our foundation at Ascot was in the business of providing funds to charities, while Baxter is in the business of acquiring funds. But these are two sides of the same coin. My experience suggests that fund-raising, like business, is all about creating incentives so that people perceive investment with your organization to be in line with their self-interest."

ZOE HENNESSY

To: j.s.whelan@baxter.com
Sent: Friday, December 6, 2013, 10:57 a.m.
Subject: Re: Re: Re: I might have neglected to mention

Complicated? You think? Everything with Will Shannon is complicated.

You are in a weakened state. You are wandering into dangerous territory. Have you seen what happens to wounded gazelles on the Discovery Channel? You're the gazelle. Don't take a stroll through lion country.

Anusha Dhaliwal says, "I was going to ask how you would persuade a donor to support the Baxter. I've been listening to you describe a process by which you would consult others about the vision for the hospital. Don't you need a clear sense of where we should be going in order to persuade donors to give? What do *you* think the vision for our organization should be?"

"Again," says Stephen, "I feel it's premature to commit myself to a vision at this juncture. I would need to loop in and really immerse myself in the organizational DNA, and complete a strategic planning process before I would feel confident that we had arrived at a collective understanding of the way forward."

"Wonderful," says Barry. "Thank you, Stephen! Would you like to make a closing statement?"

"Only that I look forward to your decision," says Stephen, rising from his seat and making his way to the door. Barry watches him go with obvious fondness, and as soon as the door closes behind him, announces: "Well, it's certainly going to be hard to top that!"

"Indeed," Lil mutters under her breath, and Jenny, sitting next to her, smothers a giggle.

J. SOPHIE WHELAN

To: wshannon@perrimanhale.com
Sent: Friday, December 6, 2013, 11:02 a.m.
Subject: Re: Re: Dinner

68 Harrison Drive. Just bring yourself! Looking forward to seeing you—6:30ish.

S

Karim Assaf is seated at the table now, a striking counterpoint to Stephen Paul. He's in his early thirties and dressed to kill in a slim-cut three-piece suit and thick-framed rectangular glasses. I've seen pictures of him, of course; he's the executive director of development for the City Arts Center and enjoys a modest, local variety of fame that involves being photographed at fund-raising events by the fashion pages.

GEOFFREY DURNFORD

To: j.s.whelan@baxter.com
Sent: Friday, December 6, 2013, 11:08 a.m.
Subject: Re: Re: Are you OK?

Let's meet after work for a drink, then. I want to see you.

G.

". . . I'm very proud that we've increased our membership by twenty-five percent over the past two years," says Karim. "I attribute this in large measure to our events portfolio. As you may know, we run several large-scale events each year, not unlike your Gala, and we also run a for-profit independent film festival. All of these events have had great press and brought our programs to a much wider audience than ever before . . ."

J. SOPHIE WHELAN

> To: zoe@hennessy.com
> Sent: Friday, December 6, 2013, 11:12 a.m.
> Subject: Fwd: Re: Re: Are you OK?
>
> Also, I'm having a little trouble managing Geoff.

". . . first priority is going to be to put the Baxter through a branding exercise. The Baxter does outstanding work, but it doesn't work hard enough to draw the community in. In the fund-raising world these days, it's not enough to have a worthy cause—saving sick children in your case, which is as worthy as they come—you have to market yourself so that people think it's hip to be associated with you. That's what we did very effectively at the CAC, and you can do it too. But you are going to need to invest in your public image and also in your events program to draw people in. I'd like to see you with a much busier social calendar, but of course, that will take more than one hundred days to put into place."

ZOE HENNESSY

> To: j.s.whelan@baxter.com
> Sent: Friday, December 6, 2013, 11:22 a.m.
> Subject: Re: Fwd: Re: Re: Are you OK?
>
> If I give you my advice, will you follow it?

". . . it will be very important to me to be present in the details as we move toward a fund-raising program that is more events-based. My practice is to treat every event with the care and attention that I would give to a party at my own home. I insist on having the final sign-off on all aspects of the event—menus, flowers, seating arrangements, entertainment—the works. It's the only way to insure that the brand is consistent . . ."

As I consider my response to Zoe, I realize that there is a worse fate imaginable than serving as director of communications for Stephen Paul, which is to become shackled to an operation whose major function is to churn out events trumpeting the global significance and essential coolness of Karim Assaf. It occurs to me that this could be the right time in my life to join the opt-out revolution, to thumb my nose at Barry and Stephen and Karim and the daycare director, to stay home and devote myself to raising better men than the ones I work with every day. In the meantime, though, I need Zoe's help.

J. SOPHIE WHELAN

> To: zoe@hennessy.com
> Sent: Friday, December 6, 2013, 11:37 a.m.
> Subject: Re: Re: Fwd: Re: Re: Are you OK?

> I promise.

". . . any pitch to a prospective donor is going to be closely linked to the Baxter's brand. For example, I wouldn't want to jump the gun and commit to a donor strategy without having the data from an impact study. I also think, incidentally, that your question highlights an antiquated approach to fund-raising that I would like to change. There is a place for face-to-face meetings, yes, but social media is changing the way we communicate with our supporters. I am a big proponent of using Facebook and Twitter to link with our donors. This approach, combined with a regular series of invitations to events, will insure that your donors regard you as a friend in their network, and not just a faceless entity with its hand out."

ZOE HENNESSY

> To: j.s.whelan@baxter.com
> Sent: Friday, December 6, 2013, 11:46 a.m.
> Subject: Re: Re: Re: Fwd: Re: Re: Are you OK?
>
> DO NOT ENGAGE. NOTHING GOOD CAN COME OF IT.
> IGNORE HIS EMAIL. DO NOT MEET HIM FOR DRINKS.
> YOUR LIFE IS COMPLICATED ENOUGH RIGHT NOW.
>
> P.S. I disinvited Richard from your party tonight.

"I want to thank you for bringing such a refreshing perspective to these issues," says Barry. "Would you like to take the opportunity to make a closing statement?"

"Indeed I would," says Karim. He straightens in his seat. "The Baxter is an integral part of the fabric of our city. For almost one hundred years, it has nurtured our children. But the world of philanthropy is changing and the Baxter is being left behind. It's time for a paradigm shift." Barry nods vigorously in the background. "I want to help redefine the Baxter as an organization of the moment. I want our events to be the must-attend highlights of the social calendar. I want to associate our brand more closely with celebrity spokespeople. The Baxter's image should be fun, youthful, and glamorous." He pauses for effect. "Once we have a new look and feel, I think you will be amazed at how quickly the dollars flow in!"

"Splendid!" Barry says. "Well, I'm sure I speak for all of us when I say that you have given us a call to action, Karim. Some very important ideas for us to think about, and I thank you for that. We will be in touch shortly."

Karim leaves, and Barry says to the table, "Well, no one could dispute the return on investment for this committee so far. We have a front runner and a strong fallback in case we can't meet Stephen's salary expectations—not bad for a morning's work." He smiles. "Let's get the last one over with and wrap this up."

CHAPTER EIGHTEEN

friday, december 6, 2013

I take advantage of the pause to check in on the personal drama unfolding on my BlackBerry, and discover, as I feared, that the more I try to contain the situation with Geoff, the further it spins out of control.

GEOFFREY DURNFORD

> To: j.s.whelan@baxter.com
> Sent: Friday, December 6, 2013, 12:05 p.m.
> Subject: Thinking of you
>
> I haven't heard back from you. I'd like to continue our conversation. What time will your meeting end?

I remind myself that Zoe's advice, which I have sworn to heed, is undoubtedly right. I can't have a scene with an employee over a rash and totally unprovoked declaration of affection, and certainly not over e-mail. It's better to take the indirect approach and let him down easily. And anyway, I feel sorry for Geoff. He has no way of knowing that he's sixteen years too late to audition for the leading male role in my road-not-taken fantasy. This thought calls to mind, in thrilling detail, the dream sequence that I've committed to excising from my con-sciousness. I remind myself, very sternly, of the many excellent quali-ties of my devoted and utterly attractive husband, take another slug of disgusting coffee, and turn my attention to the door, which swishes open to admit the next candidate.

At first glance, Margaret Anderson is the furthest thing from striking, with pale, doughy skin and an unruly mop of graying hair. She is, charitably speaking, stout, and I know in my sinking heart that nothing Margaret is going to say will be able to sway Barry. It is a terrible fate to be a plain woman. But as Margaret takes her seat and surveys the group around the table, something amazing happens: she smiles. And Margaret Anderson has a smile that transforms her in a second from forgettable to magnetic. Every-one turns toward her like flowers opening to the sun, and there is a moment of silence, broken by the sound of Barry choking on a mouthful of water.

Margaret launches in, and within moments she is creaming the com-petition with her fund-raising experience and her plans for the Baxter. My shoulders relax as I realize that she doesn't need my help. I've only met two other people who could command a room like this. One is grinning far too widely at the end of the table, and the other . . . *damn.* I'm thinking about him naked again.

JESSE WALKER

> To: j.s.whelan@baxter.com
> Sent: Friday, December 6, 2013, 12:26 p.m.
> Subject: Dinner
>
> Don't forget that Anya is sensitive to dairy and garlic.

J. SOPHIE WHELAN

> To: jesse.walker@greenfielddesign.com
> Sent: Friday, December 6, 2013, 12:35 p.m.
> Subject: Re: Dinner
>
> Wouldn't dream of it.

GEOFFREY DURNFORD

To: j.s.whelan@baxter.com
Sent: Friday, December 6, 2013, 12:40 p.m.
Subject: Are you avoiding me?

Jenny catches my eye and mimics a typing motion with her thumbs. I drop the BlackBerry into my lap, fold my hands on the table, and pay strict attention as Margaret explains her strategy for donor engagement. I don't think of Will once.

"Thank you," says Barry. "Those are all of our questions. At this stage in the process, we invite you to make a closing statement."

"Not quite all of the questions, I think," says a voice at the end of the table. Barry looks up, a warning in his eyes.

"Ms. Anderson," says Lil, "I understand that you are a single mother. This has been a matter of some . . . concern to certain members of our committee. It is my understanding that some members of the committee are worried about your ability to participate in evening events as a result of your parenting responsibilities. I thought you might wish to have an opportunity to respond to the concern directly."

"You are not required to answer that question," Barry sputters. "It is highly inappropriate."

"On the contrary," says Margaret. "I'm delighted to answer that question. I always think it is preferable to have people ask than to have them wonder and draw conclusions without information. I am a single mother of a fourteen-year-old son. And for many years, I have had a very elaborate set of arrangements that allow me to work demanding jobs and still raise my son. Primarily, I rely on my mother, who lives with me, and who has been an active partner in my parenting. The fact that I am a single mother has never affected my ability to attend events, or to discharge any of my responsibilities to my donors or my employer. I do think that it has made me a more compassionate manager."

"Thank you, Ms. Anderson," says Barry severely. "That is all for today. We will be in touch."

"Would you like to make a closing statement of some kind?" asks Jenny.

"Certainly," says Margaret. "The Baxter has some remarkable strengths, and it should be at the forefront of donors' minds in this city. The fact that this is not the case suggests to me that your major gift program has been neglected over the past few years. I think it's quite common for organizations like this one to overinvest in events. Events can bring the existing community together, but they don't replace the important work of meeting with donors and persuading them to support the life-saving health care that takes place here. This is what I do best, and I think it's a good fit for what you need. I believe deeply in the work that the Baxter does, and I'd love to be part of it."

Jenny shows Margaret out, and the rest of us settle in for what is obviously going to be a long meeting. Barry is whispering furiously to Carl at one end of the table, while Carolyn and Marvin are in a huddle by the coffee station. Lil sits slightly apart from the group, looking queenly. "All right, everyone," says Jenny, as she resumes her seat. "I'll facilitate the discussion. Let's deal with the strengths and weaknesses of each candidate first, and then we'll deal with them comparatively."

"I'll begin," says Barry. "In my opinion, we were incredibly fortunate to have attracted Stephen Paul in the first place. He is by far the most qualified candidate, in terms of professional experience and stature. He's just what we need: tough, strategic, and business-minded."

"I couldn't agree more," says Carl. "His focus on strategic planning is clearly well-placed, and his vision is realistic and achievable."

"With respect," says Marvin, "I don't believe that I heard him articulate a vision. I think he said that he'd rather not do that without engaging in some kind of process first." He looks at Carolyn. "What process was it? Stakeholding?"

"Stakeholdering, I believe," says Carolyn. "I don't mind telling you that I didn't understand a word that man was saying. It was complete gibberish."

"I agree," says Lil. "I question the wisdom of having as our lead fund-raiser someone who uses the word 'actionable' when he means 'able to be done.' 'Actionable' means 'giving rise to legal action,' for heaven's sake. The man's routine butchery of the English language might actually get us embroiled in a lawsuit."

Carl bursts out laughing. "You can't be serious. Give the man a break. I didn't know the meaning of 'actionable' until just now either."

Lil sniffs. "Your ignorance is nothing to celebrate," she says.

"Let's talk for a moment about his professional experience," says Jenny. "No one is disputing the fact that Mr. Paul has had a lengthy career in senior business roles. But are people confident that his specific experience is relevant for the position here?"

"I can't say that I am," says Anusha. "I've been thinking about what Sophie said in our last meeting—that fund-raising organizations are different from charitable foundations. I didn't hear Stephen say anything that persuaded me that he knew how to run a fund-raising department."

"I can assure you that it's not rocket science," says Barry, giving the Blowfish a workout at the end of the table. "If he can run a public company, he won't have any difficulty running our fund-raising operation. And I think we should be very careful about how influenced we are by Sophie's opinions on the subject. She is hardly a fund-raising expert herself, and her views are basically hearsay. In a court of law, you wouldn't be able to consider that evidence at all."

I consider Barry's florid complexion, hear his braying voice ringing in my ears, and am overtaken with unhealthy fantasies of revenge—Barry falling down an elevator shaft, Barry being hit by a bus, Barry being arrested for investor fraud—before I remember that actual retribution is within reach. I don't have to work here. I have a job offer. I could stand up right now, walk out for the last time as an employee, and walk back in as someone with clout and influence: a funder. The prospect of reversing the balance of power with Barry is delicious. So what's stopping me?

"Happily, this isn't a court of law, and in the context of the search committee, Sophie's views as a staff member in the advancement department are considered relevant and useful," says Jenny coldly. "The very reason that we require search committees to have staff representation is so we can have access to direct information about how specific departments work."

Patti has been silent throughout the meeting, but now says, "I feel compelled to mention that we have two equity candidates and that Stephen Paul is not one of them. If we end up hiring an older white male, we are going to have to be convinced that he is far and away the best person for the job. I'm not hearing people say that so far. Why don't we talk about the others and come back to Stephen?"

"Exactly," says Jenny. "What are people's views on Karim Assaf?"

"Very impressive," says the female board member, whose name I still haven't figured out. "I've been to several events at the CAC since he took over, and they've been terrific. He's got a tremendous vision for where he wants to take this organization."

"But is it where we want to go?" asks Marvin. "We need to raise large amounts of money for pretty pedestrian things like staff positions and equipment. We are very different from an arts organization. Listening to Mr. Assaf made me wonder if his experience is easily transferable."

"I think your concerns are overstated, Marvin," says Carl. "We raise a lot of money from our Gala every year."

"That's true," I say. "But we don't raise anywhere near as much money from our Gala as we raise from our other fund-raising efforts. Events are a pretty inefficient way to fundraise. They cost a lot, and they consume huge amounts of staff time. I personally wouldn't want to see us do a lot more events."

"Of course, Sophie is biased," Barry interjects. "She's supervising the Gala at the moment, somewhat against her wishes."

"Isn't that all the more reason to take her views into account?" asks Carolyn. "I'm also concerned that Mr. Assaf is too junior in his career for a move like this. I don't think he has the experience to build our major gift program. Our average donor is well over sixty years old. In my opinion, Margaret Anderson is far and away the most suitable candidate. She has ten years of relevant experience and her fund-raising plan makes sense. And I could understand the words she used."

"I agree," says Marvin. "I thought she seemed like a terrific person. Lots of positive energy and ideas, a very pleasing personality. I think our donors will like dealing with her, and she'll be able to talk to the medical staff."

Barry looks shocked. "No one is suggesting that she isn't nice. She's obviously nice. But nice isn't going to bring in the bucks! We need someone who is prepared to look our donors in the eye and shake them down. You need someone who knows how to make a deal. Stephen is clearly the front-runner on that score."

"Speaking as a donor," says Lil, "I think that the shakedown strategy is overrated. I'd much rather deal with someone who can make a rational case for why my assistance is needed than someone who tries to bully me into it. I'd much rather take Margaret Anderson's calls than Stephen Paul's."

"Is this about 'equity'?" says Barry. "Because if you are turning down one of the leading business figures in the country because he's a white male, it is political correctness run wild. And anyway, it's not at all clear to me that a woman should be given special 'equity' consideration. It's not as though there are no women in management here."

"I'd like to point out that you are the one who was prepared to disqualify Ms. Anderson on the basis of her family status," says Lil. "But to answer your question, no, this is not about equity. It might be if I thought the candidates were close on other measures. I don't."

"I don't think we're giving enough consideration to Mr. Assaf," says the female board member. "He's young, dynamic, and he wants to put the hospital on the map. If he can do for us what he did for the CAC, we'll be bringing in tons of new donors."

"I didn't hear him say that his major gift program showed any signs of increasing," I say. "He threw a bunch of great parties, and he managed to get a bunch of new members— but they offered discounted ticket prices to members, so the increase to the bottom line is probably negligible."

"Well," says Jenny, "this might be a good moment to take a straw poll and see if we are arriving at any kind of consensus."

"Nonsense," blusters Barry. "That would be premature. I think we would all benefit from a period of reflection. I suggest that we adjourn the meeting and reconvene in a week's time."

"I disagree," says Lil. "We will get to the right decision a lot faster if we let people vote while their impressions of the candidates are fresh in their minds."

"That is consistent with our regular practice," says Jenny. "I'm very reluctant to expose committee members to pressure—however well-intentioned—to back one candidate or another. People should commit to a candidate based on their honest reactions to the interviews and not because they have had outside discussions with other members of the committee. *Not* that I'm saying that anyone would do that, you understand, just that it is a risk if we adjourn."

Barry's face is purple, and everyone around the table is studiously avoiding any eye contact with him.

"Let's just get an initial feel of the room," says Jenny, "and that will tell us how we should proceed. How many people support Mr. Paul for the position?"

Barry and Carl raise their hands.

"Two," says Jenny. "How many people support Mr. Assaf?" The female board member raises her hand.

"One," says Jenny. "And how many people support Ms. Anderson?"

Six hands shoot up: Carolyn, Marvin, Anusha, Patti, Lil, and me. "Six," says Jenny, "plus my vote is seven." She pauses. "That was intended to be a straw poll, but we have such a strong majority vote that it may not be necessary to continue. Does anyone feel that further discussion might change their vote?"

"I'm on the fence," says the female board member. "It's possible that with further discussion, I might vote for Margaret Anderson."

"And with further discussion, you might come to support Stephen Paul," says Barry.

"No, I don't think so," says the female board member, and Barry looks deflated.

"That being the case, it seems that we have a new vice president," says Jenny. "My office will prepare an offer in consultation with the board, and we will report back to you if and when the candidate accepts. And the communications people will need to start thinking about the press release and public announcement."

"Of course," I say. I am trying not to smile too broadly.

Barry inclines his head, acknowledging the defeat, and says: "I may not agree with the choice that we've made here today, but I respect the will of the majority. This is an important moment for the Baxter Children's Hospital, and we need to present a united front. I'll start the ball rolling on the public announcement today. We'll need some strong, professional communications advice on this." Barry looks at me. "Don't you agree, Sophie?"

"Absolutely," I say. "This is a great opportunity to create some real buzz about the hospital, and we don't want to miss it. When would you like to meet to talk about the PR strategy?"

"Oh, you misunderstand me," says Barry, smiling slightly. "I don't think a meeting will be necessary. I just need you to send me the contact information for the best PR folks in town and I'll get in touch with them myself."

I have an odd shrinking sensation, almost as if Barry has punctured the bubble of elation in my chest. My cheeks are hot with humiliation. "You don't want my office to help with the announcement?" I ask.

Barry regards me with undisguised malice. "Oh, I think we've had the benefit of more than enough help from you this week," says Barry. "And as I said, it's an important moment. We can't leave the job to amateurs."

CHAPTER NINETEEN

friday, december 6, 2013

I rush out of the meeting room as the committee breaks up, pausing only to whisper congratulations in Lil's ear and to promise to see her at her party on Saturday night. She shoots me a sympathetic look, but doesn't try to stop me.

In my office, I scoop up a file of all of the things that I'm not going to read tonight, and I inform Joy that I'll be working at home this afternoon to prepare for tomorrow's shoot. Joy doesn't believe me, but she won't undermine me this time; I've just given her license to surf the Internet all afternoon with no threat of discovery. And after Barry's poisonous send-off, I feel blessedly free of guilt despite the fact that I plan to spend the entire afternoon preparing for a dinner party.

There was a time in grad school when, suffering from a mild form of writer's block, which may have resulted from a fundamental lack of interest in my topic, I spent what any objective observer would have said was too much time playing Tetris. Tetris is a simple video game that involves putting falling puzzle pieces in exactly the right spot in a limited window of time. Eventually, I had to go cold turkey on Tetris, but the closest equivalent I have found in recent years is in the design of a perfect menu for a dinner party of friends. The initial request for dietary restrictions always unearths the usual religious and cultural prohibitions, but then there are the vegetarians, or God forbid, the vegans, and the lactose intolerant, and those afflicted with various and sundry allergies to ingredients like barley or blueberries. The trick is to have a constellation of dishes in which any one person can eat at least three of them.

I'm thrilled that Richard isn't coming, not just because he is a notorious conversation hog, but also because he is a vegan. Without him, I have a group I can work with. Those who can eat everything will feast on warm goat cheese salad, beef tenderloin, mushroom risotto, wilted rapini, and pear tart with whipped cream. The vegetarians can eat everything except the beef; the lactose intolerant can eat everything except the risotto and the whipped cream; and Anya, who is apparently "sensitive" to dairy and garlic, can just suck it up.

I make it home with the groceries just before three o'clock. First up is the pear tart, and by four-thirty, I have a perfect little round of homemade pastry browning in the oven. So many people just buy dessert these days, but they are really missing out on the tactile satisfaction of baking. I love the measuring, the rolling, the patting; it takes me back to the best parts of childhood.

Next I assemble the little patties of goat cheese for the salads. I mince herbs and coat the cheese with them, and then throw some slightly stale bread in the food processor to make fresh crumbs. I bread the goat cheese patties and put them in the fridge so that I can bake them just before serving. Then I whip up a delicate citrus vinaigrette, which also goes into the fridge. I'm making excellent time, congratulating myself, when I hear the door open.

"Hello?" I call, but hear only a strange thumping sound from the front porch. I wipe my hands on my apron and head to the front door to investigate, where I am nearly taken out by the business end of a Christmas tree being pushed, battering-ram style, through the front door.

"Yikes!" I shout, leaping out of the way, and Jesse's head appears at the other end of the tree.

"Oops. Sorry about that," he says.

"I wasn't expecting you for another hour," I say. "You escaped from the office?"

"I thought you could probably use some help with the party prep."

"Fantastic," I say, concealing my surprise. Jesse isn't usually this adept at anticipating my needs when it comes to entertaining, and it's a development to be encouraged. "But why don't you just stick the tree in the garage for now, and we'll put it up on the weekend?"

"No, no," says Jesse. "I want to put it up for the party. Don't you think that would be great? I'm just going to run down to the basement and find the stand. Do you know where it is?"

"In the storage room," I say. "But, Jess, are you sure we have time for this?"

"Of course," says Jesse. "People are coming at seven, right? It's only five-thirty now. Lots of time." And he disappears down the basement stairs.

I exhale forcefully and adjust my shoulders down. Jesse is right. There's lots of time, and the Christmas tree is always beautiful. I put the dried morels for the risotto into some hot water to soak, and am washing the rapini when I hear a crash and a shout from the basement.

"Are you all right?" I call down the stairs.

Jesse appears, limping. "The fucking stand fell on my foot," he says. "Jesus, Sophie! Why did you leave it up against the wall like that? I moved the toboggans and it tipped over. I nearly lost a toe down there!"

"As I said," I say stiffly, "are you sure that this is a good time to put up the tree?"

"It'll take ten minutes," he says. "I just need you to give me a hand."

I follow Jesse into the living room. He points to the corner by the window. "That's where we usually put it, right?"

"No. We usually put it over there." I point to the opposite corner. "But we can put it here. It doesn't really matter."

"OK, then. Help me move the armchair?"

We clear a spot for the tree and Jesse puts the stand in place. "Good," he says. "Now, I just need you to hold the tree while I screw the supports in. Can you get me a screwdriver?"

I run down to the basement, find a screwdriver, and run back up to find Jesse holding the tree up with an expression of pure exasperation. "Did you have to go to the hardware store? How hard is it to find a screwdriver in the basement?"

I bite back the very unpleasant comment that I'm tempted to make and say instead, "It's just about six, Jesse. I need to get back to the cooking."

"Hold the tree and we'll be done before you know it." Jesse gets down on his belly under the tree and starts twisting the first support. His soft grunts emanate up through the pine needles. "Is it straight?"

"It's hard to tell standing right next to it, but I think so."

Jesse moves to the next screw and then the next one. He slithers out to examine his handiwork. "Goddamn it! It's leaning to the left. Push it right!"

I try to fix the angle, but the tree is locked in place. Jesse mutters and gets back under the tree, which vibrates as he wrenches the right support loose. He climbs out and looks again. He's sweating and there are pine needles in his hair. "Hold it exactly like that. Don't let it move!" He dives under the tree again, and I hold on for dear life as the tree sways with the violence of whatever Jesse is doing to its trunk. I am reminded, as I am every year, that nothing says, "Why did I marry this man?" like putting up a tree together.

"Perfect," he pronounces, surveying the tree with obvious pride. "Now for the decorations." He looks at me expectantly.

"You're on your own, pal," I say. "Dinner party in forty-five minutes. I'll be in the kitchen."

"OK, fair enough. Just tell me where the ornaments are."

"Upstairs closet, top shelf," I say.

I'm browning shallots for the risotto when Jesse reappears. "Didn't you hear me calling you?" he asks.

"Nope," I say, pointing to the fan above the stove. "What's the problem?"

"I found a box of ornaments but no lights."

"Same shelf, in a garbage bag."

He sighs heavily. "Why didn't you say so?"

I add morels and porcini mushrooms and stir them while they soften.

"Do we have an extension cord?" Jesse calls from the living room.

"Hanging on the back of the furnace room door," I call back, and add the arborio rice and some vegetable stock. Jesse darts into the kitchen to grab the stepladder.

"Smells awesome," he says. "Can I borrow you for a second?"

"No can do," I say. "The rice is in the pan. The cardinal rule of risotto is that you can't turn your back once the rice is in." I pour a couple of ladles of stock into the pan.

"OK. I'll manage," he says, but ten minutes later, I hear a shout of alarm and I sprint into the living room. "It's tilting!" he says, eyes wide.

"Hold it," I say, "I'll be right back." I race to the risotto, pour the remaining stock in and give it a good stir.

We adjust the tree again and I stand while Jesse looks for a diagnosis. "Aha! The shim slipped." He rummages around for a few minutes and emerges with a glow of victory. "It won't be going anywhere now!" He hands me the star for the top of the tree. "I know you're picky about the placement of the star. Go to it. I'll spot you."

I reach up and feel Jesse's hands resting on my waist. It's lovely, and for the first time in ages, I wish that we could forget the whole dinner party and race upstairs to bed. But then an acrid smell wafts in from the kitchen, and I leap off the stepladder, leaving the star askew, and bolt to the stove. Smoke is rising from the pan, curling around the edges of the dense risotto. "Oh no, no, no," I say, as I pull it from the heat and reach in with a spoon to assess the damage. About two-thirds of the risotto comes out easily; the rest is caked to the bottom of the pan. I taste the rescued portion, which is a bit dry but still tasty.

Jesse appears by my side. "Oh, shit. Sorry about that," he says. "How bad is it?" And as I open my mouth to answer, the smoke alarm goes off. I cover my ears as Jesse grabs a broom from the closet. He knocks the smoke alarm off the ceiling with one swing and beats it with the broom handle until it stops shrieking, suggesting that he is expelling some residual frustration from the Christmas tree project.

"Feel better?" I ask, looking at the mangled plastic on the floor.

"Much," he says. "What's the risotto situation?"

"It's not enough to feed everyone," I say. "I'm going to have to make risotto cakes to make it stretch. Do you think that will be OK?"

"Of course," he says. "It will be terrific. By the way, where are the kids?"

"Oh, right, the kids," I say. "I forgot about them."

"You forgot about them?"

I roll my eyes, and then catch myself. I heard about a study on the radio that predicted marital success by watching couples interact. Eye rolling was singled out as fatal evidence of underlying contempt, which caused marriages to fail in statistically significant numbers. "I'm kidding, honey," I say. "They're sleeping over at your parents'."

"Oh," he says. "Anyway, the tree's done and it looks great, so I'm going to jump in the shower before the guests arrive."

I fill the dishwasher and put the ruined pan in the sink to soak while I regroup. I put the risotto in a bowl and set it aside, and take the beef out of the fridge to bring it to room temperature. I'm assembling a cheese tray when I glance at the clock and realize that I'm out of time. I sprint upstairs, strip off my sweats and throw on a dress and some stockings. I run a comb through my hair and am digging through my makeup kit for some inspiration when the doorbell rings. "Can you get that?" I call to Jesse.

"I'm wearing a towel," he calls back. "Sorry."

I loop a few strands of beads around my neck as I dash downstairs and throw open the door to our neighbors, Daniel and Claire, who live across the street. "Come on in," I say. "It's so great to see you!"

Claire gives me a big hug. "It's been way too long!" she says. She steps back. "I know I'm not supposed to say this, but you look tired."

"That's just because you don't usually see me without concealer under my eyes. I'm fine. What can I get you to drink?"

I get them settled in the living room, admiring the tree, when the bell rings again.

"Oh, thank God," I say, finding Zoe standing in the doorway. "I need to put you to work."

"I'm all yours," she says. "Is he here yet?"

"Will? No. How are you doing, by the way?"

"Mostly enraged, with moments of sadness, which is probably better than the reverse. But I don't want to talk about it tonight. Much like the way you don't want to talk about what's going on with Will." She lifts one eyebrow and gives me a penetrating look.

"Not now, Zoe. We'll find some time this weekend, I promise. I have to go into the office tomorrow for the holiday ad shoot; maybe we could meet after that. Let's connect in the morning once I have a better sense of how long the shoot will take."

"Fine," she says. "Just as long as you don't think you're off the hook." The doorbell rings again and she saves me from answering. This time it's Paul, Jesse's closest friend from grad school, and his wife, Lila. I introduce them to Daniel and Claire, put Zoe in charge of drinks, deposit the cheese tray on the coffee table, and head back to the kitchen to assess the dinner situation.

Conservatively, I seem to be behind schedule by at least an hour. Why, why did I bake dessert? When will I learn that the first impression is what counts? It is a truth universally acknowledged that by the time you get to dessert, your guests will always be too drunk or too tired to notice your efforts. I pour a large glass of Chianti to calm my nerves and address myself to the beef tenderloin. As I slide it into the oven, I hear the doorbell ring again, and I dash out in my apron.

Jesse beats me to it. "Will," he says. "It's been a long time." He holds out a hand and they shake.

"Great house," says Will, stepping past Jesse and into the foyer. "Hi, Sophie," he says, leaning down and brushing my cheek with a kiss.

"Have you never been here before?" I say, knowing full well that he hasn't. "That's terrible! It's long overdue, then." The foyer is small, but it seems smaller than usual with the three of us packed in together. I hope Jesse doesn't notice how flustered I am. But his attention is on the last arrival.

"Anya, you look incredible," Jesse says. She does, too, in a fitted black jersey dress and high black boots. She waves at me and brushes her cheek. "You have something on your face," she says, and when I reach up to investigate, my hand comes away with a greasy smear of beef fat.

"Thanks," I manage, mesmerized with loathing at the way her hip-bones jut out like ridges framing the flatlands of her abs. "Sit down and relax, everyone! Dinner in half an hour!"

Back in the kitchen, I realize that I haven't baked the goat cheese yet. The tenderloin will be in for twenty-two minutes at 500 degrees; the goat cheese needs ten minutes at 375 degrees. It can't be helped: I'll put them in with the beef for a shorter time and hope for the best. Which reminds me—I haven't set the timer for the beef. I put my head in my hands for a second and guesstimate the remaining cooking time, set the clock for fourteen minutes, and send a small prayer upward to the cooking gods. Then I pull out all of the exotic lettuces from the organic market and begin chopping. I cast my mind back to the moment in the market when I decided that I was too good for the prewashed box of mixed greens, and I curse aloud.

Zoe appears at my elbow. "He's aging well," she murmurs.

"Working here," I say, and hand her a salad spinner. "Can you wash the lettuce?"

"Can I do anything to help?" asks Will, coming into the kitchen.

"Why don't you see if anyone needs a fresh drink?" I suggest, filling a pot to boil water for blanching the rapini. I can't have him in the room right now; I need to focus all of my concentration on getting the meal on the table.

I hear the soothing sound of goat cheese bubbling away in the oven, and then remember that it's not actually supposed to be bubbling. Pulling open the oven door, I discover that yet another cooking gamble has failed—the patties have lost structural integrity and are now little pools of simmering goat cheese dotted with herbs and crumbs. But the show must go on, so Zoe and I toss the salad in the vinaigrette, divide it among nine plates, and spoon a shiny glob of cheese onto each of them. Zoe calls everyone to the table, and I parade out with the first course.

Claire looks stricken as I put the salad in front of her. "Sophie, I'm so sorry," she says. "I thought you knew I was lactose intolerant."

"I did," I say. "But I thought it was only cows' milk. This is goat."

She shakes her head sorrowfully. "All cheese, I'm afraid."

"Not a problem," I say. "It just needs a small adjustment." And I rush back into the kitchen, where I realize that we have used up all of the salad, so I set about removing the offending cheese with surgical precision and returning a much-reduced portion to Claire, hoping all the while that I've eradicated every trace of lactose and that she won't have a bilious attack at the table.

Jesse fills the wineglasses, and everyone digs into their salads and makes appreciative noises. The oven timer goes off, and I dash back into the kitchen to pull out the beef and cover it, then throw the rapini into the boiling water and heat some oil. I grab handfuls of the ill-fated risotto, shape them into little sliders and toss them in. I manage to get ten little cakes out of the risotto, which is one per person, minus Claire the non-cheese-eater, plus one extra for Zoe the vegetarian. And now the beef is ready for serving, so I drain the rapini, call to Jesse to bring the dinner plates in, serve everyone exactly the right combination of foods to satisfy their physical and mental health requirements, and sit down to dinner with the satisfaction of one who has finished a marathon. It's true that Zoe's plate looks a bit sad, with two lonely risotto cakes and some stalks of rapini, but presumably this is a situation that you have to get used to if you eschew meat, and anyway, Zoe is giving me a big smile and saying that the risotto cakes are beautiful. The beef is perfectly done, thanks to the cooking gods, and the rapini is not overdone, if a little flavorless, and it complements the beef nicely. I'm so pleased, in fact, that I'm prepared to overlook the fact that Anya refers to my risotto cakes as "cute."

I clear the main course and am loading the dishwasher when I turn around to find Zoe standing right behind me with an intense expression on her face.

"Zoe, I can't talk about Will right now," I say.

"This isn't about Will. What's going on with Jesse and Anya?"

"What do you mean? Why are you whispering?"

"Maybe I'm being overly sensitive, but they seem . . . close. Take a look."

I sidle up to the dining room door and position myself so that I have an angle on the two of them. And I can see immediately what Zoe is talking about. Anya is leaning in toward Jesse, with her back to the rest of the table. She is speaking in a low voice, and as I watch, she reaches out and strokes his arm. The gesture is undeniably intimate, and Jesse responds in kind by touching her hand. The rest of the guests are all immersed in their own chatter, unaware that my world has just tilted on its axis. I step back from the door and take a breath to steady myself.

"Are you OK?" asks Zoe.

I nod, not trusting myself to speak, and reach under the counter for my mixer. I love making whipped cream, even in the most trying of circumstances; unlike most other activities in life, it is invariably easy, predictable, and satisfying, not to mention incredibly loud and distracting. And this is necessary because I feel a sense of loss so powerful I think I am going to be physically ill.

I am just starting to feel calmer when Jesse appears, and I realize that whatever comes out of his mouth is going to have more importance than it should. Which is unfortunate, because what comes out of his mouth is "Sophie, how long is that going to take? It's so loud that no one can hear themselves speak."

Another great thing about whipped cream is its use in the comic tradition as a weapon, and now that it's ready, I wonder how many more times I can appeal to my better self today. I turn off the mixer, remove the paddles, and take them over to the sink in order to put a little distance between myself and the whipped cream. It's startling how much I want to throw it in Jesse's face.

Instead, I say, "Would you mind getting out the dessert plates and helping me serve?" I carve up the pear tart, placing a healthy dollop of cream on the pieces destined for guests who embrace dairy, and hand them to Jesse just as the phone rings.

"Sophie? Are you all right?"

I struggle to place the voice for a fraction of a second and then give up. It's too much. "Who is this?" I ask.

"It's Geoff," he says, sounding hurt.

"What happened?" I ask. I have a horrible premonition that we've had another fatal outbreak at the hospital, and the press has somehow gotten hold of the story.

"I was going to ask you the same thing," he says. "I didn't hear from you. I thought we were going to get together tonight."

"Oh," I say, stupidly. "You're not calling about work."

"No," he says, exasperated. "I'm calling about us."

Us? "Just a minute," I say, covering the receiver with my hand and racing up the stairs to the bedroom. I close the door firmly behind me. "This isn't a good time," I say. "I've got people here for dinner."

"Sophie," says Geoff, "what's going on? I tell you how I feel about you and then you ignore me? That's not like you."

"I don't know, Geoff," I say. "Maybe this is exactly like me. I've never been put in this situation before."

"And what situation is that?" he asks.

It's his tone that finally does it. "You're *angry* with me?" I ask. "If anyone is going to be angry here, I think it should be me." I hear him suck in his breath but I keep going. "You work for me. You come into my office and drop a bomb on me and then harass me over e-mail all day because I don't respond quickly enough. And then you call me at home, where I am having dinner with my husband and our friends, and want to talk about 'us.' There is no 'us,' Geoff. There is never going to be an 'us.'"

There is a long silence. "That's your answer?" he asks.

"Yes."

"Well, I should thank you," he says formally. "You could not have been clearer. I appreciate your candor and apologize for any discomfort I may have caused you."

"Geoff, I'm sorry," I say. "I like you. I like working with you. I . . ."

"It's fine," he says. "I have to go now."

I walk back to the kitchen, still holding the phone in my hand. I fill a wineglass to the brim with Chianti and drink it down in long gulps. I'm refilling when I hear the dining room door slide open and then close behind me. "Are you coming back to the party?" asks Will.

I turn and attempt a sunny smile. "In a minute," I say. "I'm just taking care of a couple of things in here."

He studies me and then says, "I was going to sneak out for a cigarette. Want to come?"

"I don't smoke," I say.

"Neither do I," he says.

"OK," I say, and we put on our coats and go out to the back patio. I brush the snow off the deck chairs and we sit. "I'm not sure I remember how to do this," I say.

"It's like riding a bike," says Will, shaking a cigarette from the package with a practiced tap. His lighter flashes in the dark. He takes a second cigarette out of the package, lights it with the tip of his own, and hands it to me. "So," he says.

"So," I say.

"Have you thought about my offer?"

"I've thought about it," I say slowly. "I'm still thinking."

He looks quizzical. "Is it that hard a decision? Lillian didn't think it would be. She said that you're underpaid, underappreciated, and ready for a new challenge. The foundation would seem to be a perfect solution. What am I missing?"

I sit back in my chair and gaze up at the sky. It's cold but clear and the stars are out. I trace the shape of the Big Dipper with the glowing end of the cigarette. It's been years since I smoked, but I remember now what I always loved about it: the sense that time stands still from the moment the match is struck until the tobacco burns down to its last ember. I know I have to make a decision, and soon. But first I have to tell Jesse about the offer, and I'm avoiding it; with Will in the picture, I'm not sure how he'll react. I want the job, but not if it makes my life harder at home. Jesse has questions about Will, and even after all these years I'm still not sure I have the answers.

I take a long swallow of wine and blow a plume of smoke up at the stars. The unfamiliar dizziness makes me reckless. "We've never talked about what happened between us," I say.

He stiffens, but his tone is gentle. "What do you mean?"

I groan. I can't believe he's going to make me say it. I've considered our relationship from every angle, tested every theory that could explain it, sifted endlessly through tiny shards of memory searching for evidence of love. Now, with the only other witness to the event captive in my backyard, I'm on the verge of a major breakthrough in my research. I'm not going to chicken out. I take a deep breath. "We slept together, Will, more than once. And it was a big deal for me. What was it for you?"

Now it's his turn to be silent. "It was a long time ago," he says finally. "Is it important to talk about it now?"

"It is if you want me to come and work at the foundation," I say.

"Closure is totally overrated," Will says.

"Be that as it may," I say, "I'd still like some."

"I don't know if this will satisfy you," he says carefully. "I knew how you felt back then. But it was confusing for me. I wanted you, obviously, but something more serious? I wasn't looking for that, and I knew that any relationship with you couldn't be casual. I know I behaved badly, that I was unfair to you. I was a young guy, an idiot. It's not really an excuse, but maybe it's an explanation."

"Do you have another cigarette?" I ask.

"It's the least I can do," he says, lighting it and leaning across to hand it to me. Our fingers touch and he meets my eye. "I'm sorry, Sophie. And if it's any consolation, I've often regretted the decisions I made back then."

"Which ones?" I ask, but I'm interrupted by the sound of the sliding door behind me.

"What's going on out here?" asks Jesse. "Are you *smoking*?"

"We were just catching up," I say, crushing the remnants of the cigarette under my toe.

"Our guests are leaving," says Jesse tightly. "They would like to say good-bye to the hostess." My mind throws out an image of Anya, touching Jesse at the dinner table. I shiver.

Will stands up. "I should get going," he says.

"Good idea," says Jesse icily, stepping aside to let Will pass. A few seconds later, I hear the front door close behind him.

Jesse is very still, his jaw set in a hard line. "We should go in," I say. "It's cold."

"That didn't seem to bother you when Will was here."

"I lost track of time," I say.

"Apparently," he says.

"Let's go in, Jesse," I say. "Come on. There's no reason to be like that." I give him what I assume is a reassuring smile, but he's having none of it.

"The sad thing is, Sophie," he says, "I bet you actually believe that."

We go into the house and bid our guests a good night. Zoe gives me a sympathetic look and mouths the words *call me* as she heads out the door. Jesse starts heading up the stairs.

"Are you going to help clean up?" I ask. The tension between us is palpable, but I'm sure relations will normalize once we start tidying and domestic order is restored. It's always worked in the past.

"I don't think so," says Jesse. "I'm going to bed." It's clear he's not inviting me to join him. Remembering Anya, I feel panic begin to rise.

"Jesse—" I begin, but he doesn't let me finish.

"How about this, Sophie," he says. "How about you tell me when I get to stop looking over my shoulder, OK? Because I would really like to know."

CHAPTER TWENTY

⁓

saturday, december 7, 2013

The alarm goes off at seven on Saturday morning. With my eyes still closed, I try to remember a time when Saturday morning meant waking up on your own, just because your body had enough sleep—not because the kids wanted you to turn on the television, and not because you had to go and oversee a crew shooting a ridiculously sentimental holiday ad airing too late in the season to make much of a difference to anyone. I try, but I can't really remember what it felt like, only that there was a time in my life when it happened routinely. I roll over and reach for Jesse, but his side of the bed is cool and empty. In the distance, I hear glasses clinking and the dishwasher door slamming shut. There's no help for it; I'm going to have to intervene before he breaks every glass in the house. I slide out of bed, wrap myself in a bathrobe, and pad downstairs.

"You're up early," I say.

"I didn't get much sleep," he says.

I pour a cup of coffee and swish a mouthful around to wash out the ashy aftertaste of my cigarette hangover, and then go over to the dishwasher and start removing the wineglasses that Jesse has just loaded. "I don't want the stems to snap," I say. Jesse watches me without speaking. I fill the sink. "Do you want to dry?" I ask.

"Not particularly," he says.

"All right," I say, bracing myself. "Do you want to tell me why you're so cranky this morning?"

"I think you misunderstand," says Jesse. "I'm not cranky. I'm completely and totally pissed off. And you can probably guess why. I'll give you a hint. It has to do with the fact that you invited Will fucking Shannon into my house and then snuck off with him in the middle of dinner."

I drop glasses into the water, watching the bowls fill and sink to the bottom. I take a couple of calming breaths. "There was no sneaking," I say reasonably. "He offered me a job. He wanted to discuss it privately."

"A job doing what, exactly?"

"Running the Baxter Foundation. He and Lil want me to replace her."

"And why didn't Lil ask you herself?"

"I don't know," I say, defensively, "Will's the chair of the board. We're old friends. Maybe they thought I'd be more likely to say yes to him."

"Because you think he walks on water?"

"Jesus, Jesse, lay off. We haven't seen each other in ages. We were catching up."

"And why is this the first time I'm hearing about this so-called job offer?"

"Are you seriously suggesting that I'm lying about the job?" My voice is getting higher with each volley. "I might well have mentioned it last night, but it was difficult to get your attention."

"My attention? You were the one in the backyard, smoking and gazing into Will's eyes."

"I don't know what you thought you saw," I say, "but—"

"I know exactly what I saw. And so would anyone else paying the slightest bit of attention. Is he your backup plan in case I don't work out? Because you might want to bear in mind that he didn't want you the first time around."

"Stop it before you say something you regret," I say.

"You're the expert on regrets around here," he says.

"What the fuck is that supposed to mean?"

"Give me some credit. Do you really think I'm that oblivious?"

"I think you're oblivious to everyone except Anya these days."

Jesse slams a hand down on the counter. "You have a lot of nerve turning this around on me. What does Anya have to do with anything?"

"She was snuggled up to you all night at the table," I say, outraged at his denial. "She kept touching you. You acted like she was the only person there. Even Zoe noticed it."

"Zoe should mind her own fucking business for once," says Jesse.

"Don't you start on Zoe."

"For Christ's sake, Sophie, I'm not interested in Anya. We were talking about business."

"And what business was that? How incredible she looks?"

Jesse's face is white. "No, actually. I needed to talk to her about how our last-chance investor failed to get the loan he needed and about how our company is going to go under as a result. Good news for you. You always hated Anya and now you won't have to deal with her anymore. Happy?"

"Of course I'm not happy!"

"Well, there's a big fucking surprise. You've been miserable for months, and here's a news flash—it's not anything that Will Shannon is going to fix for you. He never sticks around for the hard stuff, and you are incredibly fucking hard to live with these days."

I feel as though I can barely breathe, my chest is so tight. "Fuck you, too, Jesse," I whisper.

In the airless silence that follows, I hear laughter as the front door opens.

Jamie and Scotty race into the kitchen and twine themselves around my legs. "Hug, Mommy," they cry, and I bend down and wrap them in my arms, hiding my face from Jesse.

"I've got to go up and shower, Jesse," I say, my voice shaky. "I'm due at the Baxter in an hour for the shoot."

"How long are you going to be gone?" He doesn't meet my eye.

"It could go all day," I say, "but it's unlikely. I think I'll be back mid-afternoon. The sitter will be here at six."

"Where are we going?"

"It's Lil's party. I promised her we'd both be there."

"Fantastic," says Jesse. "Another chance to catch up with my old friend Will. That sounds wonderful. Can't wait."

My hands clutch the steering wheel to keep them from shaking as I drive to the office, rehearsing our argument over and over in my mind. Jesse and I rarely fight, and this one has been apocalyptic by our standards. By the time I arrive at the office, I'm in a complete state. And, as luck would have it, Nigel is clocking some overtime by working the germ desk on Saturday morning. His eyes light up as he sees me, but I find, suddenly, that I've lost my will to fight. He pulls out his clipboard.

"You don't need to do that," I say. "I've had a sinus infection for the past week. I've had a fever, but I'm not contagious. I'm taking antibiotics. Here's a note from my doctor." I rummage around in my purse and produce the note from Beverley. "Truce?"

Nigel scrutinizes the document as if it contains paragraphs instead of ten words. He looks up at me with a sour expression. "It's not easy doing this job, you know."

"I appreciate that," I say. "I certainly wouldn't want to do it." Nigel looks suspicious. "I think what you do is really important," I add hastily. "And I'm sorry if I've been rude to you. It's been a stressful time at work, but that's not an excuse."

Nigel looks surprised and mildly disappointed. He obviously has a fight or two left in him, but I'm no longer a worthy opponent. "You can go in," he says.

I make a mental note to tell Jenny that I've circumvented Nigel's grievance. At least I can claim one achievement today. I wonder if I have to tell HR that Geoff is in love with me and may decide to quit at any moment, which reminds me that I'm really, really dreading seeing Geoff.

I make my way to the conference room on the second floor, which has been transformed into a tiny ecosystem populated with young people dressed in black and wearing headsets. I watch them for a few minutes while I get my bearings, observing them buzz back and forth from the perimeter of the room to a point in the center, where the maestro is holding court. Claudio is in a slim white suit today, with snakeskin loafers and aviator glasses. It gladdens my heart to see that he's prepared to treat my holiday ad with all the seriousness of an Oscar-contending Hollywood production.

"Sophie!" Claudio swans over, arms outstretched, and kisses me on both cheeks.

"I can't thank you enough for doing this, Claudio," I say, completely sincerely. "We would have been sunk without you."

"True," he says. "But the Baxter holds a special place in my heart. I am at her service." He hooks an arm through my elbow and pulls me over to the corner, waving off a couple of black-clad assistants. "I have to ask you," he says in a low voice, "is something wrong with Geoff? He seems upset with me. Did I offend him? I like to tease him, you know, but it's all in fun. It's just too delicious to poke the straight boys with sticks. But I have been known to go too far. Can you talk to him?"

I scan the room for Geoff. The sight of him makes me uncomfortable and anxious; it reminds me of the morning after an ill-advised pickup at the pub. *Prince Charming always looks like a frog when the beer goggles come off,* as Zoe used to say. But the feeling seems misplaced and more than a little unfair here: I'm suffering for my sins without the preceding pleasure of any transgression. Geoff knows I'm here, which is evident from the fact that he hasn't so much as glanced in my direction. He's not going to make this easy for me. "It's not you, Claudio," I say. "Geoff had a bad week. I think the best thing would be to go a bit easy on him today. Let's just give him some space, OK? I don't think it would help for me to speak to him."

"Ah," says Claudio. "That poor man. I always suspected that he played for your team—your team specifically, I mean. I take it that things were said?"

"It's a little awkward," I say.

"It's not your fault," says Claudio. "Better out than in and all that.

He'll get over it." He turns and points to one of the assistants hovering a discreet distance away. "Kara, can you fill Sophie in on the shoot schedule? I'm going to get started with the doctor. Showtime, people!"

Kara shows me her clipboard. "We have a three-hour shooting schedule," she says. "We're doing the first hour in here for the interviews with Dr. Waldron and the patient. We're working from a basic script, but we're still going to use an interviewer to make the conversation as natural as possible. We'll edit out the interviewer and select the best clips in the studio. Geoff is doing the interviews, since he's done the script prep. Then we're spending a couple of hours up on the oncology ward. We've got permission from a couple of families to film them interacting with Dr. Waldron, and then we're going into the recreation room for some shots of the kids playing. We've got a couple of people up there explaining the process and timing to the parents and handing out waiver forms."

"You guys are amazing," I say. "What's the timeline for production?"

"It depends a bit on the quality of the interviews, but Claudio's got the editing team booked in for the rest of today and tomorrow. He says we'll have it to you on Monday."

"Quiet, please!" Claudio commands.

"Why don't you wait in the green room?" says Kara, as she escorts me out.

The green room is an office down the hall, which is empty except for one teenage girl sitting at the desk, typing on a laptop. She's very pale and tall, with lively brown eyes and a red bandanna covering her head.

"You must be Taylor," I say. "I'm Sophie. Thanks so much for agreeing to help us out with the shoot."

"That's OK," she says. "Do you work here?"

"Yes. I'm the director of communications for the hospital, so my office is kind of in charge of the shoot. They're just starting with Dr. Waldron now, so they'll probably call you in a half hour or so."

"Director of communications," she says. "Do you mind if I ask you a few questions?"

"Go ahead."

"I'm going to take some notes."

"OK."

"What does a director of communications do?"

"Can I ask you a question first? Why are you taking notes?"

"I'm doing some research on different careers and what people like about them."

"For a school project?" I ask.

"Not exactly," says Taylor, "but it could be, I guess, if that makes a difference to you."

"No," I say. "I was just making conversation. I work with a group of people to produce materials that tell the outside world what the Baxter is all about. Those materials include our website, annual reports to people who give us money, public statements about our research that we hope will get picked up by the media, and then various projects like the one we're doing today that are designed to encourage people in the community to support us financially. And then I do a bunch of other things that aren't really part of my job at all, like organizing fund-raising events, and sitting on committees, and things like that."

"Do you like it?"

"Sometimes," I say. "I like working with other people who are good at what they do—and the Baxter is full of people like that, which is unusual. I like being part of something that matters in a larger way in the world. Most people aren't like Dr. Waldron. We don't save lives at work. But it's nice to feel that your work makes it easier for people like Dr. Waldron to save lives, if you follow me."

"So why do you only like it sometimes?" Taylor asks.

"I've been doing it for a while," I say. "Some days I think I'd like to do something new. And sometimes I worry that I spend too much time on my work and not enough with my kids. Or I worry that when I'm with them, they aren't getting me at my best." Taylor doesn't say anything but she isn't taking notes. It's a bad sign. I try for a better answer.

"Have you heard of work-life balance?" I ask her.

"Sure," she says. "Do you have it?"

"I don't think anyone has it. I don't think it exists." Taylor starts typing as I warm to my subject. "In lots of ways we're lucky," I say. "Women don't have to choose between having a family and having a career. We can have it all, right? That's the promise. But the reality? It's hard, every single day. So you have to *want* it. And when I have a bad day at work, I wonder if I want it badly enough." I am very grateful that there is no one else in the room to hear me unburden myself on a fifteen-year-old cancer survivor. It feels like yet another new low.

"So what about you?" I ask. "What's the reason for your research project?"

"For years, people asked me what I wanted to be when I grew up," she says. "And then I got cancer. I knew it was serious when I realized that it had been months since anyone had asked me that question. But now I'm supposed to be cured, so maybe people will start asking me again. And I wanted to have a good answer this time."

"What's your answer?"

She smiles. "I'm still doing my research, but I think I want to be a kindergarten teacher."

"Really?" I say. "I mean, that's a great job, but . . ."

"But I'm so bright that I could do anything I want?"

"Yes."

"I bet you thought I'd want to be a doctor so that I could help people the way I've been helped?"

"No," I say, although this is exactly what I was thinking.

"I've spent the last two years in hospitals. I don't want to work in one. But I've been doing an art program with the kids in the oncology ward every week when I'm not too sick to do it, and I like being around them. Also you get the summers off."

"You can always have kids," I say, and then regret it as soon as my brain catches up with my mouth.

But Taylor is made of tough stuff. "Probably not," she says. "I've had a lot of chemo."

Kara appears in the doorway. "You're up, Taylor," she says.

"Do you mind if I come and watch you?" I ask.

"That would be great," she says. "You can tell me how my hair looks." She grins. "That was a joke."

Back on the set, Claudio is fluttering around Carolyn, who looks embarrassed and delighted at the same time. "Brilliant!" he effuses. "Spectacular! You should get an agent. Your bone structure is sublime."

"Claudio, this is Taylor," I say.

"You aren't going to wear that bandanna, are you?" Claudio wrinkles his nose.

"No, I'm going commando," she says. "But you probably have to do something about the shine."

"Omar!" shouts Claudio, and Omar scuttles over with his makeup cart and settles Taylor under the lights.

"The shoot's going well so far?"

"Couldn't be better," says Claudio. "That doctor gave us a dozen perfect clips. No tics, no spitting, no ums—she'll be a dream to edit. And Geoff is a genius. Here he comes now."

"Hi there," I say. "Claudio was just singing your praises."

Geoff can't meet my eye. "Thanks," he says.

"I really appreciate everything you've done to make this happen," I say. "I know it hasn't been easy." And I'm saved from having to say anything else, as Claudio calls for quiet, and Geoff takes his seat facing Taylor.

It's strangely restful watching the shoot. Everything is out of my hands now, and still unfolding as it should. And Claudio is right; Geoff is terrific. I trust him so completely that I don't often watch him work, and it's obvious that he's too seasoned to be my right-hand man any longer. I'm ashamed to realize how much has escaped my notice lately.

The interview wraps up, and Claudio issues orders to the crew for the second stage of the shoot on the ward. Taylor comes over to say good-bye.

"You were great," I say. "It's been a pleasure to meet you."

"You too," she says. "Thanks for being so honest."

I wince a little, feeling some residual shame at my oversharing. "No problem," I say.

Taylor shakes my hand. "I appreciated it, honestly," she says. "You'd be surprised how often adults lie to kids."

"Don't take it personally," I say. "They lie to themselves all the time too."

CHAPTER TWENTY-ONE

march 1995

I wake up on a beautiful spring morning, weeping. I've been crying every morning without fail for the past three weeks. There is something almost religious about it, like saying morning prayers. And I don't mind it, really, because the tears remind me that I haven't died as a result of Will's rejection. I'll only allow myself fifteen minutes, and then I'll force myself to get out of bed, eat, go to class or the library or the paper, and interact with the world in the way that other normal, living people do. I don't smile much, or laugh these days, but exams are coming up, so there's not a lot of levity in the library stacks; and red, swollen eyes are practically a fashion accessory at the newspaper office, evidence of the general pain of life. So no one notices that I've become a hollowed-out husk of my former self—other than A.J., that is, who keeps asking if I'm sick. I tell him I'm not, but I wonder if I'm right. The condition of my heart, broken as it is, won't be fatal, but it seems likely that it could be debilitating, chronic, and lifelong.

My tear-soaked letters to Paris have prompted more than one late-night call from a concerned Zoe, whose furious rants against Will do little to raise my spirits. Why should they? I have only myself to blame. After a glorious week in which Will and I got out of bed only to eat, watch movies, and visit his grandmother in the hospital, I was lulled into an insane belief that our relationship lacked permanence and stability only because we had failed to give words to it; whereas I can now see, too late, that it was nothing more than a hopelessly fragile bubble of sexual satisfaction that would vanish the second we tried to define it as something more. Which is, of course, exactly what I did.

It's a conversation that I have on an endless loop as I work my way through box after box of tissues: my head on his shoulder in this very bed, his arm curved around my back. I can tell by his breathing that he is about to fall asleep. I've restrained myself all week, but A.J. will be back tomorrow, and we need to agree on a common strategy. If it were up to me, I'd have Will take A.J. aside, as I imagine men do, and explain that we can no longer deny our attraction to each other, and that we hope he won't be uncomfortable with our new bedtime arrangements. But Will may have his own ideas on how to tell A.J., and I don't want to make things awkward for him.

So I say, "We need to tell A.J."

To which Will replies, "Tell him what?"

"About us, obviously. About this."

"What about this?"

I push myself up on my elbow so that I'm looking down at him. "He may not be the most observant guy in the world, but I think he's going to notice if his two roommates are sleeping together."

"I'm sure he would," says Will.

"So are you going to talk to him about it?"

Will sits up, swings his feet over the side of the bed, and starts to pull on the clothes that are scattered on the floor next to it. With his back to me, he says, "No. I'm not."

"You want me to do it?" I cringe at the thought.

"No."

"I don't understand," I say. "If we're seeing each other, I think we should tell him."

"We're not."

"We're not telling him?"

Will stands, dressed now, and looks down at me with an expression that I can't interpret, but that makes me want to cover myself with the sheet. "We're not seeing each other," he says. "Sophie, we've had a lot of fun this week, but we can't be . . ." He seems to search for a word, shrugs, and then says, "We need to stop now. We live together. We aren't going to tell A.J. because there won't be anything to tell him. We need to go back to the way things were."

There are tears streaming down my face and I don't trust myself to speak, so I just shake my head. There is nothing in Will's declaration that I accept. What he is suggesting violates everything that I believe about the nature of love. I've read my way through the literary pantheon devoted to unrequited love but, fundamentally, I've never truly believed that love can catch fire without an answering spark from its object. Can he really think that we could go back to the way things were before? Is it possible that I could have been altered so completely in the past week, reinvented as a person whose deepest purpose is to love and be loved by Will, while he has emerged unsullied, able to slip back into his life as if returning from vacation? Based on the way he's looking at me now, a soul-shriveling combination of pity and horror without a visible scrap of inner torment or regret, it appears that the answer is yes.

"Will," I croak, "I—"

He holds up a hand to ward me off. "Don't, Sophie." And he crosses the room in a few short steps and is out the door before I can say, "I love you."

I've said it since, many times. Whispered it in the dark, sobbed it into my pillow, but never to him. A.J. is confused about our relationship after all, but not because of any inappropriate affection; he can't understand why our necessary interactions are fraught with strained civility. Our family dinners are all business now, with either Will or me leaving the table at the earliest polite opportunity. It's desperately uncomfortable, and all of us are finding excuses to study later at the library in the evenings. Every day brings a new, searing wave of loss; Will has clearly decided, perhaps with good reason, that I will interpret even the most innocent gesture of friendship as evidence of deeper emotions, and so he keeps his distance. He pours himself a coffee without offering one to me, I have to ask him to pass the arts section of the paper, and he leaves the house without checking to see if I want to walk to campus with him. Each omission is a fresh rejection.

The telephone is ringing, but I don't answer it. It's a long-distance ring, so it's either my parents or A.J.'s parents, and I'm in no state to speak to mine. Someone else in the house picks it up eventually, and after a long while I hear footsteps padding along the hall and a knock at the door.

My adrenaline spikes: is it Will? But I hear A.J.'s voice instead. "Sophie? Can I come in?"

"Just a sec," I say, wiping my face and blowing my nose, sliding out of bed and wrapping myself in a bathrobe in a few economical movements. "Come on in."

A.J. opens the door slowly. He's still dressed for bed, too, in a college T-shirt and loose cotton pants, but there's nothing sleepy about him. His jaw is tight, his brow furrowed, and he stands in the doorway as if he would give anything to be somewhere else.

He clears his throat. "You need to call your mom," he says. "There's been an accident."

"What kind of accident?"

"It's your dad," he says. "You need to go home. I'll drive you."

"What happened?" I say.

"Just call your mom, Sophie."

I find that I can see everything in the room very clearly. There's dust swirling in the shafts of light from the gap in the curtains, and I think that it's been too long since I vacuumed in here. The specks whirl around me as I take four steps toward the door, until I'm standing right in front of A.J., and I say, "Tell me."

He straightens his shoulders, steeling himself, and says, "There was a car accident. He hit a patch of ice."

"Is he going to be OK?" I know the answer already but I want to hear A.J. say it. With his rumpled pajamas and messy brown hair, he is reassuringly solid. I know that whatever he says will be true.

"No," he says, and I feel the cold wash through me. A.J. steps in, reaches out; he's afraid I'll fall.

"I need to tell Will," I say.

"I'll tell him," says A.J. "I'm going to borrow his car. You get dressed and pack, OK? I'll be back in a few minutes."

"I want to see Will." I've held myself back for weeks, crushed myself into a tiny box of good behavior, and now my whole life has exploded, shattering all of my self-imposed boundaries. I don't care if I embarrass myself or Will now, and it's almost liberating.

"That's not a good idea, Sophie."

"You don't know anything!" The scream surprises both of us, but I can't seem to stop once I've started. "Get out of my way!"

He swallows hard, and then moves back so he's blocking the door completely. "Sophie," he says, "You don't want to see him right now." He closes his eyes briefly. "He's not alone."

"Oh," I say, and then I begin sobbing, great racking sobs that relieve the need to look at A.J. or think about Will, because all I can do is concentrate on gasping for air so that I don't die. I'm vaguely aware of voices in the hallway, and then my door closes and Lil appears next to me, wraps her arms around me, and sits me down on my bed.

"That's it," she says, stroking my hair. "Let it all go." And I do. I cry for all of the dreams that Will has disappointed—proposals and weddings and babies and a whole future together—and for all of the dreams that my mother realized and has now lost. I cry for all of the conversations that I never had with my dad, for the week that I should have spent with him and spent with Will instead, and for the knowledge that my memory of our time together, the pinnacle of my romantic life, is now fatally tainted with regret. I cry for all the ways in which my selfishness disgusts me: that I can even think about Will when my father is dead, that I haven't yet picked up the phone to call my devastated mother, that I screamed at A.J., who has been nothing but generous and dutiful, and that I'm channeling even a tiny fraction of my distress into the fact that Will has another girl in his room right now. I cry until I'm too tired to cry anymore, and then I say, "What will I do now?"

"Now you'll take a shower, which will prove to you that you are capable of feeling better than this." The certainty in her voice reminds me how much Lil has lost in her long life. "And while you're in the shower, I'll lay out some clothes for you, and then we'll pack them together, and then A.J. will drive you home in my car."

"That's not what I meant."

"I know," says Lil. "But it's the best advice I can give you. Just keep putting one foot in front of the other and, at some point, you'll realize that you feel less awful. That's the goal."

On the morning of my father's funeral, I sit in the front pew next to my mother, listening to the rustling and creaking of people filling the seats behind me. I keep my head down in an attitude of prayer to deter anyone from speaking to me. My legs feel thin under my black skirt, which I'm grateful to Lil for packing. Through my lashes I watch the blocks of colored light from the stained glass stretching across the stone floor, and I grip the folded papers in my lap. I've agreed to give the eulogy. My mother is a mess, my brother has never been much for verbal communication, and my dad's friends are all strong, silent types. The minister could do it, but we all know that my father didn't have a religious bone in his body. I'm not sure I can get through it.

The minister calls the congregation to order and we all stand for a hymn. I close my eyes. My mother shakes with silent sobs next to me. The music stops and I'm called up to the pulpit. I've asked to speak first. I settle my papers in front of me and adjust the microphone. I can't bear the sight of my mother's grief, so I pitch my gaze out toward the back of the church and catch my breath. The room is full, so full that people are standing up in the aisles near the exit. So many of my parents' friends and neighbors are here, of course, not just from Port Alice but from the city, and so are Mike's friends, and mine; for some reason this is unexpected, and painfully moving. It makes the whole experience achingly real: if all of these people have come to mourn, my father must really be dead.

I fight the choking tears in my throat and remember Lil's advice—one foot in front of the other—and I begin. "On behalf of my mother, Mary, and my brother, Mike, I want to thank all of you for being with us today. My father was taken from us much too young, and all of us feel robbed of the many years of his advice, companionship, and love that we assumed we would have. I want to thank everyone who has supported us since the accident. Many of you have come by the house to see us or bring us food, or have sent beautiful letters telling us what Dad meant to you, and we are grateful for all of these acts of kindness." So far, so good: the church is quiet. I brace myself to depart from the safe formality of the first paragraph. I stick to my text and don't look up.

"Dad was immensely talented in obvious and also unexpected ways. He was a brilliant student who became a brilliant lawyer. Many of his friends and colleagues were mystified when, almost a decade ago, he moved to Port Alice to become a small-town solicitor. There were those who thought he'd thrown his talents away. But Dad never doubted his decision. He was the most self-aware person I've ever known. He knew what he wanted, and he was utterly unmoved by considerations of public opinion." I risk a glance up and see Lil sitting on an aisle; the seats beside her are empty. She smiles at me, and it strikes me that my dad would have gotten quite a kick out of her. The thought makes me sad.

"Dad believed that the most important things in life were simple—love of family, investment in community, self-respect, and the reward of good work done with integrity. For him, these things came into focus much more clearly when he was out of the city. He was at home in the country. He was in his element here."

Almost done. I take a final breath and launch into the last paragraph. "Of all the things my dad valued, he treasured his family above all. His love for us—my mother, my brother, and me—was uncomplicated and unconditional. He wanted nothing more than our happiness. He taught us so much about how to live." And now my voice cracks as I fight to hang on, and I manage to squeak, "We'll carry him with us always," and I run down the stairs, crash down in the pew, and bury my face in my hands, as my mother whispers in a thick voice, "He would have been so proud of you today."

The rest of the service passes mercifully quickly, and soon we're spilling out onto the front lawn. Few people linger; the pale sunlight doesn't cut through the harsh wind, and most of the guests are planning to come to our house this afternoon anyway. But Lil is standing at the bottom of the stairs, a little off to the side, surrounded by A.J., Will, and Zoe. I promptly burst into tears again and throw myself into Zoe's arms. I'm so happy to see her that I almost forget for a few seconds how incredibly wretched I feel, and from the expression of satisfaction on Lil's face as she watches us, I wonder if she's responsible.

"How did you know?"

"Lil called me," Zoe confirms. "She tracked me down somehow and got me on a flight."

"Thank you so much," I say to Lil and give her a hug.

"You're welcome, sweet girl," says Lil. "You were very brave in there." Tears well up in my eyes again, and I see Will and A.J. shrinking back collectively.

"Will you come back to the house?" I ask.

"No, my dear. The boys and I are going to head home. But Zoe's going to stay with you until tomorrow if you want her to." Lil shivers. "I'm going to wait in the car, boys." She squeezes my hand. "I'm so sorry, Sophie. I'll see you when you come home."

A.J. moves to follow her, but I stop him. "Wait," I say. "I never thanked you properly for everything you did for me the other day. You were a really good friend." And before he can deflect me I reach up and give him a kiss on the cheek. He blushes scarlet, mumbles his condolences, and rushes after Lil, leaving Will and Zoe and me in a huddle. I haven't been this close to Will in weeks, and as thrilled as I am to see Zoe, I want her to vanish for five minutes.

"Zoe," I say, pointing to the waiting black limousine. "Can you let Mike know that you're coming with us?"

"Sure," she says, giving me an odd look, but complying.

I'm getting colder by the second, and my family is waiting. Today of all days, my pathetic drama with Will should be banished from my mind. But he's here, on the worst day of my life, and if he won't take me in his arms, he's not climbing back in the car without giving me something more than a pat on the shoulder. "You came," I say.

"Lil thought you'd want me to. Was she wrong?"

"No," I say, trying not to be hurt that his presence here is not entirely his own doing. I remind myself that excessive emotion, like hospitals, makes him squeamish, and smother a fleeting sense of irritation. "It's good to see you."

"I don't know what to say, Sophie," he says. "I'm sorry about your dad. I'm sorry about everything."

"Me too," I say. And then, knowing that he won't deny me anything today, I say, "You owe me a conversation. I want to talk to you about what happened between us when I come back. Promise me."

He looks down at his shoes. "I promise," he says. I wonder, uncharitably, if he has his fingers crossed behind his back, and before I can say anything else, Zoe sprints up, panting.

"Your mom wants to get going, Sophie." She tucks an arm through mine. "Come on. It's freezing out here." She pulls me away from Will, toward the car.

"See you, Will," she calls over her shoulder. He waves at her, but his eyes are on me.

"Take care, Sophie," he says.

"You poor baby," she says. "I missed a lot this year, didn't I?" I sniff, and she says hastily, "Listen, I've got an idea. I want you to come and stay with me in Paris this summer. Come for your birthday. You'll love it there and it will give you something to look forward to. Sound good?"

I smile at her, and I think, *This is what Lil was talking about.* Someday, maybe in Paris, I'll be able to smile without finding it strange that I still can, without feeling the corners of my mouth turn up and wondering how the muscles move of their own accord. "It sounds perfect," I say.

CHAPTER TWENTY-TWO

saturday, december 7, 2013

I follow the film crew up to the ward and stand around for a while until it becomes clear that I am not needed. I touch Geoff's arm to get his attention and he jumps back as if stung; his involuntary reaction makes both of us feel terrible.

"Do you think I could go up to my office for a while? It looks like things are under control."

"It's going great," Geoff says stiffly. "Really, Sophie, you don't need to be here. Go home. Be with your family." It feels like the rebuke that it is, and I don't know what to say, so we stand there for an awkward moment or two until I can't stand it anymore and beat a hasty retreat. I wonder how many parts of my life I can screw up in one week. From the vantage point of Saturday morning, it looks like one for the record books.

I'm standing in front of the elevator, awash in indecision, when my cell phone rings. It's Zoe.

"I know you're busy," she says, "but when can you get out of there? I need an intervention."

I hesitate only for a fraction of a second, realizing that I can't afford to lose any more karmic points by being a fair-weather friend, and that if I meet Zoe for lunch in her time of need, I might actually earn some back. I also know that conventions of female friendship demand that I deliver a full and frank airing of the Will issue in the wake of my disappearance at dinner last night. That and, let's face it, I'm desperate to get away from Geoff and Claudio and everything to do with the Baxter Children's Hospital. Plus the idea of going home and dealing with the aftermath of my fight with Jesse makes me want to put my head in my hands.

"I'm leaving now," I say. "Where do you want to meet?"

"We're going to the Four Seasons," she says. "They have a really expensive wine list and Richard is paying."

I look at my watch. "Isn't it a bit early?"

"Nonsense," says Zoe. "By the time you get here it will practically be lunchtime."

"Are we eating lunch?"

"If you want," she says indifferently.

When I arrive at the restaurant, Zoe is already working her way through an impressive-looking bottle of red.

"Are we celebrating or commiserating?"

"A little of both," says Zoe. "I kicked Richard out last night."

"Wow," I say. "For good?"

"Oh, yes."

"Oh my God," I say. "This is huge. I'm so sorry, Zoe."

"Don't be sorry," she says. "I know you never liked him."

"Zoe, I . . ."

She holds up a hand. "You were right. He was an arrogant, humorless bastard."

I'm in dangerous territory here. A breakup is a fragile thing in its early days, and I know from bitter experience that the friend who shares fully in the piling on of insults can find herself shivering in cold and lonely isolation while the once-again happy couple basks in the afterglow of reunion sex. In such moments, therefore, it is critical to be mindful of all possible outcomes, and to employ a contextual filter to any remarks about the maligned partner's conduct that you might be tempted to make. "I never said that," I say.

Zoe laughs. "I admire your caution," she says. "But you can relax. There is no prospect of reconciliation. When I got home last night, earlier than expected, there was a Prius in the driveway. So I let myself in the back door and kind of tiptoed into the living room, and surprise! There's Richard making out with some girl on the couch. And I recognized her but I couldn't quite place her, you know, and then I realized that it was the salesgirl from Hiker's Haven who sold us the kayak for Richard's birthday."

"Mr. Intellectual is banging a girl who sells kayaks for a living?" I say, as my filter slips ever so slightly.

"Oh, yes," says Zoe. "And now we understand the sudden interest in camping. Can you believe it?"

"God, what a jerk," I say, filter now entirely disengaged.

"That's more like it," says Zoe. "But wait, there's more. According to Richard, this is my fault because I kept him in a 'box of urbanity' and prevented him from accessing his 'primitive soul.'"

"I don't even know what that means," I say.

"It means that I never have to listen to him whine about his sinuses again. I never have to pretend to like conceptual jazz or experimental theater. *He* can figure out what to buy his odious parents for Christmas. I am *so* finished with all of his bullshit." Zoe takes a long drink and looks thoughtful. "You know, it's funny," she says. "I always thought there was a possibility that Richard would leave me, but I never thought it would be for some pretty little dimwit."

I adjust my face into what I think is a neutral but supportive expression.

Zoe laughs. "You still think he's gay?"

"I never said that either!" I say, horrified.

"True. You never did, but you have a lousy poker face. It never bothered me in the least, though, because your instincts on that front are hopeless, as you demonstrated again this week."

"Fair comment," I concede.

"Honestly, one of the only things I'll really miss about being married to Richard is watching you try to figure out how to like him," says

Zoe. I start to protest and she puts up her hand. "I'm not criticizing. I've really appreciated the effort you put into it all these years." She smiles. "I think I was always afraid that Richard would leave me for someone more creative or intellectual or political. Someone more like you, actually. Book smart rather than street smart."

I bristle at the backhanded compliment. "What's that supposed to mean?"

"It means that you can speak intelligently about virtually any topic but have trouble seeing things that are right in front of you."

"Such as?" I say sharply.

"Take your pick: the fact that your office lapdog is in love with you, or that your husband is being pursued by his business partner, or that you're still half in love with Will Shannon, or that you're having a full-fledged midlife crisis," says Zoe.

"I'm not having a midlife crisis. You're projecting. I'm not the one leaving my husband," I say unkindly.

"I'm not trying to be mean," says Zoe. "I don't deny that I married a flaming asshole—clearly a mistake. But aside from that admittedly large issue, I'm happier with my life than you are."

My indignation evaporates in the sure knowledge that Zoe is right about this. "You know what?" I say, as if changing the subject, "I was sitting in a meeting this week and I had this fantasy that I quit my job to stay home with the kids."

"I suspect that would be a bad result all around," says Zoe. "You might want to consider some options in between. In the meantime, though, what's going on with you and Will?"

It's a good question. If I read back a transcript of everything that Will and I have said to each other in the past several days, there would be no outward sign of the tectonic shift occurring beneath the surface. But since his return, my world has been clearer and sharper and more colorful, as if he's adjusted the dial to eliminate the gray static around me. "I have no idea," I say. "It's very confusing. He offered me a job."

"What job?"

"Running the Baxter Foundation with a view to taking it over from Lil."

"Interesting," says Zoe. "What does Jesse say about it?"

"He thinks it sounds interesting," I lie.

"And what do you think?"

"It's a dream job," I say. "It's all the things I love to do, and almost none of the things I hate, not to mention better pay and way more autonomy and flexibility."

"But it feels like a handout?" Zoe guesses.

"It *is* a handout," I say. "They're only offering it to me because of the personal relationship I have with Lil."

"Does that have to be a bad thing?" asks Zoe. "Is it absolutely necessary that you earn everything by yourself without any help from anyone else? They know and like you, yes, but they wouldn't want you if you weren't capable of doing a fantastic job."

"Possibly," I say. "But then there's the issue of working for Will. He's the chair of the board. I'd report to him, at least technically. And I'm not sure that's smart."

"Because?"

"You know why."

"Tell me anyway."

"Because of what happened the year you were in Paris. Because it's never been resolved or discussed or even acknowledged between us. Because he makes me feel like I'm twenty all over again whenever I see him. Because it drives me insane that I still don't know what's going on in his head and probably never will. Because for all of these reasons, I'm in a state of complete anxiety when he's around, and I don't want to have that kind of relationship with my boss."

"OK," says Zoe. "Let's focus on the anxiety. I have a theory about that."

"You don't say."

"I think that you are terrified of really examining your feelings for Will, because you think that if you do, you'll discover that you married the wrong man." I half rise from my seat, and she holds up a hand. "Let me finish. I also think that you're mistaken about Will. According to my theory, you married the right man."

I exhale slowly, beating back my flight instinct. For all of her new age zaniness, I have to admit that Zoe is unexpectedly perceptive, and I'm willing to seize on any theory, no matter how implausible, if it validates the core decision of my adult life. "Enlighten me," I say.

"The idea is that all women have a dominant romantic archetype that drives their choice of partners. Most women are also influenced by one or more secondary archetypes, which can complicate their choices. I think that's what's happening with you."

"Uh-huh," I say, by which I mean, *Is there a reason why self-help devotees are never content with mere self-help? Is the process of salvation incomplete unless you commit yourself to showing others the light?*

"I've identified six major archetypes. You, for example, are dominated by the Jane Austen. The Jane Austen's romantic narrative is about rescue, but Jane won't agree to be rescued until the rescuer demonstrates that he recognizes her as an intellectual equal. She's like Cinderella with a university degree. She wants the Prince to see her for who she really is inside."

"You should write this stuff down," I say, by which I mean, *Carl Jung is spinning in his grave.*

"You also have a strong Amelia Earhart, which means that you are looking for an impossible challenge in love. You're attracted to the danger and sheer unlikelihood of success. You're determined to beat the odds or die trying, metaphorically. It's your Amelia Earhart that can't let go of Will Shannon."

"What does the theory say about you?" I ask.

"My dominant archetype is the Jerry Maguire." She gives me a withering look. "Don't laugh. My romantic narrative is that I'm looking for someone to complete me. To summarize a very long story, my role in my family was to be the pretty, sociable one, so that my brother Zack could be the smart one, which he needed to be since he was pretty dorky. But my romantic choices have all been about trying to find someone to help me reclaim the smart side."

I am reminded, not for the first time, how little we understand the people we most love. "Zoe," I say, "I've always thought of you as one of the smartest people I know."

Zoe blinks hard and squeezes my hand, and then continues. "I was flattered that Richard thought I was intellectual enough to share his life. It made me feel whole. And my choice was reinforced by my secondary archetypes. Like you, I've got a lot of Amelia Earhart in me, and Richard was always a challenge. But he also appealed to my Mother Teresa." I bite my lip, taking in Zoe's flawless makeup, her Victoria's Secret model hair, her designer skinny jeans, and the shimmering rope of semiprecious stones looped casually around her neck, but I don't laugh. "Mother Teresa's romantic narrative is about finding a partner who genuinely needs her and who can be transformed by her love. I thought I could do that for Richard. I thought his sarcasm was a defense mechanism against vulnerability. I thought his coldness was a fear of expressing his true feelings. I thought his selfishness would melt away when he realized that I wanted to take care of him. I thought he was a Jerry Maguire. But he's actually a Material Girl."

"I thought the archetypes only apply to women," I say, mostly to avoid engaging with the topic of Richard as Material Girl.

"It's a work in progress," she says. "The Material Girl is the opposite of the Mother Teresa. Her narrative is about finding a partner who meets all of her needs. She's doesn't value permanence. Relationships are commodities to her. Once she extracts everything useful from the relationship, she moves on."

"Is that what happened with Richard?"

"I think so. In hindsight, things started changing when my career took off. He was cranky about my hours and my travel schedule, but I assumed it was because I wasn't around to go to dinner parties and openings with him. I thought he missed my company, but he was uncomfortable with my success. He wanted me to be smart and successful enough to make him look good, but not enough to overshadow him. Through our entire marriage, I thought I was evolving into the partner he wanted, but what I was really doing was destroying what he loved best about our relationship."

"Which was?"

"Hero worship. When I stopped providing it, he decided to move on. And judging from his new girlfriend, he's figured out that he's going to have to move further down the food chain to get that kind of attention."

"Far be it from me to defend Richard, but I don't think your relationship would have lasted this long if that was all it had going for it. You *did* share common interests, not just the ones that Richard dictated. Maybe not conceptual jazz, I'll give you that, but lots of other things that kept you going in the same direction all these years."

"I guess," she says, sadly. "But looking at it now, it seems like our shared purpose was in trying to compensate for each other's insecurities. It wasn't a strong enough foundation to withstand a shock, and it was never going to fill me up or make me feel complete, even if Richard hadn't made the first move out the door."

We sit in silence for a few moments. "Another bottle?" asks Zoe, and waves to the waiter.

"What's Megan?" I ask, changing the subject.

"Sorry?"

"Megan. What archetype is she?"

Zoe laughs, and it's good to see. "A Material Girl–Amelia Earhart combo. I'm not sure what the proportions are."

"Laura?"

"Jane Austen–Mother Teresa."

"Sara?"

"Mother Teresa–Jerry Maguire."

"Nora?"

"Pure Jane Austen. But I'm still not done with you," says Zoe. "I got off track. We were discussing your love triangle."

"Don't call it that."

Zoe ignores me. "As I was saying, you are a Jane Austen. And Jesse, whatever his faults, is your intellectual equal as well as being a good husband, father, and all-around nice guy."

"Agreed. So why does Will Shannon have any hold on me when I have a perfect husband, according to your theory?"

"Three reasons. There's your Amelia Earhart, as we discussed. Will has always been fundamentally unattainable, which makes him irresistible to you. Then there's your other secondary archetype, the Groucho Marx." I burst out laughing, but Zoe's exposition continues unabated. "You don't want to join any club that would have you as a member. Jesse chose you. Therefore there must be something wrong with him."

"And?"

"And lastly, part of you believes that you settled for Jesse because you don't see that he rescued you."

"He didn't."

"Of course he did," says Zoe. "He rescued you from Will."

I don't have a snappy recovery line, so I change the subject. "I didn't get a chance to tell you that we hired a new VP yesterday."

"Barry the Blowfish's friend?"

I smile. "Happily, no. It's a woman. Lil staged a coup on the committee. Barry nearly had a stroke."

The wine arrives, and Zoe raises her glass. "To the Blowfish," she says. "Karma's a bitch."

"Amen to that," I say, and we clink.

"Do you have a lawyer yet?" I ask.

"I'm doing some research," she says. "I'm looking for someone with a scorched-earth, retributive, make-him-wish-he-never-met-me kind of approach. Let me know if you have any recommendations."

"I'll think on it," I say.

"I meant to ask you," says Zoe. "Have you filled your prescription yet?"

"Yes."

"I'm not talking about the one for your sinus infection."

"Oh," I say. "Not yet. I've been busy."

"You're stalling."

"I'll get around to it," I say defensively.

"No time like the present," says Zoe. "I'll escort you to the pharmacy myself. But first, we deal with more pressing priorities. Trust Dr. Zoe. She knows what you need."

Half an hour later, I'm teetering in front of a full-length mirror in black strappy stiletto heels, with a zipper up the back. Zoe looks on approvingly. "Perfect!" she declares.

"These shoes aren't really my style, Zoe," I say. "When would I wear them?"

"First of all, these are not merely shoes, Sophie. These are fuck-me shoes," says Zoe.

The clerk nods. "It's an industry term," he affirms.

"Second of all, you will wear them out tonight to the party, and after that you'll wear them whenever you feel like it, which will be a lot more often than you can imagine right now."

"Tell me the truth. Are these made by young girls in developing countries who are forced to work in factories instead of going to school?"

"I seriously doubt it," says Zoe. "They're really expensive."

"Zoe, I can't afford to spend a fortune on shoes."

"You can't put a price on the health of your marriage. You need them. It's an emergency situation."

"About that," I say. "According to you, I've found my perfect mate. So how does your theory explain the fact that it's not exactly romance central at our place these days?"

"My theory just tells you if you got off to the right start, Sophie. You still have to *try*."

"Shoes are not going to fix whatever is wrong with my marriage."

Zoe sighs. "I've known you for twenty-two years, and still you underestimate the power of shoes. Have I achieved nothing?"

"I'm drunk. My judgment is impaired. I'll think about it and come back another day."

The clerk looks concerned.

"You will not," says Zoe, pulling out a credit card and handing it to the clerk. "The shoes are on Richard. Consider it repayment for all of the times you had to listen to him go on about the marginalization of organic cheese farmers."

"Are you really telling me that the perfect marriage is within my grasp with the help of sexy shoes and antidepressants, Zoe? I thought we'd dispensed with that particular fantasy sometime after the 1950s."

"You might also try some red lipstick," says Zoe. "The no-makeup thing isn't really working for you." She puts an arm around my shoulder and gives me a squeeze. "Relax. This isn't an intervention for Jesse. It's for you. You need to get out of your own way and start having more fun. I mean, what do you want that you don't already have?"

CHAPTER TWENTY-THREE

saturday, december 7, 2013

Standing in front of the full-length mirror in my bedroom, I think about Zoe's question. What *do* I want? I have a long and growing list of things I don't want, like turning forty and having a fifteen-year-old cancer survivor know more about achieving happiness than I do, but my desires are harder to pinpoint. It's more efficient to focus on need, and what I need at this moment is something to wear to Lil's party.

I rummage around in my closet, considering and rejecting a host of blameless garments by throwing them on the bed. As the closet empties, though, I start to find treasures that I'd forgotten I owned. I slide my grandmother's mink coat along the rail, and there, just behind it, I find the old Dior dress. The tailoring is stunning, and it occurs to me that it's probably worth some money. I hold it out in front of me and wonder if I can still fit into it. I slip it over my head, tentatively, but it hangs in a way that assures me it's not ridiculous to try to do it up. I have to struggle with the zipper at the waist, but not for long, and with a final tug at the nape of my neck, I turn and examine myself in the mirror. The dress is curvier than I remembered, but no one would say it doesn't fit. It's womanly, for sure, but not matronly, so I dig through my accessories drawer and find a triple strand of vintage crystal beads. Then I turn my attention to my face: mascara and blush and red lipstick and some liquid liner so ancient that I'm slightly worried about its safety. And then I slide into Zoe's shoes and fasten the straps. I'm assessing the finished product in the mirror when I see Jesse appear behind me.

"The babysitter's here," he says.

He looks exhausted. I could be brittle and polite, which is my standard post-fight stance. But any residual anger I feel is overshadowed by a sickening sense of remorse. How could I have been so distracted that I failed to notice what was happening with his business? It's like I've been cutting class on our marriage lately, only to be hit with a surprise quiz worth twenty percent of the final grade.

"Are we OK?" I ask.

"I honestly don't know," he says.

"Do you want to talk about it?" I ask.

"Not even a little bit," he says, coolly. "You look very nice. Let's try to have a good time. I'm going to call a cab."

Our taxi pulls up in front of Lil's house and I get out and stand for a moment on the sidewalk while Jesse pays the driver. The past feels palpable tonight, and I can almost see my twenty-year-old self bounding up the front stairs and reaching into my pocket for my key. I wonder what she would think of my life now. Jesse breaks my reverie. "It's cold out here, Soph. Let's go in."

The door is unlocked and we let ourselves in. The house is packed with people of all ages, most of whom I don't recognize at all. "Do you want to take our coats upstairs?" he says. "I'll try to find us some drinks." He turns without meeting my eye and heads for the kitchen.

I find the coatroom at the end of the second-floor hall, my old bedroom, and I hear Lil's unmistakable voice behind me.

"Taking a trip down memory lane?"

I turn. "Hi, Lil," I say. She is radiant in silk palazzo pants and a beaded jacket.

"Come upstairs for a minute," she says.

"I should get back to Jesse." Will has obviously told her about our conversation, or at least the part of it that concerns her. And tonight, I'm in no condition to withstand the full onslaught of her persuasion.

"I won't keep you long," she promises, managing, despite my intentions, to spirit me upstairs and into her apartment.

"Have a seat," she says, disappearing for a minute and then returning with two champagne glasses and a small bottle. "We need to toast our great victory!" We clink glasses and drink. "Thank you for your help," she says.

"It was my pleasure," I say, warily. "Margaret will be fabulous."

"And are you going to stay and work with her?"

I sigh inwardly. Trust Lil to get straight to the point. "I haven't decided yet."

"So William told me. The foundation job would be perfect for you, Sophie. I practically designed it for you. You need a change. What's the obstacle?"

I hesitate. "I'd be reporting to you and Will. I have a suspicion that it might be too . . . close."

"Too close to me, or too close to Will?"

I parry. "Independence is important to me," I say.

"Hmmm." Lil stands. "Let me show you something," she says.

We go into her bedroom. She sits down on a bench facing the blue portrait above the bed and pats the seat next to her. I sit.

"What do you think?" she asks.

"It's gorgeous," I say, hoping that we are talking about the painting.

"It's a portrait of me," she says. "It was painted in 1950, when I was twenty-two, the year before I was married." She pauses. "I've never told anyone that."

"Oh." I can understand why. The painting is intensely intimate, and knowing that Lil is the subject makes me feel uncomfortably voyeuristic. She glances at me and continues.

"I hired Isaac to give me painting lessons. He had a studio near the university and took private students to pay his expenses. He was an extraordinary talent. I insisted that he paint me." She smiles. "He was scandalized."

"Why?"

"My parents were well-off society people, and he was a struggling Jewish artist. He had seen much more of the world than I had. His family had been through terrible things during the war. You probably know that he changed his name to Wallace from Weinberg." I nod. "He wanted people to notice his art, but he was a very private person. He had no appetite for defying social conventions."

"You did?"

"I was an incurable romantic. And I was madly in love with him. I would have run off with him, happily, and turned my back on my family and all of the comforts of my life."

"But you married Monty," I say.

"Isaac didn't return my feelings. He finally agreed to paint me, but that was all it was. And if I couldn't have him, it didn't matter to me who I married. I thought I might as well make my parents happy." She sighs. "I was very young, although I didn't appreciate it at the time. I thought I would feel numb for the rest of my life."

I contemplate the raw sensuality of the figure in the painting and the lush flowers blooming behind her, in throbbing shades of red. Everywhere the canvas vibrates with passionate emotion. How could the creator have been indifferent to the subject and still have produced such a painting? "Are you sure he didn't love you?" I say.

"No," she says. "I've been looking for an answer to that question in this painting for the past sixty years."

"And?"

"And I've come to the conclusion that the line between unrequited and unresolved love doesn't matter that much. Both leave scars."

I can see that we're not talking just about Lil and her painter any longer. "And when you have those scars, shouldn't you keep your distance from the person who gave them to you? Shouldn't you, at the very least, avoid taking a job working for him?"

"It all depends," she says. "What if it's the right job? If you didn't take it, you might be giving that person just as much influence over you as you fear he would have if you took it."

"Food for thought," I say. My throat feels tight all of a sudden.

I stand and she does too, putting her hands gently on my shoulders and turning me so that I face the full-length mirror on the wall opposite. "I always liked that dress on you," she says. "But it fits you better now than it did then."

I clear my throat and try for levity. "It's the babies," I say. "I'm fatter now."

"You're a woman now," she says. "And this is a dress for a woman, not a girl." She squeezes my shoulder. "The past is always with us," she says, gesturing to the painting. "But it doesn't have to drive all of our decisions. Scars or not, you need to live your life. Shall we go back to the party?"

We walk down together to the second-floor landing and look down at the crowd, friends of Lil's representing every age and stage of life, and all of them honoring her request to dress in their holiday finery. My eyes are drawn to a contingent of impossibly young-looking guests who can only be Lil's boarders and their friends. The men, having made an early start on the free alcohol, are clustered in packs, the most significant concentration being in front of the television in the den, which is now set to a football game. The women, vibrating at a much higher frequency, flutter about, cheeks flushed with champagne, tossing their hair and giggling and looking over their shoulders at the men, who are engaged far more deeply in the sport on-screen than the one playing out in the room. The mating ritual reminds me of my early anthropological studies of my roommates, and I smile. "I can see why you never tire of having tenants," I say.

"Riveting, isn't it?" asks Lil. "My young friends give me such a healthy perspective on life."

Against my better judgment, I say, "That time in my life feels more present right now than it has in years. I used to say that you couldn't pay me to relive university life. I was so anxious about the future all the time, terrified that one misstep would condemn me to a life of lonely nights watching movies in a crappy apartment, folding sweaters for a living."

"And now?"

"And now I remember how vivid it all was—even how things smelled and tasted. I think I was more alive then."

"That's the hole in the middle," says Lil.

"Sorry?"

"My cousin Eleanor used to call your stage of life 'the donut years.' The first half of life is about getting as far away from your past as you can. And then, just when you've established yourself as a full-fledged adult, a hole opens up in the middle of life and the past comes rushing back in. By the time you're my age, if you aren't careful, the past is more real than the present."

"What do I do?" I ask.

"You make your peace with it," she says, and we watch the crowd below for a few moments in silence. I pick out a few people that I recognize: Marvin Shapiro from the Baxter, and a collection of writers, artists, and actors that have been part of Lil's circle for decades. Jesse is in the thick of it, talking to Margaret, and to Will.

"Margaret's here?" I'm a bit surprised. "That was nice of you. You wanted to welcome her to the fold?"

"Not exactly," she says. "I've known Margaret for years. Marvelous woman. I just didn't think I would mention it while the whole search business was going on."

Not for the first time tonight, I wonder how well I know Lil. Jesse looks up and waves hesitantly.

"I'll tell you one thing," says Lil. "That one has been madly in love with you since the first time he laid eyes on you."

"You think?"

"I know. Hold on to him with both hands."

"Are you giving advice?"

"Certainly not," she says. "I never give advice. It's rarely useful and always boring. Now, come and meet my tenants." We make our way down the stairs and into a crowd of young people. "Here's my current crop, full-time and itinerant," she says merrily. "Aren't they adorable?"

They are, too, and a couple of them blush at Lil's gentle reference to their status as regular evening guests. "Introduce yourselves," Lil says. "I need to do my rounds."

I turn my attention to a young woman with a diamond stud in her nose and jet-black hair that can't possibly be natural. She holds out her hand. "Chelsea Moss. Full-time, not itinerant."

"Sophie Whelan," I say. There's something familiar about Chelsea's delicate bone structure. "Moss?" I ask.

She sighs and says in a resigned tone, "You've met my mother?"

"Janelle?"

"That's the one," she says, grudgingly.

"No kidding!" I say. "You must be the one who went to Harvard."

Chelsea snorts. "Is she still telling people that?"

"That you went to Harvard?" I ask. "Didn't you?"

"I interviewed at Harvard. I think it's safe to say that it was a more significant event in my mother's life than it was in mine. We did mock interviews every weekend for months beforehand. She grilled the parents of every kid she knew who had interviewed at an Ivy League school so that she could anticipate the questions and prepare detailed answers for me." Chelsea rolls her eyes. "She's a little controlling. I think she may have blocked out the fact that I went to music school instead."

"So," I say, casually, "family dinners were a big deal in your house growing up?"

"Not in the sense of being the most significant event of my life, no," she says. "Dropping out of music school, moving to New York, and starting my own band was." She gives me a sidelong glance. "You really shouldn't let her get under your skin. Although she's good at it, I'll give you that."

"So what are you doing now?" I say.

"I'm trying to make a living as a musician, so I do a few things. I do some vocals for a jazz quartet and teach some private students. And I just started my own band."

Her roommate joins the conversation. "Chelsea's being modest. Her band is amazing. They're turning away bookings."

"What kind of band is it?" I ask.

"We do eighties covers," she says. "I love those old songs. My mom used to play them all the time."

I can't help myself. "What year were you born, Chelsea? If you don't mind my asking, that is?"

"In 1988," she says.

"Great meeting you," I say, and I strike out for the kitchen on the theory that Jesse will eventually gravitate there and I'll have someone my own age to drink with, but first I bump right into Marvin Shapiro. He looks relieved to see me. "Sophie!" he says. "What a nice surprise." He's sweating profusely. "It's really very warm in here," he says, dabbing his bald patch with a cocktail napkin. "I meant to thank you for all of your help managing the publicity for Dr. Viggars. Did you see the feature in the paper today?"

"I did," I lie. "I thought it was terrific."

Marvin beams. "I'm so pleased to hear you say that," he says. "It's certainly causing quite a stir!"

"Why do you say that?"

"Dr. Viggars has been getting requests for radio and television interviews all day. Apparently, he's the hottest topic in the blogosphere today, not that I have a particularly good sense of what that means. But he's younger than I am and he says it's a good thing. This will be excellent for his career."

"Oh," I say, trying to muster some semblance of enthusiasm. "Well, that's great. He deserves it." I pause. "Marvin, can I ask you something?"

"Of course."

"About the study," I say. "How concerned should I be about the amount of television my sons are watching?"

Marvin looks at me kindly. "Sophie, parenting is all about instincts, and judging from what I know of you, your instincts are excellent. It's an interesting finding, that's all. It's not a reason to change your parenting strategy."

"Certainly not," says another voice, and Margaret appears at Marvin's elbow with a drink. "Here you are, Marvin."

"Bless you," he says fervently, taking a long gulp.

"How do you know Lil? I didn't realize that you were friends."

"I've known her for years," says Margaret. "I was one of her first students. I don't want to tell you how long ago."

"You lived in this house?"

"For three years, during nursing school. It hasn't changed much since then. Lil gave me the most extraordinary break on the rent in return for my looking after a pair of diabetic cats."

"Cats?" I can't imagine Lil with pets.

"They weren't exactly her cats," says Margaret. "A dear friend of hers had died and she felt duty-bound to take in the poor woman's pets. They needed insulin injections twice a day and had a raft of other health problems, but Lillian felt too guilty to euthanize them. They were in quite a sad state. Eventually the poor things expired, but Lil never raised my rent." Her face lights up as she smiles. "You know, I was just telling your husband this story in the kitchen. He's very charming."

"He can be," I say.

"That's the best you can hope for," she says. "Right, Marvin?"

"Absolutely," he says, clinking his glass against hers, and I realize that Marvin has plans this evening with Margaret that don't include chatting about diabetic cats. So I excuse myself and wander off in search of my husband.

I pause at the entrance to the kitchen and watch Lil, Jesse, and Will in conversation. I can tell from here that Jesse has turned off the charm; he looks as though he wishes he were anywhere else, and I'm reminded suddenly of the quiet endurance that my father used to exude at cocktail parties. I don't think about my dad that often; for so many years, it hurt too much, but lately I've found myself wondering what he would say about some of the choices I've made. I've never asked myself what he would have thought of Will, though, and I'm surprised to realize that I'm dead certain of his answer. *You're easy to love, sweetheart,* he would have said. *Anyone who thinks it's complicated isn't right for you.*

I sidle up to Jesse.

"Hi," I say.

"Hello there," he says. "I was about to send out a search party."

"We were telling Jesse about our plan to recruit you to the foundation," says Lil.

"Oh?" I say, chagrined. The last thing I need tonight is to reopen our earlier fight by reminding Jesse that this conversation about my future employment has been going on without him for some time.

Will turns to Jesse. "It would be a great move for her, don't you think?"

"That's up to her," says Jesse. "I have no doubt that Sophie would be wonderful at anything she decided to do."

"I said I'd consider it," I say. "But I haven't had a chance to talk it over properly with Jesse yet. It's been a crazy week."

"Isn't it your decision?" Will's tone is playful but there's no mistaking the challenge in his question.

Most of the time, the events that alter and define us are invisible, mere background noise in the dramas of other people's lives. Usually, you can get away with saying, *I have something in my eye,* or *I stayed up too late last night watching reruns,* and no one will suspect that you just broke up with your boyfriend or had a fight with your mother or bombed an interview. But there is no anonymity in the way Will and Jesse and Lil stand and wait for my answer. This is one of those rare occasions when I won't be able to rewrite a version of events in which I behaved better, or was at least funnier and better looking. All of us know that my answer matters.

I lace my fingers through Jesse's. "It's a family decision," I say, and I feel him relax, while Lil smiles and Will looks away.

Jesse squeezes my hand. "Lil," he says, "would you be horribly offended if we ducked out early? We're bagged."

"Certainly not," says Lil, beaming her approval. "If my date looked like yours, I'd leave early too. Off you go, my dears." She gives us both a kiss.

It's quiet out on the street now, and there's no traffic at all. "Can you make it a couple of blocks in your shoes?" Jesse asks. "It'll be easier to grab a cab on the main road."

"I'm tough," I say.

"You're not really," he says, and we start walking. "I was chatting with your future boss. Margaret, is it? I didn't realize that you had finished the search. She seems great."

"I hope so," I say. "I'm ready to swap pompous, insulting, and unlikable for great. That's a change I could get behind. At the moment I'm just happy not to be on the search committee any longer."

"But you're thinking about leaving."

"Maybe," I say. "There's a lot to consider. I want to talk it through with you, but not now, OK?"

"OK," he says, and we walk the length of the next block without speaking, fingers laced together. "I'm sorry about this morning," he says. I squeeze his hand. "I've been thinking about what you said about Anya."

"I'm sorry too, Jesse. I didn't know what was going on with the business. I don't know why I reacted like that. She gets under my skin."

"I know she does. I'm beginning to see that she tries to do that to you. Sometimes I think she's a bit lonely. But you must know there's nothing going on between us. I would never let anything threaten our family. It's the only thing that matters."

"I know," I say, hope rising so hard in my throat that I can barely speak. "I feel the same way."

Jesse strokes his thumb along the side of my hand, and we make our way out to the main road and hail a taxi. There's a lot more to be said, but we won't say it tonight. This tentative peace between us is sweet and hard-won and desperately needed.

At home, Jesse goes to check on the boys while I take off my makeup, wriggle out of my pantyhose, and kick off my shoes. When he returns, I'm sitting on the bed, examining the damage.

"I talk a good game," I say, "but I think I might be crippled tomorrow."

"Your friend Zoe would say it's a small price to pay for fashion." Jesse sits down next to me and pats his lap. "Let's have a look." I lie down and put my feet across his lap, and he massages my arch with his thumb.

"That she would," I say. "She calls these 'fuck-me' shoes."

Jesse's eyebrows shoot up.

"It's an industry term," I say. "Mmmm. That's amazing. I might actually walk again."

"What were you and Lil caballing about at the party?"

"Oh, nothing. She likes you. She thinks you're a catch."

"Smart lady," he says, moving his hands up to work the muscle in my calf. "What did you say?"

"I said that she has no idea," I say, in my best attempt at a sultry tone.

Jesse's hands move a bit higher. I bite my lip and close my eyes. "You know," he says, conversationally, "I could do a much better job if I didn't have all this fabric in the way."

"Hmmm. Can I help you with that?"

"No, no. I've got it covered," he says. I feel the bed shift as Jesse stretches out beside me. He slides one hand under my shoulder, wraps the other around my hip, and pulls me onto my side so that I'm facing him. I open my eyes and hold his gaze; it's dark and steady and knowing, and I swallow hard. And then he grins and, with one fluid motion, scoops me up, rolls me on top of him, and unzips the back of my dress. "Did I mention that I like your new shoes?" he says.

And for the first time in ages, as I lean down to kiss him, I know exactly what I want.

CHAPTER TWENTY-FOUR

sunday, december 8, 2013

When I wake up, my first thought is one of panic. "What time is it?" I ask, poking Jesse's shoulder.

He lifts his head slightly to see the clock on the bedside table. "Six-thirty."

I sit up. "Do you think the kids are OK?"

Jesse looks puzzled. "Why wouldn't they be?"

"They haven't made a sound all night!"

"Well," says Jesse, "I'm going to assume that's because they're sleeping, as opposed to dead. We want them to sleep through the night, right?"

"Good point," I say. I lie back down and put my arm across Jesse's chest. "That was fun last night."

He smiles. I wait for a few minutes, but he doesn't say anything.

"Was it fun for you?" I prompt.

"Very fun." Nothing further appears to be forthcoming.

"That's it?"

"Baby," he says, "one of the best things about being married is that you can have sex without having to talk about it in the morning. Don't take that away from me."

Six boyfriends, one husband, and twenty years of dating, and my natural instincts about what men think and feel are still dead wrong. With mountains of evidence to the contrary, I still cling to the theory that a man is an onion, with layers of complexity to be peeled back by a woman who cares enough to discover what is at the core. But a man is not an onion. There is nothing buried at the core; it's all visible right on the surface. You can spend years looking for the complex inner spirit of your mate, but you'll drive yourself crazy. As Gertrude Stein famously observed about Oakland, there is no there there. Women, on the other hand, are all layers. But men, if they give thought to such things, don't think of women in such benign vegetable terms; to them, we are as dangerous and unpredictable as explosive devices. We fester below the surface, ready to blow at the first wrong step.

"OK," I say in a small voice. "Maybe I'll check on the kids."

"I want to register my strong objection," says Jesse. "If they wake up, which they will, you're on duty."

"Duly noted," I say.

I slip out of bed, tiptoe up the stairs, and peek into Scotty's room. I see his curls peeking up over the top of the covers and hear the sound of gentle breathing. Truly, there is no sweeter sound in the world than that of a sleeping baby. Filled with a sense of well-being, I retreat back into the hallway and turn toward Jamie's room, stepping squarely on a creaky floorboard. I hold my breath. Nothing. And then, "Mommy?"

I groan, and hear a faint chuckle from downstairs. I retrace my steps, and find Scotty sitting up in bed. "Hi, Mommy!" he says. "I'm ready to get up!"

"Are you sure, honey?" I ask. He nods vigorously. "OK," I say. "Do you want to come and cuddle in Mommy's bed for a while?"

"No," says Scotty. "Playroom!"

"It's a little early for that. Why don't I read you a story?"

"Playroom!" Scotty says, stubbornly and too loudly.

"Shhh. Your brother is sleeping," I whisper, even as I hear Jamie's door opening behind me.

"Is it morning?" he asks.

"Sort of," I say. "It's still really early, though. Are you sure you don't want to go back to bed for a while?" I hear a snort of laughter from downstairs.

"No," says Jamie. "I want to go to the playroom."

"Me too!" says Scotty.

"All right, then. The playroom it is." We all troop downstairs, past my bedroom, where Jesse is snoring pointedly to indicate that I should look elsewhere for childcare assistance.

I brew some very strong coffee and get out the giant bin of Lego. We construct an elaborate space station, and then attack it repeatedly with star fighters; it's hungry work, so we decide to break for pancakes. The boys help mix the batter and we make shapes in the hot pan: Scotty has Mickey Mouse and Jamie has a Death Star. With the holiday ad in progress, I can't implement the weekend phase of the BlackBerry diet, so the device sits and hums on the kitchen counter, generating a corresponding hum of anxiety in the recesses of my consciousness. By the time breakfast is finished, the hum is as distracting as microphone static. I hustle the boys back to the playroom, convince myself that I've provided as much stimulation as their developing brains can absorb for now, and turn on the cartoons. "I'll be right back," I say, and scoop my BlackBerry off the counter into the pocket of my bathrobe. Then I sneak into the powder room down the hall and close the door. With the kids distracted, I can probably clear fifty e-mails if I focus for a half hour. I'm making good progress when the door opens.

"Busted," says Jesse, leaning on the doorframe with a grin.

"This is a bathroom," I say. "Knocking would be appropriate."

"The kids were looking for you."

"Oh," I say. "Sorry about that." I'm more than a little embarrassed. How did I not hear the kids?

"That's OK," says Jesse. "What's going on? Anything urgent?"

"Just backlog. I thought I'd try to catch up while the kids were watching TV."

"I have a thought," says Jesse. "What do you say to a trip to the museum?"

Jesse has always been a fan of excursions, and to be fair, the kids love them. I resist, which is one of many reasons why I am the less fun parent. Excursions are always so much work—the organization, the packing, the removal of overtired children from the public location of the excursion over their screaming protests.

"Did you ask the boys?"

"They already have their coats on."

"Did you pack snacks?"

"Yes, ma'am." Jesse salutes.

I sigh. "A trip to the museum sounds perfect, then."

"Trust me," says Jesse. "It'll be fun. Run and get dressed."

I throw on some jeans and race back down to find the kids standing and waiting at the door. I put on my coat and sling my purse over my arm. "I just need to grab my BlackBerry," I say. "Have you seen it? I thought I left it here."

"I put it away," says Jesse. "We're going to make a deal and both leave our BlackBerrys here. No e-mail for a couple of hours. Just us, the kids, and some dinosaurs. I think we could both use a little separation."

"You stole my BlackBerry?"

"That's a very uncharitable way of putting it. I'm giving it a well-deserved rest for a couple of hours," he says.

"Fine," I say. I'm too tired to argue with him, and too unwilling to disrupt our fragile peace.

We are the first in line when the doors open, and we make our way straight to the dinosaur exhibit. Jamie and Scotty have the hall to themselves and they run in circles with their arms outstretched, cawing. "Pterodactyls?" I guess.

"Pteranodons," says Jesse.

"What are pteranodons?"

"Flying dinosaurs. They changed the name."

"Who changed the name?"

"Search me." He points to the description on the wall of the skeleton suspended from the ceiling. "Also, apparently they weren't technically dinosaurs. See for yourself."

"I believe you," I say, although I don't.

Jesse laughs. "OK, smarty-pants. Guess what they call the giant dinosaur with the long neck and tail now?"

"Brontosaurus?"

"I'm sorry to be the one to tell you this, but the brontosaurus is no more," says Jesse, looking not at all sorry. "They call him apatosaurus now. There's a femur over there."

"Jamie," I call, and he swoops over. "What dinosaur are you pretending to be?"

"A pteranodon," he says, with a look that I know I'll be seeing a lot more of in his teenage years.

"Wait until you tell him he can't borrow the car," says Jesse.

"Where did you learn so much about dinosaurs?" I ask Jamie.

"We learned about them in school," says Jamie. "We came here on our field trip. Emmett's mom came with us. Why didn't you come?"

I swallow hard. "I was working, sweetie," I say. "Emmett's mom doesn't have a job, so it's easier for her to come on field trips."

Jamie looks confused. "Emmett's mom says that she has the most important job in the world."

Jesse steps in. "Emmett's mom is right. Raising kids is a really important job. Your mom is so amazing that she can do two jobs at once."

"OK," says Jamie. "Can we get some ice cream?"

Jesse laughs. "It's a little early for that. Are you guys finished with the dinosaurs? Do you want to go and see the knights now?"

The boys cheer, and Jesse leads the way to the armor exhibit. "I'm right behind you," I call, and dart over to the wall to read about the flying non-dinosaur, swing by the femur that does not belong to a brontosaurus, and then run to catch up to my family.

"So?" asks Jesse.

"It appears that you may have been telling the truth."

"I ask you," he says to the room, "eight years of marriage, and where's the trust?"

"How did I not know this?"

"The International Association of Paleontologists didn't call to consult you? We should write a letter." I punch him lightly on the shoulder. "This is actually bothering you, isn't it?"

"Yes," I admit. I feel remarkably unsettled, not unlike the day I learned that Pluto had been demoted from planetary status. Bit by bit, everything I learned in elementary school is becoming irrelevant, which is pretty serious since I don't remember anything that I learned in high school or university.

Jesse puts his arms around me and kisses the top of my head. "Sophie, I think you might feel better if you could come to grips with the fact that you are not in control of everything."

"There is absolutely no doubt in my mind that I'm not in control of everything. Most days, I'm pretty confident that I'm not in control of anything," I say, and my lip starts to quiver.

The boys are temporarily occupied with an imaginary duel, so Jesse pulls me over to a bench, sits down, and puts an arm around me. "I know the feeling," he says.

Tears roll down my cheeks, as the anxiety of the last week returns in a rush. "I'm sorry I didn't know how bad things were for you with the business," I say. "Why didn't you tell me?"

"I should have," he says. "But you've been so unhappy at work and it never seemed like the right time. And then Will showed up."

"What does Will have to do with it?"

Jesse shoves a lock of hair out of his eyes, and when he speaks the warmth is gone from his voice. "Oh, I don't know, Sophie. Maybe I didn't want to give you another reason to think you'd picked the wrong door."

"What do you mean?"

"Behind Door Number One," he intones, "independently wealthy, hot young Manhattan lawyer and deal-maker, who also happens to look like a *GQ* model. And behind Door Number Two, failed entrepreneur and perpetually exhausted father of two."

I'm shocked to hear Jesse describe himself in these terms. He has always been so comfortable in his own skin, so sure of his place in the world. I'm horrified to think that Will's visit, and my reaction to it, have rattled him so profoundly. *And for what?* I can hear Zoe's voice in my head asking. *What has Will ever really offered you behind Door Number One? If you believed you could have him, you'd have paid attention long before now to all of the reasons that he's completely wrong for you.* I hold Jesse's hand tightly in my own as a fierce protectiveness rushes through me.

"That's not fair," I say. "You're adorable and hilarious. You can cook. And," I pull his head down and whisper in his ear, "you're good in bed."

He laughs and kisses my forehead. "Not our best week, was it?"

"No."

"Leaving aside our mutual friend, what's making you so crazy?"

I sigh. "I hate my boss, my assistant hates me, Geoff is going to quit, and I can't think of a theme for the Gala. The HR director thinks I'm completely unhinged. My doctor gave me a prescription for antidepressants. We're going to get kicked out of the daycare because I'm an incompetent mother and I'm late every day and Scotty bites. The Parent Council at Jamie's school is stalking me because I don't volunteer." I'm working up a good head of steam now. "The kids have terrible eating habits. They're never going to get into Harvard because we don't sit down together for family dinner. I let the kids watch too much TV, which probably causes ADHD. God, what if the biting is the first symptom?" I put my head in my hands and groan. "I have to make a decision about the job offer from Lil, which is obviously complicated. And my mother's mad at me."

"Why?"

"Because I quit Family Yoga and didn't return any of her calls about Christmas."

Jesse shakes his head. "Let's have a reality check here. You're working very hard at a big job that you are very good at. You have two great kids. And you're married to a guy who loves you and apparently has certain attributes that you like." He squeezes my hand. "But let's deal with your list systematically. You hate Family Yoga. So you should tell your mother, quit, and move on."

"She'll be upset."

"Who cares? She's already upset. Next, you hate your boss. But he's on his way out the door and you like the look of the new one. There's a problem solved without you doing anything at all. Next, you believe that Killjoy hates you. Whether or not this is true really doesn't matter. You have both lost sight of the fact that her job is to make your job easier. If she can't do that, she'll have to go."

"She's unionized. I can't fire her."

"Again, whether or not that is true, she doesn't have to work for you. Have a meeting with the director of HR and tell her that your assistant is giving you a nervous breakdown and that she has to deal with it. That should kill two birds with one stone. Next, why is Geoff going to quit?"

I bite my lip. "Aha," says Jesse. "He finally told you, did he?"

"He likes me," I say.

"Of course he does."

"It doesn't bother you?" I ask.

"It bothers me that you're upset about it. But I know what a serious threat looks like, and that guy sure isn't it."

Jamie and Scotty race up, pink and breathless from their duel. "Can we go to the bat cave, Daddy?" asks Jamie.

"Absolutely," says Jesse. "Mommy was just saying how much she loves the bat cave." He turns to me. "To be continued," he says.

We head downstairs to the natural history exhibits. The boys never tire of the bat habitat, a dark corridor echoing with the whooshing sound of bats in flight, and occupied by Count Dracula, a.k.a. Jesse.

"Velcome to your dooooom," Jesse intones, and Jamie shrieks with delight. Scotty turns on his heel, races over into my arms, and clings to my neck.

"It's just Daddy being silly," I whisper. I cuddle him against my chest and ache with the pleasure of being able to dispense comfort and ease by simply wrapping my arms around him. I wish, profoundly, that I could figure out how to do the same for myself. "Do you want to go outside with me?" I ask, and Scotty nods, his head still buried in my neck.

We sit at the exit and wait. Jamie races out of the bat cave with Jesse chasing him, both of them giggling. Jesse scoops Scotty from my lap and tosses him in the air. "Did I scare you, buddy?" he asks, and gives him a kiss. "Sorry about that. I was just having some fun with your brother. Are we ready to go home?"

I brace myself for a double meltdown, but none comes. Instead, the boys race over to Jesse, each grabbing one of his hands. "OK," I say. "That is totally unfair."

"What?"

"That they just agreed to leave with you. If I suggested such a terrible thing, there would be so much screaming that I'd have to persuade the security guards not to call the Children's Aid Society."

"There is little justice in the world," agrees Jesse.

"I am the one who vomited every day for nine months, got an episiotomy the size of the Grand Canyon, and walked around with sore breasts for two years of my life."

"All true," he says. "We can add that to your list of grievances if you want. What do you kids want for lunch?"

"Pizza!" they yell.

"Perfect," says Jesse. He glances over at me. "Let's solve eating habits another day."

After lunch, we take the kids upstairs to their rooms for some quiet time, then bolt into our own room and fling ourselves on the bed.

"Emmett's mother may be on to something," says Jesse. "I don't know if it's the most important job in the world, but it's got to be one of the hardest. I'm paralyzed." He holds up a hand. "I realize I just opened the door for a discussion about how it's not surprising that I find it tiring since I never do it, but let's hold that thought, OK?"

"I wasn't going to say anything of the kind," I say, which is an outright lie and we both know it.

"Now," says Jesse. "To recap our earlier discussion, I've solved all of your problems except for the daycare, the volunteer stalker, the theme for your Gala, your new job opportunity, and the fact that your doctor thinks you're depressed."

"And the kids watch too much TV, and they aren't going to get into Harvard because they don't have family dinners with us."

"Ah, well," says Jesse. "We can't afford to send them to Harvard anyway. No biggie."

"Be serious!" I elbow him.

"I'm sort of serious. Do you know how much tuition is at Harvard?" I elbow him again. "Sophie, we'll have family dinners with the kids when they are old enough to eat after we get home from work. We'll get there. Can we agree not to obsess about issues more than five years in the future, at least for the next few minutes?"

"If we must," I say.

"On the TV issue, which I'm not sure even merits a discussion, the kids are fine. We have two busy, healthy, normal little boys, and that makes us very, very lucky. I'm not saying they're perfect. I'm saying that we need to keep things in perspective. Let's stop diagnosing the kids with imaginary problems and deal with some real ones. Scotty isn't biting because he watches too much TV—he just doesn't like his daycare. You can hardly blame him for that since you don't like it either. We need to figure out another solution for him, but we're not going to do that until we've sorted out our jobs."

I feel the tension unwinding in my neck and shoulders. This is Jesse at his best: solving concrete problems. I've always loved and half-envied his unselfconscious pragmatism. "The volunteer stalker is easy. Ignore her or, if ignoring her is too stressful, tell her politely that you can't help. You don't have any extra time. If other parents do, they can pick up the slack. The school won't crumble without you."

"It's not that easy," I say.

"It really is," he says. "On the Gala issue, I have no idea what the theme should be, and I think you know that it doesn't actually matter. I have every confidence that you'll come up with the perfect solution if we can get your stress level down to sustainable levels. So let's talk about why you're having so much trouble doing that."

"I don't know," I say. "I'm incredibly fortunate by any objective measure.

I know I have first-world problems. But I feel like I should have some greater sense of purpose or something. Maybe I thought I'd have achieved more by now, or that I'd have made peace with not achieving more. But instead I'm restless and anxious and tired all the time. Last night at Lil's party I looked around the room at all of those students, and I felt really, really old."

"Compared to them, you are," says Jesse.

I muster a half-smile. "This is you trying to make me feel better?"

"This is me trying to give you a little perspective. We're not in university anymore. That's a good thing. Adult life has a lot to recommend it, even if it's tiring. We're building our careers and raising our kids and it's a lot of work. Being tired is just part of the package. Being miserable is a problem. Do you want to change your job?"

"Yes," I say. "I think so. And this offer from Lil . . . it's a dream come true in a lot of ways. But it comes with some strings."

"Will."

"Not just him, but yes."

"Sophie," he says, "I trust you. It's your decision. If I'm honest, I wouldn't shed a tear if Will disappeared off the face of the earth. I don't like what he does to you. He unsettles you, and that has an effect on me. If you go to the foundation, you'll have more contact, and I'll have more angst. But I can live with that, if it's what you want."

"You know," I say, "for what it's worth, according to Zoe's new theory about relationships, I married the right person."

"What a relief," says Jesse drily.

I shift a bit closer and put my head on Jesse's shoulder. "What about you?" I ask. "What are you going to do about your business?"

"In the immediate term, I'm going to have to give notice to most of my employees. I can pay the bills for another six weeks, but if I haven't found a new investor by the end of the month, the lights go out. I called a headhunter on Friday who seemed optimistic about my options, so I guess I'll put on a suit and lick my wounds in a corporate job for a few years. The good news is that I have technical expertise in one of the few growth areas in the economy, and I can always do some consulting until I find something permanent."

"But it was your dream," I say.

"It was my dream *job*," he corrects me. "My job, not my life. You and the kids are my life. There's difference."

I find myself crying again for the umpteenth time this week.

"Now you see?" says Jesse. "If you want me to shower you with affection, you can't go bursting into tears. It's a major deterrent."

I give him a watery smile.

"Better," he says. "Here's the goal for this week. You are going to get rid of all the noise in your life—by which I mean the stupid problems that are distracting you from dealing with the real ones. And then you are going to try to figure out how to have more fun."

"Operation Fun," I say. "I'm on it. But I need a nap first."

Jesse throws an arm over my waist and pulls me close. "I have a better idea," he murmurs in my ear, as his hand eases up under my shirt. I bite my lip as his hand moves higher, and I hear him chuckle, and I remember that what married sex lacks in anticipation, it makes up for in certainty. I shiver as he plants a delicate row of kisses along my cheekbone. "You know what I was thinking last night at the party?" he asks.

"Mmmm."

"I was thinking how lucky I was to be able to take you home at the end of the night."

I run my hands up under his shirt, grounding myself in the familiar texture of muscle and bone. "I love you," I murmur.

"I love you, too," he says. "You were always the girl I wanted to go home with."

CHAPTER TWENTY-FIVE

monday, december 9, 2013

Monday morning finds me sitting at the breakfast bar in the kitchen with a pencil and paper, scribbling a set of calculations.

Jesse watches me for a few minutes over the rim of his coffee mug and then says, "I can't help noticing that you appear to be doing math."

"I'm trying to get rid of the noise in my life, as per your instructions."

"You're taking my advice? There's a positive improvement already." I throw a strawberry at him, which he catches with the precision of a natural athlete. He takes a bite and grins at me. "You were talking in your sleep last night. I figured you were fretting."

"What was I saying?"

"I couldn't really understand it. I heard the word 'selfishness,' and something about behaving like a grown-up. Were you dreaming about me, by any chance?"

"Believe it or not, I was solving a complex algorithm that assigns numeric values to the necessity of performing specific tasks."

"Do tell," he says. "That kind of thing is a major turn-on for an engineer."

I laugh. "Don't mock me."

"I wouldn't dream of it."

"I've created an equation that I call the Requirement of Action Rating, or ROAR for short," I say. Jesse raises his eyebrows. "You take your desire to perform an activity, expressed as a number between zero and ten, add a number representing the amount of guilt that would result from your failure to perform the activity, then add a number representing the extent of your need to behave like a grown-up, and then subtract any points that you think you deserve, which I call 'allowable selfishness.' In the end, you get a number that tells you how urgent the priority is. I'm trying to plan my day."

To his credit, Jesse nods seriously. "And what have you concluded?" he asks.

"That the things I want to do least are also the things that I need to do most in order to preserve my self-identity as a mature and responsible adult."

"I appreciate that this is new math for me, but shouldn't extreme lack of desire to perform an action lower the overall score?"

"Not when you start with the proposition that your desire to do any of it is zero. You can't use negative numbers. That's cheating."

Now he laughs. "Would you like me to continue humoring you?"

"Yes, please."

"What's on the list for today?"

"Five things. Performance reviews for Erica and Geoff; a phone call to my mother to explain why I'm dropping out of Family Yoga; a discussion with Janelle Moss, in which I present a fresh and compelling theme for the Gala, which, to be clear, I have not yet invented; and, if I can find the inner strength, a conversation with Joy in which I assert my authority and reclaim the balance of power in our relationship."

"And how are the priorities shaking out?"

"Well, my mother is obviously at the top of the list with sixteen, in recognition of the exceptional level of guilt that she inspires as well as my pathological need to show her, however futilely, that I'm an adult. Geoff's next with thirteen, because I feel incredibly guilty that I was so oblivious to his feelings for me and that I hurt him so badly. And I need to be a grown-up about the situation because if he gets any angrier, he'll either quit or complain to HR that he can't work with me anymore, and I'll end up having to explain the whole situation to Jenny Dixon, which I am absolutely not prepared to do." I take a breath and continue. "Joy is an eight because I can't even take myself seriously as a grown-up if I can't get my own assistant to do what I want. Janelle's a seven, which is low considering how behind I am on the Gala, and how correspondingly high my guilt factor should be, but I'm allowing myself extra selfishness as a result of the family dinner episode. And Erica gets a score of five, mostly because I gave her a big opportunity this week, so for once I don't feel that guilty about her." Jesse looks skeptical. "What do you think?"

"I think that your system oddly reminds me of the theories of birth control that I learned at Catholic school, but if it works for you, carry on." He kisses the top of my head. "I've got to run. I've got a horrible day ahead myself. I'm meeting with our lawyer to talk about layoff notices for the staff."

I squirm inwardly, and remind myself that I am a lucky woman to be married to a man without a flair for the dramatic. "Are you sure you don't want me to do some ROAR calculations for you?"

He laughs. "Thanks for the offer, but I think I'll stick with what I know: sports metaphors."

"Go for the flag," I say. "I'll drop the kids." Jesse waves and heads out the door.

Two packed lunches, two parking-lot traffic jams, and two reluctant good-byes later, I'm back at the germ checkpoint, struggling to dredge up a modicum of optimism for the day ahead. It could just be the depression talking; on the other hand, studies show that depressed people predict outcomes more accurately than their mentally healthy counterparts. So if I can't come up with a scenario for the day that doesn't make me want to run screaming from the building, I probably have good reasons. Not that I'm completely incapable of finding a bright side: thanks to antibiotics and the ministrations of Beverley Chen, for the first time in what feels like weeks, I'm not sick.

I step up to the front of the line and brace myself for my daily dose of

Nigel. But what I find instead is a miracle, nothing less than concrete evidence of the power of prayer: Nigel is gone, and Max is back in his place.

"Sophie!" says Max. "Great to see you!"

"Max! Where's Nigel?" I ask.

"Oh, he was just filling in for me while I was on vacation. He's probably back in the Records Department."

"You were on vacation?"

"You bet. Went to see the grandchildren."

"Vacation," I repeat. I'm having trouble processing.

Max is puzzled. "Didn't I tell you before I left? Hey, I brought some pictures. Want to see them?"

"I'd love to, Max," I say, "but I'm late for a meeting upstairs."

"Too bad," he says, looking disappointed. "Maybe tomorrow?"

"I'm counting on it," I say, fingering the medical note in my pocket like a talisman. With such a radical shift in fortune at the germ desk, the day ahead seems less daunting. Still, I'm going to ease in, starting with the least dreadful task on my list and working up to the truly horrific. I'm silently rehearsing my constructive criticism for Erica as I pass Joy's desk; she glowers and waves a pink message slip at me. *Will*, I think immediately, which begins a mental conversation that swings between guilt (*You owe your excellent husband better than this*) and self-justification (*I'm just anxious because I haven't made a decision about the foundation job*) until Joy puts a stop to it.

"Urgent message," she says. "Janelle Moss wanted to speak to you as soon as you came in."

"That may be," I say, giving myself a mental kick. I cannot get thrown off my plan within fifteen minutes of entering the building. "But I need to see Erica first thing this morning. Could you call her for me?"

While I'm waiting, I jot down a few notes to limber up for the big event. I'm aiming for a tone of restrained praise: firm but fair, kind but constructive, and friendly without suggesting for a moment that we are friends. I know my own proclivities only too well, and I'm determined not to leave Erica with the mistaken impression that she is the most talented person in this or any department in the history of professional communications. There's a knock at the door.

"Are you ready for me?" Erica says expectantly.

"Come in," I say. "Have a seat." She does. "I'm sorry for taking so long to do your annual performance review," I say, inwardly cursing myself for opening with an apology. "First, I want to take a few minutes to hear from you before I give you my comments. What do you think have been the highlights of your work here this year?"

Erica launches into a lengthy recitation of her greatest hits, culminating in the ADHD press conference last week. It's fascinating to have a window into Erica's psyche; in her overweening confidence, I see a photo negative of myself. Where my satisfaction in a project is always diminished by the rec-ollection of missteps and false starts along the way, Erica's pleasure in a good result appears to obliterate the memory of any and all past errors. It is striking to hear her describe an assignment from last summer as a success, when I recall the anxiety attack that ensued when I realized, almost too late, that her draft was completely off the mark and I had to pull Geoff in to do emergency triage. In her shoes, the mere thought of that assignment would still make me blush with shame, but Erica is not similarly burdened. In her mind, the end result was positive, and therefore should be celebrated as yet another example of her indispensable value to our team.

Erica is prepared to continue enumerating her triumphs for longer than I would have thought possible, so I wait for her to draw a breath and offer some comments of my own. "You have lots of energy and ambition," I tell her, "and those are important. But at your level, you need to be working more independently. You still require a lot of direc-tion from me at the beginning of a project, and Geoff usually does a heavy edit at the end. There's no doubt that you are a talented writer, and I'd like to see you moving in a direction where your work needs very little oversight. I thought your work last week on the press confer-ence was excellent, and it demonstrated to me that you can be self-sufficient when you're motivated. I'd like to see that kind of focus on all of your projects. That's how you're going to get to the next level."

Erica nods enthusiastically, and I'm relieved. I was prepared for an argument, but Erica seems to agree with everything I've said. Perhaps I've been uncharitable. "It's important to me that you continue to develop your skills and that you feel challenged and supported here. Is there anything that I can do to help you achieve your goals?" I ask.

I'm not really expecting anything other than a pitch for money to attend a conference, but Erica says, "Absolutely. I agree that my performance this year has been outstanding, and I'd like to work with you on a timeline for moving up in the organization."

"OK," I say, although I'm a little confused. I thought I'd been clear that my feelings were in the range of somewhat satisfied to occasionally pleased, but it appears that something has been lost in translation. "Tell me what you have in mind."

"I feel that I've been playing an increasingly important role on the team, and it's great to see that you recognize my talent," says Erica. "I'm glad you see that it's time for me to move to the next level. I'd like you to consider promoting me now, but I'd be prepared to settle for a pay increase as long as I had your assurance that I could expect a title jump within the year."

I look at Erica with a mixture of envy and incredulity. What would my life be, I wonder, if I had even a modicum of Erica's confidence in her own talent, and in the inexorability of her success in the world? I can't even imagine. Is everyone in Erica's generation as sure of herself as she is? Is everyone in mine as afflicted with crippling Imposter Syndrome?

I clear my throat. "It may be that I wasn't as clear as I could have been just now," I say. "You are doing some very good work. But I'm not going to reward you with a promotion and a raise just because you are starting to perform at the level that I expect for someone in your position. You're still learning. Keep up the good work and we'll talk in a year about whether it's time for you to move."

Erica looks surprised but not particularly offended. "Oh, well," she says, nonchalantly. "You'll never get what you want if you don't ask for it."

"So I hear," I say. "But just because you ask for it doesn't mean that you'll get it."

"Touché," she says, and we sit in silence for a moment while I fantasize about a workplace where no one says things like "touché."

"So, have you decided on a theme for the Gala yet?" she asks.

"We have, and it's very exciting," I lie. "But it's under wraps for now while we run the details to ground." I put my hand over the telephone and affect my best expression of managerial authority. "I'm going to have to get back to it now, but I'll share the details with you as soon as I can."

"Can't wait," says Erica, rising to go.

"Me neither," I say.

"You have a message," Joy says, walking in and handing me a pink slip. "He didn't want to be put through to voice mail." She rolls her eyes, marveling at the sheer laziness of a caller who would put her to the trouble of penning a message, and stalks out. I glance at it and catch my breath. "WHAT IS YOUR ANSWER?" reads the message from caller Will Shannon.

I don't have an answer yet, but I have questions. I know that when you choose a path in life, you can't go back. You can undo the choices you've made, but the undoing won't take you back to the place where you started. I'm not reckless enough to consider throwing my life away—my kind husband, my beautiful children—but even if I were, there no longer exists a path to an uncomplicated requited love with Will. I want to know if it ever existed at all.

I log into my e-mail, which seems less immediately threatening today, still dangerous, but more in the nature of slow-rising floodwaters than a rampaging army thirsty for enemy blood; it's a good sign, so I seize my courage and start typing.

J. SOPHIE WHELAN

> To: wshannon@perrimanhale.com
> Sent: Monday, December 9, 2013, 10:08 a.m.
> Subject: Answer

I'll answer your question when you answer mine. What
do you regret?

My trigger finger hovers as I contemplate hitting *Send*, but it doesn't
feel quite right. Maybe he needs a little more guidance on what I'm
looking for here. I add a couple of sentences and delete them. Then I
copy the whole thing and paste it into an e-mail to Zoe.

J. SOPHIE WHELAN

> To: zoe@hennessy.com
> Sent: Monday, December 9, 2013, 10:20 a.m.
> Subject: More advice
>
> See draft e-mail below. Any edits?

While I wait for her reply, I review my ROAR list, which is sitting
in the middle of my desk, reproaching me for my lack of focus. But now
that I've knocked off the one easy thing on the list, my options are all
relatively unattractive. Should I start with my mother or with Joy?
With love, however complicated, or with hate, however pale a version
of it? Put that way, the choice is clear, so I pick up the phone and call
my mother, who may be demanding and intrusive and crazy-making,
but who loves me with an elemental force that will expire only when
one of us passes from the earth, and probably not even then.

"Hi, Mom," I say, bracing myself for a tidal wave of admonishments.

"Oh, honey," she says. "Are you all right? I've been so worried about
you. Leo told me that you quit Family Yoga the other night."

"I'm sorry, Mom. I should have called. Leo and I had a disagree-
ment, and I lost my temper. I should have told you before that it's been
too stressful for me to try to get to yoga during the week, but I didn't
want to disappoint you."

"Well," she says. "I gave Leo a piece of my mind. I don't know who
he thinks he is. Pretty affected if you ask me! Dana and I quit in solidarity."

I'm both stunned and unexpectedly touched. Although I'm unlikely to disagree that Leo is precious, I have some sympathy for his position. My mother, on the other hand, is indifferent to my confession that I tainted Leo's sanctuary with hateful, karma-destroying technology. She instead blasts Leo with a stream of vitriol that reminds me she has always been much tougher than I give her credit for, and an amazing person to have in your corner. Why is my default memory of her that of a broken widow in the months following my dad's death? I imagine that my mother is incapable of astonishing me, but in truth, she has been doing just that for years: moving back to the city after burying my dad, growing her business, rebuilding her life. Why do I cast her as someone who wants far more from me than I can possibly give, when she wants so little?

I'm reminded again of her many e-mails about Christmas, and press on. "I'm so sorry, Mom," I say. "I know I've been dismissive lately. It's not that I don't care about Christmas. I've been under a huge amount of pressure, and I've been struggling to stay above water."

"I know, sweetie," she says.

And I truly believe she does know. I continue. "I think Jamie would love to have a robot kit for Christmas. And you should forget the turducken. Let's go with tradition this year. I'm trying to simplify."

"Done," says my mother. She sounds a little choked up. "I'm so proud of you. Your dad would be, too. Now go back to work and stop worrying about me."

"OK," I say. "I'll talk to you later."

I shed a few quiet tears at my desk, then blow my nose, pull out my compact, and get rid of the evidence. "Joy," I call. She takes her time coming in.

"Could you get Geoff for me?" I ask.

Joy looks sullen. "Why don't you call him?" she says, pointing at my phone. "I'm in the middle of some work."

I should be furious, but instead I feel strangely cool. Is this a side effect of my wholehearted embrace of the ROAR system? If you commit to organizing your day around the systemic eradication of dreaded tasks, can you trade roiling emotions for clinical detachment at will?

I've been reluctant to initiate a confrontation with Joy, but it seems that the moment has arrived without any impetus from me.

"No, you're not," I say. "Because, as we both know, I don't give you any work." Joy blinks. "That's going to change starting today. I need an assistant who views it as an occupational requirement to make my life easier. That can be you or it can be someone else."

We stare at each other for a long moment, and then Joy nods stiffly. "I'll get Geoff," she says and walks out.

And just like that, I see the world as I imagine men see it, a giant map of relationships about which strategic decisions must be made, like a game of Risk. The decisions you make might bring happiness or unhappiness, but the strategy should be selected in a state of essential coolness and rationality. I've always secretly wanted to be cool—really cool, as in not caring about what others think, as opposed to self-consciously cool and caring desperately about what others think—and maybe, for the first time in my life, I'm in striking distance.

A few minutes later, Geoff appears in the doorway.

"I'm supposed to give you a performance review today," I say.

He lingers at the door, and then takes a couple of steps into the office, keeping his distance. "I'm still working through the feedback you gave me on Friday," he says, and then catches himself. "I'm sorry. That was rude. Let's hold off until next week. It's going to be a busy day getting the holiday ad out the door."

"You're missing out," I say brightly. "I was planning to put a rave review together for HR and tell them that you are perfectly capable of doing my job and that we're lucky we've managed to keep you this long. With any luck, they'll decide to give you the raise that you should have had last year. But we don't have to meet about it today if it's too awkward for you."

"I think it is," he says.

"Fair enough," I say, but then I find that there is something that can't wait after all. "You've been an amazing colleague and a friend, and I've absolutely loved working with you," I say. Geoff stiffens and I take a deep breath and forge ahead. "I feel sick that I've made you miserable.

It was completely unintentional and I'm sorry." I stop myself from saying that I wish things could be different for us; it's the easy way out, and it's not true.

"I know you are," he says. "I'm sure you understand that I can't keep working for you. I'm going to be looking for a fresh start."

"If you need to leave, I'll give you the best reference in the world," I say. "But can you hold off, just for a couple of weeks? Take some vacation if you need to? There may be an opportunity here and I wouldn't want you to miss out."

"I'll consider it," he says. And then his face lifts in a wan smile, a pale shadow of his old one, but progress all the same. "What did you say to Joy?"

"We had a meeting of the minds," I say.

"Lucky Joy," says Geoff, and walks out.

I turn to my computer screen and see that I have an e-mail from Claudio. It's the final cut of the holiday ad. I'm just about to play it when I notice that Joy is back in the doorway, looking oddly sheepish. "I should probably have mentioned this before," she says. "Your senior management meeting started half an hour ago."

Everyone turns to stare as I slink into the boardroom, and I realize with a sinking heart that Margaret Anderson is at the head of the table.

"I'm so sorry," I say, mortified. "I got caught up in a performance review. We usually meet on Tuesdays, and I didn't know that the schedule had changed."

"Not to worry, Sophie," says Margaret. "It's not a formal meeting. I was in the office today and thought I'd take the opportunity to learn about the organization from the people running it. We were just wrapping up, although now that you're here, maybe you could give us an update on the annual appeal? I understand that you did some emergency filming this weekend."

"Actually, I have the final cut right here," I say. "I haven't seen it yet. Give me a minute to boot up my laptop and we can all watch it together."

"While we're waiting, Margaret," says Marni, "I just want to say how excited we all are to be working under your leadership. The selection committee made an inspired choice. We stand ready to help you execute your vision."

"Thanks," says Margaret, not looking at Marni.

"Here we go," I say, as I pull up the file and run it. From the opening frame, I can tell that it's absolutely perfect. The music is stirring, Carolyn is the epitome of caring and professionalism, and Taylor is so heartbreakingly brave that I want to leap out of my chair and write a check.

"You did this on how many days' notice?" asks Margaret.

"Not many," I say.

"Five," says Bill, the director of the Annual Fund. "Honestly, I don't know how you did it. You're my hero."

"When is it going to air?" asks Margaret.

"That's the really, really good news," I say. "We got two stations to donate time in exchange for interviews with Dr. Viggars, our star ADHD researcher, so it's airing all week, starting tonight."

"Remarkable," says Margaret. "Sounds like you pulled off a miracle."

"It was my staff, really," I say. "And our filmmaker, Claudio. They deserve the credit."

"All the same," says Margaret. "This is a job very well done." She turns to the rest of the group. "That's all for today, everyone. I'm looking forward to working with you." Everyone stands up to leave, except for Marni, who lingers expectantly for the post-meeting debrief, ready to mark her territory in the inner circle of the new regime. Alas, poor Barry, I think. The King is dead; long live the Queen.

"Sophie, would you mind staying for a few minutes?" asks Margaret. She turns to Marni. "Was there something else you wanted to ask me?"

"Uh, no," says Marni. "I just thought we could talk for a few minutes about my business plan."

"I look forward to that discussion," says Margaret, "but I won't be able to have it today. I'll have my assistant book one-on-one meetings with all of the managers over the next few weeks. Would you excuse us?" Margaret closes the door behind Marni's unwilling back and takes a seat across from me.

"Truly, Sophie, congratulations," she says. "I couldn't believe my ears when Barry told me about the ridiculous deadline he imposed on you."

"We've got a great team," I say.

"You're too modest," says Margaret. "But that's not what I want to talk to you about. I understand that Lillian Parker has made you a job offer."

I feel myself flushing. "I'm sorry that you had to hear about it from someone other than me," I say stiffly, conscious of the poor impression I must be making on my new boss. "I haven't made any decisions."

"Relax, Sophie," says Margaret. "There's nothing to be embarrassed about. I wanted you to know my position, and to know that you can discuss it with me if you want to. It's entirely your decision. Everyone I've spoken to here—with one exception—says that you are a huge asset to the hospital. But Lillian's foundation is our biggest donor, and it would be good for us to have you there. If you want to go, we can talk about how to manage without you. I understand that your second-in-command—Geoff, is it?—is excellent, so that might be a solution. The only advice I'll give you—and this is advice not as your future boss but as a professional woman who got into the game a few years ahead of you—is this: do what you want to do, not what Lillian wants you to do, or what you think I want you to do. It's easy to make decisions to please other people, especially when they are as persuasive as our friend Lillian. It's often easier than figuring out how to please ourselves."

"I really appreciate that, Margaret," I say. "Thanks. I don't know what I'm going to do yet. There are a lot of things to consider."

"Of course there are," she says. "I remember your stage of life so vividly." I wait for the usual refrain: *These are the best years of your life. Enjoy every minute. You won't believe how quickly it goes.* But Margaret surprises me. "I'll never forget the sheer relentlessness of it! Everyone tells you to enjoy it, but most of the time it's too much of a grind—not to mention the constant noise. I was exhausted for years."

I nod, and she smiles her wonderful smile at me.

"It gets easier," she says. "I promise. But in the meantime, you should try to remember that it's your life too, and have a little fun when you can." She gets up. "It's not always possible—I have a meeting now, for example, which has zero prospect of being fun—but there's honor in the striving." She winks.

"Margaret?" I ask, as she prepares to leave. "Can I ask who the exception is?"

"Oh, it wouldn't be appropriate for me to tell you that," she says. "Let's just say that he lost his day job recently and his name rhymes with 'hairy.' And I'm on my way to meet with him now. But you shouldn't give it any thought, because no one, least of all me, is listening."

My BlackBerry hums on the table. "Go ahead and answer that," says Margaret. "We'll speak again soon."

I recognize the number. "Hi, Lil," I say.

"Sophie!" Lil shouts over the noise of a busy restaurant. "I'm at the Four Seasons with the Gala gals."

"Who?"

"Addie, Katerina, Jane, and Janelle. We've come up with the most divine idea for the Gala. Did you know that the eighties are back in vogue? Absurd, really, since that decade seems like last week to me and wasn't all that fabulous the first time around."

"I did know that," I say.

"Do you remember Janelle's daughter, Chelsea?"

"I met her at your party," I say. "Doesn't she have a band that does eighties covers?"

"Exactly, you clever girl." Her voice fades slightly. "Don't be silly, Janelle, you're too modest. Chelsea is a major talent. This could be her big breakthrough. Imagine how proud you'll be!"

I hear the buzzing of voices in the background, and Lil says, "Yes, Jane, Chelsea's band would be an excellent choice from a budgetary perspective." More buzzing, and then Lil again. "Costumes! What a marvelous idea, Addie." The volume cranks up as Lil yells into the phone again. "Sophie, are you there? What do you think of costumes?"

"Why not?" I say. "Tell her she can wear as little as she likes." Lil snickers and says, "Sophie says it will be very fashionable, very *now*. Just the theme we were looking for, Katerina."

"Do we have your blessing, Sophie?" Lil shouts. I picture Janelle being berated by Lil over Cobb salad, hoisted with the petard of her own maternal pride, silently calculating the social cost of a failed event featuring her daughter in place of an aging rock star. It makes me smile.

"You do," I say. "Actually, I love it."

"I knew you would," says Lil, and hangs up.

I shake my head and cross one more item off my mental ROAR list as I head back to my office. Really, it's been a remarkable day, and I feel stronger and more in control of my life than I have in weeks, maybe even years. I scroll lazily through my e-mail, safe in the conviction that today, there's nothing the universe can dish out that I can't handle. And then the phone rings.

"What are you doing?" says Zoe.

"What do you mean?" I ask.

"I *mean*, Sophie," she says, "what are you doing with Will Shannon? You can't send this e-mail."

"Why not?" I ask. "Don't I deserve an answer after all these years?"

"It's not a question of what you deserve," says Zoe. "It's a question of what it will cost to get the answer—an answer, I might add, that doesn't actually matter."

"How can you say that?"

"Sophie," she says. "You have to let go of the idea that there's some alternative reality out there in which you and Will live happily ever after. It was never going to happen. You keep picking at this old scab and it's going to bleed. You're better than this." Her voice softens. "Every woman has a 'what if' guy somewhere in her past, Sophie. But that's where he belongs—in the past. You can't let him mess with your future."

"Fine," I say, my voice rough. I know that she's right. "I won't send it."

"Good," she says. "Because I don't think you even know what you want from him."

But for once, Zoe's dead wrong. I know exactly what I want from Will. I want to know that he regrets Paris.

CHAPTER TWENTY-SIX

august 20, 2014, and august 20, 1995

"Sophie!"

Jesse's voice is insistent, which is somewhat justified since I assured him that I would be ready to go fifteen minutes ago. But I'm taking my time tonight. After all, it's not every day a girl turns forty, and I'm pulling out all the stops; I'm not naïve enough to believe that we're headed out for a quiet dinner, and I want to appear as well-preserved as possible.

"Sophie!" The bathroom door opens, and Jesse appears. "Wow," he says, taking in my form-fitting black sheath dress. "You look fantastic."

"Really?"

"Really," he says, and pulls me in for a kiss.

"Good luck, my friend," I tell him. "I've got some serious body armor under here. You're not getting through it without help."

Jesse laughs. "That's probably just as well. We're going to be late for our reservation." He catches sight of the journal with the watermark cover on the vanity. "I didn't know you still had that," he says.

"I was feeling nostalgic," I say. "It's my fortieth birthday, after all." I raise an eyebrow. "Do you want to tell me what Zoe has planned?"

"It's just a little party," he says.

"Head count?"

"Not sure," he says, evasively.

I shake my head. "You're a terrible liar, you know," I say.

"True," he says. "And if you let on that I spilled the beans, there will be serious consequences for all concerned."

"At least we're not in costumes this time," I grumble, thinking back to the Baxter Just Wanna Have Fun Eighties Dance Party Gala this past spring and the sight of Jesse in a white suit with a tightly curled black wig, a silver glove, and stuffed chimpanzee. "How did she get you to wear that outfit, anyway?" Of all the things I've seen Lil pull out of the hat in the past twenty years, Jesse in a Michael Jackson costume is one of the most astonishing.

He shrugs uncomfortably. "She called in an old favor," he says.

"Must have been some favor," I say.

Jesse declines to elaborate. "Let's not keep your fans waiting," he says.

Jesse calls a taxi while I give some final instructions to Dulcie. Six months after hiring her as our nanny, I can hardly remember what misguided philosophy persuaded us that daycare was a viable option. "Go on," she says, making a shooing motion with her hands. "Have fun. We'll be fine." She turns to the boys. "Who wants to build a pillow fort?" The boys shriek in unison and sprint for the playroom without a backward glance. Jesse helps me into my coat. "Are you ready?" he says, holding out a hand.

"Are you ready to order?" asks the waiter. He addresses me in English, having determined early in our acquaintance that the table will be liberated more quickly if we stick to my native tongue. He's not contemptuous, though, being an expat himself, Australian possibly. Zoe, who made the reservation for me, assured me that this little wine bar, a haven for English speakers in Paris, is perfect for a date with destiny. In the event that destiny fails to unfold in the way I intend, Zoe has promised to take me dancing later.

I've been sitting here for half an hour already, nursing a glass of red wine and Waiting for Will. In the thirty-two excruciating minutes that have elapsed, I've descended from Frank Capra–land to Samuel Beckett territory, recording the entire psychological journey in my journal for posterity. I've moved on from my initial reticence to use A.J.'s gift to preserve in writing my feelings for Will; perhaps someday I'll become a writer and draw inspiration from this sordid episode, and thank A.J. in the acknowledgments. I've been told that young writers come to Paris to do exactly this: sit alone in restaurants and wallow in red wine and sorrow. I should feel romantic and free of confining social norms, but actually, I feel like a loser.

This is exactly what Zoe has anticipated, I know, although she's been gentle with me in the way that people are careful around the very ill: she neither wants to raise nor dash my most desperate hopes. Since my arrival in Paris, we haven't talked much about my relationship with Will or what I'm hoping will happen when we meet. Neither of us wants to hear Zoe say aloud that Will is a manipulative man-slut or that I'm a deluded fantasist, which is why we're both avoiding the subject.

I order the duck with marmalade sauce and another glass of wine, and then rashly call the waiter back to add a starter. I've saved up for this birthday party, working at my mother's side to deliver one picture-perfect wedding after another all summer for a parade of young women blissfully content with conventional social norms and their place in them; I can afford a few leaves of lettuce and some goat cheese. And although my hope that Will might still walk through the door is flickering out, and being replaced minute by awful minute with the sure knowledge that I will be alone forever, I can't make a spectacle of myself by sobbing or rending my clothes or running out into the street, because Zoe is dropping by at nine to pick me up. So I continue drinking and torture myself by remembering the last conversation I had with Will.

I hadn't been around much; I'd been going home every weekend since my dad's funeral and logging long hours at the library to make up for the weeks I'd missed. Still, I'd managed to write all of my exams on schedule and submit my honors paper with a couple of weeks to spare. And now I was surrounded by cardboard boxes, at various stages of assembly, preparing to move home to Port Alice for the summer. I'd originally planned to stay in the house and get a job temping downtown, but my mother had wedding bookings every weekend all summer and was so shattered by my dad's death that she could barely get out of bed, let alone run her wedding factory at full production. I'd agreed to help her get through the season, provided that I could take the last two weeks of August off to visit Zoe in Paris.

I was acutely conscious of Will's comings and goings: I knew when he was in the bathroom or the kitchen; I knew the sound of his footsteps on the stairs; I could distinguish from all the other doors in the house the distinctive creak his bedroom hinge made when it opened or closed; I knew that he hadn't had any overnight guests. But I didn't seek him out. It was painful to make small talk with him, and I was too weary to attempt anything more. Oddly, my relationship with A.J. had altered in unspoken ways as well. Since the awful day that he drove me home to Port Alice, we'd become friends. It wasn't like any other friendship I'd ever had, in the sense that I didn't know much about what made A.J. tick, but I felt comfortable being quiet around him. We'd do things side by side, like watching television in the evenings and sharing the paper in the mornings, and occasionally we'd talk, about school or our families, but never about Will. I'd discovered many things over the course of my yearlong experiment in male anthropology, and one of them was this: the lives of boys and men are full of white space, where no dialogue occurs and the plot doesn't seem to advance, but, in fact, many exchanges of significance happen there. I thought there was a good chance that A.J. and I might stay in touch after graduation, maybe grab a coffee or a beer once in a while.

I heard Will's bedroom door open, and listened to him take a few steps. Was he going to the bathroom, or down the stairs? But the footsteps came closer and he appeared in the doorway, movie-star handsome in ripped jeans and a white T-shirt.

"Hey," he said.

I sat back on my heels. "Hey," I replied.

"You're packing up?" I nodded. "When are you leaving?"

"In the morning. My brother rented a van and we're going up together."

"I thought you were going to keep your room here for the summer."

"I was," I said. "But my mom needs me home, and realistically, I won't get back here very often. And Zoe will be back in the fall, so we'll get a place again." I couldn't resist asking, "Why? Will you miss me?"

"Of course," he said lightly. "Good roommates are hard to come by." He shoved his hands into his pockets and leaned in against the door frame. I waited. "I know I made you a promise," he said. "I haven't forgotten. But I'd like to request an extension."

"Well," I said, "you have to have a good reason to get an extension. It can't just be that you'd rather stick hot needles in your eyes than have an awkwardly personal conversation."

"Yeah," he said, not meeting my eye, "I get it. So here it is. I had a lot of fun with you over Reading Week. But everything about this situation is too intense and I can't figure out how I feel about it. So what I'm proposing is that we both get a little distance and postpone the analysis."

This is heady stuff and I'm careful to keep my tone even. "What did you have in mind?" I asked.

"You're going to Paris in August, right?" I nodded. "I'm traveling this summer too. What if we made a date to meet there?"

"In Paris?"

"Right. We could go on a date, have dinner maybe. See how we feel without all the pressure."

In fact, Will's plan to meet in the most romantic city in the world for a scheduled dinner to discuss the possibility of a future together seems inescapably fraught with pressure, but I'm not going to tell him that. I'm in. "August twentieth," I said. "It's my birthday."

"August twentieth it is," he said. "We'll have dinner at Willi's Wine Bar. Zoe knows it. Get her to make a reservation at seven."

"You'll be there?"

"I'll be there," he said.

And now here I am, in Willi's Wine Bar in Paris. I check my watch again. Seven-forty-five. I know now that Will isn't coming. I wonder, briefly, if he ever intended to, but I push the thought away. I couldn't have been so mistaken in him. I might eventually believe that Will never loved me, but I won't believe that he intended this humiliation. My salad arrives and I'm just about to ask the waiter to cancel the rest of my order and bring me my bill when a voice that isn't Will's says, "Hi, Sophie."

I look up. "Hi, A.J.," I say. His hair is longer than it was in April, and it's curlier than I would have guessed. He looks determined, in freshly pressed khakis and a blue dress shirt, open at the neck, and holding a bunch of orange tulips. Everything about his arrival is unexpected. A.J. never mentioned that he was coming to Paris this summer. And it's such an odd coincidence that he should turn up, tonight of all nights.

I'm about to ask him what he's doing here when he hands me the tulips and says, "Can I join you?"

"Sure," I say. "Of course." I stand up, come around the table, and give him an awkward hug. "It's great to see you." I check behind him. "What are you doing here?"

"I'm here to see you," he says.

"These are for me?" I ask. He nods. I bury my nose in the flowers to buy myself a few seconds, knowing perfectly well that tulips don't smell like much of anything. My brain feels sluggish, though, and I'm having trouble keeping up.

"It's your birthday," he says. "I didn't want to come empty-handed."

"Ah," says the waiter, "here he is. You shouldn't keep a beautiful woman waiting like that, mate. You'll have to make it up to her." He fills A.J.'s glass and hands him a menu.

"Do you have steak frites?"

"Of course," says the waiter.

"I'll have that," says A.J., handing back the menu.

"A man who knows what he wants," says the waiter.

"That I do," says A.J., looking at me.

"How long are you in Paris?" I ask, leaping into the silence that has followed his last remark.

"I'm not sure," he says. "I have a job starting in a couple of weeks, so I'll probably stay as long as I can afford to and then fly back standby. I thought I'd make it for the full two weeks, but I got in this morning and I've already way overspent my daily budget. The town is crazy expensive."

"I know," I say, happy to be back on safer ground. "I've been sleeping on Zoe's floor and cooking at her place, and I'm still going through money like mad. Where are you staying?"

"On the Left Bank," he says. "Not too far."

"Congratulations on your job," I say. "What is it?"

His face lights up. "It's amazing. It's for a little company that's building photovoltaic systems." He sees my bemused expression and hastens to add, "That convert solar energy into electricity. They're experimenting with new types of batteries that store the energy. It's an incredible area. If we can make the technology more cost-effective, everyone will want to adopt it." His face falls. "Sorry. I don't mean to be boring."

"You're not boring," I say, and I mean it. "Where is it?"

"About five subway stops from Lil's house," he says. "I'm going to stick around for another year or so."

"That's great," I say. "It'll be nice to have you in town."

The waiter arrives with our meals. "Another bottle?" he asks.

I shake my head, but A.J. says, "A bottle of Veuve Clicquot, please."

"Very good, sir," says the waiter.

"A.J.," I whisper, "we can't afford that."

"I can," he says. "I've been working all summer." I open my mouth to argue, but A.J. holds up a hand. "I came a long way to do this," he says. "And you're going to let me, OK?"

"OK," I say, and I tuck into my dinner while A.J. tells me about the cast of characters from his summer internship at the water filtration plant; I, in return, tell him about the Bridezilla sisters, their equally awful mother, and the two weddings that ate my July. The food is wonderful and so is the champagne, and when the waiter comes back with the dessert menus, I'm ready to tackle the profiteroles. But A.J. says, "Let's walk for a bit. I've got another plan."

"I'm supposed to meet Zoe here at nine," I say.

"I called her," he said. "She's going to meet us for dessert."

"I'm in your hands," I say. I should put a stronger effort into putting the pieces of this evening together, but my head is cloudy with unshed tears and I'm exhausted from whipsawing between despair and something that feels more like hope. For once in my life, I think I might just let things unfold around me. Out on the street, A.J. holds out his arm and I take it. We walk through the Palais Royal gardens and past the Louvre and down to the Seine. "We cross here," he says, pointing to the Pont des Arts. "Not much farther, I promise."

"I don't mind," I say, and I don't. I'm more than a little tipsy, but A.J.'s arm is steady and the night air is warm and silky. Given how horribly the evening started, I'm frankly thrilled to be doing anything other than sobbing on Zoe's floor. Walking across the Seine arm-in-arm with an attractive male acquaintance may not be my perfect-world scenario, but it's a long way from the worst case. "I never asked you," I say. "Why did you take a year off school?"

A.J. looks surprised, but he says, "My mom got sick, really sick, with cancer. My family thought . . . we weren't sure what was going to happen. And I was too far away to see her as much as I wanted to. I could have transferred schools, but I decided to work for a year instead."

"Oh," I say. "That sounds awful."

"It was," he says. "But we were lucky. She beat the cancer and now she's fine. And I got some work experience, too, which probably made me more employable than the other million engineers that I graduated with." We're on the other side of the river now, and A.J. turns onto a narrow street. "Just one more block," he says.

"This must be some dessert," I say, as we stop outside an ancient gray building festooned with trailing geraniums in window boxes. Plumes of cigarette smoke and gales of throaty laughter ring out from the café tables on the sidewalk, and the bright blue signs declare that we have arrived at Café Laurent.

"She's here," shouts a voice I recognize, and Zoe springs up from one of the tables and wraps me in a hug. "Surprise!"

"Happy birthday, my dear Sophie," says another voice, and when I extricate myself from Zoe's embrace, I see Lil, smoking a cigarette from a long black holder and regarding her surroundings with the bearing of a queen surveying her lands and subjects. "Do be a darling," she says to A.J., "and tell the waiter that our party has arrived, won't you?" A.J. disappears into the restaurant.

"What are you doing in Paris?" I ask Lil.

"Miss a surprise party in Paris? Moi?" says Lil, grinning. I kiss her on the cheek.

"Thank you so much," I say to both of them. "I don't know what to say. I'm overwhelmed."

Zoe pulls me off to the side. "Are you all right?" she asks in a low voice.

"I'm not sure yet," I say. "Did you know that Will wasn't going to show?"

"I didn't know for sure," she says. "If Will had been at the restaurant, A.J. would have brought both of you here." She squeezes my hand. "I'm so sorry, Sophie."

"Me too," I murmur, and then raise my voice and ask very casually, "Lil, you haven't heard from Will lately, have you? We thought he might be in Paris this weekend."

"I spoke to him this morning, as a matter of fact," she says. "I thought he might like to join us. But he's on Mykonos with a group of friends, no doubt getting into all kinds of trouble. Too bad! He would have been a fine addition to our merry band. He sends birthday wishes."

"Thanks for passing the message along," I manage. "Are the toilets in the back?" I saunter to the rear of the restaurant, blinking rapidly, and barricade myself inside a toilet stall for a few minutes, until I feel more composed. In one way, I suppose I should feel grateful for the definitive information that Lil has just handed me. I won't be able to persuade myself that Will forgot, or got the date wrong; he decided not to come, unlike the three people sitting and waiting for me outside. And I am not going to make them sorry that they went to all this trouble to give me a perfect birthday.

I return to the table at the same moment that A.J. appears with a waiter bearing a bottle of champagne and four glasses.

"I'm not sure it's a good idea to drink any more champagne," I say.

"It's always a good idea to drink more champagne," says Lil. "You just need to soak it up with some dessert." And on cue, another waiter appears with a tower of cream puffs held together with spun sugar and impaled with lit sparklers. Zoe leads the other patrons in a round of "Bon Anniversaire," and I take a bow to general cheering.

"Now," says Zoe, swallowing a mouthful of whipped cream, "are we still going dancing?"

"Of course you are," says Lil. "It's Paris! Life begins after dark! In fact, there used to be a famous nightclub on this very site, Le Tabou. The Existentialists adored it. They were quite the partygoers—not nearly as dreary as history suggests. I'm going to bed, but you should make the most of the evening."

"Where are you staying?" I ask.

"Here," says Lil. "Hotel d'Aubusson is attached to the café. I always stay here. You're staying here too."

"I'm staying here?"

"You and Jesse both have rooms here for the next four nights. Yours is a double, so Zoe can stay too, if you want a roommate. I've got a big agenda planned starting at eleven tomorrow morning. It's my birthday present to you, sweet girl."

"I don't know what to say. Thank you so much." I process the rest of Lil's last statement. "What did you call A.J.?"

"Jesse. He doesn't like being called A.J., apparently. Well, who can blame him? It's a ridiculous name for anyone over the age of ten. I don't know why he didn't mention it earlier."

"Oh," I say, turning to A.J. "Do you want me to call you Jesse?"

He smiles shyly. "I'll understand if it's too weird for you to make the switch, but I prefer it. A.J. was just a camp nickname that followed me to university. The important people in my life call me Jesse. I'd like it if you did, too."

"Surprise!" The room erupts as Jesse and I make our entrance. There must be a hundred people here, some of whom I haven't seen in ages.

"Smile," Jesse murmurs, and I oblige.

Zoe bounds over. "Were you surprised?"

"Absolutely," I say, giving her a kiss on the cheek. "Thank you for doing this."

"You know how much I love throwing a surprise party," says Zoe.

"That I do," I say.

The speakers suddenly crackle to life and Lil appears on the stage with a microphone in her hand. "Good evening, friends. Welcome to Sophie's fortieth birthday party! Come on up, birthday girl." Amid general cheering, I am pushed up to the stage, where Lil beams at me.

"Sophie and I have been friends for many years, and it is a great honor to be able to celebrate with her tonight. I'm sure you'll all agree with me that she makes forty look fabulous." Riotous applause ensues, including a few wolf whistles that I recognize as Jesse's. "As you may know, Sophie is a big eighties fan, so we have another surprise for her. Please welcome our special guests, the Legwarmers, to the stage!"

Chelsea Moss and her band appear from the wings; Lil hands over the microphone and we climb down as the first set begins.

"You're completely ungovernable," I tell her.

"You're not the first to say so," she says, grinning from ear to ear. "Happy birthday, my dear." She glances over my shoulder. "Perfect timing," she says. "I wanted to have a chat with Jesse. Entertain the guest of honor for me, Will."

"Yes, ma'am," says Will. "Care to dance?"

"Is it a good idea to dance with your boss?" I ask.

He looks surprised, laughs a little. "Is that what I am to you now?"

"Don't underestimate it," I say, smiling. "You're the best boss I've ever had. I'm glad I accepted your offer to come to the foundation, Will. It's been amazing."

"You're amazing," he says. "But for tonight, why don't we call it a dance with an old friend, instead?"

"Is that what I am to you now?"

"I like to think so." Will pulls me onto the dance floor and we move together, stiffly at first, more like seventh-graders than grown-ups with a history. "Are you having a good birthday?"

"Better than the one I had in Paris," I say. "Although you weren't there for that one, as I recall."

"Ouch. I was hoping I'd been forgiven by now."

"I'd have considered it if you'd ever offered an apology or an expla-nation," I say mildly.

Will steps back and sighs. "You still want one?"

"You bet. And I'm the birthday girl, so I get my wish. Cough it up."

He waits, and then says, "I lost my nerve."

"What?"

"I was planning to come and meet you. But I got cold feet. I knew what you wanted from me, but I didn't think I could deliver. And then I got an offer to go to Greece, so I ran." He runs a hand through his hair. "I wish it were a better story. I'm not proud of it. But that's what hap-pened. And I'm sorry."

"OK," I say.

"OK, what?"

"I accept your explanation. And I accept your apology. We can stop talking about it now."

"Excellent," says Will. "Because I find these conversations very awkward."

"I've got one more awkward conversation in my arsenal tonight," I say. "But don't worry—it's not for you."

"Lucky me," he says, and spins me around. Now that we're both more relaxed, he pulls me a bit closer. And because it's dark in this corner of the dance floor, I rest my head on his shoulder and close my eyes. I let myself remember how it felt to love him, and the terrible hole it left when I knew he would never love me back. But I remember other things too: who healed me; who offered me friendship and understanding; and later, when he knew I was ready, love, who assembled IKEA furniture for our first apartment; who let my mother plan our wedding down to the last Martha Stewart bow; who told me I was beautiful when I was nine months pregnant and wild with hormones; who gave my sons their warm brown eyes—and I know that I don't regret Paris. In the end, I don't regret Paris at all.

The song ends, and we step apart. "It's good to have you back in my life, Will," I say. "I missed you."

Will gives me a kiss on the forehead. "Thanks," he says. "Me too."

I find Lil and Jesse off in a quiet corner of the room. "What are you two plotting?" I ask.

"No plotting," says Lil. "Jesse was just telling me about his consulting practice. Isn't he clever?"

"He is," I say, dispatching him in search of drinks. Six months after dismantling his business with Anya, Jesse is scrambling to keep up with the demand for his consulting services. He's wary about expanding too quickly, but he's decided to hire a couple of employees. "He's amazing."

"He always was," says Lil. "So, are you enjoying your party? I know you think you hate surprises, but you don't, not really. Remember how much fun we had in Paris?"

"Actually, that trip's been on my mind lately," I say. "And I wanted to ask you a question about it."

Lil looks wary. "Yes?"

"Why didn't Will come to Paris? I think you know. I want you to tell me."

She regards me evenly for a moment, and then says, "He didn't come to Paris because I offered him a rental house on Mykonos."

"Why?" I ask. It's strange to feel so calm, knowing that Lil saw my heart so clearly and still thwarted its desire. I should be furious at her betrayal, but I'm more curious than angry. "Didn't you think I was good enough for him?"

She shakes her head. "You know me better than that," she says. "I thought you were far too good for him, and I still do."

"Do you always get what you want?" I ask, and there's an edge in my voice that isn't entirely nice.

"No," she says, sharply. "I don't. If I did, I'd have what you have."
Her tone softens. "You never noticed the way Jesse looked at you back
then. That party in Paris was his idea, you know. Even knowing that
you were hoping to meet Will, he still flew across an ocean for you. So
I gave Will a choice, which he made of his own free will, and I gave
Jesse a chance to prove that he was the one who deserved you all along.
I have regrets, Sophie, but that isn't one of them."

I blink back unexpected tears, reach for her hand, and squeeze, and
see the relief pass across her face. And I think of all the gifts Lil has
given me over the years—clothes and fancy dinners and hotel rooms in
Paris, to be sure, but also joy and fellowship and an interest in the
minutiae of my existence that can only spring from love.

Lil's interest in me has always been a puzzle, but I've never doubted
her affection or loyalty. Maybe, as she once told me, I remind her of her
younger self. Maybe I'm the daughter she never had. With love, it's not the
why that matters. It's the how. It's the millions of ways we reach out and
connect with the people we love and try to make them happy and protect
them from harm. All of Lil's gifts to me have been expressions of love, but
now I see, more than ever before, that my life with Jesse is a gift too.

"I never thanked you properly for bringing me over to the foundation," I say. "I love it."

"That makes me very happy," she says. "Now, stop wasting your
time with old people, and go have fun at your party."

"You'll never be old," I say.

She touches my cheek. "Not if I can help it," she says. "Embrace the
present. Release the past. That's the secret." She looks over my shoulder. "I see your date coming back with your drink," she says. "Why
don't the two of you go and have a dance?"

Jesse holds me close and we shuffle in a slow circle as the Legwarmers
belt out a few classic rock ballads.

"Chelsea's band is pretty amazing," I say.

"It is," he says. "Lil knows how to pick them."

"She was certainly right about you," I say, and I step back so that I can see his face. "I know what the favor was, Jesse. I know what Lil did for you. I know about Paris."

Other couples swirl around us but we don't move. When he speaks, his words come out in a rush. "I'm so sorry, Sophie," he says. "I should have told you a long time ago. I convinced myself that it didn't matter, that we hadn't taken away a real choice from you, but since Will came back . . . I wonder now. I may have misjudged him then. I didn't think he was serious about you, and I wanted you more than I had ever wanted anything before or since, so I felt justified. But maybe he was serious. How could he not have been? How could he not have wanted to spend the rest of his life with you?"

I hold him close, and when I rest my cheek on his chest, it feels like home.

"Good birthday?" he asks.

"As good as forty could possibly be," I say. "I'm shooting for less drama now that I've officially crossed over."

He laughs. "No argument here," he says.

"I put you through a lot," I say. "I'm sorry."

"Sophie," he says, "it's going to take a lot more than that to get rid of me. I'm in this for the long haul."

"I never loved him the way I love you," I say.

"I know," he says. "I was just waiting for you to figure it out."

The room recedes as we complete another circle in time to the music. And then I look up at him and say, "You wanted me to tell you when."

"When what?" he asks.

"When you could stop looking over your shoulder," I say.

I reach up and put a hand on either side of his face and pull him down for a long, sweet kiss.

"Now," I tell him.

His arms tighten around me, and I feel all the parts of my life knit together into a whole. And for one perfect moment, I think I know what it means to have it all.

ACKNOWLEDGMENTS

It is quite something to be in a position to acknowledge people in the back of your very own book. It feels more than a little bit miraculous. And so I am endlessly, eternally grateful to:

My editors, Claire Zion in the United States and Jennifer Lambert in Canada, for falling in love with Sophie Whelan and cheering her all the way to the finish line.

My agent and friend, Beverley Slopen, for her breathtaking tenacity and her unwavering support of my work.

My early readers and supporters, including Sara Angel, Alexis Archbold, Amy Ballon, Danielle Botterell, Sarah Brohman, Melissa Bubb-Clarke, Marie Budworth, Marie Campbell, Kirby Chown, Sari Diamond, Brenda Doig, Todd Ducharme, Leah Eichler, Bronwen Evans, Sara Faherty, Rivi Frankle, Deborah Glatter, Bonnie Goldberg, Melanie Gruer, Lily Harmer, Ana Maria Hobrough, Martha Hundert, Tamara Jordan, Reva Katz, Jane Kidner, Judith Lavin, Susan Lee, Suzanne Lewis, Leena Malik, Judith McCormack, Mayo Moran, Stacia Morris, Heather Morrison, Molly Naber-Sykes, Amreen Omar, Susy Opler, Kerry Owen, Ira Parghi, Beth Parker, Lesley Parrott, Laurie Pawlitza, Nancy Reid, Patricia Smith, Jenny Thompson, Brianna Caryll Valihora and Maureen Whelton, for sharing thoughtful suggestions that made the book so much better and for making me a believer in the power of the social network.

My writer friends, including Heather A. Clark, Jon Evans, Chantel Guertin, Guy Gavriel Kay, Andrew Pyper, Roberta Rich, Jennifer Robson,

Reva Seth and Marissa Stapley, for their wise counsel on writing matters great and small.

My tennis ladies, for keeping my sanity intact.

My first family, the Hiltons—Margo and Jim and Anne and Betsy—for being a home to come back to.

And my children, Jack and Charlie, for being the whole point.

the hole in the middle

KATE HILTON

*This Conversation Guide is intended to enrich the
individual reading experience, as well as encourage us
to explore these topics together—because books,
and life, are meant for sharing.*

QUESTIONS FOR
DISCUSSION

1. *The Hole in the Middle* takes place in two different time periods—1994–1995 and 2013–2014. How does this technique enrich our understanding of the characters and their actions?

2. Is *The Hole in the Middle* a contemporary fairy tale? Why or why not?

3. The character of Lillian Parker plays a key role in Sophie's life, both in the past and the present. What do you think motivates Lil's interest in Sophie? How do you feel about her interference in Sophie's choices?

4. Much of the novel is set in Sophie's office. Why do you think the author placed such an emphasis on Sophie's work relationships? What do these relationships tell us about Sophie? Are the power dynamics in Sophie's office typical of an average workplace? Why or why not?

5. Do you think that Sophie and Jesse have a good marriage? Do you think that Will poses a serious threat to their relationship at any point in the book? If so, do you think he continues to pose a threat at the end of the book?

6. Toward the end of the novel, Lil says: "The first half of life is about getting as far away from your past as you can. And then, just when you've established yourself as a full-fledged adult, a hole opens up in

the middle of life and the past comes rushing back in. By the time you're my age, if you aren't careful, the past is more real than the present." Do you agree with her?

7. Does Sophie experience a true midlife crisis in the book? Do you feel that she is at a genuine crossroads in her life, or is she merely having a very difficult week?

8. Zoe tells Sophie: "Every woman has a 'what if' guy somewhere in her past." Do you think this is true? How do you think our past romantic relationships affect our sense of satisfaction with present-day choices, either positively or negatively?

9. What do you think of Zoe's "romantic archetype" theory? How would Zoe characterize your romantic choices?

10. Sophie's journey is, in part, a search for work-life balance. Do you think that work-life balance is achievable? Does Sophie find it at the end of the novel?

11. Sophie bears far more responsibility for household management and child care than Jesse does. Why do you think their family has evolved in this way? Do you think it is possible for men and women to share parenting equally?

The Hole in the Middle is **Kate Hilton**'s first novel. Before turning to fiction, Kate worked in law, higher education, public relations and major gift fund-raising. She has an English degree from McGill University and a law degree from the University of Toronto. She is a working mother, a community volunteer, a voracious reader and a pretty decent cook. On good days, she thinks she might have it all. On bad days, she wants a nap. Kate lives with her family in Toronto.